# A GODDESS ARRIVES

by

## GERALD B. GARDNER

A Goddess Arrives

First published in 1939

Copyright © Karen Dales/Dark Dragon Publishing 1993.

Ebook: 978-1-928104-38-4
Trade Paperback: 978-1-928104-37-7
Hardback: 978-1-928104-39-1

Cover Reconstruction by Evan Dales, WAV Studios

Dark Dragon Publishing
88 Charleswood Drive,
Toronto, Ontario.
M3H 1X6
CANADA
www.darkdragonpublishing.com
Printed in the United States of America

# A GODDESS ARRIVES

by

GERALD B. GARDNER

# CONTENTS

# INTRODUCTION

A long time ago, after I had purchased and read Gerald Gardner's novel *High Magic's Aid*, I found out that it was not his first written work. Of course, I had already read his non-fiction works, *Witchcraft Today* and *The Meaning of Witchcraft*, so when I discovered that his first creative adventure was *A Goddess Arrives* I knew I had to get my hands on a copy. Easier said than done!

*A Goddess Arrives* had been originally published through a vanity press in 1939, and only a certain number of them had been in the print run. As a vanity press, Gerald had to pay for the privilege of seeing this work in print. Of this original printing, it is unknown how many copies are still circulating. The publishing and copyrights remained with Gerald. In 1997, thirty-three years after Gerald's passing into the Summerlands, Gavin and Yvonne Frost reprinted it, but never had the copyright to do so. This was a book that was going to slip into the obscurity of time, something that should not ever be allowed.

It was during the republication process of *High Magic's Aid* that Philip Heselton suggested I republish *A Goddess Arrives*—thanks Philip for putting that massive bug in my brain. I delved into the research of *who* exactly held the copyright of *A Goddess Arrives*. It took a lot of internet work and reaching out to several people to discover that it was, what we call in the publishing business, an orphan, and I gleaned to obtain the orphan rights to it so that Dark Dragon Publishing could publish it. It took time and lots of red tape, but I managed to gain the copyright to publish this soon-to-be-lost gem. Needless to say, I was

i

thrilled.

The next step was to find a copy of A *Goddess Arrives* since my copy seems to have been devoured by the immenseness of my library. All I can say is a MASSIVE thank you to Matt Daughenbaugh who lent me his copy a year ago. I kept it safe and sound until I could figure out how to get the text from the paperback into my computer. One thought was to scan each page and convert it into text, but that would have broken the spine and destroyed the trade paperback. That was out of the question! This meant only one option: I had to manually type all 130,000 words into my computer! Thank the Gods I learned how to touch-type when I was in High School.

From start to finish, it took me months to complete. In the process, I was pulled into a story that was quite remarkable and extremely well written by today's standards. Gerald's vocabulary was immense and he used it masterfully. For someone who had never written a fiction piece before, he did a wonderful job.

Considering that this book was written in the 1930's and published in 1939, there were some eye opening situations that would never be written in books today. So, my friend, when you read this tale, keep in mind that Gerald Gardner was a product of his time—someone who was born and raised during the Victorian Era. As such, the representation of Dayonis and how she is treated by Kinyras and other men is perceived through that Victorian lens, despite being a strong warrior who is also a lover. By today's standards such presentation would not fly well by modern conventions, but despite that, given the era in which this book was written, Dayonis is a remarkably strong and brave woman who knows her own mind and heart and isn't afraid to act upon them.

Another aspect to be aware of is the very minor character of the Jewish man, Yakub, who Gerald describes as *a Jew, a lank, dark man with long curling ringlets, a beak of a nose and a small, twinkling, intelligent black eyes came in with a curious mixture of cringing and self-importance.* Unfortunately, anti-Semitism was rife at that time and influenced Gerald's portrayal of this character. Was Gerald an anti-Semite? I seriously doubt it, but the representation of Yakub is considered problematic in modern times, so bear that in mind.

One thing I was surprised about was the extent of the research Gerald must have done to create this engaging narrative. Though the story is historical fiction, the places and the circumstances are real, showing how incredibly well read Gerald was.

I'm thrilled to be able to have this book back in print for current and future generations to enjoy!

Karen Dales
June 2024
Toronto, Canada

# FOREWORD

**G**erald Gardner always dreaded the cold weather of winter and the effect which it would have on his health. So, when he retired to England in 1936 after a working life 'out East', he initiated a pattern of wintering abroad that continued, apart from the war years, for the rest of his life. For the winter of 1936/37, he planned to go to Cyprus. The reason for choosing this island dated back some time.

For many years Gerald had had, not a recurring dream exactly, but a succession of dreams, events and experiences which gradually built up into what seemed to him a very real life. It was set in ancient times, in a hot country, and Gerald was in charge of having a wall built, to repel invaders. As well as being the designer of the wall and supervising its construction, he was also responsible for organising the melting down of bronze cooking utensils for making weapons.

Gerald probably strongly suspected that these were memories of a previous lifetime, though not as coherent or detailed as those brought through by Joan Grant, whose memories of a life in ancient Egypt were to be published by Arthur Barker as the novel, *Winged Pharaoh*, in October 1937. These dreams did not engage Gerald's attention unduly. He felt that they might be a real place, and that it might be somewhere in the Middle East, as for some years he had had the strange feeling of 'belonging' to that area.

The extent to which the work which became *A Goddess Arrives* is an account of a former life which Gerald remembered is uncertain. We have, for example, the unequivocal statement in his *Witchcraft Today* (Rider 1954).

> ... *I must say that, though I believe in reincarnation, as most people do who have lived in the East, I do not remember any past lives, albeit I have had curious experiences. I only wish I did.*

Yet, six years later, J. L. Bracelin, in the book *Gerald Gardner, Witch* (Octagon 1960), certainly implies memory of a previous lifetime when he writes:

> *A curious succession of dreams, almost as if he was living another, yet coherent and connected life, had been frequent experiences for many years. In this strange serial story, Gardner was in an ancient world where he was having a mighty wall built, to keep out invaders. It was like a Roman wall, it was in a hot country, because he was involved partly as an armourer. He "remembered" seizing all the bronze pots and kettles he could to cast into spears and other weapons. He had a strong curiosity about this secret life.*

Probably the truth of the matter is that Gerald did have the series of dreams that Bracelin wrote about but they were never so clear or detailed that he could be sure that they were memories of a previous lifetime: he just suspected that they were, and was frustrated that he could not bring them into focus.

I think Gerald somehow recognised that the place that he was having dreams about was probably Cyprus. Certainly it was worth a visit, and, as he needed to go to a Mediterranean climate over the winter anyway, Cyprus it was.

His interest in, and knowledge of, ancient weapons provided a focus for the trip. Indeed, he may have been put on the track of Cypriot weapons by others who attended a gathering in Denmark in April 1936, particularly Holger Jacobsen, who was to become a lifelong friend.

# Gerald B. Gardner

His interest may have dated back to the 1932 Conference which Gerald attended in London where there was a talk given by Dr. Porphyrios Dikaios on 'Early Bronze Age Cults in Cyprus as revealed by the Excavations at "Vounous", Bellapais'. When Gerald arrived in Cyprus, probably in early 1937, he went straight to the Museum in Nicosia, by which time Dikaios was Curator. He may have been given a letter of introduction by Jacobsen, who almost certainly knew Dikaios. Bracelin tells what happened when they met:

> ... the Curator said: 'You are interested in weapons. Tell me how the ancient Cypriots hafted their swords'.

Gardner didn't know and eventually gave up an analytical approach, allowing his mind to slip into contemplation:

> Then, suddenly and extraordinarily, my hands felt as if they knew. I said, 'Will you give me an old blade. These people had bronze saws, chisels and knives, and bores. Lend me some modern ones, and I will try'. My hands told me what to do. Next day I brought the sword back, hafted. They tried it many ways and found it good, and then they said: 'Take it out, and show us how you did it'. And it would not come. We had to get an axe and split it to get the haft off.

Gerald subsequently wrote an article entitled 'The Problem of the Cypriot Bronze Age Dagger Hilt'. As far as I know, this was never published in English, but he did send copies to the Journal of the Société Prehistorique Française, who translated it and published it in their Bulletin No. 12 in 1937 as 'Le Problème de la Garde de l'Epée Cypriote de l'Age du Bronze'. He also sent it to Jacobsen, who translated it and published it in the Transactions of the Vaabenhistorisk Selskab in 1938 under the title of 'Problemet: Det cypriskesvaerdfaeste'.

I suspect that it may have been the experience with hafting the blade that made Gerald think that he might have been a sword-maker in Cyprus in a previous lifetime. He would then probably have made the connection with the dreams he had been having, and would have come to the conclusion that they were related to a previous lifetime in Cyprus.

In September 1937, Gerald applied for, and subsequently received, a diploma bestowing on him the degree of Doctor of Philosophy. However, this is not what it appears at first glance. The institution from which he obtained this diploma was known as the 'Meta Collegiate Extension of the National Electronic Institute', an organisation that is not recognised by most academic institutions.

Gerald had never had any formal education: he never went to school or college. Indeed, he probably always felt as if he had been living in the shadow of his father's achievements, and that he needed to rectify things somehow. I think that when he started to meet archaeologists and anthropologists at conferences where he was talking with them about his excavations at Johor Lama and his work on the Malay magical knife, the keris, he began to feel as if he ought to have the formal qualifications that the others had got. And after the genuine praise he received following the publication of *Keris and Other Malay Weapons* (Progressive Publishing Company Singapore 1936) he felt he deserved such qualification and in particular a PhD (Doctor of Philosophy).

Gerald certainly knew that it wasn't worth very much but felt that it was important to get some sort of qualification, however dubious, for it was only after he received his diploma that he started calling himself 'Dr. Gardner'.

The excavations that he had planned to join in the winter of 1937/38 had been abandoned, but he needed to escape from the English winter quickly, so, on an impulse, he arranged to go back to Cyprus. This was on a slow orange-boat, which took a month to get there.

On the eve of his departure he had another extraordinary dream. Bracelin described it as being 'about a man who found that he was not wanted at home: so he dived into the past, seemingly with ease—where he *was* wanted.'

Whether this in some way was to do with his relationship with Donna (the wife of Denvers, the hero of *A Goddess Arrives*, is called 'Domina') I do not know, but I suspect that this dream was the first of a series which Gerald began to write down and which formed the basis for that novel (A H Stockwell 1939).

On the boat, the other passengers seemed intent on drinking and playing bridge, which didn't interest Gerald at all, so he made a decision at that time to write a novel based on his dreams. I think he probably guessed that he would find the landscape of those dreams when he reached Cyprus, and so it proved to be.

Gerald was keen to try and find the site of some of the locations which he remembered from his dreams sufficiently clearly to have reasonable hope that he would be able to identify them. He particularly wanted to identify a small round hill at the mouth of a small river, which had featured prominently in his dreams.

He went to Famagusta and, in circumstances which Bracelin does not explain, he met a '*wild-eyed semi-Mexican woman who said that she was English*'. Bracelin said: '*He hired her to look for the dream-place which he had found the previous winter.*' Why it should be necessary to hire someone to find somewhere that he had already found, I do not know, but Gerald was directed to a site on the southern coast of the Karpas or Karpasia peninsula, which forms the north-eastern extremity of the island. Here was a hill known locally as Stronglos or Stronglas, upon which had been built the Castle of Gastria by the Knights Templar in the 12th Century. It was at the mouth of a stream known as the ArgakitouKastrou.

It is a very good defensive position since the hill descends steeply on its eastern side into the sea. To the west is an area, now dried up, but which had been a marsh through which the stream, now silted up, winds to the sea. There is a sheltered harbour at the mouth of the river where ships would be hidden from view by the hill itself.

All this was familiar to Gerald, apart from the castle, presumably because it dated from an era later than that of his memories. He identified the area of former marsh and a ravine, between which he thought he had had to build a wall in a previous lifetime. As Bracelin remarks: '*He remembers it all–foundations, earthworks, stones in position, towers. He even knew instinctively the points of the compass–the river flowed from north to south*'.

Now that he knew for sure that his dreams were memories of real places, he became more convinced than ever that he had the pieces of a real lifetime lived in ancient Cyprus. And it had been lived in the landscape that he was now in.

On an impulse Gerald bought some land here with the intention of building a house on it, but the war intervened and nothing came of the project.

At some stage, Gerald must have had the idea of writing about these experiences. He had previously written *Keris and Other Malay Weapons* and I suspect he initially thought he would just write a factual account of his experiences, but he very quickly realised that the narrative would be much too short, so he started writing a work of fiction. Whether he had previously tried to write fiction I do not know but, if so, none appears to have survived.

From the time he returned from Cyprus, probably in April 1938, until summer 1939, Gerald was busy writing his novel, which was to be entitled *A Goddess Arrives*. It is a very competent first work of fiction, in many ways better written than his next book, *High Magic's Aid*, which was published ten years later. It is certainly a long book and I think it almost certain that Gerald paid the costs of publication, as it seems highly doubtful that a publisher like Stockwell would otherwise have been interested in a first novel running to over 380 pages.

*A Goddess Arrives* is important because its writing spans the roughly two and a half years from Gerald's retirement in January 1936 to his claimed initiation into 'the witch cult' in September 1939. It may therefore reveal something of his thinking during that period. Certain themes, for example, may have been added in later revisions of the text as new ideas occurred to him. As an author myself, I appreciate how this is a natural and expected part of the process.

Gerald couldn't spell. Also he found it difficult to arrange material in a sensible order, so he always needed someone to help him in preparing a book for publication. In his other books, he had help with spelling and other stylistic techniques. It is clear that someone must have helped him but, as no-one is acknowledged, it was obviously someone who didn't want their name to appear. I know from other sources that this person was Edith Woodford-Grimes, whom he knew as Dafo. She knew Gerald well, certainly had the skills to act as editor, and would not have wanted any publicity for what she did.

In outline, the book tells of the Egyptian Invasion of Cyprus in 1450 BCE and of the legend of Venus emerging from the sea. As Gardner says in his introduction:

> How it would be possible for a woman to be received as
> a Goddess, rising from the sea, I have endeavoured to show.

So, what were the raw materials from which Gerald fashioned the pages of his novel? First, as I have mentioned, there were these memories, both vague and precise, of a previous lifetime in Cyprus. He probably used these as a starting point and read up all he could about the history of the island, using the resources of the British Museum.

It starts in the London of the 1930s. Robert Denvers, the hero, obviously based on Gardner, is concerned that his wife, Mina (short for Domina) is having an affair with his former boss, Hank Heyward. He finds some comfort in a bronze snail which he had acquired from somewhere and which had resurfaced in a drawer after several years.

> When he was in the presence of any object of genuine
> antiquity he had a curious sense of complete familiarity with
> it, as though, through its medium, he could recreate the life

*which had surrounded it from its inception.*

Whether this is based on a technique which Gerald himself adopted, I do not know, but it is interesting that Joan Grant used exactly the same technique, in her case an Egyptian scarab, to bring through the memories that were subsequently published as her novel, *Winged Pharaoh.* It was a long time after *A Goddess Arrives* was published that Joan Grant revealed that this was what she did.

Denvers gradually drifted into a sleep which, to all outward appearances resembled a cataleptic trance. Inwardly he was able to re-live, in great detail, the most exciting part of one of his previous lives, as Kinyras, a citizen of Karpas, in Cyprus in the 15th Century BCE.

The book was being written in the 1937-1939 period, one that was crucial in the history of Europe. The rise of Nazi Germany and its threat to the stability of the whole of the continent was something of which everyone in England was fully aware, not least Gerald, who experienced some of it first-hand on his way through Germany back to England.

He was highly critical of the policy of 'appeasement' which was typified by Chamberlain's 'Munich Agreement' with Hitler in1938. This is certainly reflected in certain passages in the book, such as that from the soon-to-become leader of the Karpasians, Erili:

> *'I am here, Karpasians, to guard you from disaster, but I know from my spies that Khem is mustering a great force against you, determined to conquer you once and for all. They are formidable warriors, they live by fighting, their engines of war are many and modern to the last degree, their troops are hardy and indomitable, their generals, men of great experience and much ability. Against such an army my own men are inadequate, being but a small force. If Karpas is to resist invasion by my aid, then Karpas must be prepared to make sacrifices.'*

The opposing viewpoints are made very clear in a subsequent exchange of opinions:

> '*I would remind you that there IS NO WAR and to prepare for war is the very way to bring it about.*'

> '*On the contrary, the country which is prepared, is the country immune from attack.*'

Erili is given the powers of a dictator and he orders the hero of the novel, Kinyras, to design and have built a defensive wall across the land which separates the Kingdom of Karpas from the rest of the island in order to defend it from the much greater force of the Khemites.

Whilst Kinyras is both brave and practically minded, he does use an unusual skill, which is to see into the future and to bring through designs for new weapons and things of that sort. He saw in detail the plan of a fortified wall in a dream and sets everyone to work to build it in as short a time as possible. One of the most useful is what he calls the staveros, which turns out to be a form of cross-bow, albeit getting on for 1000 years earlier than the period when they were actually found in the Mediterranean. It had the advantage of being capable of use by someone with little training and still have great strength and accuracy.

Gerald included 'love interest' into the story in the character of Dayonis, Queen of the Aghirda tribe who, escaping from capture by the Khemites, fights naked alongside Kinyras and subsequently becomes his lover and wife.

Dayonis was some sort of ideal woman as far as Gerald was concerned, perhaps even a 'dream woman', and not like Donna or Edith in personality. In fact, the individual whom she most closely resembles is Rosanne, Edith's daughter, who, from all accounts, was outgoing and adventurous and popular with the opposite sex.

Now, at one level, Gerald was attracted by naked young ladies and to introduce one into his story is probably to be expected. However, whilst in some respects she conformed to societal expectations of the time with regard to her behaviour and attitudes, in other ways she certainly did not.

The plot of the story is complex, with many attacks, counter-attacks, spying and other treachery. Dayonis escapes from her captors and, after being found by Kinyras and helping him defeat an attack by the Khemites, is brought back to his house to rest. An attempted invasion by sea by the Khemites is defeated.

Kinyras is married to Dayonis at an underground temple in her own land. This has a vivid description of a series of large underground caves reached through a fissure in the ground from which vapours emerged. This was the dwelling-place of their god, Jaske, and where Kinyras and Dayonis were married.

The cave formations as described by Gerald are largely imaginary, although based on the so-called Hot Cave north of the village of Agirdag (Agirda) on the southern slopes of the Kyrenia Mountains (Pentadaktylos Range). It is described as a partially collapsed natural formation from which warm air emanates, which can be felt from a quarter of a mile away.

It is interesting, in view of the later development of the Craft, that Gerald did not focus on the Mother Goddess cult centred on Vounous, less than six miles away from the cave, which Dikaios had spoken about back in 1932 and which I mention above.

The climax of the book is set near Paphos, the site of Venus' legendary emergence from the ocean. Two religious factions are in conflict with each other. The Tamiradae, who were wool-merchants and owned dye-works, abhorred the sight of the naked human body and worshipped Hera. The worshippers of Ashtoreth, the more ancient goddess, loved nakedness.

Dayonis, having escaped capture a second time by diving naked into the sea, swam ashore where she was identified as Ashtoreth/Aphrodite. The Tamiradae were defeated.

Meanwhile, Hange is unmasked as a traitor. It is learnt that the Khemite king, Thothmes, is dead and the Khemite troops are withdrawn and return to Khem because it is seething with rebellion about his successor.

Back in the London of the 1930s, Heyward forces the snail from Denvers' grasp. Having slept for a fortnight, he wakes up, realising that Heyward and Hange are the same person. His wife, Mina, realises how much she loves him and wants to stay with him. The book ends with Denvers telling his wife about Steiner's theory of group reincarnation.

That, in outline, is the story. And it is a good one and an accomplished one for a first novel.

Nakedness is a frequent theme in the book, particularly of Dayonis. Whilst this may be an indication that Gerald was already familiar with, and active in, naturism during this period, it must not be forgotten that nakedness, particularly when fighting, was quite usual in the Mediterranean area during the period in which the book is set.

One particular passage is very striking, where Dayonis escapes from her captors on board ship:

> For some brief seconds Dayonis saw a clear passage to the stern. It was now or never. She was naked, her hair was hidden and she had her sword for attack. If she sped lightly, in the rush she might escape recognition and it would be difficult to snatch at her naked body, which she had taken the precaution to oil well.

The idea that it is difficult to capture someone in the nude, whose body was well oiled, also occurs in *Witchcraft Today*:

> ... they found that the soldiers would usually let a naked girl go, but would take a clothed one prisoner. The slippery oiled bodies also made them hard to catch hold of.

It is important for us is to look at Gerald's references to witchcraft, how he saw it at that time, and other themes which would prove important in his later writings. It is clear that Dayonis is presented as being a witch, although this is rarely stated unambiguously. For example, Kinyras exclaims 'You must be a witch!' and she replies: 'Well, cannot a witch have her uses, sometimes?', in other words not confirming the statement, but implying its veracity.

However, Kinyras' brother, Zadoug, had been spying on Dayonis and her captors and says:

> "She passed most of the time at her witch-tricks. ... It was well known that she was a true Cabire and had invoked these Lords [of Fate] and acquired mighty powers. I discovered that the Cabire were a secret witch cult."

This statement unambiguously suggests that Dayonis was a member of a 'secret witch cult'. The use of the term 'witch cult' is interesting, as Gerald uses it right through until *Gerald Gardner, Witch* was published in 1960. It was, of course, the term which Margaret Murray used in *The Witch Cult in Western Europe*, published by Oxford University Press in 1921.

The Cabeiri or Cabiri were in fact Greek deities who were worshiped in a mystery fertility cult or cults on the Greek island of Lemnos and Samothrace. So, in fact, they were the gods rather than a cult.

Gerald attributes healing qualities to Dayonis and it is clear from the context that these are derived from her being a witch:

Dayonis also says: 'I have the gift of sight from the Old Ones.' Later, she reveals other magical techniques to Kinyras, who in turn reveals his own techniques:

> 'I do nothing but leave my mind open for what will be put into it. I come and I go, up and down Time according to my need, sometimes without voluntary effort.'

She, by contrast, makes a dense smoke and the gods speak to her out of it. It is clear also that she makes sacrifices, both human and animal, as part of her magical workings. For example, she slaughters a jailer, not directly in order to escape, but as an offering:

*'I knew that to obtain real power I must have a human sacrifice, but I always hated to do it. But when I was a help-less prisoner, and my country lost, it was another thing. And he was a beast of an enemy. So I did what was needful, and it worked, for the very next day Ammunz broke through the wall and led me to freedom.'*

So, what conclusions can we draw from an examination of *A Goddess Arrives?*

In this context, the date of publication of *A Goddess Arrives* becomes particularly significant. There is no date in the book and the records of the publishers (Arthur H. Stockwell Ltd.) were destroyed when their premises in Ludgate Hill, London were bombed during the war. The firm moved out to Ilfra-combe in Devon and is still in existence.

However, the British Library received their copy on 6th December 1939. Under the Copyright Act 1911, publishers have to send copies of all new books published to the British Library, and this is obviously likely to happen shortly after copies have been received from the printers. According to Richard Price, the British Library's Curator of Modern British collections, it was not unknown for publishers to omit the date of publication around the end of the year 'so as not to make their work seem quickly out-of-date'. This might well apply to *A Goddess Arrives*, particularly as it was being published not just towards the end of the year but towards the end of the decade as well. We can, I think, with reasonable confidence, give the date of publication as the very beginning of December 1939.

We have another clue. A review of *A Goddess Arrives* appeared in the *Christchurch Times* of 27th January 1940, presumably as the result of a review copy sent by Gardner. Assuming that the review copy was sent out shortly after Gardner received it and giving the reviewer time to read the book thoroughly (which he obviously did) the above publica-tion date seems reasonable.

Gerald therefore probably submitted the book to the

publishers no later than the summer of 1939.

It is clear that Gerald had been interested in many of the main themes of the book for some years—weapons and warfare, reincarnation, secret societies and magical powers, not to mention naked young ladies!

Perhaps it is not surprising that the heroine of his story is made a member of a witch cult but it does mean that by the summer of 1939 at the latest he was writing confidently about a witch performing naked rituals in a circle ringed with lamps, with an altar upon which were bowls, holding a wand and sword, with circumambulation, incense and anointing, all of which would form part of the rituals which Gerald wrote about in *High Magic's Aid* following his initiation.

I think by this time Gerald had read the Key of Solomon and other magical texts, and all these elements could have been obtained from such sources.

Indeed, it was not primarily a book centred on witchcraft as his next book, *High Magic's Aid*, was. It was about warfare and love in ancient Cyprus and about how the legend of Aphrodite rising from the waves may have originated. The psychic or occult element is present in the actions of both hero and heroine but the role taken by witchcraft plays a relatively minor role: it is certainly not a book extolling its virtues or advocating its use.

It seems to me a book by someone interested in witchcraft as one of several interests, someone who had read about it but who had misconceptions about it, for example, the place of animal sacrifice. Indeed, Bracelin says as much about Gerald's initiation:

> *Until then his opinion of witchcraft had been based upon the idea that witches killed for the purpose of gaining or raising power, and he had thought the persecutions of them fully justified.*

The hero, Kinyras, who is based on Gerald, clearly

disapproves of much of Dayonis' activity, as we can tell from the passage where she wants one of Kinyras' men as a human sacrifice, to which he replies: 'Have done, lady. Human sacrifice is an abomination, of which I will have none'. And following the ritual, Kinyras remarks: 'Hark ye, mistress, it's the last time ye play these tricks aboard my ship. I'll have none of it.'

One can imagine that Edith was in a rather difficult position. She had agreed to put Gerald's book into a readable form and was therefore well aware that he was writing about the witch cult. She was a very secretive person and it is clear that she did not reveal herself as being a member of the witch cult herself until half way through his initiation in September 1939, so any influence she had on what Gerald wrote would have been done in a very subtle way. She obviously kept quiet when Gerald introduced ideas which were alien to the Craft as she knew it, including animal and even human sacrifice. Of course, we don't know what Gerald's first draft was like and how much she may have influenced the final version.

Regardless of any such arguments, A Goddess Arrives is a good book, with much to reveal about Gerald Gardner's thoughts and feelings in the late 1930s. As Walter Forder says in his review of the book in the Christchurch Times:

> It is a grand yarn, and on many occasions a most schol-arly and informative narrative, and throughout is a romance that grips. Mr G.B. Gardner may take the unction in his soul that he has accomplished something of which he must be justly proud.

Philip Heselton
January 2024
Hull, UK.

# CHAPTER I

# THE AWAKENING

It was nine o'clock when Denvers let himself out of the flat. He stood on the top stair and peered down the well of the staircase, listening, every line of his figure tense with strain. The old, tall house in Maiden Lane, of which he occupied the top floor, was silent, not as though it was dead but as if it slept, breathing deeply and evenly, giving that impression of a fullness of suspended life, of every board and brick being charged with forgotten tragedies, which is characteristic of ancient dwellings.

Robert Denvers listened, his tall, wiry body stretched far over the banisters, his white, sensitive fingers gripping the handrail. He had unusually beautiful hands, young looking in contrast with his thin, worn face, his greying dark hair waving away from the broad, benevolent brow, the lines of experience and sadness bitten round the fine, generous mouth. His eyes, blue-grey, handsome, clear and intelligent, searched the regions below as keenly as his ears listened. Even in its weariness and misery it was a good and quietly appealing face. In perfect health and happiness it would have been exceptionally well-favoured.

With surprising suddenness he straightened himself and ran lightly down the top flight to the landing below. For such a big man his movements were extraordinarily active, lithe and silent as those of a panther and strangely at variance with that pale, spiritual face, with its brooding expression of permanent unhappiness. Arrived at the landing he turned and, with a series of silent, agile strides, taking two stairs at a time rapidly, reached the top again without making a sound, inserted his key, which turned in the newly-oiled lock with a silky action, and entered the flat and closed the door softly.

'I can do it... perfectly!' he muttered.

But should he? For five minutes he stood debating the question, the emotions struggling in his mind written plainly on his ravaged face.

'I must! I must!' he whispered feverishly. 'I can't stand another day, another hour of this misery and suspense. I must know where I am.'

Crushing down the repugnance and delicacy which was always rising to balk his resolution, he flung open the wardrobe in the hall, which was a large landing boarded in from the stairs, struggled into his great-coat, snatched his hat and once more left his flat, this time banging the door loudly behind him and clattering down the polished uncarpeted stairs. In the hall below, the porter, sorting letters, glanced up and touched his cap as Denvers went out into the street.

A scud of cold rain slapped into his face, so that he shuddered and heaved his coat collar up round his ears with a grimace of distaste. Long years in Malaya had thinned his blood and made of these English winters a torment. Half a gale was blowing, the mingled scents of flowers, fruit and decayed vegetable exhaled from the market nearby, sickening him. With his long stride he quickly reached the end of the lane, doubled up through the market, turned back down Henrietta Street, and re-entered from the other end. Opposite his flat he had discovered a small Italian cafe and tobacconist, where sweets, ice-cream coffee and chocolate were always on sale. After one quick look up and down the street he dived into the shop and seated himself at a little marble table tucked away in a corner, ordered coffee, and waited.

From where he sat he could see the large hall of the old house opposite, brightly lit, the porter reading his paper and yawning convulsively now and then. With the exception of the shop-keepers, very few residents inhabited the lane. Most of the houses had been turned into offices long ago. He glanced at his watch. Almost time for them to come, now. They thought he was safely out of the way, dining with Rogers. What cause had he given them to deem him such a silly, unsuspecting fool? Their contemptuous dismissal of him as such stung him to a twisted smile of misery and self-hatred.

A thin, sallow Italian girl brought his coffee and stood smiling while he paid her. Something in her lustrous dark eyes, the sweet curve of the lids to their outer corner, the starry iris and flutter of deep black lashes reminded him of his wife. There was the same trick of suddenly lowering the white lids without apparent cause, very reminiscent of Mina. Give this girl beauty, a dazzling skin and colour, a laughing, pouting, ripe and roguish mouth, a provocative nose, and there stood Mina when he had first met her. Even now his blood gave a faint stir at the recollection of what Mina had been and still was, lovely, alluring, slim as a slip of hazel. No wonder Heyward loved her.

He did not mind how much Heyward, or any other man, loved her, provided her heart and mind remained uninfluenced, but he was afraid, terribly afraid! There had been too much manoeuvring for his peace. Heyward, as acting Resident in the same Malayan district as himself, high official where Denvers held a minor position, had been able to send him on duty long distances away, so that he could have a free hand with Mina. Then, when Denvers finally retired on his small pension, Heyward had dug up all the long arrears of leave due to him, had followed by the next boat and had spent most of it in so-to-say friendly attentions to Mina. Now he was due to return in a week or so, and they were spending one of their last evenings together, dining at Verey's. Soon they would return to the flat together, where he, Denvers, was not expected back until midnight.

He glanced at his watch again. Half-past nine, not long to wait now. Yet, supposing he was mistaken? Supposing his harassed mind had distorted simple facts into mountains of disaster? Women to-day expected and took for themselves great liberty of action, demanded friendships taboo to their mothers, unthinkable to their grandmothers. The sight of the Italian girl had veered him round to Mina's side, pleaded for him to judge his wife leniently, better still not to judge her at all. Heyward was going away to-morrow, why not ignore it all, try to restore the crumbing fabric of his marriage? His great love for his wife swept over him in a wave of tenderness, flooding his soul and bringing him momentary surcease, transitory peace.

Denvers ordered another cup of coffee and took another long, refreshing look at the girl. She was not really like Mina, it was the eyes and the expression, that gentleness and the beaming smile in them. In Mina they promised what the mouth and nose contradicted, in this girl the other features were so nondescript that they might not have existed. The coffee was brought, Denvers helped himself to sugar and by some devil's trick of visualization suddenly saw Heyward standing in characteristic attitude, silver tongs poised over a cup in his thin brown hand, talking to Mina in his lazy drawl, smiling his slow, Oriental smile, born not of mirth but of irony.

With the involuntary vision Denvers' torments leapt again to scourge him, and his face, which had gained in colour as he thought tenderly of Domina, his wife, paled to its former sickly hue and the strain returned to his clever eyes. His former suspicions and distrust of the man were magnified to certainty. There was a yellow streak in Heyward, of that there was little doubt to Denvers' informed mind. He had studied races too deeply not to know the signs of the black blood inherited from three or four generations back. Heyward's dark skin was not due to the bronze acquired by a life spent in the East, the sombre magnificent eyes were not those of Southern Europe, the veiled insolence of his normal manner to Denvers, so intangible that active resentment was impossible, was never born of anything but Eastern subtlety. While Denvers was writhing again in the grip of a dozen remorseless recollections, a taxi hooted and drew up at the house opposite. They had arrived.

He watched them alight, saw Mina, swathed to the crown in the costly fur wrap he had given her, skip lightly to the shelter of the hall, her little feet pearly in satin slippers gleaming from beneath a froth of lace and ninon, tinted like the surf beneath the rosy clouds of Malayan dawn. She was ten years younger than Denvers and looked twenty. His heart contracted at the sight of her and then began to hammer fiercely, thudding distractingly in his ears.

Give them time to get indoors, upstairs to... settle down. The taxi drove off, they were gone. An immense loneliness, a devastating desolation assailed Denvers. With their departure the whole world seemed emptied of life, as though cataclysm had struck it, wrenched it from its orbit and sent it whirling through space, with himself conscious and awaiting destruction, perched dizzily on some blasted crag. Presently the vertigo passed and he was calm again.

God, would that light never go up in the top front room? In any case what was he going to do? That long debated question had yet to be answered. Involuntarily his hand sought the revolver in his outside jacket pocket. It seemed the easiest, the only possible, answer. Suddenly the light for which he had been watching sprang into being. He must give them another quarter of an hour.

Thought was not suspended in an immensity of waiting. A soft babble of Italian came from the back of the shop, broken every now and then by the entry of a customer. Presently Denvers arose.

'Good night,' h said to the proprietor, 'your coffee is excellent, as usual,' and went out with a grave gesture of farewell. The girl, looking after him, burst into a torrent of excited approbation, to be met with chaff and laughter from her parents.

In the hall the porter was still yawning, and stopped in the middle of a sleepy stretch as Denvers entered and strode towards the stairs.

'Good night, sir,' he answered, stifling another gape.

At the foot of the top flight Denvers paused to listen. No one was moving in the floor above, they had... settled. With those former light, noiseless springs he reached the flat door and entered. Had Mina noticed, he wondered, how silkily the lock worked under his constant oiling? Perhaps not, she was not unduly observant, otherwise his scheme to-night of finding out once and for all would not succeed. He stood within the door, stealthily stowing hat and overcoat in the hall wardrobe, his ears stretched to the murmur of voices which came from the big front room. There was the smell of freshly-brewed coffee, the chink of cups. He crept to the door of the back room, took a new key from his pocket and inserted it in the lock. In a second he was inside the room, behind the heavy bookcase which had been placed across the corner to hide the door, and which he had been pulling, inch by inch, further into the room for the past month, so that ingress by that way would be possible.

The folding doors dividing the two rooms had been removed and a wide arch built in their place, so that Denvers had a clear view into the room. Mina, sylphine and lovely in her long, diaphanous blush-tinted gown, stood by the fire, which made a ruddy, leaping background for her airy figure. She affected period dresses and this one, billowing and froth-ing about her, made her look like Gainsborough picture. She had the extraordinary buoyancy of bearing, as though she floated rather than moved to any other way, which is peculiar to his work and which no other artist had captured and portrayed in the same manner.

'What was that?' she demanded quickly, turning a startled face to the dim interior of the back room, 'put on the light, Hank.'

Heyward obeyed and stood with his hand on the switch, staring searchingly into the room as the light flooded it. Denvers stood like a rock, though his heart thumped suffocat-ingly.

'What?' Heyward asked, dropping his hand and moving back to her side, 'there's nothing there. Did you hear anything?'

'No, but I felt a strong draught. It made me shiver.'

'You're nervous, darling. It's a blowy night, and these old houses are full of unaccountable draughts.'

'Yes, of course. I suppose so,' she said, dubiously.

'Have some more coffee,' Heyward suggested, stretching out his hand for her cup.

She yielded it up with a smile and watched him refill it.

'How neat-handed you are, Hank. I do think it's important in a man.'

'Not like poor old Robert, who seems to spill everything.'

Mina frowned into her cup as she stirred slowly.

'That's only because he's been so wretchedly nervous lately. He used not to do that. Hank, I can't help thinking he suspects.'

Heyward's ironical laugh burst out.

'I see in him every sign of premature senile decay, but we should worry!'

Again Mina Denvers frowned and her red mouth pouted mutinously as she eyed her lover discontentedly. There were times when some smothered inner self made abortive struggles towards life, when its dying voice endeavoured to articulate... what? At such times the jar of Heyward's manner could pierce even her bemused infatuation. She did not want to think, to reason, to consider her conduct and its effects, all she desired was to be lapped in a rosy dream of impossible delights, to keep the nightmare of advancing age at a distance, to feel exotically, passionately, to live in the world of forbidden pleasures heed-less of rough expulsion, which stalked a haunting shadow by her side from the moment of entrance.

'Why do you always sneer so abominably at Robert? It's hardly decent.'

The almost querulous tones in the beautiful voice warned Heyward of danger, stabbed him with a sharp fear that his case was not yet won and showed him that his first curious, instinc-tive detestation of Denvers, experienced at their first meeting and increasing abnormally with the growth of their intercourse, must be curbed. He had often pondered the question and sought for the reason of this hatred, which he was assured Denvers reciprocated, and which had sprung to life at their first encounter as though it had been the revival of some old, bitter feud, started in their childhood and which must inevitably last until their death. Heyward hated things which he could not explain away and had tried honestly to account for this, even to fight against it.

He stood silent, staring at Mina, who was looking at him in a mutinous discontent which, in an ordinary woman of her age would have been ridiculous. In her it was captivating and he wondered if her charm was of that enduring kind which lasted into extreme old age. He adored her, was hers body and soul, but he was not sure of her, yet. Damn Denvers! How this persistent hatred of the fellow had power to rise up and come between Mina and himself, as though the man were actually in the room. When he first met Mina he remembered how her obvious devotion and loyalty to her husband had irritated him to that point of making every effort to seduce her away from her duty. That sudden, instinctive hatred alone had impelled him to the action and not love or even attraction for Mina. He thought of how he had excited her, and led her to tire herself out, so that feeling ill she, in the absence of her husband, turning to him for sympathy, and had the more easily become his prey.

At the time he was still in love with Mary, who had given him long years of happiness, and whose love he was rewarding with shameful cruelty. Then suddenly he was aware that he was hoist with his own petard, a slave to Mina Denvers, experiencing in the acutest form feelings which he had affected out of animosity to an utterly inoffensive subordinate, who should have been protected from him by every law of decency and rectitude. But he did not want to think, either of his wife or of Denvers. He wanted Mina with every ounce of his strength and here was she reverting to some of her old loyalties. It was unthinkable!

'You don't like it?' he asked, slowly.

She made a sudden, fierce gesture of repudiation. 'No, I don't. I want to forget. Besides, it's rotten of you, Hank. Why do you hate him so?'

'Hate him, oh, I don't hate him. I only despise him. It's funny, I liked him at first, he was so uncommon; I like uncommon people, then I found how wrapped up he was in you, how proud he was of you. No one could talk to him for five minutes without knowing that. So I thought what fun it would be to make the one he loves hate him, and I have, and he's miserable about it.'

Suddenly, as though in a blinding flash, she had a true picture of the man, knew his cruelty and unscrupulousness for what they were worth, was the yellow streak in him and drew back repulsed before it. Almost immediately this flare of insight was over, as thought it had never been, irreparable loss. The feeling was so intolerable that her face grew white, her eyes darkened until they looked like a clear pool beneath a night sky, and she shivered again.

'What is it?' he demanded, torn with anxiety by her looks and manner.

Mina did not know, the impression had been too fleeting to be aught but a miserable one, but she answered what she believed to be the truth. 'I was thinking of Mary.'

Denvers wondered how Heyward would take this. Standing in his cramped position close to the wall, he felt that all sensation had left his body and mind. He was like a tense spectator in the grip of a strong drama, too concentrated upon the actors to be conscious of his own reactions and emotions. When the play was over awareness of self would return.

Hardened as he was, Heyward replied with a cynicism that surprised himself. 'She'll sue for divorce. She won't be able to stand much more of me. I've been driving her to it and I know how! When I go back I'll put the finishing touches.'

'She may not divorce,' Mina whispered, her eyes fixed on his dark face in a sort of fascinated stare.

'Don't be afraid. She's proud and... squeamish. By the time I've done with her she'll take to it as a sort of bath. Leave all that to me. I'll manage it. I've got away with quite a bit. No one suspects us. She knows, but she'd bite her tongue out before she'd breathe a word against me.'

'I can't bear to hear you talk like that. It's all so horribly cruel. You'll be like that to me when you get fed up with me, I know you will.' She began to cry wretchedly, sobs growing more and more convulsive.

They tore at Denvers' heart and drove Heyward desperate. 'Mina, darling!' he implored. He snatched her into his arms, holding her closer with each second of mounting passion, his torrid blood thudding through his heart and clouding his brain, his hungry lips on her. At first she struggled against him, doubling his excitement by her resistance, but his hot mouth pressed to hers, covering her face and neck with ardent kisses, his ever tightening clasp of her slender, thinly-clad form against his vibrant body, fired her to an equal expression. He carried her to the couch by the fire and set her roughly in the corner, flinging himself beside her in panting haste. The diaphanous clouds were pushed from her shoulders, all their intoxicating softness and curves lay bare to his adorning eyes, his hands and mouth questing avidly.

Sickened and convinced, Denvers, feeling more like a man of ice than a human being, slipped through the door out into the hall again. Disgust held him in frigid thrall. He stepped quickly to the door of the flat, opened it and sent it slamming with a clap that reverberated through the whole house and set the upper floor ashake. He pulled open the wardrobe door with a click and shut it carelessly and noisily. Having given these evidences of his return he walked to the sitting-room door and paused to light a cigarette, observing as he did so with a curious detachment that his hands were steady as rocks. Then he went in.

His first rapid glance showed him Mina with her back to him, feverishly poking the fire. Heyward lay back in a deep armchair, his long legs outstretched to the blaze Mina was making. H was lighting a cigarette and his hands were shaking so that the lighter wavered. His face was hidden by his clasped hands. Disdaining all attempts at concealment, Denvers walked deliberately to the mirror on the wall between the windows and scrutinized his face. It was white, but rigidly calm. It might have been carved in granite save for the burning eyes, gazing back at him in tortured misery. Well, he could not hope to control them and they had betrayed him already, he knew. He pretended to straighten his tie. 'Good evening!' he said belatedly, 'beastly night.'

Neither was capable of answering him and he did not expect one. He walked over to Heyward's chair and stood looking down on him with an openly contemptuous scrutiny. His financial security no longer could be imperilled by this man, he was his own master at last. 'You appear to be having some difficulty with that,' he said in quiet scorn, 'allow me.'

He took the lighter from Heyward's fluttering fingers and held it, poised just out of reach, so that it lighted the dark face thrown into vivid relief by the jade cushion behind it. A small contest of wills between the two men followed. Heyward was resolved he would neither life his eyes nor bend his head, Denvers that he should do both. Mina continued to rattle the poker frantically, while the glare from the steady flame on his face was intolerable to Heyward. Still he was determined and endured it.

An icy race possessed Denvers, in which all his former anguish was swamped in an ache to humiliate his enemy. The steady, waiting flame never wavered. The maddening clatter at the grate went on. 'There's no necessity for that din, Mina. The fire was quite good before you started on it and you know it.'

The power fell with a crash to the hearth, but he did not turn to look at her. Something deep in his mind asked him why he should feel such monumental scorn of these two people. He dismissed it with the bald assertion that he did so feel. Suddenly endurance snapped, Heyward's lowered lids flickered up and down, there was a flashing glance of unbearable insolence and triumph, and he bent his head to the flame. For what seemed an age Denvers continued to hold it, then he extinguished it and put it back into the other's hand. Then, with equal suddenness his clenched fist shot out and crashed into the face before him with all his might, smashing the glowing cigarette up into his eye and holding it there. He could feel it burning into his own knuckles, but was incapable of all sensation of physical pain. Then he withdrew his hand and turned to look at Mina. She was standing with her back to them, trying to control her unruly breath, rectifying the disorder of her hair with furtive touches of trembling fingers. Denvers turned back to Heyward. He had risen from his chair, his left eye was closed and there was blood on his cheek where the bevel of Denvers' big signet ring had made a deep gash, the cigarette lay smouldering on the carpet. Denvers extinguished it with his foot and made and expressive gesture towards the door. Less than a minute later the flat door slammed behind Heyward.

The sound roused Mina and she swung around startled, thinking it was her husband who had gone. When she saw him standing behind her she gave a strangled exclamation of dismay. 'He's gone?' she said incredulously.

Denvers nodded and stooped to retrieve the cigarette, which he tossed into the fire. The wild exhilaration and satisfaction caused by his blow had evaporated, the icy rage was gone, the anguish of desolation flowed back upon him and he was sunk once more in the gulf of misery where he had been lying so long.

Mina made no attempt to conceal her dismay and agitation. 'Why has he gone like that, without saying good night, or anything?' she demanded, fixing wistful eyes on her husband, like a child disappointed of some cherished hope.

'He hadn't the nerve to stay any longer, I think.'

'Hadn't the nerve! Hank? Are you crazy?'

'I wish I was.'

She shrugged impatiently and glanced at the clock. You're home early.'

'You thought I'd be safely out of the way, I suppose?'

'Safely?' she echoed scornfully, flaunting him with eyes and lips.

12

'Yes. I came back half an hour ago and more.'

Her gaze fixed him steadily but she disdained reply.

'The draught you felt was me opening the door behind the bookcase.'

If he hoped to move her by this explanation he was mistaken, for whatever were her sensations she kept them to herself, merely commenting acidly, 'You must have had a very unpleasant experience.'

He found himself on the verge of offering excuses. 'I simply had to know for certain, Mina. I couldn't go on like that any longer, suspecting you and then cursing myself for doubting. It's being going on a long time, now.'

She threw out her hands in a sudden gesture of futility. Anger, despair, impatience, hopelessness, all seemed to be written on her face at once. 'I can't help it, Robert, it's all beyond me. Things just happen like this. I didn't do it deliberately, didn't even want to, for a long.'

'If only I could understand where I'd failed you. If I hadn't loved you...'

He was interrupted by her gesture and look of impatience and distaste, a look which pierced him fiercely and drove the words from his lips. For a moment or two there was silent between them, she experiencing all the crude disgust evoked in a woman by protestations of affection from the wrong man, when she is in a state of excitement about the right one, he feeling that if he knew why she preferred his obvious inferior, some of the smart would be taken from his wound. The urge to discuss this had been strong upon him for months, and was the last feeble defence of the defeated in love. 'Tell me, honestly, where he is a better man than I?'

She looked at him, obliged to acknowledge Denvers' patent superiority, both physically and mentally. Yet she loved Heyward. 'He is a wonderful lover.'

Denvers winced and knew a moment of blinding jealousy, the potency of which staggered him. 'You're infatuated,' he gasped in a choking voice. 'You're in the dangerous years when a woman claws desperately at any kind of animal passion offered her, knowing the time is short.'

The blood stole into her pale cheeks at this insult. For a moment or two she was silent. The long mirror between the windows showed her lovely in her clouds of chiffon and lace. She looked at the reflection, was comforted and smiled, forgiving him because of what she saw there. 'And men never do that.'

Shamed, he did not answer and she went on.

'I'm not your sort, Robert. I want life and gaiety, you're dull and bookish in your musty old museums. You get passed over, given all the hard jobs while other men get the credit, so we're boor and obscure. Oh, yes, you're clever and handsome and that makes it worse, because everyone wants to know why you haven't got on, and pities us. I hate pity and I'm sick of poverty.'

'God knows I've tried hard enough and worked like a galley -slave all my life. I've found hard for security and tried every damn thing to get it. Times have been fightfully difficult, Mina. It's been no joke having one's life cut in half by a bloody war, able to get only temporary jobs, going constantly in terror of being axed. That's been the life of hundreds of us men, while you women have sat and grumbled and sulked. You might give a thought to that. Anyhow, we're not paupers. We've six hundred a year.'

'What's the use of going over all that? It just happens, like everything else.'

'Once you loved me, Mina. You were everything a man could wish till you met that swine.'

'I tried to be, at any rate.'

'D'you mean to say it was an effort?'

'No. I did care, tremendously, and we promised each other that if either met someone else, we should both be free to do as we liked. Well, now there's Hank, but it might just as well have been you who changed your mind.'

'I never should. I always loved you and I always shall.'

Again a pettish motion of her shoulders expressed her distaste, as tough she shook off noxious insect. 'It's no use hanging on to what's dead and gone, Robert. These things just happen and arguing won't get us anywhere. I'm tired.'

'What are you going to do?'

'Oh, don't bother. I'm not going to leave you yet awhile. Hank has got heaps of things to arrange and we simply mustn't do anything in a hurry. I shall just carry on as usual until he's ready for me.' She began to move towards the door, blissfully unaware of the outrageousness of her attitude.

'Of all the impudence!' Denvers commented quietly. 'That swine of a half-caste won't come out into the open about you and risk his precious position for your sake, that's obvious. I didn't think you were such a blind fool, Mina.'

She paused by the door and looked back at him. 'You're jealous and incapable of seeing anything in a sensible and reasonable light,' she said quietly. 'You know how we stand, now, and I think you might accept things decently. At least there's nothing to be gained by talking any more to more to-night. You won't change me, Robert.'

With that the door opened and she drifted through, closing it softly behind her.

# CHAPTER II

# ESCAPE

For some minutes after Mina left the room Denvers stood staring at the closed door. He felt a horrible flatness, realising that for the past few months he had been living in a state of much excitement, rising to the peak of this night's crisis. Now all uncertainty was over and he knew exactly the extent of the calamity which had befallen him, and it was not until this moment that he fully comprehended how large a part hope and trust had played in buoying him up. Now he knew the vast difference between apprehension of disaster and its actuality. The completeness of his overthrow was appalling.

Mental and spiritual pain overwhelmed him and he longed for oblivion. The desire alone was a torment, was worse than any physical torture, because there was nothing which could give him assuagement or forgetfulness. Fractious and disagreeable as Mina had been to him for some time past, hard as she had made life for him with his doubts and fears about her conduct, these trials paled into insignificance before the desolation of her utter loss. The needless cruelty of life, the horrible, ironical twists of its petty pace revolted him with a sense of inescapable futility. It was not that he was a coward who shrank from adversity, unable to bear the sting of the lash, but it was the purposelessness of it all which crushed him. Deep in his soul the conviction was born and thrived in spite

16

of all thwarting, that Mina's love was not given to Heyward. Had it been, he told himself he would have resigned her with less foreboding. Out of his own great love for her Denvers had obtained a knowledge and understanding of his wife which was almost feminine in its delicacy of perception and intuition.

Mina was dual natured. One side of her was shrewd, practical, highly intelligent, the other was childish and childlike, frivolous, craving amusement, attracted by highly coloured and meretricious personalities. Until recently she had preserved the balance between these conflicting characteristics and the result had been a disposition of great charm and variety. But of late she had given the reign to her worst impulses. There was little doubt to any onlooker who had watched them so closely as had Denvers, the Heyward appealed to and roused in her all her worst qualities. Equally there was no doubt whatever that she had loved Denvers deeply and devotedly, and during the years of his hard struggle to secure even the most meagre footing, she had been his loyal, understanding, loving and comforting ally. She had made his bitter efforts possible, had been the supreme consolation for his innumerable disappointments, their domestic happiness had been a by-word. Then had come the encounter with Heyward, the hostility which had instantly sprung into being between the two men, Heyward's veiled enmity evidenced in a thousand petty details, and the gradual change in Mina. Denvers, with his uncanny insight, was firmly persuaded that the man's pursuit and conquest of his wife was due, not to an overwhelming attraction towards her, but to an overweening vanity and egotism, which could not tolerate the thought of happiness so unusual possessed by an enemy, or of a woman so beautify remaining impervious to his own very superior and purely imaginary attractions. The undermining of Mina's loyalty and content had been a very insidious affair, yielding considerable enjoyment to the operator. Looking back, Denvers could see all this plainly.

And Mina? What of her, when he bemused infatuation was over and she came to her sense, when she saw Heyward for what he was, a mere fly-by-night, when an equal intensity of disgust would supplant her present obsession? From past experience he knew the depths of her emotional nature, her passions of repentance for small lapses, her extravagant self-reproach for trifling unkindnesses to which she gave expression now and then in capricious moods, what of her when she had offended her own delicacy and pride past self-forgiveness? No matter how deep, how complete would be his own over-looking of her conduct, the memory of the wrong she had done him and herself, her betrayal of their love and life together would never more be effaced from her mind, and would for ever stand between them.

It was this knowledge of her and the conviction that neither had power to avert the impending stroke, which maddened Denvers. The thought of Mina at the mercy of such as Heyward, of what would be her ultimate fate, was insupportable to Denvers. Like all far-seeing, deeply understanding people, he could see the future stretching ahead, his warnings passing unheeded, and plumbed the depths of the worst kind of suffering. Surely it was no act of murder to shoot Heyward? Would it not be the height of sanity to end such a life for himself and his wife? Or better still, to shoot himself.

Mechanically he groped his way to his room and fumbled for the switch. His limbs seemed to have lost their usual, clean-cut agility and to be invested with a creeping paralysis. The light sprang on and he sank heavily on the side of his bed, sitting there with hunched shoulders, his sensitive, expressive hands hanging hopelessly between his knees, eyes staring unseeing before him. So he sat for an hour, until his knees, eyes staring unseeing before him. So he sat for an hour, until he was chilled to the bone and in a fit of nervous shivering crawled over to the fire-place, lit the gas-fire and slumped into the easy chair, to sit staring at the flickering flames, his mind pursuing the dreary treadmill of unconstructive thought. Presently he roused himself and tried the distraction of reading, quite uselessly.

In a corner of the room stood a small table holding an exquisite model of an ancient temple. Next it and beneath the window was a bench on which lay many delicate tools and another model half finished. Denvers rose, switched on a second light, and sat down before the bench, to try the effect of work, in which normally he could become utterly absorbed. For years he had been making models for museums and as an expert in his special subjects enjoyed a great reputation. Had he neglected Mina? While he was so engrossed in his archaeological research and reconstruction, had she been intolerably dull and bored? His mind was swinging round the old dizzy track and he turned away from the section, laying down his tool with a gesture of despair.

He began to walk the room with his soft, long stride hating the ferment of his mind, yet caught in its seething swirl. How long would this go on? Would this sleepless, boiling activity eventually drive him mad? Could he stand another night, another hour of it. The bed in the next room creaked, as though its occupant had turned over in an ecstasy of impatience. He must not disturb Mina with his restless misery.

If he could unload his mind perhaps he could find relief. The impulse to write down all his feelings and thoughts about themselves to Mina was urgent, and he sat down at his desk, sweeping away a litter of notes and MS. With an impatient hand. In doing so he came across a small object wrapped in white tissue paper, which had fallen out of one o the drawers where he kept it. The Snail. Strange that it should come to hand just now. It was years since he had looked at it. Idly his fingers began to unfasten its wrapping until they disclosed a piece of fine bronze, exquisitely worked in the form of some strange creature, like, yet unlike, a snail.

Denvers sat staring at it, turning it about and about. It had a strange fascination for him, this relic of the Bronze Age, with its unpronounceable name, Karaolous. He did not know where it had come from nor how he had obtained possession of it. As long as he could remember anything he could remember this. And the curious words associated with it, where had they come from? 'A new life for an old life when all life has lost its value, but not till all life has lost its value.' Who had told him this?

Denvers passed his hand wearily across his aching head. There was so much he knew which he had neither read nor been told, and which he could never have observed for himself. Where did all his curious, out of the way knowledge come from, so that he could make his models of forts and houses as though he was rebuilding them from memory?

He laid the Snail down beside him because, in an extraordinary way, it comforted him to have it near him, and began to write to Mina. He wrote all his aching thoughts, his abiding love for her, his efforts and aspirations on her behalf, all his fears for her welfare, his certainty that her old, wonderful love for him was not gone but only buried, preserved like a rare vase of exquisite workmanship which could lie unharmed beneath the ruins of Pompeii, and he implored her when she knew her old love was brought to light again, not to let the period of its obscuring come between them and separate them for ever. We could learn the truth about ourselves only by experience.

When he had finished it was close upon five o'clock and some of the pain was assuaged. His eyes smarted and an ineffable weariness overcame him. Hastily he thrust the letter into a drawer. Mina would never see it but a measure of ease had come to him in the effort of putting his emotions into words. Shivering with cold in spite of the heat of the room, he undressed and crept into bed and almost immediately fell into a troubled sleep, haunted by dreams in which his brother Zadoug flitted phantom-like just before him and with whom he could never catch up. Then he was at a council meeting, where loud, angry voices rose in a babble of confused statement, amongst which his own was the loudest and angriest because something of vital importance pressed urgently upon his consciousness without achieving clarity, and some action was demanded of him upon which no one would come to an agreement. He wakened to find himself grasping the Snail and to an awareness of impending calamity, though its exact nature was as yet hidden from him.

A moment's thought served to enlighten him and he was back again in all the old pain and heaviness of spirit. He rose, shaved and dressed, hoping to escape from the flat before his wife came out, but she had risen early for her and came into the sitting-room with the same set white face she had worn for days past, the same scornful gleam bordering on hate in her dark eyes, a cigarette dangling from her lip.

Whether it was due to the wretched night he had passed, or to the fact that his endurance was ebbing fast, he could not tell, but this morning Denvers felt a great deal more anger than sorrow at the calamity which had overtaken them both. His wife irritated him, her petulance bored him.

'Good morning, Mina,' he said, staring at her disparagingly.

'Good!' she sneered. 'What's good about it? You look like a wet week. Why can't you put a good face on things, for a change?'

'I seem to have heard the same remark from you before, many times. Need you imitate a parrot?'

Mina cast a glance into the mirror, unconsciously assuming a pleasant expression she always took when so doing. Like most people, it is doubtful if she ever saw her true self. Reassured, she returned to her grievance. 'If you really loved me you'd look happy, when you know how I detest dull, miserable people. I'm sick of your hang-dog air. After all, I haven't left you yet. When we were first married you always looked bright and cheerful. I'm ten years younger than you.'

'And don't look it... at the moment.'

'That's only your beastly envy. Everyone tells me I look years younger than my age. Hank's as young as I and we fit in together. We're sick of dull and dusty old fogeys. We're both young and jolly.' She poured a cup of coffee and sank into her chair to sip it and eye him resentfully over the rim.

Denvers simply glared at her, amazed at his own animosity. 'You're neither of you young nor jolly, but just a couple of silly, middle-aged fools, who'll never see forty again. You tag around with the young people, who tolerate you because they're polite, and who tell you all sorts of silly stuff just to see how much you will swallow, and then laugh at you behind your backs. You, and all like you.'

Mina glared at him in speechless fury, too non-plussed at this sudden turning of the worm to be able to think of any suitable retort. Denvers, beginning to feel elated at this opposite swing of his pendulum, and believing he had reached emancipation, helped himself to eggs and back and began to eat with more appetite than he had known for weeks. For some time silence reighed, while Mina sat turning over various biting remarks in her mind and rejecting them all because they lacked the necessary sting. Presently Denvers finished eating and pushed away his plate, poured more coffee and lit a cigarette. Precious time was slipping and soon he would take himself off before she had achieved a verbal victory.

'Hank's the same age as me and I'm no forty-three yet,' she blurted out at last.

Denvers flicked ash into tray with a judicial air. 'Old enough to know better. Old enough to have given beauty a background of dignity. You should be reaping, not ploughing for your crop of wild oats.'

The scorn in face and tone were intolerable and futile hatred blazed in her, to find equally futile utterance. 'How dare you!'

His level eyes met her furious ones. Denvers thought of Heyward and wondered how he was looking this morning. A certain grim satisfaction warmed his chilled being. He rose, remembered his coffee, drained then cup and stood looking at her with a cold and merciless scrutiny. Instinctively she shrank back.

'You needn't be afraid,' he told her icily.

For some little time after he had stalked from the room and walked down to the Museum, his glow of satisfaction at this self-assertion continued to warm him, though with gradually diminishing effect. When the last vestige of it had disappeared he was in the fell grip of momentary hatred swamped and drowning in his revived love for her. He loathed himself for having forgotten his manhood. Though he had no very clear recollection of what he had said, doubtless his words were utterly outrageous and unforgivable. Yet he must have her forgiveness and after a day which was several degrees more wretched than any which had gone before, he returned early to obtain it.

The flat was empty, but a good fire burned in the grate and the kettle steamed away on the trivet. On a table drawn up beside the fire a meal was set for one. The white square of an envelope leaning against the clock gleamed at him in the dusk. Wearily he took it, switched on the light and tore it open.

It began without preamble. 'I'm off to cousin Bette for the day. How could you be so cruel as to hurt Hank like that? I think it is very mean of you. I haven't left you yet and until I do I think you might at least be decent. If you loved me at all, you'd not inflict sour faces on me. You know how I hate them. I've always been good to you and done what i could to make you happy and be a good and loyal wife to you. We promised each other freedom if either should want it. If it had been you I would have given it cheerfully, but because it is me you go about like a wet week and vent your spite on poor Hank.'

The same old parry cry that he'd been listening to for some time lately.

'Why can't you take life easily and be pleasant? You used not to be so glum and sour. I don't like disagreeable and ugly faces. It isn't as though I'd left you yet, and until I do you might at least be bright and cheerful. I like young and gay people, not old, dusty fossils, with the weight of the world on their shoulders. I'm tired to death of your sullen temper. Perhaps, by the time I come back you'll have got over the sulks and be prepared to treat me nicely, until Hank is ready to take me. After all, I've given you the best years of my life and you oughtn't to grudge me a little happiness now. Why don't you find somebody for yourself? There are heaps of girls knocking about, trying to get off with every man they meet, who'd jump at you. All you've got to do is to look about you and wear a smile. Some nice girl is bound to fall for you, I give you my word. There, I've tried to cheer you up by showing you what to do. Reward me by being nice and cheerful when I come back.'

It ended without a signature and Denvers read it through twice, searching in vain for any little expression which could give him a ray of hope. He found none and finally laid it down, feeling such a sickness of misery that it was physically nauseating. He must pull himself together, somehow, make an effort to face things. Thoughts of suicide haunted him, but that way out was repugnant to him. What a bloody business life was, and he might live for years, carrying this ache of wretchedness perpetually, always longing for the release of Death, who, like a cat, would come only when he was not wanted.

He sat down by the fire and ate his meal, trying to distract his thoughts with a book, reading avidly and turning a great many pages without comprehending a single paragraph. When at length he had finished eating, he went into his bedroom and set himself resolutely to work at the model fort upon which he had been engaged for some time; Phoenician, with its force of tiny lead soldiers. He arranged them lovingly, wondering if ever again he should get back his old, ardent enthusiasm for his work. Beside him the Snail lay on the bench, gleaming dully in the light. He took it up and turned it about and about.

Queer that it should give him that vague feeling of consolation! It must be pure imagination on his part, due to memories of his childhood and youth which it evoked. Yet why carp at any mean is of obtaining relief? His long, delicate, artist's fingers traced the dim lines that were still discernible on the bronze lying in his palm, and he fell into one of his day-dreams as he called them. When he was in the presence of any object of genuine antiquity he had a curious sense of complete familiarity with it, as though, through its medium, he could recreate the life which had surrounded it from its inception. Denvers never had determined whether this was some curious psychic power he possessed, or merely the effort of a vivid imagination. He was inclined to attribute it to the latter, for he was extraordinarily well balanced mentally and gifted with amazing powers of visualization. The process of thought with him was a series of vivid mental pictures. Not only did he see everything he thought, but he heard his thoughts in a voice speaking to him.

It was because of this keenness and rareness of his mentality that his unhappiness smote him with such intensity. It was because of this sensitiveness that he was so successful with his forts, modelling them and their garrisons with an accuracy as though he worked from memory of things seen and not from facts acquired through reading alone.

He laid the Snail down gently on the bench before him and went on with his work. At the far end was another model, of a Roman fortress, each little figure of the garrison exact in every detail of its harness. Beside it was a Viking ship, a thing of great beauty with its crew and warriors of Northmen, looking as though but yesterday it had made the passage of the mighty waterways from Constantinople to Novgorod. Denvers contemplated this example of his skill, of which he was justly but secretly proud, for some time, delighting as good craftsmen always must don in their own efficiency. After all, there was always his work and through, according to modern superficiality of thought and observation, such perpetual dwelling in the past as it entailed was of no interest and of little value to humanity to-day, Denvers knew better. With his accustomed profundity of thought he realize that past, present and future were inseparable, bound together in one vast whole and that without a knowledge of the first, humanity could not live safely and well in the second, nor build for the third. People to-day were too ignorant and too shallow-minding, preferring to dwell upon the surface of things, too cowardly to plunge into the depths... people like Mina and Heyward. There he was, back again in the centre of his circle, when he thought he had walked out of it.

He plunged into work, his hands moving swiftly and delicately, his fine face, illuminated by the table-lamp, brought into vivid relief, so that all its clear-cut lines, the broad, thoughtful, benevolent brow, the dark intensity of the intuitive eyes, the firm set of the sensitive lips, which life had refined, strengthened and sweetened, were strongly etched against the background of the dim room, with a play of light and shade which would have delighted the heart and eye of Rembrandt.

So he worked, keeping misery at bay, apparently absorbed in nothing but his task, until the early hours of the morning, when his eyes were so fatigued that he deemed sleep must be inevitable. With a shy smile at his own folly, he took the Snail in his hand, experiencing once more that intangible sensation of consolation, of companionship, such as he had felt when, as a small child, refusing his favourite disreputable Gollywog, he would clamour until this same Snail was found and given to him and he would fall into a sweet, profound sleep

Resolutely he put out the light and composed himself, deliberately setting his mind on sleep. Kipling's lines floated through his mind—

'Now we are come to our Kingdom and the crown is ours to take,
With a naked sword at the council board and under the throne the snake.
Now we have come to our kingdom, but my love's eyelids fall.
All that I wroght for, all that I fought for, avail me nothing at all.
My crown is of withered leaves for she sits on the ground and grieves.
Now we have come to our Kingdom...'

Well, he had come to his kingdom and a kingdom of despair it proved!

But now there was a feeling of dust falling, falling, a period of calm, peaceful, restful thought, a delightful sensation of sliding gently down a soft, grassy slope...

# CHAPTER III

# IN A NEW LAND THAT WAS OLD

Slowly consciousness began to dawn again upon Denvers. He became aware of many men sitting round him and a hated voice droning on interminably, Heyward's voice, uttering its usual stream of specious lies. A sense of outrage began to burn in Denvers. By the gods, if someone did not silence him he would hurl a knife through Heyward's throat! His fingers sought the bronze dagger at his waist.

Someone was shaking him violently by the shoulder, calling him, 'Kinyras! I say, Kinyras!'

Denvers struggled, reluctant to emerge from sleep. He was infinitely weary, he must sleep if he was to be fit for anything. A final rough shake brought him effectually awake. It was his brother Zadoug sitting beside him, the council in full conclave, Hange, the law-giver, was making one of his endless speeches.

Denvers glanced round the massive, rough-hewn halls wall of the council hall. The supporting pillars of wood were painted black and red in the chequered design, the upper air so wreathed with blue veils of smoke from the many earthenware lamps, that the roof was obscured. His surroundings seemed strange to him, though vaguely familiar, as the home of one's childhood is familiar after years of absence from it. He had been dreaming one of his strange, intensely vivid dreams, in which he was living in a curious age among millions of people who rushed pell-mell morning and evening into underground tunnels, or clambered aboard huge vehicles which moved of their own volition at an incredible speed, so that many were killed daily through falling beneath their wheels. These people worked in great buildings, where there was much noise, both of a large and small kind, from irritating clickings to vast roarings, and there was an infinity of rain, always rain, against which one wore a harsh, flapping garment, cold and clammy to the skin. A violent shudder seized Denvers at this recollection and he glanced down at his own clothes, a loin cloth, and the broad leather of his sword-belt, the comforting feel of the hilt beneath his hand. These were clothes indeed, something a man could move and fight in.

Already the effect of his nightmare was fading rapidly as he came back to life again. Thank the gods that horrible experience was only a dream. It was so unnatural, only one thing was the same there, women betrayed you there, as they did in real life!

He turned to Zadoug smiling. 'I was wearing and sleep overtook me. And I dreamed...gods, what a dream!'

Zadoug shifted impatiently and dismissed it with a gesture. 'Dreams, Kinyras! You are too prone to them. Listen to that braying ass and silence him, if you would save the country from ruin.'

Denvers glanced satirically at the law-giver. Heyward... no, that strange, uncouth word belonged to the man in his dreams, the enemy who had poisoned his life. Curious that his instinctive hatred of Hange should pursue him even into the realms of sleep, to haunt him there, too. Hange had been in his dream, dark, lithe, insolent, taunting him, making a fool of him, his handsome, swarthy face, which showed so clearly the black blood flowing in his veins, full of a mocking triumph. What was it he had done to Hange in his dream? He couldn't recollect. No matter. It was much more important to circumvent Hange in life than to worry about his actions in dreams.

'My lords,' Hange was saying, one hand thrust negligently inside his sword-belt, the other resting on the table, partly supporting his weight, 'we are told by some scare-mongers that the country is in imminent peril. We Karpasians are in danger from the men of Khem. Now, sirs, I put it to you, is this likely? With the Khemites invading Dali as they are busily engaged in doing, and with Aghirda and Damastes holding out so vigorously against them in his pathless mountains, what can they do against Karpas? It is obvious Khem will never dare to attack us while Aghirda is on their flank, to say nothing of the fact that the distance to our frontier is so great and that first they must pass through the wild forest and over the awful hills, where only a barbarian like Aghirda and his hordes can life and survive the dangers. No, Karpas is safe, I tell you.'

'Liar and swine!' Zadoug muttered restlessly.

Kinyras made a restraining gesture. 'Patience,' he whispered, 'it's a dog that will hang itself, given time.'

'Time,' Zadoug echoed, 'it is time we lack.'

'Nevertheless, patience. Look around you, listen.'

Involuntarily Zadoug obeyed, and saw that the Council was in an uproar of excitement and dissension which gradually found vent in words and cries, some verging upon the abusive. Hange still stood negligently leaning upon one hand, silent, half smiling with that twist of the lip so characteristic of him and which always looked like a half-formed sneer, glancing from face to face, seemingly unmindful of the growing discontent about him, which even the shouts and howls of his lick-spittle following could not disguise. At length Kinyras sprang to his feet and struck the table with his clenched fist. 'Silence!' he demanded, in a tense, carrying voice.

Hange, with a suppressed start of surprise, turned reluctant eyes upon him. 'Is it you, Kinyras, who cries out so imperiously?'

The two men exchanged a long stare and it was Hange who found occasion to brush a beetle off the table which had fallen from the rafters.

'Yes, it is I,' Kinyras answered when the other had removed

his gaze, and not before.

'Well, Kinyras.'

'We have listened to you, sir, at great length. You are a law-giver and doubtless your words contain much wisdom... in law. But this is a season for soldiers and Erili is here, asking to be allowed to address the Council. I ask that we hear Erili.'

Slowly Hange raised his eyes to those of Kinyras and again that long, steely look was exchanged, while the latter stood as though cut in rock, inflexible with purpose, and the other looked supple and slippery as an adder. Once more he was unable to sustain the encounter and he turned with a gesture, all affability, to the rest of the council. 'Is it your wish to hear the leader of the Mercenaries?'

'No! No! Speak on,' shouted his followers.

'Erili! Erili! Let us hear him,' bellowed the majority, and with another gesture Hange resumed his seat.

Kinyras sat down and near to him a tall, powerful man rose, mid another shout of approbation. He was bare headed and his yellow hair clung about his forehead in damp curls, for the chamber was hot from the flare of many lamps. His eyes, a greenish hazel, were commanding, clever, forceful, his head, small and compact, showed good capacity and he carried it well. His skin was fair and ruddy, his features bold and handsome and likable, his manner assured to the point of arrogance, indicating that contradiction and opposition to his views and wishes was not only unusual but unthinkable, combined with a carelessness of look and demeanour which goes with unquestioned authority. He was as big a contrast to the long, owl-eyed, sallow visage law-giver as vanity could wish. Erili's voice was a clear tenor and he managed it with instinc-tive artistry, speaking well and easily, though with a strong foreign accent.

'Sirs, I thank you. I am a soldier and my tongue has learnt no tricks of subtlety. I am used to say, "Do this," and it is done. I do not beat about the bush. You will pardon me, therefore, if my speech is blunt and to the point. I have no wish to anger ye, but to speak plain facts.'

'Yes, yes. Speak. Erili.'

'With your permission, then. Men of Karpas, you have called upon me to defend your frontiers against the men of Khem, who are about to invade you. Is it not so?'

The assent was vigorous and with one accord. Erili raised his hands for silence with a commanding gesture. 'Karpasians, you are farmers, fishers, townsmen, merchants, men of industry and of peace and you never have been warriors, nor do you desire to be so. Am I speaking truth?'

'Absolute truth, Erily.'

'Once the men of Khem swept over Karpas, firing the land, putting the people to the sword, torturing the old and feeble, carrying off the young into slavery.'

A groan of dismay and despair seemed to split the assembly asunder at this reminder. Hange listened with scarcely veiled impatience, drumming his fingers rapidly on the table before him, but Erili held his audience and proceeded, with an ironical glance at the lay-giver. 'Ever since that day you have gone in terror of Khem, and now you know that the enemy is preparing yet another raid against which the last is but a flea-bite, is already marching for your border and you have called upon me and my men to defend you. I have come to answer to that call.'

A shout of acclaim swept through the vast, smoke-wreathed chamber, and again Erili commanded silence with a gesture.

'I am here, Karpasians, to guard you from disaster, but I know from my spies that Khem is mustering a great force against you, determined to conquer you once and for all. They are formidable warriors, they live by fighting, their engines of war are many and modern to the last degree, their troops are hardly indomitable, their generals, men of great experience and much ability. Against such an army my own men are inadequate, being but a small force. If Karpsas is to resist invasion by my aid, then Karpas must be prepared to make sacrifices.']

A deep silence pervaded the chamber and the silky voice of Hange came from his seat. 'What sacrifices, Erili?'

His yellow haired opponent did not immediately answer the question, but resumed calmly— 'I came hither on the understanding that I should have men placed at my disposal, together with the resources of the country. My men were promised pay and permission for such of them who wished to settle in the country to do so. I have letters to them effect and believing in the faith of Karpas I brought my men to your aid. Now, we find ourselves without pay, without means of proper defence, with none of these promises fulfilled, and in danger of being cut to pieces with the rest of Karpas by the invading Khemites. That is our position, sirs.'

Cries of 'No, no, outrageous! You are mistaken. We mean you well!' burst from all sides, to die down as Hange once more addressed Erili.

'We mean you well, sir. Fortify the frontier, drive away any raiding parties, protect us from acts of brigandage and trust to the well-known generosity and hospitality of Karpas for your reward.'

'The situation is too serious for that.'

'If your men want titles, well, each chief can be made Ban of the lower nobility, but without covering power over any free-born Karpasian. Such power could neer be given to aliens. It is vested only in members of the Council, who would be betraying the nation if such power were given to foreigners.'

Erili dismissed this protest and assurance with a wave of his large hand. 'Such toys can await a more peaceful settlement, when we have leisure to consider them, sir. The time is urgent, the enemy almost at our very gates, yet we bandy words and talk of promises. Karpasians, if I am to defend you successfully from Khem, I must be given supreme powers while the state of war lasts. I must be able to call upon all classes of men and women for aid, some to be trained as speedily as possible to carry arms and to fight, others to build fortifications. The whole resources of the country must be placed at my disposal for purposes of maintenance and defence.'

At these bold words, uttered calmly and with all the conviction of the force of reason, a wild hubbub broke out. Cries, yells and catcalls from the followers of Hange rose above the more steady acclaim of his opponents. Many leapt to their feet, waving their arms in frantic excitement, brandishing their fists under Erili's nose. Zadoug and Kinyras moved to his side and slipped into seats vacated by some of Hange's men who had rushed round to his support, and were responsible for most of the clamour. Many of Erili's men, scattered about the chamber, moved up to his aid until they sat or stood solidly at his back. Ugly looks were exchanged between men of conflicting parties, many threatening gestures, but Erili stood calm amidst the rumpus, looking not a little contemptuous, as though he was surrounded by a crowd of heady, unruly children. At length, when Hange through the demonstration had reached the necessary pitch of discord, he stilled it by rising from his seat and assuming his former negligent pose, his air one of tolerant amusement. Watching him Kinyras wondered if he was indeed a fool, or in secret league with the enemy? How he detested the man! Every instinct he possessed warned him to be on his guard against this schemer, to outwit him or die in the attempt.

Suavely Hange spoke, looking silkily into Erili's eyes. 'What you ask, sir, is impossible. The council holds the supreme power as a sacred trust. It can never be given into the hands of a foreigner, no matter how skilful a warrior he be, or how great the necessity may appear.'

'Nevertheless, I repeat my demand,' Erili answered steadily.

'You are trying to bring back the curse of a king upon Karpas. We have had a bitter struggle to abolish monarchy.'

A general murmur of assent greeted this, but Erili answered it with a shrug. 'In war there must be supreme control or the country will perish.'

Another murmur, of equal assent, rippled through the chamber, accompanied by renewed uneasiness.

'I would remind you that there is NO WAR and to prepare for war is the very want to bring it about.'

'On the contrary, the country which is prepared, is the country immune from attack.'

'There is an aspect of your position which has escaped your attention.' Erili's eyes narrowed ominously and Kinyras laid his hand upon his sword-hily.

'So?'

'You are in very bad odour with Khem, since it is owing to your action on behalf of her enemies that she has met with defeat. Unless you defend Karpas, and defend her adequately, you and every one of your men will get his throat slit.'

'The notion does you credit, sir. I and my bands march from Karpas without an instant of delay. Kinyras, convey that order to my captains.'

Kinyras jumped to his feet and saluted, but such an uproar now arose that all others were dwarfed by comparison. Hange saw that he had gone too far, and Kinyras, reading the man, lingered.

'I but made the suggestion.'

'Speak on, Erili,' cried one.

'I want the power of a dictator. I want each of my captains to be appointed to the government of a section of territory, from which he can requisition food, labour and men to form an army. Only trained warriors can make a successful defence against such an army as will be sent against us. I have such an army, but it is too small for the purpose. If I start to recruit and train a militia now, so that it will be ready when the time comes, such a force can be officered by your countrymen, if you wish, but such officers must be under the command of my own captains. If you cannot keep your promise to pay us, then give us permission to settle in the land if we wish. We are wandering folk and some of us need homes. Men will fight for their homes and their country without payment. If you refuse my counsel then I shall retreat at once. I shall not remain in the plains but retreat to the Kastros hill. I have some ships, and from thence I shall slowly transport my men by sea across into the band lands of Kush.'

Again cries of 'No! No!' interrupted him.

Erili spread his hands with a shrug and waited for them to die down before he resumed. 'War is certain. It is no myth, but a definite disaster advancing rapidly upon Karpas. Knowing we have received no pay and that Karpas has broken every promise made to me, I shall not risk the lives of my men by undertaking an unsuccessful defence. Unless I have the powers given to me to organize the country, I retreat, and the whole country must perish.' He paused to gauge the temper of his audience and saw signs of great disquiet, whilst Hange sat listening with a frown of attention and a sulky expression.

'The shortest line we could defend is from Stronglos across the hills to the sea. This is a distance of ten miles and though part of it is hilly, I have only two thousand five hundred men, say two hundred and fifty men to a mile. The Khemites can put thirty men into the field against every man of ours, and we must dispose of our forces to the best advantage. I shall have to scatter my men all along the line because I cannot tell where the enemy will attack.'

Kinyras saw that the council was caught in the grip of Erili's earnestness and their own fears, and he laughed internally as he noted the effect of this upon Hange, saw his evil scowl of mingled hate and defeat.

Erili, well satisfied at the close attention he was receiving, elaborated his plans, speaking in the quiet, reasonable tones so characteristic of the man. 'Therefore, it is useless for me to attempt defence at all, unless I can claim the authority necessary for success. In order to succeed I must have power to commandeer every man I need, some to train as militia, others as labourers. These companies can be under their own commanders, but such must be officered by my own captains. We discovered the cost of divided control at Carium. Such disaster never shall happen again under my command.'

Fresh murmurs broke out as he ceased speaking and one of Hange's followers sprang to his feet to address the assembly, his voice conciliating, his smile suggestive of desire to compromise. Erili eyed him with calm penetration and little favour.

'My lords, if the noble strangers will undertake to defend the frontiers and apply to the council to commandeer the necessary men, the council will immediately call up such men as will be required. These bands can be under the command of their own leaders, subject to the advice of the novel Erili to their mutual advantage. The enemy are unlikely to attack by the difficult ways. I submit, with all due deference to expert opinion'—here he bowed gracefully to Erili and then to Hange—'that they would attack only where they could use their chariots. This reduces the danger spot from an area of ten miles to a mere four or five at the most. Twenty-five hundred men could easily defend this area, especially as the enemy would hardly dare to attack in force, with Damastes on their flank.'

He sat down, a little breathed with his long speech and elated by the looks of renewed confidence with which his fellows viewed him. Erili's measured speech broke through again—

'Doubtless the Khemites will prefer to attack by an easy path, but they have such numbers at command that, if checked at any one spot they could feel for another, a weaker one, using their archers and spearmen to consolidate the breach made. Once this breach was forced, defence would be impossible, because we have neither chariots nor men to cope with the large forces which the enemy could bring up at incredibly short notice, and to drive them back and reform the line would be out of the question.'

Gloom had descended once more upon the assembly as the weight of this argument sunk deep into every mind present. A depressed murmur buzzed through the great chamber, which subsided into a tense silence as Hange rose leisurely, outwardly composed and utterly unimpressed by all which had gone before. He spread his hands and slightly lifted his shoulders, a gesture which made Erili set his teeth together with a snap and Kinyras long to get his fingers round the lean, dark throat.

'It is all on the knees of the High Gods. My lords, the council has laboured over long to-day. To-morrow we will assemble to discuss the matter again. Perhaps the gods will smile and we shall find our noble guests in a more reasonable frame of mind. Panic is to be avoided at all costs. Fears, which stalk huge in the dark, have a trick of vanishing in the sunlight. We will meet in the morning at the ninth hour.'

A movement of relief rippled through the gathering, the eyes of Erili and Kinyras met and exchanged a long, intelligent look. Some rose, others began to talk apart, exchanging gossip and stories of the day. Hange was soon surrounded by his following, and from the group bursts of laughter rose frequently. A general motion of exit was preparing when a disturbance arose at the door. The hanging was flung aside, the lamps flared and smoked in the sudden draught, the crowd swayed as a pair of arms thrashed their way towards the table, and a hoarse voice chanted—

'Hail, O Most Noble Council! Vent on me not the punishment of the bearer of evil tidings!'

Hange strode out from his thronging admirers, thrusting some aside with rude gestures, until he stood clear, facing the messenger. His sallow face was tinged with green, the nostrils of his long nose quivered and fear lurked in his shifty eyes. In a voice indescribably altered from its old, cocksure drawl, he replied mechanically in the customary way—'The blame be on the evil news and not upon you, O Messenger.'

The man bowed his head in mute acknowledgement and amid a deep silence Hange's voice sounded metallically—'What... what are your tidings?'

'My lords, Karpas is in peril. Khem has penetrated through the hills to the heart of Aghirda. Damastes is dead, his people have fled to the mountain-tops, those that still live. His cities are ravished. Khem is lord of all.'

A groan burst simultaneously from all lips, succeeded by an appalled silence as the dire nature of these tidings became more and more apparent. Then a murmur began and grew to a great shout. 'Accept the terms of the strangers, or we are lost. Erili alone can save the country. Make Erili King. Erili! Erili! All hail, King Erili!'

A perfect pandemonium broke loose, the council was in confusion, men ran from group to group, all talking and gesticulating wildly. Hange drew apart, arguing fiercely with his followers, bitterly opposing some measure thrust upon him. At last he pushed them aside, hurried to the centre of the chamber with impatient strides and threw up his arms angrily for silence. 'My hands are tied! To-morrow we will deliberate how to give the power to these strangers, what restrictions to impose upon them, what measures to safeguard our liberty.'

But Erili strode towards him and faced him. 'Now or never!' he roared. 'I have been called by the council to be your King. Acknowledge me as your sovereign, with full powers to defend the country, or I leave to-night, our ships shall sail in the morning. Damastes is dead and we may be invaded at any moment.'

Again the shout went up. 'Accept the stranger's terms. Long live King Erili.'

Such a tumult now filled the hall, so much resolution was now stamped upon every face, even those of his followers expressing agreement, that Hange answered—'We accept Erili for our King if he will swear to be guided on all points by his council.'

Erili raised his arm solemnly. 'I swear, by all the Gods, yours and min.' A yell of acclamation broke out, but he stood with his raised right arm, until the uproar died away into silence. 'I swear always to be guided by my council. But, men of Karpas, my council will consist of myself as head, my chiefs and anyone else I may see fit to appoint. Now choose and choose quickly.'

From all sides again the cry burst out—'We accept! We accept!'

Kinyras watched the scene in amazement, not unmixed with contempt. He felt his arm twitched, and looking, saw Zadoug, grinning from ear to ear in delight at the defeat of Hange and the triumph of Erili. 'Gods! What a sight,' he whispered.

Kinyras shrugged, scornful, as one councillor after another pushed and jostled and scrambled for place to advance and kneel, to kiss the hand and take the oath of allegiance to his commander. It was a lengthy and tiresome business, and every time the ceremony was repeated, the smaller fry yelled 'Hail! King Erili!' amid a great clapping of hands and stamping of feet and waving of torches so that the vast chamber was filled with the din of every degree of vocal timbre and the stench of smoking oil lamps. Voices were hoarse and throats parched, lungs gasped for air and eyes smarted and reddened till tears rose.

It came to an end at last and again Erili raised his arm for silence, which fell like magic in obedience to the summons. He called—'To me, my chiefs,' and as they stepped forward and clustered around him, he addressed them in a loud voice which reached to the farthest limits of the chamber. 'I have spoken to ye ere this of my plans for the defence of this country. We must build lines from sea to sea. Plans have been prepared, with which you are acquainted. Each of you knows the position I assign to him. Is that not so?'

'It is, Erili,' they answered, some merely bowing their heads in assent.

He shot a glance of approval over them, marking with satisfaction their fine proportions, alert bearing, their quick, intelligent eyes. 'As the first act of my reign, I give to each chief the lordship of that tract of land for six miles behind his lines. He will work through the local mayors and magistrates to the greatest possible extent, but if they refuse obedience to his orders he can dismiss them and appoint others. Each chief will immediately call up every able-bodied man to form a militia, training to being without delay. Is that clear?'

A murmur of assent answered him, of approbation from the listening council. Erili passed a hand of his smarting eyes and cleared his throat. 'Good!' he croaked, 'at the same time each chief will form labour companies of every available man who is fit and above fighting age, of boys too young for military service and of women and girls between the ages of ten and sixty'

The orders went on, pouring out from that untiring brain. Nothing was forgotten, proclamations were written and sent forth, every measure considered from the safety of Karpas. Dawn was breaking and rain falling heavily, before the weary council was at length free to stumble out of the reek and murk of the great hall into the reek and drench of the pelting storm, and to seek what rest they might find from the fears and apprehensions of their minds in the doubtful safety of their homes.

Mina Denvers came home the following evening in no very amiable frame of mind. Her cousin Bette had put her out badly. She was such a prude.

Discontentedly she slouched into the sitting-room and rid herself of her furs with one pettish jerk of her shoulders. The place was cold and cheerless, the fireless grate, with its little of dead ash, was the most depressing sight in the world. She felt profoundly unhappy, dissatisfied with everything and everyone, her world, her life, her lover, her husband, and most especially with herself. Tears of self-pity flooded her eyes and dripped off her chin as a chill wind howled down the Lane, sending a scud of icy rain driving against the exposed windows. She seized the curtains and dragged them across to shut out the bitter night. Just like Robert to let the fire out.

Where to go, what to do? She stood pondering. Useless to expect Hank to take her out with a face like that. How odious was Robert. Hank did not like her to o to his flat. Still, she could ring him.

How cold and still was the flat, how horribly silent. With another shiver she went out into the little hall, determined to ring Heyward and to make some coffee. Then she saw several letters on the floor, showing by their differing hours of postage that they represented three different deliveries.

So Robert was away somewhere? She shrugged negligently, and put the letters on the table as she passed into her bedroom to take off her out-door things. Mina lit the gas-fire and sat warming her cold ankles. Heavens, how horribly silent everything was. For some reason even the gas refused to roar as usual, even though she tried to make it by turning it full on.

Where had Robert gone? He had no friends in London with whom he could stay. Suddenly an idea struck her and at the bare thought of it the colour drained from her face. Was it possible that Robert had left her, gone for good?

It has never occurred to her that this might be his answer to her conduct and her talk. She could not imagine Robert as anything but the patient and long-suffering beast of burden for any load she might choose to inflict upon him. Gone! Left her high and dry! Oh, but that was incredible, he couldn't treat her like that. What on earth should she do? How could she find him? She had money of her own, but not enough to keep her, she would have to work again. Horrible thought! In a panic she rushed into his room to try to find some evidence of his intentions.

What she did find sent a scream to her lips, which she stifled with the back of her hand and stood staring at the bed, sick with dismay. Denvers lay there flat on his back beneath the bed-clothes, very rigid. Not a sound broke the horrible, brooding silence of the room. When she could master her shaking legs enough to move, she turned and fled to the telephone.

'Hank! Hank!' she whispered frantically after what seemed an eternity of waiting for him to come to the instrument, 'You must come at once. Robert has killed himself.'

And she hung up the receiver because she could not bear to say any more.

Ten minutes later she admitted Heyward. His eye was covered with a black shade and his face was yellow with agitation. 'This is awful,' he muttered, 'it means ruin, for both of us. Has he left any letter, or anything?'

'I don't know,' she faltered, staring at him with wide eyes of horror. 'I never thought of it, Hank.'

'Then think of it now,' he retorted, in a savage undertone, 'And go and look.'

'Oh, I can't. I CAN'T go in there again,' she whimpered, 'he looks—awful.'

'Good God. What has he done? Show himself, or what? Come, Mina, pull yourself together. I'll go.'

Heyward hurried into the bedroom, giving one quick, comprehensive glance at Denvers' still form out of his available eye, and began to search the room, but there was nothing to find. He went out again to Mina, who lurked uncertainly in the open doorway, averting her eyes from the bed. 'It's all right, dear. We know nothing, mind. I'll run for a doctor.'

'There's one just round the corner,' she whispered.

Hank returned with a rather frowsy, bent little man, with a grey beard and short-sighted weak, blue eyes peering through thick glasses. Mina made a supreme effort to be rational.

'This is Dr. Groves, Mrs. Denvers.'

'Oh, doctors, I'm so glad you've come. I returned home from a visit to a friend to find my husband ill.'

'What's the matter with him?' grunted the doctor, elbowing his way unceremoniously into the bedroom and setting his bag down on the table beside the bed. He made a lengthy and exhaustive examination, wheezing bronchially as he moved. He noted Denvers' hand was closed over a piece of dark metal.

'Is he dead? Mina breathed fearfully.

The doctor stood erect, put one doubled hand upon his hip, and scowled thoughtfully at the patient. 'No,' he pronounced, after a long pause.

'Thank God for that!' ejaculated Heyward, and wiped his face with his handkerchief. 'Phew!'

Mina clasped her hands in silent relief. Hank's manner had filled her with a great fear. She need no longer dread the loss of his love because scandal had come upon them. 'What is the matter?' she asked timidly. 'I was dreadfully frightened, doctor.'

'Yes, yes,' he murmured absently, still gazing intently at the patient, as though he would read the nature of this mysterious illness written upon Denvers' face. He bent down and raised an eyelid, then shook his head, then put back the bed-clothes, again revealing that curious bronze object tightly clasped in the patient's fingers. 'What is this, Mrs. Denvers?'

'I don't know. I've never seen it before.'

The doctor tried to unclasp the rigid fingers, but he could not move them. 'let it alone, it can't hurt.'

'But, doctor, what is wrong with him?' Mina insisted naturally enough.

'I'm damned if I know,' he might have answered truthfully, but that would never do. Instead he pursed his lips and shook his head portentously, then seeing a repetition of the question in Mina's eyes, he barked with a sudden snap 'Catalepsy!'

'What in God's name's that?' Heyward demanded, feeling the necessity of and glad of the chance of being profane.

'A trance. You can do nothing until he comes out of it. Has he ever been like this before, Mrs. Denvers?'

'No,' said the wondering Mina.

'Oh, well! You can do nothing until he comes out of it. Keep him warm with hot water bottles and sit by him. Don't attempt to rouse him, but if he comes round give him some warm milk and ring me. I'll look in again in the morning.'

He curried off home to read up on catalepsy, muttering to himself all the way. 'Very strange case. Most unusual! Practically unique. Most interesting.'

# CHAPTER IV

# THE PLAN OF COMPAIGN

inyras, I give you the line from the Kastnon river tot the rest of Hap Hill. As you have ships you must take this coast. The enemy may try to land men by sea, but praise the gods, they cannot fight our ships. Old, slow but sure, many men follow the banner of the Snail. You are a builder. Build surely, though not too slowly.'

With these words from Erili, Kinyras had risen and with his brother Zadoug passed into the night.

The rain was falling in torrents and with a curse Zadoug muffled himself deeply in his cloak and with a stifled word of farewell departed on some business of his own which he did not disclose. Kinyras shouldered his way through the crowd gathered outside the council chamber. Hasvan, his household slave, came forward with a cloak, threw it round his master and together and in silence the two plunged into the darkness towards the quarter where his men were encamped.

Kinyras was too deep in anxious thought to pay heed to anything but the dangers and difficulties ahead of the Mercenaries. The crassness of the Karpasians, the follow of the delay which had imperilled all their lives, the possible treachery of Hange the Law-giver, were no longer paramount considerations. When action was called for, the Snail, the Dreamer,

Kinyras came promptly to action. He was no idle dreamer but an constructive one, had strange powers to see the objects his mind sought after stand forth in pictures, clear cut in every detail. Truly it might be said that, as the Khemites wrote in pictures, so did he think. The little houses he passed, from which lights twinkled dimly, were so many quiet homes, so many shelters from this rough night, little communities of courage and thrift, fighting the unequal battle of life gallantly. He must protect them, give them security, justify the trust they reposed in him.

Then suddenly, disconcertingly, the picture of his young wife rose clear before him in all her dark, alluring beauty. Strange how her image would rise before him at odd times. Six years before, Eune had run away from him, seeking a younger, gayer man. She was by now drudge to some swarthy Khemite, or Negro, no doubt her delicate loveliness lost in the bearing of many brats. He dismissed her impatiently, she had gone over to the enemy.

Splashing and floundering through the driving rain over the uneven ground, Kinyras tramped on doggedly, with bent head and body inclining forward to meet the storm, the patient Hazvan plodding behind.

The enemy! Were they still deep in the plundering of Aghirdi, chasing the red-haired barbarians round the cliffs they lived in, or were they already marching on the border? They might well be over it before he could get there. No fortification, no ditch yet built had ever kept Khem out. In his mind he saw them, swarming like locusts, everything giving way before them. One ditch was useless, but two?

At this point a shout startled him back to reality. He paused, for it was his brother's voice, and presently Zadough splashed up to him. 'Gods, what a night,' he exclaimed. 'I'm wet to the skink and famished. Will Pheretime have anything like a meal ready for us?'

Kinyras shrugged. 'I doubt it. She is more like to snore than to cook at this hour.'

'Women!' snorted Zadoug, 'the gods created them to

plague us.'

This was so obvious a remark that Kinyras left it unan-
swered and soon they came upon his encampment, a few huts
built of mud bricks covered in plaster, which was falling off in
places. They were roofed with stout beams, painted in crude
blue and red where visible, and over which were spread canes,
on which the roof of rammed clay was set. A long line of tents
showed dimly, for the night was not pitch dark and from the
cluster of small farm buildings, where his officers were
quartered, shadowy figures came running.

'Hail, mighty chief,' one shouted, 'what news?'

'Good news. Erili has been made King,' Kinyras answered,
saluting immediately. 'We march in two hours or less.'

Miklos, a young Greek, cheered, and his two companions
muttered hoarse approval. 'Where is our line, noble Kinyras?'
Miklos asked eagerly.

'From the Kastnon to the hills. A night's march will bring
us to Gastri. Send word to Kinuis to bring the ships round to
the Kastnon to meet us there.'

'Very good, sir. Thenk the gods this misery of waiting is
over at last.'

Kinyras did not answer, but turned to Hasvan. 'Run and
waken Pheretime. Bid her prepare food for us now and pack
for the march. We must take the road in an hour. Miklos, call
all troop leaders, muster the men quietly without sounding
alarm. Advise me as each troop is ready. The first ready the first
off. To the first there is the best choice of billets. Understand
and march.'

Without further words he swung round and made his way
towards the largest of the huts, where light now showed. As he
entered he shouted—'Waken, Pheretime, bring us food. We are
wet and famished.' He threw off his saturated cloak and shook
it vigorously, saying over his shoulder to Zadoug as he did so,
'Snoring, as I expected.'

As he spoke a plump, good-looking girl of medium height,
wrapped in a big cloak, huddled and shivering, came from the
inner room, knuckling the sleep from her eyes. 'Hail, mighty

chief,' she yawned copiously. 'I'd have you know I am not the snorer when I sleep, whoever else may be.' She set her hands on her hips and nodded at him defiantly.

Kinyras responded with a mocking gesture and seated himself on a stool at the table, pushing out another from beneath it for Zadoug and motioning him to take his place.

'So we march at last, praise the gods.' The woman continued, abandoning one grievance to take up another. 'And not before time, neither. I'm sick to death of this place. The folk about are nothing but fools. There is no life, no gaiety anywhere.'

Kinyras was stung by memories of the past, when such complaints had been his daily portion. Was he never to escape? 'Life, gaiety?' he echoed, his dark face flushing swarthily, his fine, aquiline nose twitching with irritation. 'Woman, you are lucky if you escape being cut to pieces in a wholesale massacre, or being strung up by your thumbs to the nearest tree until your body rots and the carrion pick your carcase clean. Be silent if sense is not in you, and serve us with food, at once!'

She screamed and ran from the room, her great cloak trailing from her naked shoulders as she went. Zadoug laughed as he kicked the stool into position and sat down. 'It passes me why, being rid of one woman, you encumber yourself with another of the breed. For my part I contrive to keep them for their proper uses.'

'And what are they?'

'For a man's entertainment and pleasure,' Zadoug laughed.

Kinyras pished impatient scorn and growled. 'I don't know why I bought her. To make me forget, probably. I don't love her, but she is useful.'

'You are a fool to let that minx, Eune, still spoil your life. She dead by now, perhaps. Have you heard of her?'

'In Salam, but nothing more. He deserted her there, and she disappeared, what usually happens to a woman in such a case.'

Pheretime here returned and set on the table with a series of bangs of platter of thin, dry oat cake, two bronze drinking cups and a vase of light, sour wine. Zadoug seized the jar and poured, drinking with a shudder of distaste, while Kinyras began to munch the cake with a resigned expression. The woman stood near, her attitude half fearful, half defiant. 'I will not march to-night. I have things to buy in Karpasia. I wish to live there, not in the country. This is bad enough, but Gastri will be awful. I—'

But Kinyras interrupted her fiercely, half rising with a threatening gesture. 'Begone, woman. Pack, or I'll beat the life out of you, and you'll be left behind in dead earnest.'

Once more she fled, wailing, and the two men ate stolidly and doggedly, in silence and without interest or enjoyment, and whickly the thoughts of Kinyras were utterly absorbed in the problem of his ditch. Zadoug watched him curiously, wondering as he had so often, at this brother of his, with his lean, dark face, illuminated by the beautiful, large, intelligent eyes. Kinyras had strange, awe-inspiring powers, of whose existence Zadoug alone knew and which he venerated, in spite of his bluff affection of dismissing them with a gibe. In his rough simplicity of mind, Zadoug shuddered at his brother's daring, knowing that Kinyras the Dreamer, the old slow-but-sure, was a bold adventurer in hidden mysteries and that these dreams of his were nothing less than journeys of the spirit into the future, long, perilous, terrifying journeys forward into times as yet unborn and backward into the dim and awful past. Kinyras had told him of these, for the two were devoted friends as well as kindred, and had made him understand faintly something of their nature and object, and Zadoug did not know which he regarded with the worst fear, the past, present or future. All were terrible when one came down to actual fact, but of the three the last held a vague comfort, because hope dwelt there.

Suddenly Kinyras looked up into the perplexed face opposite, which studied him so earnestly and questioningly, and smiled. The brothers bore a strong family resemblance to each other, especially noticeable when they smiled, as did Kinyras now, though Zadoug was shorter and stockier than his companion, and his intelligence went little further than was required from an accomplished and reliable officer and soldier.

'This question of the ditch,' said Kinyras, swallowing hard upon a piece of cake which had stuck in his throat. Tears glittered in his eyes and he snatched hastily at the cup and drank deep. 'This dry stuff is poor fare for fasting men, though we shall be glad enough of it before the campaign is over and Khem thrust back.'

'Do you think we're in time to drive them back?' Zadoug asked seriously.

'I pray the gods we are—it shan't be my fault if we don't. We shall be lucky if we can check them with fortifications.'

'But how, Kinyras? No ditch known to man can stay the onrush of Khem. Numbers equal to their own alone will serve us.'

'In a dream,' began Kinyras and Zadoug nodded comprehension and sympathy, for it was the formula used and recognised between them to describe his habit of adventuring, 'I saw a new fortification.'

'Well enough for you to copy?'

Kinyras nodded. 'The Khemites are victorious because of their good organization. All are under one leader, their action is concerted instead of being split up and enervating their force through lack of direction. They are supremely skilled in the art of beleaguering and they take positions regarded as impregnable by filling in ditches with brushwood, earth or any available material, stockades they scale or burn through, high stone walls they scale with ladders, or if checked in scaling, burn through by piling up thousands of bundles of brushwood, incidentally smothering the inhabitants of the city in the process.'

'All this we have suffered,' Zadoug agreed, 'but the new ditch?'

'I am coming to that. One ditch is useless, but how about two?'

'Two?' echoed Zadoug. 'That seems merely to prolong the attack without ultimately saving the town.'

'Listen. The first ditch is a broad, flat one, studded with

sharpened stakes. On its near side is raised a steep, almost vertical bank, so narrow at the top that a man can find no foothold. Falling sharply behind this a deep V-shaped ditch, so narrow at the bottom that a man's feet must be placed sideways, rendering it difficult to climb the inner bank. Above this a stockade with a platform built near the top of a row of archers. Thus, this stockade has a double line of archers through it and from above, the top line being able to command the bottom of the ditch.

Zadoug drew a sharp breath and looked at his brother with glowing eyes. 'Brilliantly conceived, Kinyras. That will keep them out, or nothing will. But archers are our trouble. You are weak, having about eighty all told good me, I have less, about another hundred and fifty can handle a bow at a pinch and we have a long line to defend. This is a weakness which we shall not easily mend These Karpasians are not the stuff to make soldiers of and we have our militia to form and train. The difficulties are insurmountable and we were wiser to collect our men and march.'

'Where?'

Zadoug shrugged and laughed. 'To some new land where the odds are less and Khem is not. We have ships. What do your dreams tell you about their possibilities, Kinyras?'

'As you say, bowmen are our chief trouble, or rather lack of them,' said Kinyras, returning to his problem patiently. 'You are wrong about the men of Karpas. In the main they are stout fellows and with time could be turned into effective machines of war, but it is time, time we need.' He beat with his clenched fist upon the table, scowling thoughtfully down upon it. Presently he burst out—'These cursed Karpasian laws! What follow to forbid men the use and carriage of arms, to cut down the standing army for the sake of economy. Now, when I need my best men so badly I must set them to training raw recruits how to handle a pike without killing their comrades and to make veteran archers of boys who have as much notion of handling a bow as a kite.'

'It takes years to make and archer,' Zadoug agreed. 'A man

must start as a child if he is to be a bowman.'

They were interrupted by the entrance of Miklos, who had come to report that his company was ready to start. Kinyras rose and clapped the boy on the shoulder. 'Good work, lad.'

The youth flushed with pleasure and Kinyras noted with approval his keenness and promptitude. Miklos, despite his age, was one of his most valuable men.

'And Witkind?' he asked.

'Almost ready, sir.'

'We shall do yet,' exclaimed Kinyras and gave certain necessary instructions tersely. 'Away with you. We shall meet in Gastri.'

Miklos saluted, turned and marched out.

'There goes a man,' said Kinyras, reseating himself at the table. 'Well, to our problem.'

'I have it, old snail. You must seek your solution in another dream.'

'I have done so, scoffer, and to some account.' Kinyras spoke quietly, but there was a slumbering gleam in his eyes fixed steadily on his brother which Zadoug affected not to see. Sometimes old Snail was touch on this subject of dreams, especially when, as now, the matter was an urgent one and Zadoug had not enough finesse to know when to jest and when to be sober.

Awed now, in spite of himself, he exclaimed–'These dreams come from the very gods themselves. Did you not make the great engines to hurl stones from one such?'

'Aye! From the gods, you say? Maybe,' answered the other, with reserve and a withdrawn look replacing the sleeping fire with which he had rewarded the clumsy thrust.

Zadoug regarded with misgiving. He had a feeling that it would be more comfortable to his skin, showing a marked tendency to creep at such times as this, if such dreaming could be attributable to some god's intervention in man's affairs, rather than to some secret power possessed by man himself, especially by his own kin. Useful as such dreams might be and undoubtedly had proved, yet to contemplate their possible origin made Zadoug feel a castaway on a fierce, perilous and unexplored ocean, full of strange monsters and incredible terrors. He hastened to speak again of the engine, to restore the shaken balance of his mind. That at least was something tangible. 'There were engines in plenty on land to hurl stones, but yours are the first to be fitted to ships. Where would we have been in the fight off Sidon but for them?'

'Land engines are too big and too heavy, require too many men to pull them, for sea-fighting, but the device of twisted hair and gut for leverage I found in my... dream.' He rose and broke off a piece of charcoal from the bronze container near the glowing brazier and reseated himself at the table. He began to draw with rapid, sure strokes. 'See here, old sceptic, what I have seen. A bow fixed to a short, stout stock, so, held bent in position by a clutch, so. The arrow is held in place in a notch, so, and by a device here, a wheel or trig is released which propels the arrow with great force.'

'The gods preserve us!' cried Zadoug, gazing down at the drawing, appalled. He poured a libation with a mental apology for the quality of the wine and a mute supplication for protection.

Kinyras watched him with a slight smile, especially when his brother almost immediately recovered self-confidence and became once more the blunt, practical soldier, as he bent over the table to study the sketch further, shifting the lamp hither and thither to get the vet light on it. At length he looked up and drew a long breath.

'Well, brother?'

'Such an instrument, if it can be made practicable, would solve much of our problem. It cuts out the question of the long training of muscle so that the bow may be held steady under great strain. It solves the problem of jerk of the bow when the string is released and of skill depending upon judgment to allow for the jerk of the arrow itself as it starts its flight. It may cure the leftward trend of flight, because from this machine the arrow should go straight for its mark, being unhampered by dependence upon human physique.'

'I see you are quick to grasp my thought. See how valuable is this power to look, and see what is hidden from most men. Why not adventure yourself, Zadoug? Such things can be learned and accomplished by certain practices.'

'I?' echoed Zadoug, astounded and horrified.

'You. Consider the benefit to us now if you, too, could see. For no two men see the same things, brother, and you might bring back from the future who knows what plans and devices to aid us now.'

'The future?' Zadoug whispered, glancing round apprehensively.

'Aye, the future, where men will become more and more skilled in the arts of war. The present is dangerous, the past useless to serve us now, for our fore-fathers have handed down to us their lore. It is the future we must capture and harness to our disastrous present, if we can do it, as I have done, dimly, once or twice. Two might accomplish much more.'

'The gods forbid, Kinyras. Put the impious thought from you.'

'There is no impiety, for all power lies within a man's true self. Such things are but the training of the muscles of mind and spirit to hit the mark aimed at, as my bowmen out yonder have trained the muscles of their bodies to shoot their arrows straight. Both become perfect through practice.'

'No. One seer in the family is enough. Your talk makes me shiver and I'm no coward, as you well know.'

'Well?' said Kinyras, turning sharply as Hasvan entered, 'are we ready?'

'Almost, lord. One Sedru, a Karpasian, craves admission.'

'Present him, quickly, but see that he stays not long. These Karpasians have over much to say. I will give him a short time and if he is not gone by then, come in again on some excuse.'

Hasvan bowed and immediately showed in a grave and important-looking elder, bearing a scroll. Kinyras knew him slightly. 'Greetings, O Sedru.'

'Greetings, O new-made Ban!' the man answered, saluting, a little sourly. He presented the roll, scroll, sealed with the arms of the council, and a great stone seal. 'These are the orders of the council to all the mayors and elders of your new province, bidding them proclaim Erili king, and giving you authority to govern the province under him. This also they must proclaim to the people. This seal is your badge of office, O Ban.'

'Many thanks, Sedru. I will acquit myself well and, under Erili, serve your council faithfully. I march immediately.'

'A rare trouble your king has given us already. He has cut up the province boundaries in a way that will take us years to disentangle. He proclaims that the new boundaries must run straight from the spot where each of the lines ends, taking no heed of the nature boundaries of the fields. So, farmers must pay half their tithes to one province and half to another. You don't know these peasants. Give them the chance and they will cheat the gods themselves out of their own back teeth.'

The brothers laughed in unison and their visitor, pleased and flattered by the ready acceptance of his wit, became more cordial. After all, these strangers were pleasant enough fellos and would save them from Knem.

'Good,' exclaimed Kinyras heartily, 'the warning is useful. Go now to Gastri, Sedru. Warn the mayor that I shall be there soon after dawn. I shall require food for four hundred men and fodder for sixty donkeys. Bid him assemble the notables from all surrounding villages, and the bigger farmers. I must see and talk with them.'

'I will, sir. Any further commission?'

Kinyras considered a moment or two. 'Yes. Ride from thence to Haptri. There proclaim Erili as king and me as Ban. Announce that I will levy men to work on the walls I build; bid them assemble with provisions and every kind of tool and implement they can collect and be ready to march when I give the word. I shall requisition materials for building labourers' huts and all bronze available in the province. This is war and I am calling up all workmen and able-bodied men and boys. Each man must bring with him the tools of his craft. Let builders be ready to start putting up huts immediately.'

'Very good, sir.'

'Finally go to Gastros, but on your way thence requisition provisions to be sent to the labourers from every village through which you pass. Make your proclamation and announcements regularly, so that there is no confusion or pretence of ignorance of the situation.'

'I will make all things clear, lord.'

'I depend upon your diligence, Sedru. If the advance of Khem is to be stemmed we have not a second of time to lose. Make the people understand that their very lives depend upon their industry and willing help, their co-operation with us, who are appointed to save them.'

'My words shall be whips to drive them. And at Gastros?'

'Oh, yes. Supplies of fish, and all men not actively engaged in fishing to go to the walls, boat-builders especially. They are the best carpenters. And arms. Don't tell me those fishermen have none! Each is allowed a spear for his trade an dmost have swords and axes tucked away somewhere, I'll swear.'

Sedru laughed and glanced at Zadoug, winking solemnly.

Kinyras, seeing Hasvan hovering unhappily in the background, called out to him. 'Bring win for our guest and bid Witkind supply him with an escort, Hasvan.' He turned again to his envoy. 'Baskets, Sedru! I shall want tens of thousands of them for carrying earth. Collect as many as you may and set the women and girls to weaving.'

Hasvan returned bearing a jar of wine and earthenware cups, decorated in lines of red.

Kinyras filled one, refilled his cup and Zadoug's and raised it. 'Here's to our wall! May we build it, may we hold to it like grim Death!'

They drank and then pledged each other.

'Come, Sedru, march. Your escort awaits you. Farewell, we shall meet up the line. Be speedy, and diligent and I shall know how to reward your services.'

'Farewell, sirs, and thanks, O Ban.' He strode out of the hut, a brisker and more enthusiastic man than he had entered, fired with some of the zeal of Kinyras and ardent to serve him.

Almost immediately Witkind, one of the lieutenants, entered. He greeted Kinyras with a grin, including Zadoug with a salutation. 'Greetings, O new-made Ban! Praise the gods they have come to their senses at last. Twelve of the men are sick and twenty-seven missing... wenching, I'll be bound. We could march in twenty minutes, but the baggage will take an hour, at least.'

'Good,' said Kinyras, 'Miklos is off already.'

'Ah, the young rogue was already three parts packed... swore he knew we should break camp to-night and march.'

'Did he, now? By what means, I wonder?'

Witkind shrugged and laughed. 'Had a special message from the gods. Come, tell me the news. I hear nothing but the wildest rumour.'

Briefly Kinyras and Zadoug told him, giving him bald outlines of what had happened in the council chamber.

Witkind lisened delightedly and finally burst into a great laugh, slapping his thigh vigorously. 'Glorious! Trust Erili to cozen them into the way he would have them go. He's a man for the main chance and his meat is another's poison.'

'True,' Zadoug agreed. 'He's got more than we ever hoped for or would have reached, but for the fall of Aghirdi. As far as I can see he is king absolute. He will establish the men here, they will get wives. War makes widows. He'll bestow lands on condition of serving as frontier guards.'

'I wonder how they will get on as mud-footed farmers?' jeered Witkind. 'Most of them are flown from the plough's tail originally and now they rend the heavens with their howlings, beseeching the gods... and Erili to stop their eternal wanderings.'

'It was a good life in the old days. Then we were young and loot was plentiful and a man liked to fight. But now these accursed Khemites secure the loot, leaving us the wounds and the hardships. It's a dog's life when you're not so young.'

'Well, let's hope this will be the end of it.' He glanced at Kinyras, whose thoughts seemed to be deeply absorbed elsewhere. 'Can we hold the wall, Kinyras?'

'It will be an almighty task. If we can hold them off for a year we can build walls that will stop them and teach them a lesson into the bargain.

Another lieutenant appeared at the door. He saluted saying, 'Men are falling in, Kinyras,' and went out again.

'Come, Witkind, split my last jar of win to drink to our success. We'll get more in Gastri. If we can't hold the wall we shall have no throats to drink with.' He filled, saying as he put down the jar, 'Here's holding on like grim death.'

The three drank deeply of the thin, new wine, holding their cups in their left hands, the right on the sword-hilt as was the custom of the brotherhood of the sword. Kinyras went out and looked at his little band, followed by Witkind and Zadoug. The light from the torches flickered over their accoutrements, their bronze helmets and big shields of hid rimmed with brazen metal. The trumpets shrilled a salute as he came out of the hut. He answered with a salute and gave the order to march.

Again the trumpets shrilled the advance and the little band started out on the narrow track that led to Gastri, the chief town in his new domain.

# CHAPTER V

# THE WALL

I t was cold and drizzling still as the two brothers rode
ahead of their army. Kinyras drew his big cloak closer
around him. What was he doing at the head of these
men at night, clad only in a sort of kilt and cloak of
skins fastened with what resembled a big nail more than anything else, with sandals on his feet coming half-way up his legs.
Where upon earth had he got this extraordinary rig-out, this
bronze helmet and sword in a broad shoulder belt? Why was he
out on a night like this, without his raincoat? His cloak was
soaked, and he'd catch his death of cold. It was years since he
had got drunk. He must have gone on an almighty binge to
find himself in a fancy-dress show like this. Yet it was funny!
He didn't feel drunk, his legs were not a bit unsteady.

'Kinyras, you told Sedru to collect arms. How in thunder
can the fellow do this when the cursed laws of this godforsaken
country forbid the carriage of arms by any but the men of the
standing army.'

Kinyras shook himself angrily and impatiently. He must
cure himself of this habit of dreaming at inopportune moments. On duty, too! No wonder he was chaffed so unmerci-
fully.

'Oh, I'll warrant there are some forthcoming, if needs be.
Most Karpasians have some weapon hidden away beneath the
thatch, a pike or sword. Perhaps a bow,' he added hopefully,

58

after a reflective pause.

'A likely chance!' laughed Zadoug, scornfully, 'they would not have so much trouble with brigands if that were so, old snail. Wake up! What will be the disposition of the standing army? Will Erili use it at the frontiers?'

Kinyras shrugged in the darkness and shivered as the rain rushed off his cloak down his neck at the movement. 'Curse this everlasting rain!' he muttered irritably, then in answer to his brother, 'Hardly, I fancy. Hange declares it must be kept frot the defence of the capital and the council. Erili is in favour of that. As he said, if the Karpasian army is doing any of the fighting, Hange and his kidney will wish to interpose. "I intend to do my own fighting," says Erili, and small blame to him.'

Zadoug nodded agreement. 'Hange is in league with Khem. I'm as sure of that, Kinyras, as though he had told me himself. Why else did he assure his countrymen they were in no danger of invasion, if not to lure them into a false security? He sent for Erili so that he could delude Karpas into feeling safe because mercenaries were on the spot, while hw used every effort to delay any active measures of defence.'

'Yes, and if we were sent to the frontiers he would see that we were in a position we could not hold. While we were being cut to pieces he would be gaining great credit for the measure he had taken. And if we were defeated he would vow we had betrayed the country.'

Zadoug cursed the absent Hange heartily. 'It's a cunning dog, but I fancy Erili knows him and will hang him as soon as maybe, on some pretext of another. If all this could be proved the people would tear him limb from limb. There is nothing so fierce as a mild and pacific people, when once thoroughly roused.'

'I will settle with Hange myself, one day.' In the meantime we have other matters more pressing. This question of suitable arms for the Karpasians troubles me sorely. Everything depends upon it and an error of judgement now will be fatal. We might teach them to use the Agkyle.'

'We might,' was the reply, given doubtfully, 'but to throw

with it you have to be in the open. Khem is so many and we so few, we can't afford to leave cover.'

'True! Though it could be used with effect from behind the battlements of a wall.'

'Yes, if we had walls. Even so half the body must be exposed and the KHemites are superb archers.'

'This question of numbers tears a man's guts out, Zadoug. While our actual line runs through open country there are adjacent woods which must be cleared, a difficult and dangerous task which may entail much loss of life should Khem come up before we get them down.'

'This accursed delay has caused us that loss, and we have Hange to thank for it. Your earth-wall and double ditch may hold off stray raids, even if made in force, but we could not resist an attack with engines, and Khem has many of them.'

'Stone is the only thing to resist engines. Well, we'll build in stone.'

'If we can hold the ditch and the wall for a year, yes. But can we?'

'The future is in the lap of the gods, Zadoug.'

At that moment his beast floundered into a hole almost pitching its rider over its head. Zadoug recovered with difficulty and retorted acidly in consequence—'Is it? I thought you had power to snatch a piece at will, Kinyras.'

'I have seen walls so highs that no scaling ladder could reach their top, so strong that no rock hurled at them by the most powerful engine could make the slightest impression upon them... walls with narrow slits in them, through which archers could shoot. I could build such and have the world dumb with amazement, had I the time. Ho there, orderly. Send me Dicios the wright.'

Down the line of wavering torches the cry went for Dicios. Presently he came running to Kinyras' stirrup. 'You sent for me, sir?'

'I need your help, good wright. Between us we must produce a new arm.'

Kinyras carefully expounded his invention while Dicios

listened, grunting assent every now and then until Kinyras had finished speaking, when he asked a few questions and thought for a moment or two.

'How will you bend it?' he asked at last, 'if it can be bent with the hands it will not have the range of an ordinary bow.'

'No. The friction of the groove will rob it of force, but as I view it, an untrained man could use it. Not all men can hold a bow steady, nor learn to release the string without plucking. It is for such I want it, if it can be made.'

'I can but try, sir. I'll make one without delay. I could use a windlass to draw it, such as we used in your engine, but it would take so long to bend and would be heavy and cumbersome to carry.'

'But it would shoot strongly, Dicios, and if it is shot from behind walls, weight would not matter. You could make the shaft heavier, so that it would drive through shield and mail.'

'Aye, to be sure. A slow rate of fire wouldn't matter, if every shaft killed. You never can tell with these things till you try, sir.'

'Thanks, good Dicios, do the best you can with it and bring it to me as soon as it is ready. I'm all impatience as you may suppose.'

Dicios fell back with a salute, muttering to himself, 'Good old slow but sure, a man might do worse than work for the Snail.'

The march continued through the wet and windy night and it was an hour past dawn before the wary men approached Gastri and saw its walls in the near distance. They halted on the level green by the banks of a little stream. Here the mayor of Gastri, on Verg, had caused a huge fire to be lighted, before which sides of deer and goat were roasting. The welcome sight and smell sent all spirits soaring and the men threw off their packs and hailed the crowd of townsfolk, who had gathered to admire their own preparations and to see the strangers, with shouts of cheerful greeting. Verg came forward slowly and with dignity to welcome Kinyras and his officers, while the crowd watched the proceedings in silence.

'Not much enthusiasm for their defenders,' muttered Zadoug, eyeing the men of Gastry askance.

Miklos, to whom he had spoke, shrugged. 'Well, 'tis their lives are at stake as well as ours, my captain. A month hence they'll tell a very different story.'

'See the fat, merry man in the long red cloak trying to look dignified,' jeered Witkind, under his breath and from the side of his mouth towards Zadoug. 'That forked beard going grey makes him look like a mountain goat. What seeks he?'

'He's mayor, judging by his long staff surmounted by the open hand of gold.'

'Well, 'tis the open hand we need at the moment,' laughed Milos, 'his smell is more to my taste than his looks.'

They all dismounted, giving their bridles to slaves, and advanced with Kinyras to meet Verg. It was nicely timed so that the parties encountered halfway between their respective supporters.

'Hail, great chief, I am Verg, Mayor of Gastri.'

'Hail, worshipful Mayor, I am Kinyras, general of Mercenaries under King Erili.'

'I have seen the orders of the council and I greet you, O new-made Ban.'

He saluted and Kinyras returned the compliment and greetings with affable condescension.

'These orders are passing strange,' Verg continued, his naturally jolly face becoming slightly discontented, 'but in fear of invasion I must obey. They press hardly on our free city, and I have much trouble with my fellow officials. With our walls we are safe and have already withstood many sieges. Enough of this, however, I came to bid you to my house. Honour me with your presence, I beg, and we will talk over meat.'

'Many thanks, O Mayor, but you have already furnished noble hospitality. Pardon me if I decline your bounty until a more fitting occasion. Speed is of the utmost importance to all of us and I will, with your permission, eat with my men.'

The mayor shrugged and looked a little rueful. 'My wife will scold, for she has provided well for your coming, but you must please yourself, Kinyras. The plan for lines of defence from sea to sea is good but who will pay? Already the people grumble at the small taxes we impose.'

'Better a grumble and a payment than a slit throat,' Kinyras informed him bluntly.

The mayor hastened to assent, with a doleful wag of his head. 'Indeed yes. Refugees are coming in fast, with horrible tales of rape, murder and torture. My wife's cousins have been killed at Aghridi.'

'My condolences, sir. And now, I pray you, issue a proclamation summoning your whole population, women, old men and children as well, to work on the lines.'

Kinyras went on to give the same instructions as Sedru had received and finally got rid of the talkative mayor, who trundled off to calm his wife and do the bidding of these tiresome strangers.

Kinyras flung himself down on the grass, wearied and anxious. 'We rest here till midday,' he told his officers, and composed himself to snatch brief sleep. Almost immediately he was wakened by Hasvan, who shocked at his master's forgetfulness of the needs of the body, had hastened to bring food. Kinyras ate with relish and sent Hasvan to summon Dicios. 'Bid him bring his bowl and eat with me,' he shouted after the retreating slave.

'Ha, Dicios. Sit you down and eat and when you have finished go into the town and collect what materials you will need to make my bows. Fetch several ox-loads. We must experiment much before we reach success. What shall we name it? Staveros would do, eh? They look like a cross.'

'Staveros is excellent, master,' declared Dicios, wolfing mutton and bacon with animal enjoyment, 'most excellent.'

With the departure of Dicios on his errand, Kinyras fell into an uneasy sleep, from which he was wakened by the calling of trumpets. He rose and mounted the fresh donkey which Hasvan brought him, a beautifully bred, dun-coloured, little animal with dark brown points and petulant, twitching ears, a very different mount from the sorry little beast which had born him thither.

'A present from the Mayor, master,' Hasvan informed him.

Kinyras stroked the soft muzzle and the little creature responded cordially. 'See, Hasvan, he likes me,' cried Kinyras, ridiculously pleased. 'I shall call him Baal-Salah, and see to it that he has of the best.'

So saying he mounted Baal-Salah, who seeming to understand his newly-conferred importance, behaved now and always with unwonted intelligence and docility. The trumpets sounded, the weary men fell in and the army marched forward again under the huge banner of a golden snail on a black ground. With the coming of morning the rain had stopped, the clouds lifted and soon the sun was shining forth, warming and heartening the men and giving everything a much improved aspect. Under its beneficent influence Kinyras found his thoughts working with great rapidity and clarity. Like many other men of vivid imagination his thoughts seemed less the product of his mind than some outward direction spoken to him by a voice, such as Socrates of a later age, and Joan of Arc knew. This voice now spoke and he listened to it with so rapt an attention in so still a manner, that he looked like a statue of bronze sitting the little fawn animal so daintily picking its way beneath the gleaming gold and black flag. Presently he roused, looking round for his brother and beckoned him.

Zadoug rode out from the group of officers and joined him. 'You were so still I thought you slept, Kinyras?'

'I've been thinking. Are you prepared and willing to undertake a dangerous mission?'

'At your service, brother. You know I love an adventure.'

'This is nothing pleasing, but full of hardship and much peril. I doubt much if I should ask it of you.'

'Come, what is it? Having whetted appetite you cannot refuse sustenance.'

'I've been thinking that if we knew the movements of Khem we should be at better advantage. I want someone to go and spy out the enemy and bring back as much intelligence as he can glean from Aghirda. You, my confidant, know exactly what I wish to know, without any telling.'

'I'll go and thank you for the office, Kinyras.'

'Then go with my blessing and thanks. Be wary, Zardoug, take no needless risk. You have a shrewd head don your shoulders. Use it to save yourself and us all from disaster. Go secretly and tell no one of your mission.'

'I'll steal away to-night, travel in the darkness and lie up all day. Trust me, Kinyras.'

'Then we'll part now, Zardoug. Farewell! The gods guard you and restore you to me in safety.'

The two clasped hands and rose on together, talking earnestly, deciding to whom among Zadoug's officers to give charge of the wall during his absence. Kinyras found his brother of great service to him in matters whoc required courage, initiative, daring and address and frequently employed him on important missions. Sometimes Kinyras would set for on such adventures himself, appointing Zadoug as his deputy during his absence. Hitherto these missions had not been unduly hazardous, but this one carried a double peril, for he was as likel to be caught and slain by the red-headed barbarians of Anghirda as by the men of Khem. Yet, should he survive, the information he would obtain would be invaluable to a country so pressed for time as Karpas at this juncture. Kinyras had no hope of avoiding the ultimate conflict, for that was inevitable. Greedy Khem, with eyes on the rich copper mines of Cyprus for their bronze, and her luxuriant forests of cedar, walnut, cypress, plane and pine for her ships, would not easily forgo so precious a prize, the fact of this booty being an island and so solving all difficulties of transport adding immensely to its wealth. The object of Kinyras was to inflict a final and crushing defeat upon Khem, to teach them such a lesson that they would not again attempt invasion.

Their march was south-west toward that gently rising ground where the long, narrow north-eastern peninsula of Karpas swells into the gulf of Salam. Here, from to south, the wall was to be built. In an hour they arrived at the foot of Gypsa Hill, where a general halt was made. Kinyras and his officers set out to survey. Zadoug lingered behind and called from his lieutenants, one Sabiah, bidding him take command of his force until he should relieve him of the authority again, and proceed with his portion of the wall under the guidance of the general. Sabiah, a thin-faced, dark-haired, sallow and wiry Phoenician, keen and zealous, saluted and quietly withdrew.

'He will do well,' thought Zadoug, watching the alert, stringy figure as it rejoined his brother officers, the strong swing of the shoulders, the confident, yet quiet carriage of the head. 'a man like Kinyras, who gets things done.'

He strode over to his brother and a glance of intelligence passed between the two. Zadoug nodded and they ascended on the north-east slope of Monarga, where the going was easy. On the south-west side, from whence attack would come, the hill fell away in a sharp declivity which, though steep, was not impossible to climb. From it the view was a long, rolling stretch of grass-land to a belt of forest, cypress and juniper. To the left lay more grass-land, with scattered farms, forest again in the middle distance merging into the swamp, which marked the winter flooding of the Kastnon. Beyond was the deep, unfathomable blue of the sea. A rocky head stood boldly out at the mouth of the Kastnon, called Stronglos, the white crests of the waves breaking leisurely at its feet gleaming in the sun. Within the curve of its jutting base would be shelter for his ships and in times of storm they could be brought out of danger into the river. Kinyras looked long. It was a fair country on that still, sunny afternoon, one worth fighting for.

He turned to his officers and pointed out the direction of the lines. They must run them across the flat land, straight to the Hill. The great strength of the enemy lay in their chariots, but as these could be operated only on flat country it followed that the first fortifications must be built where this cavalry attack could be stopped. There were two roads, narrow tracks, little better than footpaths leading across the frontier from Salam to Karpas which, though seemingly unimportant, would yet indicate the route to the enemy, who would quickly build them in order to bring up their chariots. Undoubtedly the first attack might be expected here.

To the north the country was more hilly right up to the southern flank of Hap Hill and, by running the line along the crest of this rising ground, natural advantages could be used to good effect. The only drawback was that by so doing the line was lengthened and there was much clearing of forest to be accomplished first. Timber gave the enemy bowmen cover, providing Khem with every means of hindrance she could desire.

Kinyras returned to camp and made his dispositions, appointing a squadron leader to every five hundred paces of line, with orders to start operations without delay. Scouts were posted, orders given to all troops to retire upon Gypsa Hill if a body of the enemy appeared from Kastnon river, and if they should come from Hap Hill to retreat up the hill. He impressed upon them the importance of keeping together, not to run the risk of being wiped out before the defences were ready.

Next morning Kinyras found that Zadoug had quietly disappeared. Workmen came up from Gastri and the day was spent in steady attention to routine, marking out the line in all flat places, cutting a ditch thirty feet wide, a fifteen-food berm with an earth valum behind it. As the earth was taken from the ditch it was piled up along the line of the valum. So the work went on, orderly, without waste of time, labour or material, all along the line and the progress made was astonishing. Later he returned to the no less important question of arms, giving instructions to his captains to weed out those who could use them from each party of workers as they arrived, to start drilling, exercising and instructing at once. All workers were classified with the most methodical exactness and such as were craftsmen set to work, each on his own business, though every man had to put in a certain number of hours at the ditch. A look-out was set on Gypsa Hill for smoke or fire signals, a watch kept for the expected ships lest for lack of a sign they sail past their anchorage; nothing was forgotten, no possibility discounted.

When all was going to his satisfaction Kinyras called for

Baal-Salah and when Hasvan brought him, ran a keen eye over its grooming. Already the little creature knew him and nuzzled into his hand with every expression of pleasure. Its trappings of leather and bronze were of the finest workmanship, and satisfied, Kinyras mounted and rode off to visit other sections towards Hap Hill. Here was the beginning of high cliffs, starting at an elevation of ten feet or so, separated by terraces each twelve feet wide. They ran along for a distance of six hundred paces, gradually increasing in height until they merged into the main cliff, which was a sheer sixty feet of unclimbable rock; and though his line ran to the crest of the hill, this portion of it caused him no present anxiety.

As he returned, his thoughts were much with his brother, working out his dangerous path through unknown lands of dense forest up to the mountains of Anghirdi, right into the heart of the barbarians, those wild men dressed in rude skins, with matted red hair and green eyes. Rumour said they were more like cats than men, could see in the dark and ate each other, having little bronze, killing with stone axes. Kinyras gave very little credit, either to their eyes, their uncanny powers or their evil habits, but his heart was heavy with anxiety for the safety of his beloved brother. Since his wife had left him he had been a very lonely man and had found consolation in Zadoug's bluff sympathy and chaff. His natural affections were soft, warm and tenacious, his deepest inclinations and hopes lay in comfort of home, wife and children. Eune had robbed him by her action of everything he valued most, and though he had bought Pheretime in order to fill the gap and heal the would she had inflicted, the slave-girl was unable to make him forget is wife. Eune had both grace and charm and he doubled whether he ever should meet a woman who could make him forget her, worthless as he had proved herself. He admitted frankly to himself that he wished another woman would come into his life.

The season of the year induced such thoughts. The warm, soft air, the heartening sun after months of rain and cold, and far yet from that torrid heat which later would wither man, beast and plant, had worked their magic upon the island. The turf upon which he rode was begemmed with violet and crocus, anemone and narcissus. Wherever his eye turned was beauty in excelsis, the hills nearby dancing in the sunlight, the distant mountains a soft lavender against the lapis sky, the occasional gleam of rock and sparkle of stone, new green of cedar spines able the reddish brown of massive bough and trunk, deep shadow of the grand forests encroaching upon the flower-decked plain, with its little, scattered houses gaily but crudely painted red, yellow and blue in ornamentation, all begirt by the sea, blue as Astarte's eyes, drowsing in the spring sun. Well might they call it 'The Sweet Scented'. Prospero's isle was never more entrancing. Kinyras reigned in Baal-Salah and looked his fill, thinking of Zadoug, or Eune, of the thing of beauty in a man might make of his home in such a blessed spot, and he prayed that he might save the land from Khem and preserve it in peace and tranquillity, if not for himself then for others.

When he reached camp he found Hasvan building a hut of the stones with which the hill-top was covered. A hollowed-out piece of cliff had offered a suitable site, having the merit of the builder's eyes of requiring only two side walls and a front to make a snug shelter for his master.

'Well done, Hasvan,' he encouraged, and made one or two helpful suggestions to lighten labour before he passed on.

A group of men were toiling at the ditch, women and girls carting the earth in baskets to the wall, so much farther than usual from the ditch.

'Why, in the name of all gods must the wall be all that way off? one grumbled, pausing to straighten his back.

His fellow tapped forehead and spat expressively. 'The old 'un's got bees in his helmet.'

Kinyras, standing behind them, grinned. 'Come, get on there!' he called sternly and grinned still more broadly as they leapt to work again.

Further on were groups of men drilling, others were practis-ing archery, very clumsily and with much blasphemy from the instructors. They stood in the hot spring sun, stripped but for a loin-cloth, striving to bend the long bows with muscles grown slack in other work and finding the task almost impossible. Kinyras stepped up and watched quietly, then, going to one man he explained patiently the construction of the weapon and the technique of the art of using it, and passing on in a more confident frame of mind as he saw that his pupil had profited a little from the lesson.

'Give them time and we could make them into a smart body of men,' he murmured to himself, pausing to watch a crowd of women and girls squatting on the grass busily weaving baskets with nimble fingers. They, too, were innocent of clothing for the heat had demanded the discarding of winter garments. The sun played lovingly on the curves and tints of young flesh.

'Hail, lord!' they greeted him, smiling with flashes of white teeth through parted lips and glances of curiosity.

'Bless you, my children,' Kinyras responded, 'work well for our salvation.'

'Aye, master,' they cried in chorus.

Everyone seemed to be in a cheerful mood, working fast and willingly, like these women. He left the bright little spot of colour, for they had flung their cloaks on the turn and these were crudely dyed in brilliant hues. As yet something of a holiday mood prevailed and the novelty of the enterprise had only just begun, enthusiasm ran high, wits were working. The eyes of Kinyras ranged along the lines of his wall, already making remarkable progress, and concentrated upon one spot. With a word to Baal-Salah he pushed forward, the little donkey breaking into a canter and halting.

Kinyras sat watching the progress of the wall. 'Ho, there! Let the foreman come hither.'

A small, muscular, clever-looking rascal, with twinkling eyes and an alert manner, ran to his stirrup. 'Hail, lord. You called?'

'What is the meaning of that?' Kinyras pointed to a low breastwork which rose at the edge of the ditch in this section. The man stared at him, hesitated and looked as though he had a mind to bolt for safety.

'Never fear, but explain and quickly. There is no time to lose.'

The man gathered his courage desperately and answered falteringly—'Pardon, lord... my presumption... the breastwork... could be defended by spearmen while archers, standing on the wall behind, could shoot over their heads.' As soon as he started speaking of his work the man's hesitation was gone.

Kinyras noted here the natural authority which belongs to the man with ideas. 'Good. What is your name, friend?'

'Ludim, master.'

'You have a brain in that head of yours, Ludim, and it is such men as you whom we need now. Raise the breastwork to four feet and make it of sharpened timbers. You will take charge of the workmen in this section under your officer. I will speak with him and if you have any more such notions, come and lay them before me at once. Even though they may be useless I shall like to hear them. Seek me and fear not. I am always accessible to those who need me, or can be of use to me. Now go and be faithful; loyalty shall reap its just reward when it comes to the final settling at the end of the war. I will not forget you, Ludim.'

The man flushed, knelt and bowed his head as Kinyras prepared to ride on. 'I will be faithful to such a master to the death, lord,' he said fervently.

Kinyras sought the officer in charge and instructed him accordingly. The incident had heartened him considerably and hope began to flourish in his heart, driving aside doubts and fears. They would beat Khem, they would accomplish the impossible, they would defeat their enemies, within and without, and he would live yet to see that villain, Hange, strung to a sturdy bough for his crimes. He rode along under the magnificent cedars, amusing himself in selecting the limb he would use for the purpose and when he came down to the Kastnon he was disappointed that his ships had not yet arrived.

However, there was no help for it, and he returned along the line, heartened again to be told that supplies of food were coming in from local farmers who, urged by memories of the terrors of past raids and the fear of those imminent, were contributing generously and without grumbling.

Work was going even better now because the reason for putting the wall so far behind the ditch had been explained, and Kinyras saw that men work more diligently intelligently when they understand the purpose of their work. Marking this down in his mind for further use, he reached the top of Gypsa Hill, where Verg, the Mayor of Gastri, was talking to Witkind. He had come with a promise of workers and tools.

Evening came, the moon rose clear and gave a brilliant light. Kinyras calculated that, with luck, they could count upon a fortnight of bright night shifts to be used, thus solving the problem of shortage of tools. Those who had been idling most of the day, lacking implements for work, were quickly rounded up into gangs, overseers appointed and the companies driven to the earth-works by the officers. The day-workers, weary from unaccustomed toil, gathered round camp fires. The air was fragrant with the burning of sweet resins from pine and cedar, great fires leapt up to the tranquil skies, where the bronze casters had already set up their furnaces, cooking pots oozed savouriness and around them the people clustered, each with his bowl of red or black pottery crudely ornamented in primitive designs, chattering noisily, while the children ran hither and thither in and out of the crowds, screaming, fighting, playing, often with yapping dogs at their heels. Garments had been resumed, for cold airs blew in from the sea and from distant mountains, and the flames danced upon vivid reds and yellows, casting monstrous shadows as they now rose and now fell when fresh fuel was thrown on. There was no lack of wood and they piled it on merrily, while the bellowing of oxen, the stamp of hooves and the roar of thousands of voices all along the line was like a fierce, rushing wind in the land.

So things went on, day in, day out, in a constant round of toil, eating, sleeping, drilling, in the practice of archery and the use of the pike. By the end of the second week the ditch averaged six feet in depth. In certain places stone was found, when they drilled it with jumpers, splitting it with wedges and sledgehammers. But after a time they hit upon igneous device of heating with fires and then pouring on cold water. Gangs of men were employed in cutting down the enormous trees which grew close to the lines, obstructing the view of the country beyond. This was dangerous work, for raiding parties of Khemites were always to be feared, yet clearing must be done and the wood was needed for the stockade.

Kinyras viewed the progress of the work with satisfaction, slow though it is seemed. Every five hundred paces a bastion was thrown out and a gateway only wide enough to admit two men at a time put in every mile. Malcontents and malingerers were bound to be found in such a large company that it practically embraced the whole population of a country. Kinyras found disaffection invariable went hand in hand with incipient treachery and laziness. These detrimental were the gravest danger to the safety of the people, and he pondered their case long and heavily, then called together his officers and sat in solemn council with them.

The offenders were arrested; each section of the line taking their worst and most stubborn cases, they were marched down to Kinyras and arraigned before him. He sat in public judgement, marshalled the evidence against them in a fair and impartial trial and condemned the two worst from every section to death. On a certain day they were taken back to their section. The workers of each were given an hour off duty and the disaffected were publicly hanged as a warning to others, the officer in charge reading the indictment against them in a loud voice, making a very impressive ceremonial of the occasion.

This procedure had a very salutary effect upon the others, who seeing that Kinyras was a fair and just master, if a firm one, decided it was wiser to yield a willing service than to kick at the end of a rope like this.

The ships had now arrived and lay at anchor in the mouth of the Kastnon. This stream spread into a marsh near the sea and Kinyras used the swamp as a means of defence. He ran his line of trenches well into it, to where it was impossible for the enemy to cross it in force, the lines starting from the edge of this swamp. The slinging machines were taken from the ships and mounted, each in a bastion as far as they would go, and such men as could be spared were set to making more.

These chariot-archers were so formidable a corps that their terror for the Cypriots often won the battle for them before they appeared on the field. Composed from sons of the nobility, they were not only of great courage, pride and daring, but were trained to such a pitch of excellence, were such magnificent archers and had such modern equipment that they were the wonder and dread of the world. The flower of the Khemite army, they would be used in the first attack both as a boastful gesture and as a means of frightening the Karpasians into a rabid submission. Kinyras hoped to be ready for them, to repulse them, to teach them a much-needed lesson and by checking them put such heart into his Karpasians that they would be induced to make a stouter resistance.

How to check their dreaded charge successfully was the greatest problem Kinyras had ever set out to solve. They could not drive through the ditch, but they could sweep up to within range, protected from fire by the long, stout shield which was carried by a bearer in every chariot. Behind this barricade they would pour in a cloud of arrows with devastating effect. Their horses could be shot, but the archers would escape and there were plenty of fresh teams behind the lines. Masked by them, the infantry would advance in thousands to the assault. Some means must be found of checking their rush. When he could get a few moments to himself he must take one of his travel flights and seek what he wanted in the future, since the present and the past could not aid him.

When he returned to camp after a conference with the masons engaged on the wall at the mouth of the Kastnon he found Dicios awaiting him with the latest pattern of Staveros in his hand. 'Ah, smith, you are the most welcome sight I've seen this day,' and he took the weapon from the man's hand, examining it minutely, while Dicios stood by with straddled legs, hands on his bare hips, a complacent smile curing his full, sensitive mouth. 'That first lot was none too successful, lord...

accurate enough, perhaps, but with none of the force of an ordinary bow.'

'No,' murmured Kinyras, holding the arm at length and squinting along the staff with one eye shut, 'ordinary arrows were useless. This short, stout arrow, with the square head is the thing. It should shoot with the maximum force. This new forked lever you have made, with the hinged arm, makes the drawing of such a stout bow as we have here practicable. A greased bolt shot from it should be driven through two shields. How does it work, Dicios?'

'As you foretold it would, master.'

'Come, we will test it together,' said Kinyras, stepping outside his house and making at a rapid stride for a secret place in a grove of cedars, where he had set up targets.

Dicios took two great hide shields of enormous thickness, bound with bronze, from a rough hut and set them up, one behind the other. Kinyras ranged himself, sighted, and fired, Dicios looking on in rapt excitement. There was a singing whirr and a thud, the smith ran to the mark and displayed both shields pierced. 'You see, master!' he called, holding them up for inspection.

Kinyras came up at a run to examine for himself. 'Well done, Dicios,' exclaimed he, in such a tone of satisfaction and commendation that the man flushed with gratification, especially when his master slapped his shoulder in his enthusiasm. 'Now we have something which will give the charioteers of Khem pause to think. Get every wright you can lay hold of, divide them into parties, make them work night and day. When some pause for food and sleep let others take their places, keep up a perpetual stream of labour on these arms until we have enough for the whole line. These square arrow heads of yours are fine, a strong bow needs a strong head.'

Dicios assented and took the staveros. 'It is a great device, lord. It passes me how a man could think of such a weapon. I believe, sir, that you walk with the High Gods and that they teach you their tricks.'

'Maybe. It is my secret, Dicios. Be diligent and I shall know how to reward you. You are master over your men, remember, so see that you have them in control and make them work their hardest. Be not harsh, but wise and just, and do not over-drive any man. A contented worker will make my staveros better than a discontented and weary one. We have a great difficulty to overcome to produce these arms against the march of time and Khem. Relieving parties are the secret. I trust you to carry through this important task to a successful issue.'

'I will be faithful, master,' the wright assured him, bowing low with a look of awe on his face, and backing as though he did indeed stand in the presence of a god.

Kinyras, weary and hungry, sought his house. Pheretime had prepared a good meal, which she began to set before him, spoiling her cooling by much grumbling. She was tired of this barbarous life, she wished to live in the capital, where there were shops, markets and merchants to gossip with. Just look at her? Was she fit to be seen. Kinyras, unheeding and suffering the storm to pass him by, ran a careless eye over her naked form, ornamented with a strip of coloured cloth at her waist and a string of bright beads around her neck. She was well enough, she smelt sweetly of unguents and when she shook her curls at him in vigorous protest, her bronze ear-rings swung heavily from her little ears and a wave of perfume issued from her pretty head. Pheretime was apt to overdo essences, but she was well enough.

He drew her roughly to his knee and kissed her shoulder. She submitted passively, watching his bronze face with critical eyes.

'Have patience, wench. You shall have all you wish, I prom-ise you, when the war is over and we march triumphant back to Karpasia.'

'The war never will be over,' she grumbled, pouting and giving his ragged hair a tweak, a little spitefully, though it passed for a caress.

'Go, bring the food. I'm hungry and thirsty and when I've eaten I wish to rest undisturbed, 'Time. See to it that I get an hour of absolute quiet, girl.'

Petulantly gratified by the use of her pet name and another careless kiss, she was about to withdraw when Hasvan entered. 'Messages from the King, lord, and a large band of his own men.'

All thoughts of food vanished and Kinyras jumped up and hastened to meet the captain in command of the new troops. Dispatches from Erili announced that he would visit the line in a week and hold a general inspection. He sent greetings to his Old Snail and bid him use these reinforcements to the best advantage.

Kinyras ordered the men to feed and rest; 'Men, you will repair to the line and dig, working at the ditch and the wall. If the lines are not finished by the time the men of Khem come up, your throats will have too big a slit in them to admit of speech, or eating. Dispurse!'

There were many black looks and much disgruntled comment, as Kinyras foresaw; but the rest round the camp-fires, the savoury cook-pots and the friendly gossip, to say nothing of the whispered warnings against the follow of rebellion, with its dire results, induced in them a better frame of mind.

It was an hour later that Kinyras re-entered his house, ate and rested for a couple of hours, sleeping deeply and tranquilly. At the end of the time he arose, wrapped himself in his cloak and, much refreshed, went out again, seeking a high, solitary spot necessary for his purpose. His way lay up the hill and along its crest to a point where a spur jutted out far from all scenes of activity. It was covered with a soft, springy sward, fragrant with violets and approached through a belt of giant walnut trees, which ended abruptly where the little plateau jutted out over the wooded valley below, from which a thousand spicy odours rose in the night air, meeting and mingling in the soft wind from the hills. It was quite dark, for the moon would be late arising, but the deep sky was full of space, a silence so profound that it seemed to stretch to the confines of the world. The fragrant earth was like a vast cup full to the brim and spilling over with this ineffable quietude, inducing in him a lightness of buoyancy of feeling as though he were borne up upon it and were drifting out into its infinite spaces, then sinking gently into it until it covered him completely.

Stillness here was not so much a soundlessness, as a profound background upon which the cadences and motivity of nature played in varying degrees, like strata of light cloud driving across the solid blueness of space.

Kinyras paused at the edge of the walnut grove and drew deep breaths of the cool air into his lungs. When he had done this for some time he knelt and offered a simple prayer, addressing no god and speaking aloud, so that his voice in the stillness had a strangely directional quality, as though he had hurled a spear at some infinitely remote target.

'Grant that I may find what I seek in the mists of time for the salvation of my people,' prayed Kinyras, then arose, walked to the edge of his plateau, spread his cloak upon the grass and lay down flat upon his back, fixing his eyes unwinkingly upon a distant star. Very soon his former sense of immersion in space deepened, the star drew him towards it, he began to float gently towards it, his spirit, released from his flesh, spread its pinions and soared.

The night airs continued to play over his motionless body stretched at full length upon the turf, the stars moved across the sky and dawn was breaking before he stirred, beating with the palm of each hand gently upon the ground beside. Leisurely was this process of coming back to earth, while the birds in the grove chanted their morning chorus and the edge of the sun appeared above the rim of the eastern sea as though in answer to their incantation. A chill wind blew over him, he rose slowly and knelt with bowed head for some time facing the sun, whose level beams bathed him in a ruddy glow as he offered these silent thanks and went with his purposeful, military stride back to camp.

Kinyras went straight to Dicios, who was already hard at work in his quarters adjoining the casting fires. He dropped his tools and went in answer to the beckoning call.

'I have been seeking a way to stop the chariot charges of Khem,' the general began and Dicios turned awed eyes upon him. Already it was known that his master had spent the night abroad, whither no one dared say. Doubtless he had been walking with the gods again, there was that in his face which lent colour to the notion and his next words went to confirm it. 'I have seen metal balls with four sharp spikes upon the, so fashioned that when and however thrown in the passage of the charge, one point always remains upward.'

A thrill ran down the spine of the smith and was conscious that the hairs of his bare arms were stiff; he looked down at them in a daw and murmured involuntarily—'Where did you see them, master?'

Kinyras smiled as he watched the fellow. 'In a dream, Dicios. You are fearful? There is no need to be. You could dream such dreams if you wished, but no matter now. This is the sort of thing I mean.' He seized a piece of charcoal, went to a table and began to draw upon it his spiked balls.

Dicios forgot the origin of the idea in his absorbing interest in their efficacy. 'Nothing could be better, master, we shall owe our salvation to you.

'All very well, smith, but we cannot spare the bronze, what can be used in substitute?'

'Stone. The old me could sit and chip them into shape out of pieces of rock.'

'Or wood, hardened by fire, and also bone.' They looked at each other and laughed. 'all three will do, Dicios. Have some made as soon as possible, keep men constantly making them. As you say, it is an occupation for the aged, and the children can collect the material. How goes the staveros?'

'A hundred have just gone out to the practice targets.'

Kinyras turned away well pleased and cheerful and went to the fortifications. The ditch would be completed in a few hours, his men were doing the digging. Then the bottom was to be planted with sharpened staves of hardwood, strengthened by fire, the points upward and bristling formidably. That morning the inner V-shaped ditch was begun.

Kinyras spent most of the next few days at the butts, watching staveros practice. His archers openly ridiculed the cross-bow among themselves, derisively stating they could loose three arrows while they were bending and firing the new arm. With an infinite patience Kinyras conceded his point, but illustrated the advantages of its accuracy, its length of range and the ease with which an untrained man could learn to use it. Again, there was the question of cover. An archer must stand with his body well exposed, or shoot through a wide loophole, while the staveros cross-bow could be fired through a narrow one and the marksman himself remain in cover. There was yet a great gain. Arrows must be made by skilled craftsmen, while any woodworker could be trusted to fashion a staveros bolt, and lastly, this type of arm could be rested on a wall of ledge to increase steadiness of aim.

In the consideration of these arguments prejudice soon gave way to admiration and soon the butts were the most popular places of amusement and recreation. The work of making the new arm went forward with enthusiasm and smaller weapons were made for young boys and girls, all of whom were eager to learn to shoot.

It was while he was watching the shooting one morning that Kinyras felt a touch on his elbow and, turning, found Zadoug quietly standing beside him.

'It goes well, Kinyras, I must have one of those without delay. Oh, well shot, sir!' and he clapped his hands enthusiastically as the officer who had fired stepped aside.

'Zadoug!' cried Kinyras, genuinely moved, embracing him heartily. 'I never was so thankful to see you before. I've been full of fears for you. Come to the house and eat and drink with me. How have you fared, lad?'

'Well enough' Zadough laughed. 'I got through into Aghirdi without meeting a soul. I kept to the forest most of the way. But the way, brother, it's a lie about them being red-headed. Many of them are, but there are hundreds of them of my own colour and some even have yellow hair, thanks be to the gods.'

'Thanks indeed!' Kinyras echoed. 'It is that fact which as caused me so much trouble. I wondered how a dark, swarthy fellow like yourself could escape detection among the red-heads.'

'I pretended to be deaf and dumb and managed very well. Gods, what a story I heard. Our suspicions of Hange are well founded.'

'I was certain of it,' said Kinyras, as they entered his house and sat down to the meal, which Pheretime had already set out. He poured wine for his brother and pressed fruit and cakes upon him. 'What of Damastes? Is he indeed killed, or taken prisoner?'

'Dead, killed in battle, and his daughter, Dayonis, taken prisoner. But listen, Kinyras. There is sedition in the ranks of Khem. Amasis, the general, plots to revolt against the Viceroy of the Pharaoh and to install himself in the office.'


Mina sitting by her husband's bedside was conscious of indescribable feelings in an indescribable atmosphere. Denvers had been lying there immovable for three days, and still Dr. Groves insisted that nothing could be done for him. Hank had gone to ask a medical friend about catalepsy, returning with the information that very often such trances lasted for weeks or months, some for as long as a year.

It was horrible, horrible, the way Robert lay there never moving an eyelash, breathing so imperceptibly that she had thought him dead and still would think so but for the doctor's assurances to the contrary.

She felt herself growing hysterical, jumped up and began to walk up and down the room, twisting her hands in an agony of nervousness. She simply could not bear it if Robert lay like that for weeks. She should go mad.

A ring at the bell startled her unbearable. It was Hank. 'Well,' he asked, after he had taken her in his arms and kissed her, 'Any change?'

Silently she shook her head and he followed her into the

bedroom, stood looking down upon his enemy's still figure. 'I don't' believe this catalepsy stuff,' he said, at length, 'the blighter's simply shamming. He's as cunning as the very devil.'

'Why should he?' she asked wonderingly.

Heyward sneered and lit a cigarette. His damaged eye was nearly well, but it still looked ugly without the shade. Mina suppressed a shudder. She hated anything unsightly. 'Because he thinks it will rouse your sympathy—bring you back to him.'

She drew closer to Heyward and slid her fingers into his. 'Nothing would ever make me do that, Hank.'

'I wish he was dead—if it wasn't for the stink it would make.'

'Let him alone, can't you? Why should you hate him so?'

'I don't hate him, I simply despise him for being such a fool. He is a fool, he trusted you!'

She shrank from the savage irony of his look and words. 'Hank—don't!' she cringed.

He seemed not to have heard her, to be almost unconscious of her presence, absorbed in some sort of diabolical communion with the still figure before him. 'Oh, I don't hate you, Denvers, but I'll ruin your life for you. I have, I know. The thought is exquisitely delicious. And that's funny, too, for at first I liked you. I like uncommon people and you are uncommon.'

'Hank! Hank!' she entreated, 'Leave him alone, can't you? It sounds horrible.'

He stared at her, his good eye snapping, the other watering and blood-shot. Again she looked away.

'Don't be so squeamish all of a sudden! He was wrapped up in you, wasn't he? How proud he was of you. It's been good sport to make the one he loves best hate him as you do.

Unexpectedly she answered in a low tone—'Do I hate him?'

His answer was a confident, careless laugh. 'You do. And I have done that. He's so miserable about it it's taken him like this. I don't pity him in the least. Once I put my hand on his shoulder. I wish it had been his throat, squeezing the life out. But what I've done is much better. I've made him squirm.'

'If that is your ambition,' she retorted, 'must we talk like this? Oh, Hank darling, let's forget him for a while.'

'You mustn't let him know anything definite until I'm well out of the country.'

'You forget. He's already found out all he wants to know.'

'That? It's nothing. Promise me, whatever happens you won't let him do anything to make a stink, so as to get me into trouble.'

'I promise,' she assured him with a strange look.

'Take all the blame yourself if anything happens. Let's hope he'll never come round—slip quietly out of things.'

'And if he does not?'

'Wait until I'm safely away, then pick a row with him and simply clear out. Where? Oh, anywhere. Then my name won't be mixed up in it. We can easily work up a case of cruelty. For instance, he wanted you to go to that queer club of his and you did. We can say he compelled you.'

She nodded mute acquiescence, still looking at him strangely. 'When are you going back?' she asked at length. 'Is the date fixed definitely?'

'In about a fortnight.'

'Oh, Hank, how ghastly. Whatever shall I do without you especially if he is still like this. And what about Mary?'

'Cheer up, darling. She knows a lot, but she'll bite her tongue out before she breathes a word against me.'

Mina sighed and he took her into his arms. She clung to him passionately, heart-brokenly.

'It won't be for long,' he whispered, 'I've thought it all out. If she won't divorce me—well, I'll have to get out of Government soon. In any case, I'm going to settle down in London and work up a practice as a barrister. I've been working at it for years. Lots of people know me. I can get them out of trouble. I'm friendly with several shyster lawyers, who'll send me clients wanting to be kept out of gaol.'

'And then?'

'Oh, you'll just come along and keep house for me, of course. Mary will have to divorce me then.'

'And if she doesn't?'

'Well, what does it matter? As long as we are happy—you'll be as faithful as she, and won't give me away either.'

# CHAPTER VI

# A NAKED PRINCESS

The two brothers stared at each other for a long moment when Zadoug had delivered himself of this statement. Kinyras poured wine for them both from a curious jar of red pottery shaped like a bird. It was one of Pheretime's latest acquisitions and very proud she was of it, too. They drank deeply and Zadoug set his cup down with a bang and a gasp of satisfaction. 'The wine is better than that vile stuff allotted to us in Karpasia.'

'It is,' Kinyras agreed somewhat grimly, 'and it had better be so, or I'll know the reason why. More?' Zadoug nodded and Kinyras refilled. 'What you have said sounds helpful and we might use it?'

'Wait until you hear the whole story. Rhadames has designed the wench for himself, bur the fame of her beauty had spread and Amasis has sent word that she is to be delivered up to him. She fought beside her father like a wild-cat, using spear and bow like a man. They say she is a witch and has great sway with her people, who will follow her to the death.'

'It is true, then, that the women of these barbarians fight beside their men and are formidable in battle?'

'She does, at any rate, but there are many lies told by these folk. They are not barbarous, though wild and untameable and desperate fighters, loving not strangers.'

'What is her name? I did not catch it.'

'Dayonis.'

'A likeable name,' Kinyras observed, repeating it several times.

'And a likely wench, with a mane of red hair curling to her knees, which have a most distracting dimple, by the way… and most unusual eyes, of much beauty and changing with every mood like the sea, sometimes a deep blue in calm weather, at others glinting and angry green or brooding grey, deep red brown brows and lashes, a mouth which provokes and promises, a body to tempt the high gods themselves.'

'You have studied her well, Zadoug,' Kinyras laughed, 'and you describe a goddess.'

'I observed her on every occasion possible and I have a use for her. She is a tit-bit which any man would desire and fight for. Already Rhadames is mad for her sake and Amasis resolved she shall be his, on mere hearsay, unless they have sent him a fancy picture. But the point is this, Rhadames not only desires her, but intends to use her as a means of compelling her people to fight for him. If he can win this Dayonis to look with favour upon him and to influence the Aghirdi to form themselves into an army, his revolt against Amasis is likely to succeed.

'I see. And is the Princess favourable to such a scheme?'

'I doubt it. She fell, fighting beside her father, and was left for dead, but her foster-father, Ammunz, searching for her body amongst the slain to give it burial, found her recovering her senses. Both he and she were taken and bound, but Ammunz escaped, leaving her unrecognised amongst a crowd of women, herded in the courtyard of the temple.₁ Later her identity was discovered and she was taken before Rhadames. She defied him, but he, anxious to please and win her, acceded to her wish to be put in a certain cell, a semi-underground room of the Temple, where she would be protected from the cold and be private. It had one very small window, but they made her comfortable with three skins to warm her, and a lamp, and sent scribes to instruct her in the language of Khem. Many a time have I crept up and watched her through this window. She passed most of the time at her witch-tricks.'

'What kind of tricks?' Kinyras asked, interested.

'Oh, mere child's play, mumbo-jumbo. She is a little impostor, in my view. She plans to save her people and to be revenged for her father's defeat and death upon Khem 'tis whispered.'

'Surely that shows her a dutiful daughter and a patriot?'

Zadoug shrugged. 'She would use her wiles on her guards and questioned them, and I, lying close to the window safe hidden while her guards gossiped, learnt much. She asked them the way to the mountains whether Pharaoh's men had ever penetrated beyond them. The man answered no, the cold made the mountains impassable, and there were Demons there. Some of the men of Bapho had fled to them and were still holding out.

'"So the Lord Pharaoh rules all of the land of Orphusa except these hills?" she asks quietly, her blue eyes guileless as a child's, the witch!

'"Yes," answers the fool, boastful as a roaring lion. "His armies have not as yet gone to Karpas, but soon they march. The people there are timid and fear war, an easy prey when we are ready for them. But there is of little value in the land in copper or precious stones, hardly worth invading, yet."

'"Yet you march?" she murmurs, dulcet as a dove.

'"Oh, yes, we march. They have no king in Karpas, but are ruled by a council and there is one who has much power there, who has sent to Pharaoh, offering to yield up the land if he is suitably rewarded, if he is made governor and given much riches. That is common talk among us here."'

'Hange!' exclaimed Kinyras fiercely.

'Without a doubt, brother. Buet we need proof before we can pull him down. At the moment we have only the word of a Khem gaoler.'

'True, but Erili visits the line in two days and we will lay the matter before him.'

'Good! Well, the more I saw and heard of this lass the longer I watched at her window, which had some convenient bushes growing thickly outside. Did I tell you I cut myself a stout staff and had become a blind cripple, as well as a deaf and dumb one?'

'No!' laughed Kinyras, 'surely that was over doing the business.'

'They are simple folk, thick-headed and inclined to be trustful with their own kind. These Aghirdis speaking a dialect which is not difficult to understand when one has got accustomed to it. And you know I can speak Khemite. Lying under the bushes with nothing to do but suck my teeth, I studied the language of Khem when the scribes came to instruct Dayonis.'

Again Kinyras laughed and slapped his brother hilariously on the shoulder, calling to Pheretime for another jar of wine.

'Also, there is much confusion in the town. The men of Aghirdi are sullen and rebellious, too occupied with their own troubles to give heed to those of a crippled beggar, who couldn't even speak to ask for alms, only make hideous noises. I would sit with my bowl beside me and the folk with but food, of a kind, into it. The way into Aghirdi lay through vast forests, but was not especially dangerous.'

'And Dayonis?' he was reminded.

'As I said, they gave her three skins and a lamp, and food, the best part of which she secreted. I soon found she had a purpose in asking for this cell. It had a slab in the floor, which she would lift at night and disappear into some chamber or cave underneath. She would roll one of her skins up and place it beneath the others on her bed, to look like her sleeping self, should the guard come in during these absences. What she did down there I can't say, but I think she was up to her mummery. They boasted in the town that she was of the true Telechines blood, enchantress, and might invoke the Lords of Fate. It was well known that she was a true Cabire and had invoked these Lords and acquired mighty powers. I discovered that the Cabire were a secret witch cult. Myrsta the blind grandmother of this girl had also great powers and had given her eyes in exchange for them. All this was common gossip.'

Kinyras made no comment but his eyes were fixed eagerly

upon his brother's face.

'She would hide her food in her bed and then demand more from her guards, so I gathered that she contemplated making some attempt at escape. Then she starts to fast and eats little for seven days and this brings me to the affair of the young Nubian.'

'Eh!' exclaimed the other, starting and frowning.

'This fellow was one of her guards and sick with desire for her. My lady sees this and indeed 'twas plain as a pike-staff. First she persuades him to give her a bar to fasten her door and when this was done, makes right royal love to him. Then, on the seventh day she whispers in his ear, he makes a clutch at her, but she evades him coyly, laughing up into his face; all very pretty play, brother.'

'Well, get on,' Kinyras ordered sharply.

'The upshot of the matter was that close upon midnight the follow comes into her cell, as expectant as a cat over a cream pot, she having left her bar down. Doubtless the Nubian had plied the guards with wine, for I heard 'em singing and shouting in their cups. He crept in softly, his teeth gleaming in an enormous grin. She looked sick and I marvelled how she could have truck with such. "Close the door... softly, softly!" she whispers.

'The fellow turned to obey and then I saw she had the bar in her hand. Quickly she swiped at the base of his head, struck two or three times and he fell without a groan. She searched him for weapons and cursed mightily that he hadn't any, listened at his chest, then tore off his loincloth and shredded it into strips, with which she bound his hands and feet together. Next she lifts the flap and drags the body down below. Hours pass, then she comes back, replaces the stone and lies on her bed, sleeping like a child. Now, why that senseless murder?'

In spite of himself Kinyras shuddered with abhorrence. 'Probably for some secret rite demanding blood sacrifice.'

Zadoug whistled and laughed, glancing curiously at his brother. 'You don't like that! Neither did I. True, I swear and very prettily and quickly done into the bargain. Well, she hadn't been asleep long before there was a faint scratching near her bed. She starts up and then her name is whispered. "Dayonis! Dayonis! 'Tis I, Ammunz!"

'She was all excitement and could barely speak for joy. "Where are you?" she demanded, looking round the cell half fearfully.

"'Behind the wall." His muffled words were only just audible to me. "I've made a tunnel to your cell with an old knife I stole. If I break through the wall can you hide the hole?"

'She considered a moment. "Not in the wall. Break through the floor, Ammunz." They had taken everything from her, even the pin of her cloak, leaving only a bronze spatula for mixing her lip-paint. She seized this and started to scrape at the floor, wetting the clay with water from her jar. In about half an hour the tousled head of this Ammunz appeared following the stone he had loosened and pushed aside. "How did you do it? What are you going to do?" woman-like she asks two questions and never waits for an answer. "Be careful. They'll be here as soon as it gets light."

"'We'll put the stone back, then," says Ammunz, "I can talk to you from the wall." So they replaced it and began their whispering again. They thought of this and that, but nothing would do. Then she tells him that she can get into the cave underneath her cell. At this the stone moves aside again and Ammunz sticks his head through. "We are saved!" were his first words, then looking round hungrily, "Have you any food to spare?" the poor devil asks, looking like a rasher of wind.

'She she gives him some of the cakes of barley she'd saved and while he was eating she spoke again of the cave. "I can get into it, easily, but there is a precipice just below the rift in the rock."

"'I have no rope, what have you?" he asked.

"'Naught but my cloak and three deer-skins for my bed."

'He grunted satisfaction. "And I have my knife. Sleep now and I will come again at nightfall." That night he came again, pushed aside the stone and entered her cell. He was covered with filth and the wound on his head had started to bleed again, but she embraced him heartily and was full of praise for his daring. "Come, daughter, we must get away at once," he urged her, but she shook her head.

"'No,' she says, "we must try the magic smoke first." With that she begins a rigmarole which I could make neither head nor tail of, but which he seemed to understand, for he nodded his head safely from time to time and gaped at her in wonder. She shows him a little figure she'd made of herself out of clay. Then she stuffs out her bed to make it look as though she slept there and both of them vanish down below with their magic smoke. After a time they both come back. "Was I successful?" she asks him. "Tell me what happened?"

"'I don't know as I can," says Ammunz, scratching his poll and looking puzzled; "I don't rightly understand."

"'Never mind that," she interrupts impatiently, "just tell me as well as you can."

"'I think we should go and not linger chattering," he says, with an anxious glance at the door. I could see the poor fellow was all on hooks to be off.

'She stamped her bare feet at him, hurt herself on the rough stone and scowled. "Tell me. It is important."

"'Well," he drawls, "after you'd lit the fire by the lamp, with the loin-cloth of the Nubian, you sprinkled on herbs and the cave was full of an awful smother of smoke. Then you kneels down and chants and soon you beings to speak in a strange voice. It sent shivers down my back."

"'Never mind that, Ammunz," she interrupts again, nearly dancing with impatience. "I know what I did, I want to know what I said."

"'I'm acoming to it," says Ammunz, looking aggrieved. "You will escape to-night and go towards Karpas. You will meet there one whom you will love, but whose love is given to another. He is a builder who seeks security. He will aid you and free your country. His weapon is shown graven on the magic stone you wear on your neck. You shall lead a mighty army and no weapon forged by the hand of man shall harm you. Beware of stones." That was what you said, then you sways and nearly

91

falls into the fire and pulls you back and presently you comes to your right mind. Now let's get hence."

'But she must first take the curious slab of green stone she wore swung from her neck and look at it in the light of her lamp. "Look, Ammunz, here on my father's stone. He gave it me before the fight. Look!" They both bent over it, turning it this way and that. I would have given much to hold it in my hand, Kinyras. "See, this man with the curious weapon, he is our saviour. We must go to Karpas." With that she begins to trace on the stone with her forefinger, describing the weapon. And, as I'm a living man, brother, her words fitted your staveros to the last inch of it.'

'It's all very strange,' mused Kinyras, 'what else passed between them?'

'Talk of the dangers of the journey. Ammunz told her there was a ledge thirty feet below. He had to lower her with the rope until she was level with it, when she must swing herself until she could land on it. He then set to work ripping up the three deer-skins and his loin-skin and knotting them into a rope. It was not long enough and he demanded her cloak, which she surrendered without a word of protest and so, stark naked save for a scrap of a loin cloth and the stone swinging round her neck, she vanished through the opening. And that was the last I saw of her. I, too, left the town that night and reached you without mishap.'

'It is a marvel to me how you escaped detection and discovered so much. One thing is clear. Hange will sell Karpas to Khem, if he can, and slit all our throats into the bargain. That was as we suspected and we still lack proof.'

'Look, Kinyras, this wench is on the way to our lines, unless both were dashed to pieces on the rocks, but somehow I thing they are safe, so far. Give instructions all along the line that she is to be taken and brought to you when she appears. You can do one of two things, hold her as a hostage and make terms with Khem, yielding her up to Amasis when he has fulfilled the conditions, or you can use her to draw Aghirdi to our side. At her command all the fighting men who are left can steal away into the mountains, where Khem cannot pursue them. When did you say Erili comes?'

'To-morrow or the day after, it is not certain. We can do nothing until we hold council with him. Refugees have been coming in constantly for some time past now, most of them fugitives from the last great fight in Aghirda. Many of them are wounded, huge mountaineers, wonderful fighters. I have tried to persuade them to stay and join our troops but, though they hate Khem, they have some superstition against serving under a commander of another race.'

'Fools!' spat Zadoug scornfully. 'They are already conquered and must yield to force eventually. Simple, obstinate and thick-headed, I know 'em. Well, our Princess, when she arrives, may help them change their minds.'

'Most of them have drifted off towards the Karpasia. Perhaps Erili can do something with them, form them into a legion. They would be most useful.'

Zadnoug yawned, nodded and stretched himself for sleep, while Kinyras went out to his line, pondering many things and wondering what he should do with this royal fugitive when she arrived.

The visit of Erili was delayed by one thing or another and refugees still continued to pour in, mostly from Salam and other of the Eastern kingdoms which had been enslaved by Khem, whence they drew their great army of slaves to work the copper mines, the object of their invasion of Cyprus. It was known through all of these states that Karpas was still free and all who could attempted an escape to the only country within reach that was not ruled by Pharaoh's tax-farmers. The farmers of Karpas, too, were beginning to come in as bidden, their ploughing and sowing being finished, and the work of digging went on apace. These farmers were a splendid body of workers, the second ditch was finished and surmounted by its little stockade.

Now began the task of building the great stockade while the women and children were put to carrying earth to heighten the wall. The weakest places were the first to be strengthened by the stockade, such timber as was already cut being used to close the gaps. The earth valum was fifteen feet high, and the stockade began to rise fifteen feet above that, so that the defence looked very formidable, loopholed as it was breast high for arrow-shooting, and a platform raised nine feet up for archers, so that the whole face of this defence had a double row of loopholes.

All who could be spared were out with the teams of oxen, cutting and carting wood from the forest. The danger of this work from raiding Khemites was considerable, and a constant look-out was kept to guard their safety.

So the work went on, at this point of the line immune from attack, though several small raids had been driving off in other sections. On the first day of June a cry from the look-out on Gypsa Hill gave warning of danger and almost immediately a party of Khemite troops were seen to be charging through the woods.

Kinyras realised at once that his working party had been cut up, but it was of no use to face needless odds.

He retreated quickly to the shelter of the lines. The Khemites advanced and, well out of bow-shot, moved up and down the lines, reconnoitring From thence they went down to the banks of the Kastnon, where they examined the swamp obviously with a view to crossing it to the high ground beyond. Constant signalling had informed Kinyras that all his other timber parties had been warned and were retreating northward until finally came them message that all were safe. In the meantime he had manoeuvred troops to attract and hold the attention of the enemy who, towards evening, retired to the woods, either to report and seek reinforcement, or merely as a strategical move. Kinyras, declining to be taken by surprise, ordered the lines to be manned, posting his own men at the points where the stockade was incomplete.

Some hours passed, but towards midnight Kinyras, making a round to be sure all was well, found one of his men standing tense. 'What is it?' he demanded.

'A curious sound, lord. I cannot tell whether it is the wind or...'

'Let me come.'

The man moved aside and Kinyras took his place, listening keenly for a moment or two. 'Light torches and throw down,' he commanded.

The order was obeyed and by their light a large body of Khemites were discovered throwing great bundles of brush-wood into the outer ditch. A ragged fire of bolts and arrows issued from the stockade, but had little effect upon the invaders, who simply threw the bodies of their falling companions into the ditch and proceeded with their task.

In a short time the outer ditch was filled and a company of men armed with copper falchions and protected by long, round-topped shields swept onwards with an ordered rush. The Staveros fire had become steadier, but the attack was at the point where no stockade was built and the archers had only the earth valum to stand on, so that only one line of fire was possible. Kinyras ordered the back line to reload while the front fired, thus keeping up a quicker and closer rate of fire.

The presence of the V-shaped ditch was utterly unsuspected by the storming party, who were attacking on a front of about one hundred paces. It was a disconcerting discovery. It checked them and had they not been of such overwhelming numbers might have broken them badly, but those behind, ignorant of the new defence, surged forward eager for the fight, pressing the front ranks into this new sabre-toothed defence.

The execution inflicted upon the enemy was frightful. Forced to yield to the pressure from behind, the front ranks had no choice but to fall to its spiky bottom, where they were either impaled upon the sharpened staves or smothered by the bodies of those who came after. In a very little time the ditch was full of the dead and dying, while the survivors continued the advance over the bodies of the fallen and began to scale the earthen rampart behind, where the defenders awaited them with pike and axe and the deadly staveros fire.

For two hours this fighting continued with the utmost savagery on both sides. The Karpasians, pacific men and slow to anger, when once roused were capable of strong resistance and only in one place did the enemy succeed in breaking through. Kinyras, prepared for such an emergency, quickly moved up his reserves standing by the purpose, and a furious charge drove the Khemites back with great slaughter. Yells of fury, hatred and defiance, the crash of desperate encounters, the curious whang of the release of deadly staveros bolts followed by smoke from flaring torches, the rank stench of sweating bodies contending for mastery, the hot smell of shed blood was picked up the distant horses, whose terrified shrieks added he last touch of horror to the clamour and were not less dreadful than the cries and moans of the dying and wounded, entreating to be put out of their agony. This violence, broadcast upon the blackness of the night, lit only but the occasional flare of a torch, gained in intensity by invisibility, waxed to a last bout of incredible fury as the darkness began to lift above the upward thrust of the morning.

With the beginning of light a very heavy staveros fire poured out from both sides of the line and from the bastions. Beneath this rain of bolts the enemy faltered, conscious for the first time of their heavy losses and that one of these deadly bolts more frequently than not transfixed two men. Retreat was sounded and they retired, leaving behind them eight hundred dead and such wounded as were too sorely stricken to be moved. These, the Karpasians, drunk with their first taste of blood, quickly dispatched.

In this attack Kinyras had lost ten of his men and eighty Karpasians. Two days were spent in clearing the ditches of the Khemite dead and wounded, and the brushwood they had thrown in, and the stockade was adorned with a row of Khemite heads. A scouting party sent out on the second day could find no trace of the enemy, though they came upon the headless, mutilated bodies of the timber cutters. Traces of the enemy's camp fires showed that the ox-teams had been killed and eaten. The bodies were carried back into the lines for burial and here Kinyras encountered his first trouble with the Karpasians. The relations of the dead men waited upon him in a body, demanding that the weapons of the dead be buried with them.

Kinyras refused, urging that the safety of the living was of more importance than the problematic safety of the dead and that, for every weapon laid in the tomb twenty men's lives were endangered. He was tactful, playing for time, wondering how he could solve this almost insurmountable difficulty of burial rite, fearing to lose his influence through what they would regard as impiety. Then the alternative for which he had been searching flashed on his mind and sent them away comforted and satisfied by ordering clay models of the weapons to be made instantly.

This immediate problem settled and the funeral rites celebrated with due solemnity, the far more important problem in his eyes of defending his timber-cutters in the future from such raids as had already cut off one party, remained to be solved. After much consideration he ordered two rough breast-works to be erected in the forest, one to the north, the other to the south of Gypsa Hill. These were made by tying long poles to the tree-trunks, and weaving branches through them. The frustration of a sudden charge and the enemy delayed long enough for the workers to collect their arms, could be secured by this obstruction.

Before these barricades, scouts were posted at intervals. By concentrating his wood-cutters in one section o the forest at a time, they would clear large blocks nearest the lines, and at the same time remove a menace in providing undesirable cover for the enemy. They also would be able to protect each other. If attacked again, by these protective measures they should be able to put up a good fight against infantry, but in case of a chariot charge the precautions were not so satisfactory. His men could move quickly enough, but the oxen, so necessary and valuable, could not be safeguarded. The speed with which the chariots of Khem brought up bowmen to the attack and the terror of their reputation made them formidable problem.

Kinyras ordered his spiked balls to be collected from various groups of makers and taking with him an escort of twelve men carrying the balls in sacks, set out to inspect the working party on the southern front. The work was progressing well and he estimated that another week would see enough timber cut to finish the stockade.

He collected the party and addressed them. 'Men of the wood-cutting corps, your greatest danger lies from a chariot-charge of the enemy. Scouts on outpost duty, your instructions are to throw out these spiked balls in front of the line immediately there is any indication of danger from chariots, then to retreat out of bow-shot behind the barricade. A horn will be sounded, warning all of the impending raid and to keep together. Remember that the ultimate safety of the land and the people depends upon maintaining the welfare of the cattle at this juncture. The stockade must be finished speedily and another week should see us through. You have worked well and truly and I have every confidence in you. Dismiss.'

Amid cheers and shouts of good-will Kinyras departed for the northern section, leaving half his spiked balls behind him. It was pleasant in the forest, where the trees were of an enormous height and girth, with its earthy, nutty odours wafting up beneath their wide-spread leafage and straying shafts of sunlight patterned the floor of its groves with jagged splashes of saffron and bronze, or where some far-flung thicket of oleander, rose and pearl against the viridity of the bocage, snared the senses with beauty and perfume, so that it was hard not to be lulled into a dream instead of suspecting a lurking enemy behind every coppice.

Kinyras trod these majestic aisles with an awareness of their loveliness which was sharpened by a feeling that he saw them with eyes and spirit accustomed to an aspect of nature less opulent, less virginal, something almost stale and world-weary in comparison with this richness of growth, this colour and scent which now engulfed him. It was as though some experience of which he had no recollection had left its indelible stamp upon him of an antithesis of life as he now knew it, heightening his instinctive delight in natural beauty. Such a feeling might come to one who, having left his native land in early youth, had kept vivid in his mind its picture, always with the intention to return and who, returning in old age, finds that memory has retained some quality of the place which no longer exists in the original. Through the passage of time he has become alien to his place of nativity. He has voluntarily abandoned the situation of his life's activity and a curious state of suspension follows in which he can establish no real contact with his immediate past or his remote past. He is an alien in time and cannot rid himself of a loneliness of spirit transcending mere description in words.

Some such sensation pervaded the life of Kinyras, with this exception, that the universe, nature, as he now knew her, was infinitely richer than any mind-picture he had retained, as a Beethoven Symphony is more stupendous than any aural memory could retain and imagination reproduce.

Thus lapped in mental sensations which could not be called thought, Kinyras strode through the forest, one side of his mind alert to the presence of enemies, the other conscious of his environment and its beauties, of himself as an entity strangely differing from those about him, of being an alien in time. The phrase stuck in his mind. The little party struck across the peaceful glade, which in periods of safety was the well-trodden track to Salam and had descended into a dell rosy with oleander, when the leader halted and lifted his hand. Kinyras went to him cautiously, ordering bows out.

'What is it?' he asked.

'Someone is hidden in the thicket, lord.'

The men hastily bent their staveros, creeping along silently, until one of them shouted—'Look there, it's white! A woman, by all the gods.'

As the men rushed up a girl started out of the thicket and Kinyras saw that a certain portion of it was hollow in the centre, some well-disposed flowering branches concealing the cavity. He saw a flash of lithe white flesh, a tumble of red curls, a glint of angry eyes, a strong bow with arrow to notch, a pair of capable, strong, elegant and unfaltering hands ready to send the dart straight to its mark, which happened to be his heart.

Her fearless eyes undaunted mien warned Kinyras to be careful. He stood still and lowered his staveros, and her eyes, which had been fixed grimly on his, shifted to his weapon, grew even more alert, and dilated in awe and surprise.

The next moment they had snapped back to his again. 'You are of Karpas!' she asserted, with conviction.

'And you of Aghirdi. Welcome to my lines, Princess.'

She lowered her weapon in answer to his salutation and inclined her head. She looked puzzled and her eyes inquired of his. Kinyras smiled, well pleased to see this imperious beauty a little disconcerted by his knowledge of her. A string of beads terminating in a curious, flat green stone and a shoulder belt holding a quiver was her only clothing. One or two bloody scratches disfigured the delicate skin, but she was unconscious of any lack, and began to speak again after a short reconnoitring silence, in which she had summed him up and recorded his measure. 'I need your aid, sir, for Ammunz, my foster-father. Help him, I beg you.' She drew aside the branches as she spoke, revealing a huge, grey-bearded man, sorely wounded and roughly bandaged with what looked like strips of her tunic. 'We were pursued and he has been hit by three arrows.'

'Cut some branches and form a litter quickly,' Kinyras directed his men.

A few blows from their swords and a rough litter was soon woven, on which the wounded man was lifted and covered with a cloak. The bearers were instructed to proceed at once to the nearest gate to the stockade, at a distance of about half a mile and to hasten.

'Quick! Quick!' urged the girl, 'we have no time to lose. He has saved me, he must be saved, too'.

'Lady, we will do our best,' Kinyras soothed her and she turned her eyes once more upon his in wonderment. 'Tell me, whereabouts are they?'

'Maybe half a mile back. A small party, but they will seek reinforcements.'

'How many?' he insisted, impatient of her lack of detail.

'A small party,' she reiterated obstinately, then, reading

something in his eyes bent upon her, added more obligingly, 'Perhaps fifty chariots and a hundred foot-men.'

'Chariots! Small!' he mocked, 'do we need more? Heth, hasten to warn the southern workers; Peleg, run to the northern section. Here, you two, take their sacks of spiked balls, we may need them.'

The two men delivered up their sacks and sped away in opposite directions, each taking what cover he could find. Kinyras grasped the girl by the wrist, but she shook him off fiercely and ran swiftly at his side. 'Double through this glade, you who have them wave your cloaks, so that if the watch see us they can warn the others.'

As she ran beside him Dayonis gave him details of her flight. 'We had escaped from the first party pursuing us and came upon another camped in the woods. Ammunz had been hit and could not move fast, but we hid and they could not find us. They grumbled much, were tired of searching for us. I overheard that they had attacked a fenced post near here, losing many men. Then the two parties met and those hunting us tried to persuade the others to spread out and comb the woods for us.'

'You were fortunate to overhear their talk, Dayonis.'

Again her eyes widened in surprise, but she made not comment upon this use of her name, being intent upon her narrative.

'While they were arguing we stole away. Our pursuers were fatigued, complaining bitterly of being ordered to take horses through the woods, where there were no tracks. They had been forced to carry the chariots half the way and to cut paths the whole of it. But if once they can get us into open ground, then the Gods help us!'

They were getting over the ground well, but the weight of the wounded man retarded them, though they were in sight of the hill. The voice of Dayonis broke in upon his inward conjectures. 'Did they attack your line? The party we met seemed to have been badly punished and did not want to fight again. They declared over and over again that they must

consult their chief. That was not like Pharaoh's men. If it got
to the Viceroy's ears they would all be impaled.'

'We drubbed them finely, lady. And will do it again if they
don't keep their distance.'

She laughed, a long, merry peal, throwing back her head
and half shutting her eyes, a trick he was to see often repeated.
A braying trumpet behind them cut her short and she flung an
anxious glance over her shoulder. 'The chariots2 have got
through and found our track, I fear.'

'Hurry, lady, the odds are sorely against us and the gate in
the stockade still five hundred paces distant.'

'I can run. Have no fear for me, sir. I know I am safe with
you.'

Here a great commotion broke from the top of Gypsa Hill
and the red flag of the alarm ran up its staff, though it showed
a tendency to cling round the pole as if the danger were negligi-
ble, Dayonis thought, watching it. Kinyras, sending a hurried
glance over his shoulder, saw a row of chariots issuing from the
forest and noted that his fleeing party was about half-distance
from them and the gate. The cavalry of Khem appeared almost
as though about to parade as it came slowly out by the narrow
forest road, forming up in line as they did so. They were unable
to charge until they were clear of the break.

'Strew the spiked balls, men,' he yelled.

Fortunately this order could be obeyed in their rush for the
gate, and it was done on a sufficiently wide front. The chariots
began their charge, but the horses were fatigued, the ground
was littered with small growth and they could go only at the
trot instead of their customary furious gallopade.

'Stretcher go forward as fast as you can and you, lady, run
with it. The rest of you halt and shoot at the horses.'

This was done, the little party standing in line bending
their staveros and sending three volleys into the midst of the
teams of Khem. A number of horses dropped, others began to
plunge furiously, and the charge had to be delayed until order
was restored and they could reform.

'Now, run!' shouted Kinyras, and turning to follow his

men, saw the girl still at his elbow. 'Why are you here?' he grunted. 'I ordered you forward with the stretcher.'

'I am Dayonis of Aghirda. I run not from my enemies and I take orders from none.'

'Yet you will take them from me and obey them, too,' he rebuked her sternly. 'I am the commander-in-chief of the forces defending Karpas and I demand implicit obedience from all within my jurisdiction.'

'You will need your breath ere we reach the gate,' she reminded him with such an angelic smile that almost involuntarily he slackened his pace to stare at her. She jolted his elbow and put on an extra spurt. She ran like an athlete who has got his second wind, easily, almost leisurely and to see her so running, so attired was a sight for gods and men.

She smiled again on the dazzled Kinyras, speaking in a voice of dulcet gentleness, 'Could I flee from my comrades, lord, when I can shoot an arrow with the best? It is me they seek, they will kill men and horses to catch me. I fear I bring great troubles upon you, sir.'

'We're used to it,' he remarked sardonically, not wishing to betray certain sensations he felt, unbecoming to the commander-in-chief, 'our troublers will find many heads of their companions bleaching on our palisades, to greet them.'

Again she laughed, this time a merry, ringing peal. 'Mercy on us, does that mean that mine will be numbered among 'em?'

Kinyras found himself laughing with her, a very bad state of affairs for discipline. 'If you are obstreperous, maybe.'

'In that case, O commander-in-chief of the forces defending Karpas, I shall be all obedience,' she mocked.

They had almost overtaken the litter again and once more he commanded a halt and a volley of staveros bolts to be fired at the enemy. A sudden thought struck Kinyras. 'Are you hungry?' he demanded.

'Famishing,' she answered him simply. 'We could bring but little food with us and that was eaten long ago, since when we have lived on berries.'

'Take this. I have but a soldier's rations, a rye cake and some dried figs.'

''Tis a royal feast,' she assured him, graciously, and began to eat avidly, but was forced to stop as she could not run and eat together.

Kinyras wished he had his cloak to give her, though he was bound to admit her unconsciousness appeared to be in no need of it. His men were firing steadily, the litter was nearly at the gate. The chariot-teams had by now reached the spiked balls and were instantly thrown into a great confusion. Horses plunged madly, shrieking with pain and fright, while a steady rain of bolts was poured into the stampeding mass. But as he watched, the rear rank of the cavalry, seeing the plight of those in front of them, made a wide detour to the left and came sweeping down in a terrific charge. Their party was cut off and all hope of first reaching the gate was quelled.

'Run to the right!' he yelled.

The chariots rushed on, the sweep of their line bringing them closer to the walls which, now manned, poured a murderous fire into them. Seeing their danger, Kinyras and his party drew heavily on their reserves of breath and strength making an extra spurt which brought them to the ditch, only to realise that they could not cross it. Dayonis pointed to the sharpened stakes, and laughed grimly.

'Blast them!' muttered Kinyras, 'but for them we could climb down and be safe from their arrows. We must make for the next gate.'

They ran on, by now sorely spent, panting hard, their legs feeling like water. Seeing the girl falter he slipped his arm round her waist and together they mustered what speed they might, but the gate seemed to retreat before their gaze. Their eyes were misty with exhaustion, the blood throbbed in their heads and laboured in their hearts. Now they could not see the gate at all and the ground seemed abnormally littered with stones and small bushes, waiting to trip their heavy feet. Yet they kept on, stumbling and lurching, the bearers clinging manfully to the stretcher, Kinyras with his arm firm behind the pliant waist, holding her up, encouraging her. A sound of a million hooves drummed in their aching ears and Kinyras, glancing aside, expecting to see the chariots upon them, found they were driving along parallel within arrow shot, while the heavy fire issued from the stockade.

In order to make range more difficult the charioteers spread out. Safe behind their huge shields, their problem was to conserve their horses. Every now and then one would drop, when the driver would spring out, rapidly cut the traces and drive on again, leaving the fallen horse lying. These chariots had no difficult task to keep up with the stumbling run, which was all the pursued could achieve, whilst they tried to shoot Kinyras without harming the Princess of Aghirda.

But now the gate was opening and yells of encouragement came from the stockade and a sortie was being made. The sallying party came out at a run, defiling to right and left, opening a gruelling fire with the Stavros. Eager hands seized the stretcher and carried it into safety, the sortie spread itself behind the pursued, firing steadily and retreating slowly, covering them. The chariots halted, weary with the former night's fighting and aware that they had lost their prey. Against the deadly staveros they could do little, since one bolt could transfix two men, pinning them together like larks on a spit. They retreated, leaving behind them those chariots which had lost all their teams, the last of the sallying party reached the stockade, and the gate slowly closed, registering the second defeat for Khem.

Kinyras and Dayonis stood in the bastion by the gate, faint with exhaustion, unable to speak, watching the stranded chariots. Their men were safe behind their shields until a large body issued again from the stockade, to attack them at close range, protected by great shields, and armed with staveros. Presently these men returned, triumphant, dragging the captured chariots behind them, while others pursued the retreating cavalry until they were out of range. Four of the pursued party had not come in but were lying somewhere outside the stockade, pierced with the arrows of Khem, or taken prisoner. Suddenly he was aware that his arm was still about that slim, vibrant waist and he looked down to find the eyes of Dayonis level with his shoulder. He looked deep into their peculiar, greenish-blue depths, in which excitement danced and bubbled with glee.

'The best sight I've seen in years!' she cried, pointing derisively at the retreating enemy. 'Are we all safe?'

'Four missing, Princess.'

A shadow darkened the merry eyes. 'The gods be good to them for they were staunch fellows? Look!' Again she pointed and he swung away from her to see that the retreating chariots had sheered to the right, that men and horses were falling before the bolts of the timber-workers, who had come up and got into action promptly. But the chariots made no stand, swept out of range and the laden wagons lumbered towards the gate. 'See! The chariots of Khem have halted and are being reinforced by that large body of infantry issuing from the wood. May the Old Ones of the Hills smite them and work them eternal mischief! I thought we had done with them.'

Dayonis uttered this malediction very much as though she meant it, and Kinyras, paying little heed to her, saw that his teams were in danger of being cut off. 'We can afford to lose neither men, wagons nor cattle,' he shouted, running to collect a rescue party.

Armed with the staveros, bows, slings and pikes they debouched from the stockade and formed a hasty line, hurrying towards the wagons. The wagons moved with what seemed incredible slowness, the teamsters trying in vain to speed their placid cattle, while men behind pushed the carts and others worked at the wheels, tugging them round and urging on the teams with noisy bellowing. Kinyras reached them and formed his men in a phalanx to cover their retreat.

Khem came up in a heavy column composed of spearmen and archers. The pikes, of Kinyras, fifteen feet long, were formidable weapons, and so too, were the staveros. The wagons were three hundred yards from the gate and Kinyras ordered half his company to retire at the run on the teams, the others to cover the retreat. As this command was carried out the enemy charged with a rush, to be met with volleys of missles from the slings and staveros. Among the archers Kinyras caught a glimpse of Dayonis who, with quiver replenished probably from that of some dead Khemite, was shooting away with the best of them, steady as a rock.

The first party, having reached the wagons, their line met the enemy's spearmen steadily, though they could not break them, while the steady shooting from others who had left the walls and sallied out, harassed the enemy's flank, tearing it to pieces with their long-range fire. But the line of the pike-men broke in one place and Kinyras leapt to the breach, his short bronze sword stabbing, darting hither and thither with a frightful rapidity as he shouted the war-cry of the Brotherhood.

'Bronze, sharp bronze!' yelled Kinyras, a dark flush of exertion mounting in his face with the fierceness of his efforts on behalf of Karpas.

'Aghirda! Anghirda!' shrilled a voice beside him, not to be outdone in vociferation or energy as two small hands clasped the hilt of an enormous blade, thrusting and parrying with equal skill if not of similar strength. She was like a Red Goddess of War, her skin flecked with crimson, her fiery mane tossed impatiently out of her eyes with a quick, eager jerk of the head which was as regular as the motion of her hands and seemed to keep pace one with the other.

With a gesture of involuntary irritation at her unnecessary irruption in a situation where she would be more of a nuisance than a help, Kinyras stepped forward to cover her with his shield and in the act of doing so exposed his own body. A Khemite archer, seeing this advantage loosed an arrow and she, seeing it coming, quick as lightning pushed the shield back again. 'Mind your own affairs,' she snapped as the arrow thudded on the hide instead of finding his heart as the mark, 'no weapon forged of man can harm me.'

He made a derisive noise, to which Dayonis responded with a fierce lunge, making one of the enemy pay for his bad manners with a life.

At that moment the Khemite push eased and the Karpasian

pike-men closed the line again. Sullenly the ranks of the enemy began to give ground and Kinyras, intent only upon defence, prudently refrained from pursuing the temporary advantage. He ordered his men to retreat, walking backwards and firing, despite sundry mutters of discontent which were intended to reach his ears.

In the lull he turned to his companion. 'A bloody sight you present,' he told her roughly; 'Princess, you should not have come into the fight, 'tis no place for women.'

'For some women, maybe, but what could I do? My arrows were spent, and besides I love to fight. What care I how I look?' She glanced down at her hands and arms, red with some of the best blood of Khem, which dripped from her elbows on to her thighs. She shook the drops off impatiently and wiped them in her long hair. 'There, my lord, it will not show on that,' she remarked, grinning up at him with an impudent glint in her eyes. 'I fear my shoulders offend your lordship, also, pray wipe them for me, my arm is something stiff.'

'Let me,' he answered, 'a bath shall be prepared for you if we get inside alive.'

'*I* shall, have no fear. It is upon you, O commander-in-chief of the forced defending Karpas, upon whom Death may fall. May a wretched vagabond runaway say you are a most excellent defender, sir?'

'Oh, say on,' he retorted, 'women's tongues run over to mockery, as their hearts to deceitfulness.'

'Now I perceive you have been badly used by one of us,' she murmured, and staggered as she spoke, her eyes closing wearily.

'Dayonis!' he croaked, catching her. 'Are you hit? Tell me?'

The dark red lashes, dusky as the deepest petals of a wall-flower, lifted and she smiled reassurance. 'My head aches and my shoulder stings,' she answered, leaning against him like a tired child.

A hasty examination revealed a gash on her shoulder and another on her head. With hands no longer steady he tore strips from his kilt and bandaged them roughly. No sooner was this done than a shout of warning recalled him to the fact that they were still outside the stockade. The enemy had drawn off only to reform and were again advancing.

The almost decimated spearmen had been withdrawn and replaced by a regiment of Ethiopians armed with maces. These came on in a disordered rush, white teeth flashing in a scarlet grin of animal ferocity, eyes fierce and wild with the smell of blood in their nostrils, brandishing their formidable weapons with shrill cries. They moved, a host of swarthy giants, their ebony skin polished like ebony, naked but for their short aprons of bull's hide, or of the skins of wild beasts with the tails drawn up through the girdle and sticking out grotesquely. Their chiefs were splendid in collars and bracelets of gold, with great golden rings pendent from their ears beneath the opulence of flying ostrich plumes.

The charge of the Ethiopians was met with a deadly fire of arrows, bolts, stones and javelins, which punished them with a terrible severity, but undaunted they continued their rush, only to fall upon the pikes until nothing was left alive of their front rank. On they came, wave upon wave of them, clashing aside the pikes with their heavy maces, fighting like demons with horrid yells imitating the animals whose skins adorned their enormous frames. It was a dogged, hand-to-hand encounter, short, stabbing bronze sword against stone club and was like to go badly for the defenders, until Zadoug sent a rock crashing among them, projected from the engine in the bastion.

Superstition broke them where bronze and death could not avail. Thinking the vast stone must have been hurtled by some angry god and dreading other similar manifestations of his disfavour and wrath, their charge had lost its dash, and cowed, at length they broke and ran. Kinyras turned panting to Dayonis. She was still at his side but faint now from hunger, exposure and exertion. He put out his arm to steady her, noting with alarm her face, white as a sheet beneath the smears and gouts of congealed blood. She drooped in his arms, leaning heavily upon him, but her eyes were undaunted through she could hardly raise their lids for languor.

The enemy were retreating, but had they had enough? Was

it safe to try to get back? As he stood watching the disordered rout of the blacks and the frantic efforts of their officers to reform their companies, he realised that blood from a wound in his head had fallen upon her shoulder. He felt a curious comfort at her nearness, despite his churlish reception of her in the fight, a happiness in this evidence of her friendship and regard for him, and he longed to bind her to him in closer ties. 'Princess, shall I make you one of us in brotherhood?' he whispered.

'If you so wish it,' she murmured back.

'See, blood from this wound of mine mingles with that from your shoulder, and blood from your shoulder falls into this wound on my hand.' He moved so that it did so and bent his lips to her shoulder, sucking the wound, offering his hand for her to do likewise, which she did. Then he drew the rough outline of a sword on her brow with blood and another on her breast, over the heart, saying—'Now you are my sword comrade, Dayonis, you are of the brotherhood of the sword.'

'Now I am your sword comrade, Kinyras,' she repeated after him with almost childish solemnity, for she had a child's delight and belief in rights of any sort. 'Now I am of the brotherhood of the sword and I swear loyalty to the death.'

'As a test of courage we all have to fight naked beside our sponsor. This you have already done and at a more convenient season I'll teach you the signs of the order.'

'Not now, I beg,' she interrupted, with a ghost of her old, merry twinkle. 'I faint from hunger and I must dress the wounds of Ammunz. He must not die.'

'Come, then,' he cried and picked her up in his arms. 'The enemy have retreated and we can return in safety.'

---

1. On the site of St. Hilarim.

2. At this period (1450B.C.) horses were used in chariots, but not for riding.

# CHAPTER VII

# GYPSOS HILL

Kinyras yelled an order to his men and he carried Dayonis in at the gate. The walls were crowded with men, women and children, cheering, laughing hysterically, crying, waving anything they could snatch from their bodies to flaunt above their heads and welcome the incoming heroes fittingly. Zadoug came hurrying up and stopped when he saw the burden in his brother's arms. He looked at kinyras, put his finger on his lip, shook a knowing head and winked. 'Well, brother, so much for the dreaded chariots of Khem. It seems they're vulnerable and you've discovered the secret of victory. They who have conquered so many nations have had their first smell of defeat. And their redoubtable infantry, too, goes limping back. So much for dreamers and dreams, old Snail.'

'Have the wounded brought in, Zadoug, and put your cloak around this lady. Princess, my brother Zadoug presents his cloak. Zadoug, the Princess of Aghirda accepts it.'

'Willingly, gracious lady,' answered the now courtly Zadoug, standing so as to shield her from curious eyes, while Kinyras stood her on her feet and the cloak was thrown round her.

Dayonis held out a languid, though extremely gracious hand, which Zadoug long pressed to his lips. Kinyras left them to give the many necessary orders, for the collecting and burial of the dead, the care of the sixk and wounded, the manning of the walls and posting of extra look-outs lest the enemy return at night and, perhaps most important of all, the gathering in of all arms, bolts and arrows from the stricken heaps without the defences.

All this don, he returned to find that Zadoug had departed and dayonis sitting in a corner, looking spent. He laid her on the litter he had brought with him and bid the bearers carry her to Monarga Hill, whither Ammunz had already been despatched in the care of a leech. She gave him a pale smile of thankgs, but he could see that she was weary with fatigue and pain and he bid the bearers hasten.

As he watched her carried away he wondered what he should do with her. He had intended to follow Zadoug's advice and use her as a pawn in any game likely to redound to his profit between him and the enemy, but now he was not so sure he could do it. The girl was lovely and spirited, had fought nobly beside him that day and undoubtedly had saved his life. Visualist as he was, her saucy, laughing face got between him and any pictured schemes to her detriment which his mind could form, scattering them piecemeal. H went in search of Zadoug, left him in charge and started out for Gypsos Hill.

As he reached the top he overtook the littler. Dayonis had recovered somewhat and was able to smile a welcome as he came to her side and asked how she did. She told him that she felt better.

'Your foster-father had been sent ahead in the care of a leech. He will tend your wounds when you arrive, lady.'

'They will do well, now, for I have already stopped the bleeding.'

'How could you?' he asked staring in astonishment. 'Are you a leech?'

She looked at him, staring provocatively and smiling mysteriously. 'I'll tend yours if you'll bid them set me down,' she answered, stretching out a hand to indicate a bloody gash on his wrist.

'Wait until we reach the house, Princess.'

'did the workers in the forest get safely home?' she asked after a pause.

'Yes, and the northern section as well, but I cannot risk sending them out again. All timber-cutting in future must be done inside the lines. We cannot afford to lose one ox, nor one man, needlessly.'

'I have brought trouble upon you, Kinyras. But for their pursuit of men you had been left in peace to finish your stockade and to clear the encroaching forest. As it stands it is a danger to your line.'

Kinyras shrugged and looked at her whimsically. 'Take heart!' he admonished her, feeling extraordinarily cheerful. 'It is not too late, I can yet throw you out to them, if you wish.'

She took no notice of this jesting, being in a mood of self depreciation. 'It is a poor return for so much service,' she objected heavily.

Kinyras pointed down into the valley, across which he could see for some distance, even though dusk was near. 'See, they are there, awaiting your ejection, lady. Several thousands of them, preparing to camp. Their scouts are prowling up and down, trying to smell out weak spots in my line. Well, let them find them and receive another dose of our medicine. To-day's work has put heart into us all. My Karpasians can fight well at a pinch, and at this moment are busy stripping the dead and wounded of Khem to arm themselves. Cheer you, Dayonis, you have brought arms to Karpas which she bitterly lacked.'

'So you say!' She pouted. 'Gods! How I pine for food and a long, long sleep. I feel I shall never waken again.

'Poor child, you shall have both in abundance, I promise you, even if only soldier's faring. Here is my mean house, Princess, very much at your service.'

The litter was set down and, calling loudly for Hasvan, Kinyras strode into the house. The slave came running at the shout to assure his master that the wounded man had been put in a hut nearby and the leech was even now attending him.

'How does it?' Kinyras asked anxiously. If Ammunz could recover he had valuable potentialities apart from the fact that he was obviously dear to Dayonis.

Hasvan pursed his lips. 'Badly, master. He will need much care.'

'Well, he must have it. Take him into your charge, Hasvan. Now send Pheretime to me, then go and secure two likely wenches, one to wait upon the Lady Dayonis, the other to help in the house. And bring suitable clothes for the Princess of Aghirda.'

Kinyras returned to the litter, where the face of Dayonis gleamed white in the gathering gloom. Kinyras lifted her and carried her into his living-room and as he did so Pheretime appeared in the doorway leading from her kitchen, a lighted lamp in her hand. She started and stared incredulous of what she saw, raising the lamp so that its beams fell full upon the figure in her master's arms. A flush mounted to her face, her lips folded in a rigid line and without a word she walked to a table and set the light in the middle of it, then turned again stared, but this time in a sullen anger. Kinyras called her sharply to attention, being in no humour to put up with any of her moods. His quiet voice had a steely edge to it. 'Come, Pheretime, smooth the couch and fetch hither my softest skin. The Princess of Aghirda has sought refuge in our lines and is sorely wounded. She will live here as my guest.'

Pheretime tossed her head and every line of her pretty, taught figure expressed outrage and mutiny. Yet she dared not disobey and set about the business with various small flings and unnecessary flappings, as was her wont, while Dayonis watched them both with a knowing smile, cynical and satiric, learning all she wished to know from this piece of by-play.

Kinyras laid Dayonis lingeringly on the couch, settling her head tenderly in the wooden rest.

With an indescribable motion of her elbows and a face which looked as though she had put a bronze padlock upon it, Pheretime edged Kinyras aside, contriving to tread heavily upon his instep as she did so, muttering something audible about blessing the man, with a reference to his clumsy great feet. Having thus thrust him into the background, she fell to examining the wounded girl, not ungently, but with a thoroughness and deftness born of long experience. At length she raised herself and turned to Kinyras with a malicious smile. 'Be not uneasy, my master, the wounds are not serious.'

For some veiled reason these simple words of reassurance were vastly irritating to Kinyras. 'Go and prepare my chamber for the princess and lend her one of your tunics, Pheretime. Hasvan has gone to buy what is necessary, but it will take time.'

'I will do what is necessary,' Pheretime snubbed him and hustled him outside determinedly before her.

Left to herself, Dayonis glanced curiously and not without awe round the room. From the lamp which the slave-girl had brought in others had been kindled, so that there was abundance of light from one handsome bronze lamp suspended from the beam in the centre of the room and from others standing about on tables. The oil used was sweet scented and the little cones of smokeless light burned clear and bright.

Notwithstanding that Kinyas had spoken of his house modestly, Dayonis found it unexpectedly rich, far in excess of anything she had known in barbarian Aghirda. The owner had a love of home ingrained in his nature and Pheretime was house-proud, Hazvan loved his lord and the result was as handsome and commodious as the time and means at disposal could achieve. Dayonis now found herself in a large room of some twenty feet square, the heavily beamed roof supported by wooden pillars, gaily painted in a chequered design of primitive quality in black, red and yellow. In a handsome brazier of wrought bronze burned a small fire of charcoal, so that the room was warm and comfortable, especially at this season of the year when the nights were chilly. The floor was of beaten earth, hard and dry, and plenty of skins lay about on chairs, stools and couches, some of them of rich, soft fur.

The furniture was of a quality and beauty of which Dayonis had not dreamt, brought probably from Egypt, or Khem as it was called, and bought from Phoenician traders. There were couches such as the one she lay on, gracefully designed with a raised head, the frame of gaily painted wood in many colours, the seat of woven thongs of hide covered with a deerskin, the legs carved to represent those of an animal. Chairs, both single and double, were of great variety and of a comfort unexperienced by Dayonis, the backs rounded to accommodate the figure, seats of woven thongs, pliant and restful, painted and carved in curious devices representing beats and birds. Thrust under the couches were stools and oblong tables, brilliantly painted and with legs outspreading in graceful curves. Large jars containing water and wine stood about, repeating the bright hues of the furniture, while others, of native Karpasian pottery were of dark brown and terra-cotta. Parts of the floor were covered by coarser skins and in the corner nearest her couch stood a small ten-stringed Khemite harp, an exquisite thing with a base shaped like a bird, whose folded wings formed the frame.

Dayonis gazed long at this piece of coloured minstrelsy, wondering what hand played it and reflecting that, much as Kinyras hated Khem in the field as an enemy, he yet was willing to profit by the civilization and art of Khem. When Pheretime entered with a bowl of water, cloths for drying and bandages, she found the stranger still gazing at the harp. Her eyes brightened with a glint of satisfaction. She drew out a table, set the things she had brought upon it and observed, without being questioned—'It is a beautiful harp, isn't it, lady?'

'Indeed, yes. Is it yours by chance?'

Pheretime spread her hands in depreciation. 'The gods forbid I should presume. My master will not suffer it to be touched. It belonged to my beloved lady and my lord still worships her.'

'Oh!' exclaimed Dayonis, as though a pin had been stuck into her, then added, to cover her exclamation, 'She is dead?'

Pheretime shook a dismal head and went on assiduously bathing the wounded shoulder. 'Alas, no, Princess. It is a sad story. My lady was taken captive and carried off and since that day lord Kinyras has sought her in vain, has never ceased to mourn her loss.'

Dayonis grunted something unintelligible and Pheretime

with a hidden smirk of satisfaction, pursued the rest of her task in silence, washing the weary limbs, anointing them with salves and perfumes, finally producing her clean linen tunic. When this was donned she then took a coarse wooden comb and began upon the long tangle of red curls, Dayonis suffering the infliction in a brooding silence with frequent winces and shuddering.

At length the toilet was complete and when Kinyras reappeared it was to find his visitor lying back upon the couch with closed eyes, the hard wooden head-rest discarded. The transformation was remarkable and he stood looking down upon her, at the dark line of lash lying upon the pale cheeks, the golden glory of shining hair spread out on each side of her and hanging down half-way to the floor. He caught his breath sharply and at the sound she opened her eyes and lay looking up at him, unsmiling.

He marvelled at the change in her that eyes hitherto so alive with vivacity could be so sombre, so profound with some dark feeling. He felt, harking back to the past six hours, that he knew her intimately as the laughing, fighting, care-free comrade who would stand by a man until he dropped and tend him afterwards. Now she was withdrawn as a cloud, remote, mysterious, brooding as an outraged goddess, impenetrable, damping to a man's spirits as a marsh in winter. He felt like an intruding oaf, and as she looked at him with an unbending greyness of aspect, his own sensitive and expressive face lengthened so comically that a glimmer lightened the opaqueness of her yes, as though someone had lit, in a darkened room, a lamp which had not yet burned up. He saw it with relief and was emboldened to ask diffidently—'You are in pain, Princess?'

Something in the dolour of his tone banished whatever it was that had douched her normal vivacity, for most unexpectedly the lamp within sprang to full flame and she laughed, rising on her elbow as she did so and shaking back the encumbering hair with her old, careless gesture. Kinyras was amazed, but determined to go warily, so he smiled in a bewildered way.

'I am clothed, as you see, sir, washed and admirably

attended. Food and wine is what I need now, and rest. Oh, Kinyras, you are a sorry sight. Your wounds still bleed and they must be painful.

Too relieved to care for aught but her restoration to her normal radiance, he dismissed them with a gesture.

'I will tend them,' she insisted. 'Bid your woman bring warm water to cleanse them and linen to bind them. Come, sit, and rest yourself.' She had got down from the couch and dragged forward the largest and most comfortable chair and was urging him into it with persuasive touches on his shoulders until he yielded, when she called to Pheretime from the door for what she wanted in no uncertain voice.

After some little delay the slave-girl came in, set down a clay bowl of hot water, wine, oil and cloths, withdrawing again without so much as a glance at Kinyras.

He raised his head to look at her and saw by the set of her back that trouble might be expected. He set his mouth sternly, refusing to be intimidated by her humours and demanded with firmness—'Have you cooked, Pheretime?'

She hesitated before answering, keeping her yes turned downward to the floor as she stood in the doorway.

'Have you, girl?' he repeated. 'Answer.'

'Yes, master.'

'Then serve and see to it that it is well done and quickly.'

'Tiresome jade!' he muttered restlessly, 'A man has his work cut out to deal with women... even the best of them.' And for a second he glowered darkly at his companion, who was busy tearing up strips of linen.

She laughed, unembarrassed. 'Now,' she said in a business-like manner, 'rest your arm across the bowl,' and as he obeyed she began to bathe the deep and ugly gashes, reprimanding him sharply when he showed a tendency to wince and flinch away. 'What cowards men are over little things, Kinyras. Here you fight light a hero, sustain a dozen cuts without a murmur, yet cannot bear the smart of a remedy.'

He swore roundly and grinned. 'It smarts damnably.'

'Of course it does. The blood is still flowing and the warm

water increases it.'

As she bathed with slow, rhythmic gestures she began to chant in a curious low croon, 'Hail Hecate! Goddess, Ruler of the Night, Hail! Aid me, who thy dread secrets share. Help me staunch this flowing blood, banish pain—cool this fever with thy breath. By all the worship I have given thee, grant this man be made whole.'

Kinyras listened with the utmost gravity as she chanted these words three times, unable to determine whether it was some magnetic quality in the slowly droned words, or some healing in the touch of her fingers which made the pain gradually leave him. The blood had stopped oozing and as he gazed the surface dried, looking like a healthy would three or four days old. 'You must be a witch!' he exclaimed, making a snatch at her fingers, which she avoided, laughing in a teasing way.

'Well, cannot a witch have her uses, sometimes? The charm is ended, Kinyras, and the spell works. Now be you the wizard and conjure up some food, I beg.'

With a yell for Pheretime he dashed into the outer room, only to find it empty. Search as he might he could find nothing of her but a chest, corded with a complication of knots standing outside and evidently waiting to be carried away. Furiously angry at this flouting of himself and their necessities by his slave girl, he strode back into the room, rumpling up his hair in a distracted way. 'She has run off,' he blurted out.

'But she has cooked?' Dayonis asked anxiously.

'Apparently, yes, I smell food... somewhere.'

'Thank the gods! Get you the vessels while I see to the pots.'

She came bustling into the outer room where Pheretime was used to do her cooking, and soon her eager little nose and prying fingers had discovered the contents of sundry pots, which were quickly transferred to the tables inside, where they drew up their eat in the fashion of Khem and not squatting on low stools as was the habit of Aghirda. Dayonis adjusted herself to the refinements of Kinyras' table with admirable aplomb and it was not until sometime later that he discovered how novel to her was all she saw and did in his house.

'Well,' observed Dayonis, when all the chicken which Pheretime had prepared so admirably for her lord's and her own supper was consumed to the last piece, 'at least she gave me her tunic before she went and for that I owe her many thanks. Likewise for supper. I have feasted nobly, Lord Kinyras and am much refreshed. How is it with you?'

'I am a new man.'

She laughed and glanced at him beneath her lashes, sideways. 'If I knew what the old was like, I might the better appreciate the new man. For all his well-being he seems strangely silent.'

'Because I cannot determine what to do with you,' he replied, torn between two desires, to keep her for himself and to use her. He could not endure the provoking picture of Dayonis in the arms of Amasis, as his mind constantly evoked it, nor was the thought of losing her as a means of wringing profitable terms from the enemy any more attractive. Therefore was Kinyras moody and preoccupied, swaying between two desires like a poplar in a gale. He ate and drank stolidly. The meal had been a silent one, save for the courtesies of the table, which he scrumpulously observed.

'What to do with me?' she echoed him sharply, and bending up him quite another kind of glance, in which acuteness and suspicion were both keenly alive.

Kinyras, sustaining it unmoved, decided he must proceed warily until he had come to some sort of a decision. He laughed easily, for he was not without subtlety. 'Yes. You are a mystery to me.' This was clever and flattering, tickling the feminine vanity which delights to think itself mysterious. Watching her swallow the bait whole, he went on before she could interrupt him. 'What are you? Are you kin to the Gods, who have given you of their beauty? Are you a goddess in disguise? Such things have been. Do you come from the Elves?'

'Well,' she answered dimpling. 'In Aghirda we do claim kin to fairy-folk. My grandma was a Telechina, but it is not wise so to boast in Karpas, I have heard. Priests cannot brook rivals and the mere suspicioius of being able to work a spell is enough to provoke a burning.'

'They do not love Cabire blood, I believe.'

'So if you are in doubt what to do with me, a straight course lies before you. I shall trouble you no more and you can warm your cold hands and colder heart at the fire which consumes me.'

'Can you suppose me guilty of such treachery?' Kinyras began and was suddenly stricken dumb by a conviction that between what she had said and what he proposed there was not much to choose. She might well prefer death, even such a death, to captivity in Khem. He sat gazing before him, tracing out the painted figures on the table beneath his hand with an abstracted forefinger.

Suddenly he was aware that her own fingers were lightly lifting the curls from his forehead, away from a gash where an arrow had ploughed the flesh. 'I like your hair,' she was murmuring, 'so dark and crisply curling,' but as he tried to capture her fingers she sprang aside with a ripple of tinkling laughter and sat down opposite him. 'From whence do you come?'

'I was born on the mainland, near Askalon, but I have travelled in many lands since then, and learnt much.'

'And I, too, have left my native land to wander. Lord, how did you know who I was, when we met out yonder?'

Now, this he had no mind to tell her and parried her question by putting another. 'How did you know me?'

She was aware of the evasion and strove in her mind to find a reason for it, at the same time being perfectly willing, nay, anxious to reveal somewhat of her powers to him. 'That was simple enough. I had been told by the Old Ones, when I invoked them by my arts, that I should meet a man, armed as you were armed, and that he would save me and deliver my people from Khem.'

'What are your arts?' he asked, smiling.

Nettled, she drew forth the magic stone and held it out for

his inspection. In order to see what was engraved upon it he must bring his head very close to hers. He examined it as closely as he might.

'You see? The stone came from the Gods. I make a dense smoke and the gods speak to me out of it. I will invoke them for you, if you will tell me how you knew me?' She was coaxing him like a child, her eyes eager and shining very brightly.

Once having looked into them he found it difficult to look away again. 'I knew you by my arts.'

'Do you, too, use the magic smoke?'

He shook his head, smiling again at the idea.

'How then?' she demanded, with an imperious little stamp of her bare foot, which was an action rather than a sound.

'I do nothing but leave my mind open for what will be put into it. I come and I go, up and down Time according to my need, sometimes without voluntary effort.'

This was uttered with great solemnity and with a portentous look, while the eyes before him grew enormous with awe and fright, as she drew a little back from him. He wanted to laugh and knew not why he spoke and acted so, being prompted by some motive which was not clearly defined, even to himself, but which he felt to be wise.

'You leave your mind open!' she repeated, incredulous and bewindered, 'do you make no sacrifices?'

'They are an abomination to those High Powers with whom I walk and from whence I derive my strength.'

'Do you walk with the Gods?' she whispered, drawing still further off and with her hands resting palms downward upon the table in a strangely vital manner, as though she held beneath them some belief in herself and all appertaining thereto, which was rabidly dwindling beneath that desperate pressure.

Kinyras slowly inclined his head in assent. 'So men say.'

'But what do *you* say?' she demanded acutely.

Again he would have smiled, but repressed the inclination and made instead a large gesture. 'I walk... Beyond,' he answered, with an involuntary solemnity.

Dayonis could make neither head nor tail of all this talk, yet was sensitive enough and wise enough to realise that here was no idle boaster, no trickster making attitudes to impress her. Neither was she so small as to suffer a sense of rivalry but was more inclined to a growing veneration, so unaccustomed with her as to surprise herself. With it there was s strange mingling of other sensations, a quickening of her pulses hitherto so regular, a desire to captivate and to hold this most unusual man, an intention to use him for her own advantage, if she could. Yet, above all these mixed motives, wonder held the whole foreground, while they flitted like shadows in the back of her mind, awaiting their turn to assume tangibility. Hesitatingly she gave voice to her thoughts—'But are your Gods ancient and powerful as my Old Ones of the Hills? I think they cannot be, for mine were the first.'

Unconsciously Kinyras grew more serious and more intense, his eyes darkening and dilating with thought as they dwelt upon hers, until their luminous beauty seemed to go past her to the utmost limits of the earth, to draw power from some source which lay beyond comprehension, bound neither by Time nor Space. 'My Powers have neither beginning nor end. Your Old Ones, as you call them, are but the creations of men's minds, subject to their wishes, while mine are the powers by which men live and are free, dwelling within each one of us.'

'But, when I make my magic smoke my Old Ones speak through me and I foretell the future.'

Kinyras shook his head. 'You stupefy your senses by your stench and smarten your eyes, then, with your eyes watering and your wits half dulled, you speak what your mind wishes and hopes will be accomplished.'

The eyes before him were very alive and flashing as she took the stone from her neck and held it out to him with fingers unsteady from the anger flaming so suddenly within her. 'Now i know you speak folly out of your own pride and vanity, Kinyas. How account you for this, which was given to my grandma by the Old Ones, whose servant she was all her life?'

He took the stone in his hand and examined it curiously and more minutely than as yet he had been able, holding it under the lamp to get a better light on it. Undoubtedly the cut figure held a curious weapon, so like the Staveros in its rude shaping that it might be take for the identical arm, if one wished to think so. But to Kinyras it presented little mystery. If he could see and fashion such a weapon, why not another, who had studied along the same lines as himself and achieved the same ability? 'This stone, Princess, was cut by a man who had learnt to See, as I have done. That is all.'

'You talk strangely and I do not understand your words. Can I, too, learn to see?'

They had both risen, he to examine the stone, she for reasons of her own, and now she stood before him, with the light from the lamp illuminating her, until her hair burned with a living fire and her breasts gleamed like pearls, while the magic stone dangled between them.

'The snowy breasted pearl,' murmured he, staring fascinated.

'What is that?' she asked softly.

'It is a song, Dayonis.'

'Then sing it to me, for I adore singing.'

Surprisingly he began to sing a lovely air in a rich baritone, which he subdued to the tender, swelling cadences of the song and the need of the moment.

She listened, wrinkling her brows in puzzlement, and when he had finished she faltered—'It is wonderful and haunting and the words in the tongue as strange as the music. Lord Kinyras, did you make the song for me?'

He passed his hand across his brow in a dazed way and stared at her as though he had expected to see something quite different from the picture she presented. 'No, no,' he answered, 'of course not. It is not known who wrote it, nor do I know where it came from. It was in my mind at that moment.'

She pouted and drew a little nearer to him. 'It is the singer, not the song, what matters and your voice is heavenly. Do you like me in your slave-girl's clothing, my lord?'

'You look lovely in anything.'

'How like a man, never caring what a woman wears, or what she wears... nothing at all,' she sighed, drooping her lids so that the beauty of the thick, curling lashes was at its best.

Kinyras made a snatch at her hands and held them closely. She felt their unsteadiness and swayed yet a little nearer.

'I have seen you in the guise of a goddess, cloaked in your glorious hair, in all the ravishment of white limbs flashing in the sunlight... Astarte–Atargatis.'

'Do you mock me for coming to your woods in so barren a way, lord?'

'I like much barrenness, it beggars all other costume, Dayonis.'

'Maybe i shall wear it yet again,' she murmured,

'When?' he breathed, trembling at the thought, 'now?'

Slowly, languidly she raised her eyes, saw the fire kindling in his, felt his breath hot almost upon her lips and drew back, snatching her hands from his to fold them, crossed high upon her breast. 'If I ever forget I am a princess of Aghirda, or what is her due.' She drew still farther off, leaving him thwarted and foolish. 'Maybe you can make me forget, Kinyras, but not now, sir, not now. I am faint from weariness and must sleep and you, too, need rest, my brother of the sword. Will you light me to my chamber, brother?'

He bowed and without a word reached for a lamp.

'What noise is that? Someone comes?' she asked.

It was Hasvan, returned with the two wenches for whom Kinyras had sent him and with a bundle of new clothing. In choosing her attendant and in examining the purchases, which were of a sufficient richness to please even a Princess of Aghirda, Dayonis once more forgot her weariness and Kinyras heard the murmur of the two women's voices, laughing and exclaiming as they tried on various garments, far into the night.


Mina, sitting in the death-like stillness of the sick room, knew a terror of the present and of the future, which never had she experienced before. It was the fifth night of Denvers' extraordinary illness. How long was this horror of immobility to go on? Must she for ever sit beside that figure whose inertness was a nightmare? It was Hank who prevented her from getting a nurse to relieve her, urging upon her the necessity for keeping silent upon what had happened. Catalepsy was a rare disease and once the papers got wind of it a stream of publicity would ensure. Such must be averted at all costs.

'I'll come in every day and stay with him for a time, while you get a few hours' sleep. And there's really no reason, darling, why you should not snooze in your chair during the night. You'd be sure to hear him if he came round.'

This was said with an air of such magnanimity that she felt she should appreciate Hank's generosity more than she did. All she could do was to bow in silence to his superior judgement. Mina was a good nurse and it was not the first time she had attended Robert with great skill and devotion. When they had married at the close of the war he had been suffering from a bad wound and the effect of gas. For many years he had been subject to recurrences of his old trouble and it was nothing but her love and care of him which had ultimately restored him to perfect health.

But that was so long ago, when they had loved each with a sweet madness and an understanding of one another which had bound them in a deep friendship and community of spirit. Of recent years Robert had enjoyed perfect fitness. Not since her meeting with Hank had she nursed him.

Mina was too frightened to read, her nerves were so frayed, her mind so distracted that she could not occupy herself in any way. All she could do was to sit staring at Robert, until she felt she must scream, or in fits of restlessness wander softly about the room, aimlessly picking up things and putting them down again, or unseeingly turning over the papers and plans upon his desk.

The great trouble with Mina was that all her old self-assertion and self-confidence was gone. Her infatuation for

Hank had received a blow, dealt by that inert hand lying palm downwards on the eiderdown, while her passion for him remained burning as brightly as ever. But now that infatuation was gone, she no longer loved blindly, irresponsibly.

This strange happening to Denvers had given back to his wife her sight and her sense of responsibility, had turned her thoughts back upon their joint past, had reminded her of much she had forgotten. His very defencelessness roused in her some pulsation of old tenderness, roused in her a subconscious instinct to protect him against herself and Hank.

Unable to endure her tormenting thoughts and the conflict of impulses warring within, she got up from her chair and began a restless movement about the room, until finally the litter of papers on the desk suggested an outlet for her feverishness. She began to tidy it up and in trying to find a place for some old letters in one of the drawers, came upon the one he had written to her. It was like a message from the dead. Slowly and fearfully she opened it and read.

Had she read this letter in her former state of impatient grievance against him, it would have roused nothing but her old petulance and intolerance for any outlook than her own. But in the interlude strange things had happened to Denvers and Mina, and she read now with an entirely new set of emotions. The love and devotion breathing in every line brought the unwilling tears smarting to her eyes and started her off upon a most ugly and unwelcome train of thought. Hank's words suddenly rose to haunt her 'Don't get *me* into trouble.' 'Take all the blame upon yourself.' 'You'll be faithful to *me*.' 'You'll come and keep house for *me*.' 'If there is no divorce, what does it matter?'

Her passion for Hank trembled at these remorseless recollections and the questions which they roused in her mind, now that infatuation was dead and she could see clearly the difference between what Hank had said only yesterday and what Robert said in this letter, how he entreated her not to let the memory of the wrong she was doing to their love prevented her from seeking reconciliation with him ,when this present madness should have passed from her and her love for him should again be burning brightly.

A ring at the bell interrupted her unquiet thoughts and she opened to admit Hank. He took her in his arms and kissed her and, savouring his kisses expertly, she knew that there was a difference in them. It was not that they were less Passionate. Hank loved her and desired as much as ever—but—he was very sure of her. There seemed to be no doubt in his mind that she was his, body and soul. The lover's doubts of pleasing and of his worthiness, all his diffidence, had departed for ever from Hank. Already he regarded Denvers as a dead man, one quietly dead without any cause of trouble for himself. Could anything be more suitable? A vain-glorious triumph over his enemy pervaded Heyward.

Mina, yielding herself to his encircling arms, repressed a shiver of apprehension, which Heyward immediately detected. 'Cold?' he whispered into her hair, then not waiting for her answer he asked his usual question, 'Will, how is he? Any change?'

She disengaged herself and shook her head. Heyward strode into the bedroom as though it belonged to him, Mina trailing weakly behind, but full of a queer, futile sense of rebellion. Hank stood looking down on Denvers, hands planted on hips, legs wide astride, shoulders hunched and head thrust forward. His damaged eye was still badly inflamed and strangely enough, all the hatred and spite of his relationship with the man on the bed seemed to be centred in this impaired member, and to glitter from its watery depths. This eye of Heyward's really was a great affliction to Mina, much more so than to him, who seemed now to be hardly conscious of it.

Abruptly Hank's attention was shifted from its occupant to fix upon the letter which Mina had dropped on the bed. He picked it up and turned it over. 'What's this? A letter from him? When did he write it? What does the drivelling imbecile say?' Quite coolly he began to read its opening sentence in a tone of savage irony. Suddenly Mina had sprung forward to snatch it from him with an equal savagery, and she hastily folded the paper and thrust it into her dress.

'Well, spitfire, and what's the matter now? D'you think I can't get it if I want it?'

He came towards her, but she stepped backward. 'Don't you dare!' she breathed tensely.

He paused and eyed her speculatively. 'Sauce piquante!' he murmured appreciatively. 'You're attractive when you're prickly and difficult, Mina.'

Her heaving breast and stormy eyes were not soothed by his tone, but their attention was diverted from themselves by a sound from the bed. With a hair-raising suddenness Denvers slumped over on his side and burled up his legs in a normal attitude of normal sleep. They both started at him fascinated, unable to speak, and as they stood so, their incredulous ears caught the sound of speech. 'Dayonis! Dayonis, my lovely dear. See, my beloved, this last year's leaf in the strong Spring Sun. It is red as your wondrous hair, my snowy-breasted pearl.'

A raucous laugh burst from the attentive Heyward. 'Did you get that, Mina? The old duffer has found a bird. Hark at him! Some bird, too, by the sound of it. I wonder who she is? Well, that lets us out, anyhow. Just listen to the old fool's ravings?'

And Mina, stiff with surprise and incredulity, did listen, with mixed feelings. Gradually comprehension returned to her brain and volition to her limbs, and soon she was at the telephone, ringing Dr. Groves.

'He's coming round, Mrs. Denvers. Thank Heaven for it. I'll be over in a minute or two.'

# Chapter VIII

# DAYONIS' STORY

inyras rose at dawn the next morning after a restless night. In his fitful periods of wakefulness his mind dwelt upon Dayonis, her beauty, her allure, his desire for her conflicting with his half-formed resolve to use her as a hostage. Never in his life before had he known such vacillation of humour and he went forth into the grey mists of the morning in a mighty dissatisfaction with himself and all about him.

For long he stood looking towards the enemy's lines, where their camp-fires glared and smoked through the haze, pondering their probable tactics, debating within himself the possibility of inflicting another defeat such as that of yesterday, should they attack again immediately. Where had this large army of infantry come from and what was its purpose? The tactics pursued yonder were unlike those of Khem in general. Were they a beleaguering force, or did they mean to attack? Perhaps Dayonis could give him some information if he questioned her.

After several hours of inspection he returned to the house. All within the lines was going smoothly and methodically. Zadoug shared much of his own talent for organization and was a valuable adjutant, the brothers being able to work together amicably and efficiently. The Karpasians, elated by victory, their confidence in their general increased to

130

stupendous efforts to make their defences impregnable. Success in arms had roused their manhood and their patriotism, the praises of their women, the songs of triumph chanted by their children were sweet to their ears and exhilarating. Therefore did Kinyras find everything going merrily, even the dead had died in the most favourable circumstances known to primitive man and would be buried like the heroes they were, with all the solemn rites due to them.

Dayonis, clad this morning in a garment of sheer white, girded at the waist and leaving her rosy, dimpled knees bare, her hair dressed and bound in order, though a few curls still strayed about her forehead and ears and the nape of her neck, was seated on the floor weaving a garland from a mass of flowers she had gathered. When Kinyras entered she sprang up alertly and flung the finished decoration round his neck, while he stood, pleased but foolish.

'There is a garland for a hero,' she exclaimed, in her teasing way, 'and a hungry one, too, I'll wager. Come to the table, my lord, and eat. Hasvan has performed wonders. Here are figs and dates and good wine with these fine nuts though you may prefer more substantial fare, and hot juniper drink.'

Kinyras clapped his hands, drew out a chair, seating her and himself, while Hasvan entered with a steaming bowl of fish and vegetables, which smelt exceedingly good and which he placed on the table with something of a flourish, grinning broadly. Kinyras felt that here was a royal welcome indeed and his spirits rose with his appetite.

He beamed kindly upon his man and his guest. 'Very good, Hazvan,' he remarked, drawing in the grateful odour with something very like a loud sniff.

'Yes, master. Pheretime has run away, but the new girl is a better cook.'

'So it seems.'

Kinyras ladled out a portion of the savoury mess into a bowl and Hasvan conveyed it to Dayonis with much ceremony, pouring her win into a painted pottery cup of great beauty. Again the Princess of Aghirda was a little awed by the appointments and service of her host's table, though she concealed the fact extremely well, but feeling more nervous in the presence of this slave than she had done with Kinyras alone. She began to eat in silence, wishing the man would go.

'Yes, lord. Her chest has been carried away in the night, and nothing is left of her here. Shall I send men to capture her?'

Kinyras shook his head, while Dayonis watched him with covert acuteness and curiosity. 'Nay, let her go. She is a slave and behaves evilly, but I give her freedom. She shall not stay here, however. Have her taken, Hasvan and conveyed to Re-Karpas, where she shall be set free to go whither she will. Have my orders carried out instantly.'

Dayonis was pleased to eat alone with Kinyras, but secretly pouted over his decision about Pheretime, thinking is action showed weakness. The princess was anxious to invoke her Old Ones as soon as maybe and in her opinion Pheretime should have been pushed immediately and brought back, to suffer the punishment she had earned by deserting her master in an emergency. What sacrifice could have been more acceptable to the Old Ones than that of a young and pretty woman? A black Ethiopian assumed proportions of poverty by contrast, and if she had attained to so much by the one, how much more might she expect to receive by the other?

Dayonis ate in hungry silence, mindful of her table manners as much as might be, while her thoughts were so preoccupied.

The voice of Kinyras, breaking in upon them suddenly, almost made her jump. 'You rested well, Princess, and your woman is in your liking?'

'Yes, indeed, sir. She will do admirably and I slept like a squirrel in winter. You have shown me noble and generous hospitality, Kinyras.'

And at the thought of his anxious solicitude for her comfort, her brooding discontent vanished like morning haze before the climbing sun and she smiled happily and gratefully into his eyes.

'It is nothing suitable to your condition, lady. If you will occupy your present chamber until another more commodious can be added to the house, I will see that you do not have to wait long for it. Hazvan tells me that some traders have come from Sidon to Karpas in two ships bearing great store of furniture, glass, ornaments in gold and enamel, rich tissues, and muslins from Khem. It is but rarely that they come to the peninsula. Maybe your gods sent them for your adorning, my princess.'

Dayonis laughed and her eyes sparkled with delight. 'How I should love to go aboard those ships and to chaffer for their merchandise, but i am bare as a stone in the desert, owing everything to your charity.'

'It is my delight to supply your needs, Dayonis. Let us have no more of such talk. If you will tell Hasvan what you need I will send him to these traders. I have enough to spare.'

'Your generosity has already exceeded my needs, Kinyras,' she assured him earnestly. 'Indeed, I live in Aghirda more simply than you may believe.'

'Tell me of your home,' he asked and she obeyed, repeating most of what Zadoug had already told him, rather inclining to enlarge upon the matter of the Nubian's slaughter. 'I knew that to obtain real power I must have a human sacrifice, but I always hated to do it. But when I was a helpless prisoner, and my country lost, it was another thing. And he was a beast of an enemy. So I did what was needful, and it worked, for the very next day Ammunze broke through the wall and led me to freedom.'

He recognised that she wished to impress him again with a recital of her powers and was tempted to humour her in the hope of learning something valuable from her prattle. 'How could you, a girl, kill so powerful a man without a weapon?' he asked curiously.

She waved a negligent hand, lids half lowered over her eyes, a little superciliously. 'No every difficult matter, lord. I stunned him with the bar and dragged him down the passage to the cave beneath, first binding his hands and feet with his loin-cloth torn in strips. She still breathed. Indeed, if he had not the sacrifice would have been useless. He had no weapons on him, not even a knife. Feared I'd snatch it, I suppose, so I had to strangle him.'

'And then?'

'I pulled him over to the altar-stone and got the bar. There was a crack below the sacred stone and into this I put one end of the bar, made the proper incantation and pressed the hither end, with his neck beneath. He spluttered and stirred and it was done.'

'Simple, as you say. And your escape from the cave?'

She shuddered and pressed her fingers into her closed eyes, as though to shut out the memory of that night's journey. 'That was far from easy. I marvel I'm here to tell the tale. There was a narrow ledge some thirty feet below the opening of the cave, situated farther inland than the cave. I mean that the rock shelved inward. Do you understand?'

'Perfectly.'

'Below the ledge there was a drop of three or four hundred feet to the rocks below. Ammunz fixed the bar across the opening of the cave, tied the rope round my waist, and lowered me slowly.' Again she shuddered and shivered. 'It was a cold, moonlit night and I was naked, but I sweated with fear as I went lower and lower down, spinning on the end of the rope and when Ammunz began to try to sway me inward to the ledge I could scarce forbear to scream the sickening terror I felt. In fact, I did screech, Kinyras, loud and long, until I came to my senses, and then I shook with fear that I had been heard.'

'Poor child! The ordeal was frightful.'

'At last i felt the ledge beneath my feet and contrived, how I know not, to grasp some roughness in the face of the rock and to cling there. After a time I recovered enough to unfasten the rope and to give Ammunz the sign. And when he had pulled it up again I was sick, oh, so sick and giddy! I nearly died again. And all the while the birds flew shrieking and crying about me, and the moon flooded the rocks and trees

with her bright light and watched me, clinging there like a
beetle. It was awful.'

There was a moment or two of silence, while she relived
those terrifying moments and he speculated upon the courage
and nerve of this slip of a wench, performing feats of daring
and endurance that well might make a man quail.

'Then the rope fell again and Ammunz came down. I held
the rope to steady it as well as I could, but as he neared the
bottom I could not pull him in,. All I could do was to pull at
the rope and let it go again, so that it swung until at last he,
too, fell in a heap beside me on the ledge and i could clutch at
him to prevent him falling over.

'When we had rested somewhat, we started to climb along
the ledge, and downwards as it wound round the cliff until we
reached the bottom and were safe.'

In spite of himself Kinyras drew a deep breath at these
words, for though she was there before him in the flesh, yet her
adventure had been so perilous and so enthralling, that its
already known conclusion seemed impossible in the
circumstances.

She smiled and went on. 'But that was by no means the
end of that night's work. For a time we lay panting, then
advanced cautiously along the crest eastward. Presently
Ammunz stopped. "A Khemite sentry!" he whispered and
pointed. There, black as ebony against the pale light of the
moon, was a giant of a Nubian. He might have been twin
brother to one I had slain in the cell. He was armed with spear,
bow and quiver, and a great knife. It was impossible to creep
past him.

'"Call him girl, Decoy him!" Ammunz commanded.

'I could do naught but obey. I called as seductively as a
dove in spring and let the moonlight reveal me to him.'

Kinyras found himself disliking this part of her narrative
profoundly and emitted several disapproving grunts of impatient assent.

Again she laughed, teasingly, but with a beguiling light in
her eyes, bent softly upon him across the table. 'I see you are

displeased, my lord!' she mocked, 'but what was a poor captive to do? While I played hide and seek with him, Ammunz seized a great rock in both hands and smote him with it on the back of his head. He fell without a murmur. We disarmed him speedily and cast him over into the Rocks. Thus I got me a bow and Ammunz a spear; I wished for his cloak and clothes, but Ammunz said no, they will search for him to-morrow and will find him. When a man falls by accident his weapons often fall clear, not so his clothes. If we take a stitch, they will know our path and follow. An hour's grace is more to us than twenty cloaks, and he spoke sooth, but o' nights I much regretted that by cloak. And so we came to your lines, Kinyras, sleeping by day and journeying by night.'

'A great adventure, lady, and bravely sustained, but I am puzzled for the reason why you were kept prisoner for so long.'

'I, too, was vexed for an answer until I learnt it was with much cunning from one and another source. Rhadames saw me among other women prisoners and had me brought before him. He questioned me and set me apart for himself. Later I learnt he was ambitious and he thought if he wed me he could draw my countrymen into his service.'

Kinyras nodded. 'That I can understand, but why confine you in a prison cell, princess?'

She raised her hand imperiously to stay his questions. 'Stay, I am coming to that. Rhadames knew that Pharaoh disliked and distrusted his viceroy, Amasis, and would welcome any means of ousting him. Because of his connection with his family and because of his powerful friends, Pharaoh dared take no action openly against Amasis fearing to raise rebellion and civil war if he did so, but he sent Amasis to conquer Cyprus, raising him to the vice-regal office. In reality it was banishment for Amasis.

'That I know, already.'

'But, Amasis, too, had heard somewhat of me and thought that he, too, could wed me and raise to himself a powerful army of my countrymen, by whose means he would dominate the Khemite troops under his command. With this additional power in his hands he could, when Pharaoh died, use his family connections, offer his services to Pharaoh's heir, or to the highest bidder, thus making himself the power behind the throne, and so put an end to his hated exile in Cyprus.'

'With that object in view he sent to Rhadames, bidding him hold you and send you to him as soon as might be under suitable escort?'

'Even so, Rhadames dared not to refuse openly, but having half-formed plans of assassinating Amasis at some future date and so obtaining favour with Pharaoh by ridding him of a powerful and dangerous enemy, made excuse to Amasis that he dared not send me until the country was in a more settled state, for fear of a rescue being attempted. He would keep me prisoner for a space, in the Hills.'

'A pretty tangle,' mused Kinyras, appearing to be thinking aloud in deep thought, but in reality throwing out feelers. 'Were Amasis put to silence, or otherwise deposed of, as I view it, the next Viceroy of Cyprus might well be a native of the island, bound to Pharaoh and his interest by ties of gratitude, held in his post by Khemite spears, but no warrior, so that the army would disdain to follow him. Such a native, in secret commune with Pharaoh, would be no petty chief of Council, of a small and insignificant state, but viceroy of the whole island and Pharaoh would deem a native governor more acceptable to the Cypriots.'

Dayonis shrugged. 'Some such notion might well rise in Pharaoh's mind, as you say.'

'In which event he would cast about for a likely man and open negotiations with him.'

'Doubtless I even heard tell of such a man.'

'What was his name, Dayonis?' He leant forward, both hands grasping the table, his knuckles showing white through his bronzed skin.

She looked at him beneath dropped lashes and shook her head slowly. 'There were rumours and rumours, whispers and much nodding of heads, but I heard no name spoken.'

'You would free your country from Khem by my aid, lady.'

'The gods have told me you would do so.'

'Bring me the name of that man, Dayonis, and your country is more than half way to freedom.'

She looked at him in a half-startled, incredulous manner, but he left the subject abruptly. 'Rhadames sent a small party in pursuit of you, and Amasis sent an army to intercept you ere you reached my lines.' He pointed through the window to the plain beyond. 'There they lie encamped, with their chariots and their infantry. Did you see, or hear anything of preparations for a big invasion before you escaped from Aghirda, was there any talk of advancing in force?'

'There was much whispering amongst my guards and those who came to teach me to speak Khem, but who can heed such?'

'Any straw will serve to show which way the wind blows.'

'True, but if I told you that Totmes himself, the Great God, had bidden them send me to Khem without delay, designing me for himself, should I not sound boastful, Kinyras? Would you believe me, or the rumour?'

Kinyras looked at her long and burst into a laugh. 'I'd believe anything about one so lovely, wise and desirable as yourself.'

She inclined her head, smiling perkily. 'Well, so my guards chattered, while I resolved that neither one should have me. I would be free, would bestow myself where it seemed to me most good. And here I am... with you, lord.'

He put out a hand to grasp her arm at this, but she drew back, aloof as a goddess for all the implication in her softly uttered words. 'There was other chatter, too. There is one in the Council at Karpasia whom Pharaoh calls friend, whose business it is to lull the people into the belief that Khem will not invade the land, even though you are here, building your wall. When the Karpasians have been lulled to sleep thinking their labours have been in vain, and have been cozened into not supporting you mercenaries in the defence of the country, then will Khem strike and conquer the land, his path having been made easy for him.'

Kinyras ground his teeth in helpless and impotent rage while Dayonis watched him with much interest. 'And you know not the name of this man?' he thundered like an angry god.

She surveyed him unmoved, shaking her head vigorously. 'Truly not, sir. You have been good to me and I need your aid. I entreat you to believe me. I would tell you instantly if I knew. But do you know, Kinyras?'

'Yes, I know,' he rasped bitterly, 'but I need proof and until I have it and can smash him with it,' and he brought his hand down with a shattering force upon the table so that it shook and the vessels upon it danced, 'you, I and the whole land, we are at his mercy.'

Dayonis was silent, her agile wits trying to find a way out of this coil.

After a brooding pause, Kinyras roused himself and spoke again. 'And you, lady, seem to be another storm-centre, with Pharaoh, his viceroy and his commander-in-chief, each determined to secure you for himself.'

'Words came through the Priests, whom neither Rhadames nor Amasis dared disobey. While they temporized, I escaped and Pharaoh will think that my escape was arranged. That is the reason why Amasis is furious and has sent his army to recapture me. He has to make a great business to convince Pharaoh of his innocence.

''Tis enough to make a plain man crazed,' Kinyras commented, clawing at his hair desperately. 'Thank the gods you are safe here.'

'Even had I not been, I had done better with the King himself than with Amasis. He is young and Pharaoh is full of years.'

'And a woman can twist an old man to her will?'

'It is not so, lord? His sons would have been mine to choose from, and the chosen, mayhap, would have seen to it speedily that Pharaoh slept with his fathers. It is better to be chose of Pharaoh when the throne has been put within his reach by his choice.'

139

Kinyras favoured her with a cold stare. 'I marvel to behold you here, princess,' he retorted ironically.

Dayonis laughed, in no wise disconcerted. 'I do but consider all things, Kinyras.'

He rose with an exasperated gesture. 'Enough of consideration,' he said roughly, 'you have brought great tidings, lady. We knew not of rival claims to Pharaoh's throne and our King will have much to ponder. When villains scheme and fight, good men come to their own... maybe.'

Dayonis rose, too, and laid her hand pleadingly on his arm. 'Nay, Kinyras, now you are angry and mistrustful. I did but plague you. I seek not Pharaoh or his sons. I would be Queen of my own people and we must be free. I would win independence for myself and my people. For that I have sought you, Kinyras.'

'So you say,' he muttered, still mistrustful, 'but your mouth is too full of Khem and its greatness for my liking, Princess.'

Dayonis considered him in silence, cursing her folly for having gone too far. 'You have only to hand me over to Khem, to be rid of your trouble, lord,' she suggested, paling a little at the thought of his doing so. 'They will promise you anything you like to ask, and maybe will give you a fraction.'

'I am no fool,' he growled disdainful, still eyeing her doubtfully. 'I can think of three good ways to force them to keep their word, one of which would be sufficient.'

'How?' she demanded, hiding her very certain fears.

'I have the habit of keeping my own council.'

Dayonis was silent a moment, then spoke with a confidence she did not feel. 'But you will not do that, lord, even though great pressure be put upon you. You will go against your King, you will abandon your wall sooner than give me up.'

'You talk folly and I'm in no humour for't. Nothing could turn me against my King, for whom I've fought and worked these twenty years. We are sworn brothers, my life is his. As for my wall, sooner would I abandon my own life than these of my companions and these people, which it represents.'

'Yet you will do all this within a month, for my sake.' The rapt, solemn expression on her face as she said this gave Kinyras pause to think and his heart turned to water within him as he gazed upon her. 'I have the gift of sight from the Old Ones,' she added, to clinch the matter. 'You are set apart, Kinyras, for me... to save my country and my people.'

He uttered a short, hard laugh to hide his discomfiture. 'Then must they be saved along with Karpas,' was his cynical retort, 'so the sooner you bring your people to heel, the sooner will the marvel be accomplished. Meanwhile, yonder lies Khem and my work,' and he made a sweeping gesture towards the valley below the window.

'That will I do,' she answered eagerly, 'my people shall serve you at my bidding, I swear by all my solemn gods.'

'We shall see, child, we shall see,' he assured her with some haste, 'now my duty takes me to the wall.'

'I will go with you.'

'Then come in God's name. Enough time as been wasted in idle talk.'

They went outside and sat on the low parapet which crowned the hill. Kinyras pointed out the lines stretching over the low country to the green bushes marking the swamp-land at the edge of the Kastnon river. The thin, blue line of the stream was lost in the grey-blue of the hill beyond, whose contour stood out against the hyacinthine distance of the sea in softened pencilling. Away to the northward, over the rolling country between it ran the wall until it could just be seen as it joined the cliffs at Hap Hill. He traced it out slowly with his forefinger, keen eyes narrowed, but instead of following, she looked at him instead, thinking how attractive was the alert, dark face, the purposeful carriage of the small, compact head, the steady poise of the erect, athletic figure. The gods had told her she would love this man, but he would not love her and at the recollection of that fateful prediction her heart was like a stone in her breast.

'Now,' said he in a grim voice, 'that thin, poor line is all that keeps the might of Khem out. If it goes all the country

141

goes with it. A million Karpasians who trust me, whom I have vowed to defend, all my comrades with whom I have marched and fought for twenty years and above all, my King, will go with that wall, lady. Now do you understand the enormity of what you predict?'

'I understand, Kinyras,' she answered softly.

With his eyes dwelling upon the distant mountains of Aghirda as though he looked into a picture he went on more gently.

# Chapter IX

# Kinyras' Story

My father was a petty noble, living in peace, escaping the fluctuating evils which befell bigger men of his caste. I grew up with my brothers and sisters among a mob of children of the household slaves and tenants, lording it very prettily until, when I reached the age of ten years, war came. The elders of the community, including my brothers and uncles, marched away and we young ones went on with our games. But one day came the enemy, putting all to the slaughter who resisted, killing the old and feeble and the small children, driving off the slaves and the young boys and girls. My father rand mother were killed, my sisters disappeared and I never saw them more. Zadoug and I were enslaved, beaten, tortured until Erili rescued Zadoug and me from the barbarity of our captors.'

'Oh, hated Khem! How much has the conquered to avenge upon them!' exclaimed Dayonis in an access of irrepressible bitterness.

He glanced at her curiously and resumed. 'From that time I worshipped Erili; to my adoring young eye he looked like a god in his beautiful bronze armour, but he had forgotten me. Then once more he intervened when my tormentors were peeling my skin off me, strip by strip. He bought me from them with two jars of wine and I'd have died if he had not cared for me. Thence onward I was under his protection and as he advanced, so also did I with him, until I am as you see me now.'

'Your King is a demi-god, I see.' Dayonis, in no vague fashion jealous of this devotion which she considered wasted upon a mere man and with which she could have been very content, permitted herself this guarded sneer, though Kinyras was too absorbed in his theme to heed it.

'Now you know something of my tale, how all I have in life and my very life itself, I owe to Erili. Think you I will desert him? Then only nation I know is the Brotherhood, shall I betray it? Look at those camps and those farms beyond the wall. I am holding them for my comrades. These women and children, am I to cast them all to Khem... for you, Dayonis?'

'No,' she retorted stoutly, 'a thousand times no, but a way will be found.'

He rose impatiently and strode back to his house, she trotting meekly at his heels. He called Hasvan to bring Baal Salah and when Dayonis saw the little beast come running to his master's whistle like a dog, his reins fastened about his neck by Hasvan, she cried out in delight at the pretty sight and nothing must serve but she, too, should have a mount and ride with Kinyras.

'But can you ride, Princess?' asked Kinyras doubtfully.

'Yes,' lied she, boldly.

So Hasvan was despatched in search of another donkey, while she sped to her chamber, returning in a short tunic to the thighs and a bright green cloak against which her vivid hair shone like living gold. The patient ass was brought by Hasvan and stood meekly, while she got nimbly enough in the saddle, and they started out for Hap Hill. 'Slowly, lord,' she urged, wondering how long she should retain her precarious seat and trying to bring her body in tune with the rhythm of the little animal beneath her, 'I am something out of it, as you may perceive.'

Kinyras smiled knowingly, all his good humour restored. 'Very much so, Dayonis,' and he checked his Selah to a gentle amble, 'maybe a few lessons from me will help you to a better acquaintance with the art.'

She laughed merrily and he gave her a lesson all the way to Hap Hill, vowing she would make a fine rider one of these days. Perfect good humour was restored between them, when suddenly he reverted to their former talk.

'Let this be clear to you, Dayonis,' he said, with much solemnity, 'duty will come first with me, and mine at the moment is to give security to these people. When that is achieved I will ask leave of my King and return with you to Aghirda. I'll go whither you will, lady, but first I must finish my task here.'

She answered him as gravely. 'Plainly and honestly spoken, Kinyras, and I believe you will keep your word. What woman could ask more of a man than that? I accept you on those terms and will plague you no further with my talk of magic smoke. Everything lies on the lap of the gods.'

She held out her hand to him and he clasped it warmly, though she thought her own thoughts the while, resolving to keep them to herself. They rode in silence for some distance, she a little weary, but disdaining to speak of it, he deep in an abstraction from which she sought to rouse him. 'Those signs of the brotherhood which I am to know...?' she suggested. 'Maybe we could sit on that bank of violets and you would instruct me further in these mysteries?'

Seeing through her ruse, Kinyras drew reign instantly, dismounted and lifted her from her mount. Tenderly he carried her to the bank where she lay back amongst the deep-scented flowers, her rosy limbs almost hidden amid their leaves. She smiled at him languorously and as he flung himself beside her, palpitating, and ardently about to clasp her close to him, she checked him with a blink of her eyes, which brought him roundly to the point while she changed not one jot of the seduction and aggravation of her enticing pose.

He sprang to his feet and stood before her, determined to repay her by a drastic obedience to her behest. 'The first sign is this, the swordsman's greeting. Upright, right hand raised to full extent, palm outward. 'Tis the common sign of peace everywhere and often you'll see it, to show there is no weapon in the hand. Your left hangs at your side.'

Dayonis made a gesture of comprehension.

'But if you think only brothers are present the third and fourth fingers of the left hand are closed, the middle finger is held straight down, representing a sword, the index touching the thumb and representing the sheath. Quietly done it is a most natural gestures, passing unnoticed though not to e used except when in the presence of brothers or if you are being tested. In such a case, give it first then draw your sword, holding it in the right hand upwards at full extent give the sign again. This is our royal salute, given only to our leaders, or at rites, or when being tested.'

'They are not difficult to remember,' she observed, watching him keenly from almost closed eyes as she lay back.

'They drinking sign again is given only when brothers are present. Drink with the cup held in your left hand, your right resting upon your hilt.'

'That, too, is simple, and had we wine we might practice.'

'You must be prepared for tests, when you'll be asked to drink to the brotherhood, or to the King. Then there are distress signals, when both hands are raised high, palms outward and are waved, four times to the right, five times to the left, so. You must never fail to help a brother and you will always be helped in turn; and remember, if one is testing you, as you give a sign he must answer it, but reversed, that is, using the right hand for the left etc., but only when being tested, and mark this well, never give the signs at random. Outsiders must not learn them at all costs. If one wishes to test you, claim to have a known brother present. Then, if you give a sign and they don't answer it reversed, the brother will question them closely, as to where they were admitted and by whom; you should get behind them while they are being questioned; if they can give good answers, and prove their claim, good; if not, the brother will nod twice. Then put your knife in, under the left shoulder blade is best if they wear no armour. In their neck if they do. The secrets of the brotherhood must be kept.'

After this half-hour of rest they resumed their ride and when they reached Hap Hill a great demonstration greeted

Kinyras. All the people who were not at the moment working on the fortifications came thronging about him, laughing, singing, shouting his name, calling him their father and saviour from the might of Khem. The boys cut fantastic capers in a kind of rude war-dance of their own invention, cursing their enemies and howling derision at their discomfiture and enjoying themselves mightily. The girls and young maidens had gathered flowers, some of which they strewed upon the ground before his donkey's feet, while others they had woven into garlands which they cast about him, chanting sweetly as they danced naked before him, their lithe young limbs glowing in the hot sun.

Of Dayonis they took little notice though one laughing rogue threw a long garland round her neck and running with the other end encircled Kinyras also in the fragrant rope, but beyond this the play was all for their victorious general and the pretty pageant accompanied them all the way down to the fortifications, where there was more cheering, though work was not interrupted. Kinyras took a simple pleasure in this exhibition of good-will from his people and dismissed them with a short speech, commending their industry and docility. He knew well the value of putting the populace in as good fettle with themselves as they were with him, though their exclusion of Dayonis caused him some disquiet. It was very necessary that they should receive her cordially and suffer her presence among them with good feeling. Dayonis loved weapons, and soon acquired a staveros, and practised with it daily' being a fine natural shot she was soon a wonderful markswoman. To her it was a magic weapon, foretold by her Gods.

Together they visited the lines and interviewed the various captains, to whom the Princess of Aghirda was made known with due ceremony and again their general felt a coldness. As they passed on there was a murmur, accompanied by looks of discontent. 'It was a hapless day when that minx ran naked out of the woods to plague us.'

'Aye, but she found bravely beside him and saved his life.

The first gambler spat derisively. 'No matter, we want no women to fight for us. She is a witch and already her toils are fast about him. Damn all women, say I, especially red-headed barbarians.'

Could Kinyras have heard these words and many like them which followed Dayonis everywhere he would have been sorely disturbed. As it was he continued in a happy ignorance and his friendship with the lovely stranger grew apace. At length, seeing that her weariness was excessive in spite of her gay attempts to hide it, he summoned a litter and sent her back home in it. 'I will overtake you ere you have covered half the distance,' he promised her when she objected and stood at salute while she was borne away, she waving to him and the solitary garland, now something faded, trailing behind deject-edly, while assembled Karpas shrugged and whispered.

Kinyras urgently needed a long talk with Zadoug and had come down the line for the purpose. Now he learnt that his brother had gone to inspect his own section of the wall and would remain there all night. Leaving instructions for Zadoug to await his coming on the morrow for a conference, he mounted and hastened after the litter, leading the little ass which had carried his guest by the bridle. When he overtook the little *cortege* Dayonis was lying with limbs relaxed, sleeping with all the abandonment of a tired child, nor did she waken even when they reached the house. Kinyras bid the slaves lower the litter beneath the shade of a giant cedar and leave it there until she roused.

As he was standing looking down on Dayonis and wonder-ing whether her coming was an unmixed blessing, he saw Hasvan coming towards him with two commanders of the Karpasian troops. Guessing what was in the wind now, he advanced to meet them.

'Hail, lord!' they exclaimed in unison.

As he responded to their greetings, Kinyras was seized with forebodings of disaster. Nothing but some act of folly could make men look so pleased with themselves, or wear so important an air, he told him cynically. 'You bring me news? I hope it is as good as your looks, sirs,' he said courteously.

'Great good news, O Commander, a glorious day for Karpas,' they chorused happily.

'Let me hear them.'

'Two envoys of Khem have come, lord, so we have brought them hither. They came, bearing the green boughs of peace to the gate of the sixth section saying they wished to discuss terms of peace.'

'And you have brought them hither? Truly, sirs, I am indebted to you. Pray give them my greetings and beg them to honour my poor house with their presence.'

The two men marched off to obey and Kinyras broke out into bitter vituperation. 'May Ran and Meroch and all the demons of the mountains and the great sea seize and destroy the damned Karpasian numbskulls. Envoys! Accursed spies, more like, evil sons of abominable mothers!'

A light touch on his arm interrupted these amenities and he swung round savagely to find Dayonis at his elbow. 'What now?' she demanded, 'why this raving?'

'Envoys bearing green branches have come from the enemy and my Karpasian lieutenants have been fooled to the extent of admitting them inside the lines.'

'So bad as that!' she exclaimed fearfully. 'Where are the Gods?'

'Snoring, as you were a moment ago,' he sneered savagely.

Dayonis uttered a short laugh at his rudeness. 'Damned zaneys!' she observed and considered a moment or two. 'Well, what's done can't be mended, but you can hear what they have to say and then give the envoys to me, Kinyras. I will sacrifice them and invoke my Gods in the magic smoke.'

'What, with victims who have borne the peace sign in their hands. Much good will they do you.'

'But they have seen the weakness of our defences and will know best where to attack. Well, so be it, we can but die fighting. But you?'

He paused to think, frowning at her, while she stood silent, wondering what was coming now. At length a plan occurred to him. 'Hasvan shall take you to my two ships at the mouth of the Kastnon, with orders to Karan that if the line breaks he is to put to sea at once. He must carry you to safety whatever happens and must prepare immediately for a long voyage.'

This scheme did not at all appeal to Dayonis, who looked her discontent. 'The line is not yet broken,' she reminded him.

'No, but its chance of remaining firm is so much reduced that I dare no longer rely upon its strength. You must be with the ships. There is no safety from Khem in the known lands, you must go out on the great sea and search for lands where the might of Khem is unknown. But first you must hide in the bad lands of Kush.'

'They sound bitter to me, and I mislike them. You have not yet heard what these envoys have to say.'

'I know it before they speak. They have come to learn the secret of the staveros and thanks to those fools have doubtless succeeded. Here they come, but they must not see you. Here into the thicket yonder. Hasten! I will stand close by this bush so that you may recognise them, maybe. Pray the gods they try to murder me, that will give me an excuse to dispatch them.'

'I will creep behind them and put my knife beneath their shoulder-blades when you give me the sign, as you told me to do to those who seek the secrets of the brotherhood,' she said, hopefully and coaxingly.

'Have you no honour, girl?' gasped Kinyras.

'But they are spies, you said so yourself, why not treat them as such?'

'I could not treat men so, who bear the green branches of peace. Can I descend to the depth of a Khemite put of iniquity?'

Dayonis shrugged, said no more, and disappeared behind the bush just as slaves brought seats. And no sooner was this done than Hasvan appeared, walking with slow, majestic strides, followed by the envoys, both elderly men of noble bearing, richly attired.

They were clad in bronze mail of exquisite workmanship. Because they were not at their ease in such accoutrements,

Kinyras judged them to be no soldiers but nobles of Khem, statesmen, true envoys; and as he considered their costly dress and jewels his heart sank. These were no murderers, he would have no excuse for killing them. He advanced a half-step to meet them and bowed in his soldierly way, and to his greeting they raised their green branches which they carried in token of their errand.

An interpreter accompanied them, a slave, a Karpasian captive. As they spoke he slowly translated. 'We are the envoys of Amasis, the viceroy and beloved of Pharaoh, who is the King and ruler of all kings and nations.'

Again Kinyras bowed. 'Speak, O Envoys of Amasis. I listen.'

'You have among you a runaway slave-girl, one Dayonis. She is not of your nation but is of Aghirda, a nation subject to our King.'

The speaker paused to clear his throat and the slave translated in a monotonous sing-song.

'Well, sir?' said Kinyras, looking utterly unimpressed.

The Khemite eyed him with a large melancholy, resuming— 'as his representatives we demand the return of this woman. Our master is not ungenerous. If she is restored we will withdraw our armies and give you peace. In addition he will return to you one hundred men and one hundred women of your nation taken captive.'

'Is that all your message?'

'You yourself, O Ban, we bear a dress of honour and a collar of gems.'

'Many thanks, O noble envoys,' returned Kinyras, bowing low in acknowledgement.

'As for these captives, we have them among our slaves, all of Karpas. Question the interpreter, if you will. He is one of them and will verify my statement, or if you prefer it we will give you gold for yourself instead of these slaves.'

'Again, many things, but we cannot give up anyone who is under our protection,' he answered them coldly.

'If you do not, we shall take.'

'If you can take, why treaty?' he riposted like lightning.

The envoy disposed of this with a large gesture of his bejewelled right arm. 'We have seen your lines, we know the weakness of your defences, how few are your real warriors. We have seen that most of your men are untrained farmers and townsmen. How can they stand against the armies of our mighty King, who has conquered the earth, may his name be praised.'

Kinyras smiled gravely and urbanely—'You have seen much, O Envoys of Khem, but there is one thing you have failed to perceive.'

'And what is that, sir?'

'I speak without offence, that is understood?'

They bowed in concert and glanced at each other.

'That, poor as are our means, we yet have inflicted two defeats upon the enemy.'

'Mere raids, sir.'

Kinyras shrugged and laughed and looked as ironical as he knew how, while his brain raced and he was so minded to order the instant execution of the men before him that he was appalled at the depths to which he might fall upon the greatest provocation. Play for time, play for time and detain them, some inner voice urged him. Suddenly he bent a scowl upon the envoys to try the effect and was in no little amaze to see then disconcerted by it.

'What scabby terms are these for a reigning Princess. The exchange of two thousand prisoners would not fit the mark. You must mend your offer, sirs. And even so I have neither power nor inclination to treat with you. I will pass you through my lines and inform my King, Erili, of your mission. It is with him you must deal.'

When this had been translated the envoys appeared none too pleased, and they eyed Kinyras with a sharp suspicion, but he appeared so careless and so contemptuous that they withdrew to confabulate between themselves. 'We can do nothing with this dog,' said the spokesman viciously, 'For two peas he'd slit our throats and seek only for a legitimate excuse to do so.'

'Then must we not give it him,' asserted the other hastily. 'I mislike his looks excessively. Let us return immediately to camp and consult the Captains of the Host. Misbegotten swine of a mercenary, he shall pay dearly for his pride and contempt. The Gods will deliver him into our hands.'

Guessing something of the nature of their talk Kinyras assumed a still more haughty and commanding bearing, and when they turned again to him, he said before they could utter a word—'For the sake of speed I pray you write a letter, commanding that a thousand men and a thousand women captives be sent to your camp, to be ready for exchange if Erili agrees. Meanwhile, let there be a truce. Neither of our people are to cross the ditch, nor your men to come within a bow-shot of it until your return. If the truce is broken the negotiations are void. Two of my men shall go to your camp with green boughs to inspect the prisoners. They must be unmutilated.'

'You know your mind, lord,' observed the first envoy, narrowing his lids most unpleasantly. 'We accept your terms, but first we will return to our lines for a further consultation.'

'That cannot be allowed. You have entered my lines, lords, and until your mission be accomplished and your terms accepted or rejected, here must you remain. If you are indeed envoys and not spies, you will go to Erili under escort.'

'Accept his terms' urged the second and more timid of the Khemites. 'The son of Set wishes to deem us spies, so he may use force to prevent our return to camp with our knowledge.'

They accepted, with no very good grace, and Kinyras bowed them affably to their table, where they sat to write the letter to their general. While they were so occupied Kinyras sent a runner to summon Zadoug and called to Hasvan to find a man who could read and understand Khemite. This man arrived just as the letter was completed. Kinyras advanced to his guests and held out his hand for their communication.

'What is this?' demanded the first, glaring in alarm.

'Merely that I wish this man, who reads your tongue, to translate to me what you have written, sir.'

With a convulsive gesture the man passionately tore up what he had written, finding the bow and smile with which

Kinyras received the action galling in the extreme. Another letter was written and dispatched and Kinyras brought wine and food with his own hands, showing himself an admirable, courteous and gracious host, while he pondered the matter of the destroyed letter, asking himself whether ample proof of treachery did not lie in it, sufficient to warrant the destruction of the envoys with a clear conscience. Almost he thought it did, but that could be decided upon later. If the envoys were detained ten days or so, there would be time to finish the stockade.

A number of most jovial and hard drinking captains were called, a banquet was prepared for which his best wines were brought forth and late that night the detested visitors were carried to bed, too drunk to know whether they were alive or dead. Zadoug arrived as they were being conveyed to their couches and with him Kinyras sat talking for the rest of the night. Just before dawn Zadoug set out on his mission to Erili.

'I will detain them here as long as may be, to give you as much time as can be squeezed from this emergency. Erili will know what to do. They have seen the defences and the staveros and know too much ever to be permitted to return.'

'Shall we set an ambush and fall upon them?'

Kinyras considered this possibility and rejected it. 'Not so. Who knows but these envoys, shut up in Karpasia, will lead us to Hange? Are they not bound to meet and to intrigue? Are these not the very men who already are trafficking with him?'

Zadoug slapped his thigh with a resounding smack. 'By the Gods, Kinyras, you've hit the mark!'

'I send no letters to Erili, they are dangerous. Tell him all I have told you, Zadoug; urge upon him the wisdom of being absent when these envoys arrive. And above all, tell him how much I crave council with him. I will send them out by the south coast road, leaving the northern track for Erili. Hasten, brother, every moment is precious now.'

# CHAPTER X

# "I LOVE YOU"

Zadoug rode away into the darkness and Kinyras lay down to snatch an hour or two of sleep. By sunrise he was up and out again inspecting the northern line of the defences, urging haste, haste, everywhere haste. The gaps in the stockade were slowly closing. More than ever were they now working against time. The problem of staking the ditch when it ran through rocky ground perpetually harassed him. There was no time to bore holes. At length he determined to cut great boughs from the trees, to sharpen each branch to a keen point and to lay them on the outer edge of the outer ditch, tied together, with points toward the enemy. When in place they looked like an array of antlers and were so effective that he had them planted along the length of the whole line.

The most dangerous place in his line he found to occur at the point where the stockade ended and the natural precipices began. They started in three rows, each perhaps ten feet high with a twenty-foot level between it and the next. These could be scaled in turn with short ladders and a man without armour could easily climb them in various places without a ladder. A stockade on the topmost cliff was necessary, but timber was short, time was shorter, and such wood as there was would be needed for the big stockade.

Kinyras surveyed the area meticulously, finding the cliff to be of solid rock with only a few inches of soil for top-dressing. There was nothing for it but a turf breast-work, to give some shelter from arrows. Upon the crest of the hill were many small trees, too small for the stockade but large enough, when sawn into logs and placed upon the turn breast-work two deep with a third on the top all along the wall, heightened it considerably. The long, narrow loop-hole thus provided was useless for bowmen, but admirable for their staveros, through which it could be fired with great effect, while the topmost log gave excellent head-cover.

Kinyras next sent for all available masons and set them to work chipping at the edge of the second cliff, the stones so derived were hauled aloft in baskets and piled in convenient heaps behind the parapet. Heavy stones dropped even from so small a height as ten feet would crush in heads and shields. The patient survey continued, while the blazing sun poured down pitilessly upon the unflagging organizer who, absorbed and faithful to his task, knew neither fatigue, hunger nor thirst.

Some four hundred paces further along the three small precipices merged into one and the cliff grew to a height of fifty feet, inaccessible for nine hundred paces. But here came another danger-spot in a small shoulder of the hill which rose up from the plain below. At its juncture with the cliff it was only forty paces wide, when the shoulder sloped steeply again, leaving the precipice to rise three hundred feet above the plain below. Examination showed that the layer of earth was fully ten feet deep. Kinyras called up a body of labourers and very quickly a ditch was cut, with a parapet, and men sent to search the hill for timber big enough to form a stockade. A guard of forty men was stationed here with instructions to build the stockade at all costs, then to build huts and to keep a constant watch upon the plain below.

From the hill there was a magnificent view over the luxuriant rolling country beyond. The enemy's camp lay beneath him and for some time he watched their movements keenly. Reinforcements were continually arriving, scouts were reconnoitring the line in all directions. This activity was ominous and Kinyras cursed it heartily, wishing more than ever that he could assassinate the envoys. Whey could he not, what was it inside himself which prevented him from doing this most necessary act? He pondered the question but was no nearer acquiescence to the deed than before.

The sound of a shrill, sweet piping drew his attention from this problem of when-was-killing-no-murder to the other slope of the hill, where he saw a number of shepherds, clad in rough goat-skins, tending their flocks. He went towards them and questioned them, asking whether there was any path up the face of the cliff from the plain below? At first they replied that there was not, but the youth who was piping, having finished his air, drew near and joining in the debate, admitted that he had climbed up the bed of a little stream which trickled down in wet weather, and offered to show Kinyras the place.

'Here it is, lord,' said he, pointing down the steep, rocky channel, where one slip would hurl a man two hundred feet below.

'There!' exclaimed Kinyras, peering over, 'impossible.'

'I was but a little lad, then, and heedless,' the shepherd boy answered, almost apologetically.

'A brave lad! Could you do it now, think you?'

The boy laughed. 'I might, but I'm no such fool as to try again.'

Kinyras sent the boy to fetch three men and sat himself down on the thymy sward to await their arrival. When they came he ordered them to keel a constant watch, turn and turn about, to build a hut there in the bushes. This point was some twelve hundred paces from the nearest post, the guard on the shoulder, and he ordered a long cord to be run, tied at inter-vals to whippy poles. By pulling this cord a bell was rung in the camp on the shoulder and the alarm given when needed. He also ordered a path to be made so that men might be moved quickly from post to post.

Satisfied and heartened by his morning's work, Kinyras re-turned home at midday to find his guests just stirring from their beds. He met them with a smiling affability and an air of so much confidence that their condition, which was pitiable enough from their tippling of the previous night, was augmented. Heavy-eyed they staggered forth, shuddering from the ample meal provided, of which their now cordial host ate heartily, striving to assuage their aching heads with fruits and more wine. After as much delay as possible, and they were in no hurry to be gone, he sent them off in litters to the charge of Hasvan, whose orders were to convey them to Karpasia by the south coast route and on no account to incommode the noble guests by any undignified haste. Grinning intelligently Hasvan saluted his lord and the *cortege* set out.

Dayonis now appeared, having remained hidden in her chamber until she could do so with safety.

'Did you recognise them?' he asked anxiously.

She shook her head, bubbling over with question and comment. He satisfied her curiosity and received her gracious approval, which made him smile and then, she being eager to ride again, he called for the asses and they set forth once more to the lines.

The earthworks were now all finished and much labour was therefore released. This meant that Kinyras could enter at last upon the fulfilment of his dream and begin to build in stone. He sent a runner to summon all the masons not engaged to meet him in a certain place, and forty paces behind the stockade he started marking out the lines for the new wall. So passed several days and still Erili did not come, though Zadoug returned with the news that Erili had set forth immediately upon his arrival in the capital and in answer to Kinyras' plea, was on his way to see him. Erili's journey was a secret one, said Zadoug, with one of his atrocious winks and further added that he must return to his section at once as the King was inspecting the whole of the line, starting with the most northern sector.

Much relieved, Kinyras returned to his masons, who were set to work chipping out the stones from the cliffs for the new wall. Dayonis and he were constantly together and her quick observation and essentially practical mind saw deficiencies and

made suggestions which were of real value to him. Their friendship and understanding of each other grew rabidly and he
found her charming, intelligent companion, one who would
enter into his schemes and his moods in a way which he had
never experienced with a woman before.

No longer did Kinyras contemplate her as anything but a
beloved mate whom he would defend with the utmost limit of
his strength and wit. The proposals of the envoys had shown
him this, to his own amazement, but Dayonis froze into regality
the very instant his ardent sentiments showed any tendency to
demand satisfaction, though it was true she did her best to
rouse them on any and every occasion which came her way.
She lured and denied almost in the same look and breath,
until Kinyras fumed and despaired alternately... a very pretty
and proper state for a lover to be in, so Dayonis thought.

Kinyras was getting stone in abundance from his chipping
out of the middle ledge, his object being to cut it entirely away,
thus heightening the lower part of the precipice. This building
of mighty stone walls, braced together with tree-trunks was a
hope he was never tired of discussing with Dayonis, but in order to be effective they must stretch the length of his line right
down to the Kastnon two leagues away. Though there was
much stone it was not suitable for his purpose, the only
durable stone able to resist all ramming and mining coming
from the neighbourhood of Hap Hill. His problem was conveyance, his only means of transport lying in teams of men
carrying the more portable material in baskets, the large blocks
dragged by oxen, both slow and difficult processes over rough
ground. A quicker means must be found if his plans were to
succeed and he must seek these means, the solution of his difficulties, in the way he had done before.

When the full moon cam he sat silent, eating his supper
quickly, his mind already concentrated upon the journey ahead
of him. Dayonis, sitting opposite, tried in vain to lure him into
their usual happy talk. He replied absently or not at all to her
merriest sallies and finally she, too, fell into a watchful silence,
puzzled by the strangeness of the man and not a little awed by

it. When at length he rose, hastily seized his cloak and strode out with nothing but a speechless salute, she was childishly vexed and frightened and sat there at the table, mechanically taking nuts from the bowl before her and cracking them with her strong, white teeth, heedless of what she did and sunk in a brooding conjecture. He was in love, he had gone to some pretty slave girl because she had held him at a distance. Fully that she was not to see this would happen, sooner or later.

After what seemed to be hours of sullen surmise she could endure her jealous doubts and fears no longer and rushed out to find him. Hasvan was sitting under a tree in the moonlight. The night was warm and filled with spicy odours and the slave was about to sleep in the pile of dried grasses he had carefully prepared. Dayonis, appearing suddenly before him in her white vesture and streaming hair, looking more than a little distraught, startled him, so that he sat staring dumbly.

'Your lord... where is he?' she demanded.

Hasvan struggled to his feet, reassured by the sound of her voice, with the very human edge to it. 'My lady, I know not. He passed me without speaking some two hours back.'

'Whither?' she demanded, with an impatient stamp.

'Toward the hill, yonder,' and he pointed.

Dayonis was too proud to follow to Hazvan's knowledge and returned to the house until he should be asleep. Later she crept forth again, saw him snoring soundly under his tree and sped away to hunt and surprise Kinyras, but when the brightness and the beauty of the night had soothed her jangled feelings, she recognised the hopelessness of her quest and sat down beneath a clump of cedars to contemplate her distress in a different and sorrowful spirit. Kinyras was lost to her, though her own caprice and folly, and now she knew how much she loved him. Fool that she had been, to reject so noble and de-voted a lover, and she pictured him in the arms of the slave, his head pillowed on her breast, sleeping.

This picture in her mind was unendurable and she sprang up again, to wander on disconsolate, heeding nothing but her woe, stumbling over the roots of the great trees until she was clear of them and stood on the little plateau of soft, thick turf which jutted out of the hillside over the valley below. For long she stood there, watching the camp fires of the distant enemy, steeped in a wretchedness which could find no relief from any external distraction, even that of her own problematical future. Gradually her eyes left the valley and became attuned to nearer vision, and then she saw a man lying flat on his back at the edge of the plateau.

She stole nearer and saw that it was Kinyras. Her lover, stretched prone beneath the moon and lying uncannily still, not lapped in sleep in the arms of some lovely slave. Reaction swept over her, such a paean of joyful relief swelled in her heart that she stood transfixed, gazing, her mind capable of appreciating only the one, tremendous fact of his innocence. But, when the first ache of rapture had passed off, something in his utter inertness gripped her with an icy chill and she fell on her knees beside him to lay her hand softly on his shoulder. He did not move. She called his name, shaking him gently. He was like a dead thing.

As swiftly as certainty of his falseness had seized her, so ws she now convinced of his death. She cried, she implored, but still he lay stark and at last she flung herself down beside him in a very tempest of despair and wept convulsively. When her weeping was spent and she lay prone, exhausted and as inert as he from the violence of her first grief, he startled her almost to death itself by beating with his hands upon the turf beside him at first gently and them with increasing energy, drawing deep breaths the while.

She started in amazement, too bewildered to move, paralyzed with another revulsion of feeling, which was stronger than any that had gone before. Presently he sat up and then she hurled herself into his arms with a shriek of joy. 'Kinyras, my lord, my love! I thought you dead, oh, I feared you were dead.'

His arms closed about her and he strained her to him, while she sobbed convulsively. 'Dayonis, how came you here? What ails you, my sweet?'

But she was incoherent and could do nothing but exclaim between her passionate kisses, her arms about his neck, clasping him in a frantic rapture of relief and love. Presently she grew calm enough to tell him all she had suffered since he left the house.

'They you do love me? You will be my wife, my beloved?'

'Yes, a thousand times, yes, Kinyras. I will love you to the end of my days, I'll follow you and fight beside you until I drop dead.'

'Oh, my adored princess, i did not think such rapture could exist for me.'

'Nor I,' she whispered, lying in is arms with closed eyes and parted lips, faint with happiness.

When they had grown a little calmer and the moon had climbed considerably higher, Dayonis spoke again of her terror when she found him lying to all appearances dead, and her fears re-awakened. 'You looked like Death himself. Are you sick, Kinyras? Have you some cruel disease which makes you so? And was that the reason for your silent humour at supper?'

He laughed and clasped her closer. 'My sweet, put away your fears for me. Nothing ails me. I am well and hearty, as you can see.'

'You look so, but my dear lord, what mystery is this, if it is not sickness?'

He hesitated for a moment or two but at last yielded to her pleading importunities, though speaking purposely in vague terms. 'I was... out... walking with my Gods.'

She grew taut in his arms, involuntarily shrinking a little from some strangeness which she knew instinctively to be genuine, and nothing like the hokus-pokus with which she was familiar.

'I needed help for my wall and I went to seek it... so,' he went on, marking her unusual silence.

'And did you find it?' she asked, in a low tone, striving to hide her fear.

'Yes, Dayonis. In that other life I was making a great fortification, much greater and stronger than any known to us and I saw the great stones being moved from place to place in a long line of wagons, joined together and running on... rails. Yes, that is the word! Made of some unknown metal. That is what I need to cart my stone quickly, but we have not enough bronze for the purpose.'

'Dreams are sent by the gods,' she answered, still in a doubtful and troubled way, knowing in her soul that these were no dreams. He might go 'out' in such a way and never come back to her again. And once more she relieved those comments of horror and panic when she had found him lying there so still and irretrievable. She wrenched her mind away from the exigencies of the moment. 'Bronze is hard to come by, lord. If the gods would only send a storm to tear down some of the wood out yonder...'

'Wood!' shouted Kinyras, joyously. 'Beloved, you have said the very word. The Gods inspire me through you, Dayonis. If the wagons can be made to run on logs without slipping off, we have found security indeed... logs, with shallow grooves cut in them and butted together. The ground slopes all the way down to the sea and we shall get over the distance with a greater weight in half the time.'

She caught fire from his enthusiasm and they talked until they slept, lying in each other's arms until dawn wakened then and they returned home. That morning Kinyras had a number or carpenters assembled, cutting logs, fitting them together and grooving them, and the second day blocks of stone were being drawn in ox-carts with ease in through the gate and stored ready for the builders, in half the time which had taken a double team of oxen previously. The foundation stones of the wall were laid with great ceremony by the Karpasian priests on the same day. Everyone living in the neighbourhood was in attendance and a public holiday proclaimed.

The stockade was finished everywhere and Kinyras heartily agreed that all workers deserved a holiday. Everyone living must attend the ceremony of propitiation of the Gods. All oxen, asses, sheep, goats, dogs and cats were driven up, large baskets containing fowls and pet birds in cages were brought.

The assemblage was indescribable.

A great hush fell upon the people as the ceremony began and the only sounds came from the beasts and the birds, chiefly from crowing cocks and agitated hens. The scene was the great foundation-stone of the wall. Beside it the altar had been set up and adjacent to it blazed a mighty fire. Three Khemite prisoners, three Karpasian criminals, three white sheep, three white goats, stood near in a forlorn group. These were the sacrifices, the men in an apathy of resignation to the inevitable, the animals sensitive of doom and trembling with apprehension. The priest officiating approached and drove the captives three times round the altar then pierced them with the Palos, the sacred spear which represented the divinity of the Gods. Their blood was caught in a vessel and poured upon the altar, while the priests chanted prayers in their secret tongue and the slaughter continued with the animals. This accomplished, fruits of the earth were cast into the fire, grapes, corn, incense, wine, oil and honey, together with the bodies of the victims and more fuel. Many prayers followed and at length the solemn rights were ended and the people free too merry-make.

No more work must be done until the great fire had burnt itself out and the Gods had accepted the sacrifice and would lend their aid by making the victims the guardians of the wall. The future duty of their spirits was to see that it did not fall. Dayonis was an interested and approving spectator of these rites and though she followed them with immense solemnity and outward show of devotion, Kinyras noticed that the priests engaged viewed her with coldness and suspicion. Kinyras, by nature a sceptic, behaved with accommodating gravity and respect before the people, but when he and the princess were wandering apart in lover's converse, he asked her curiously—'Do you indeed believe that these same Khemite ghosts will defend the enemy's wall against their own countrymen?'

Now this question was in the nature of a poser, an answer to which did not immediately occur to her naturally practical and sensible mind, so she hedged, not without a note of asperity which made Kinyras smile internally. 'My lord is excessively impious and it is well neither the people nor the priests hear him.'

He encircled her waist with his arm and drew her to his side. 'My lordship speaks in confidence to his dearly beloved heart, knowing he can open his mind freely to her.'

She smiled up at him, her eyes softened and deep with feeling. 'And rightly so, my dearest. In their secret tongue the priests have told the Earth Gods that a wall is to be built in their territory and that they would receive certain presents of sacrificed animals, if they would have the foundations in their keeping.'

'Telling them if they do not wish to accept and will have none of us and our schemes, they will show their will by ejecting the stone from its hole before the fire dies down?'

Dayonis gravely inclined her head, not at all relishing the light tone in which these mysteries were spoken of by her companion. She had an uneasy sense that the Gods were listening, even though they had sent her for deliverance to this man, and she glanced round apprehensively. 'even so, lord,' she said.

'We must in fact, buy the ground rights from them?'

'How strangely and unwisely you speak, Kinyras. Shall we question the doings of the High Gods themselves?'

'No, my sweet. Have no fear, I have no impiety but only curiosity. It is the Khemite sacrifice that perplexes me.'

'Such ghosts have not human wishes, they know only duty. It is an honour to these men's spirits to safeguard the wall 'gainst all comers, even their own countrymen and it is a disgrace to the enemy to try to destroy a wall when the ghosts of their own men are guarding it.'

'And will it stay them, think you, Dayonis?' he asked, with suitable solemnity.

But she burst out into a merry laugh, triumphing in her own superior cleverness to the priests of Karpas, for whom she had no love. 'Have done with plaguing me, Kinyras. To make terms with the Earth Gods as well, but Jaske the God of the Earthquake they have forgotten, and he can do more destruction than all the rest put together. Obtain me a prisoner or two, lord, and I'll put matters right with him to-night. He's no proud god, demanding attendance of a whole population, but asks only sincerity and truth from those concerned. Some of those great, strong Nubians are the very thing to please him best.'

'Aye!' he acquiesced, pleased with the chatter of her lilting voice and not much heeding her words, being occupied with other secret matters.

'There's a valley leading up to Aghirda, east of the Giant's Hand, a very good way to get up to the hills from the north,. He split one of his mountains there, a curious crack, one can step across at most points, yet the mountain is cleft in two to the depth of a mile or more and smoke issues forth. 3 If a suitable sacrifice is made and thrown down with rocks kept ready for the purpose, the God will send forth fire and stones and choking smoke for days afterwards, keeping away all invaders.'

Kinyras made noises of attention as she paused with a bright glance at him and she continued blithely—'In my great-great-grandfather's time an enemy came upon us suddenly from the sea. There was no time to make sacrifice, but my ancestor made Jaske the promise of one, throwing in the stones, Jaske worked excellently well and the sacrifice was paid in due course. It never pays to cheat the gods. He has a strange temple. It lies deep down in the great crack that he made. You must turn your palms to the earth when you worship him, Kinyras. He likes you to wear a cloth steeped in wine over your mouth and nose, so that you may breathe through it when you go down to worship him in his own caves. Sometimes he gets angry and if then you are not so covered you fall asleep and die. If you are not quickly carried out.'

'Do many worship?' asked he, a little ironically.

'I will tell you a secret of my family, if you will vow never to disclose it.'

'I swear, by the swordsman's oath.'

'In my father's father's father's time, if there were any whose power was becoming too great, he would take such down to pray in the secret Temple. Very loosely woven cloth would be given them, barely damped. The honour was much desired and they would go without question. My sire would bid them kneel to pray whilst he stood performing the rites. When they slept he would leave them so for a time before he had them carried out, knowing just how long to leave them there. Though he would revive them with cold water and strong wines and though they recovered a semblance of their good health, yet would they die within a few days. So would I serve Pharaoh and all his men, if I might. To-night I will build a little altar in the cave in the side of the hill and sacrifice three Nubians, three black goats and three black cats. These Karpasians have called upon their God, the man-bull, the god of the land's surface, but Jaske is the god of the underground and will hold the wall strong for us.'

'Nay, there has been enough of bloodshed, Dayonis. The good gods will guard the wall with our wits and strength and courage, and for these I thank the High Gods and will always serve them.'

He finished with a gesture like a salute and she, awed but sullen, fell into a silence from which he must woo her with diverse coaxings and pettings. These she enjoyed so much that she would not too soon relax her sulkiness.

The bonfire died down in due course without the foundation-stone being spewed forth from the earth, and the building went on merrily. Wagons rumbled down the log road, dumping their loads of cut stone all along the line and returned by another route. A certain amount of stone had been taken up when cutting the ditch, much was available and building could start on the line's entire length. Though the best stone for facing came from the quarry, as the foundations were laid, more and more good building stone was uncovered and, as this was always quarried on the outer wise of the wall, so was a trench, or moat, cut at the same time and work progressed at a pace. Everyone was pleased with the scheme and worked at the peak of enthusiasm, knowing that in the wall they had at last found security against mining, battering-rams and crows of the type of ram with the spear point, that picks and dislodges stones instead of crushing them. Big frameworks of squared logs bolted together were built into the wall for additional strength.

All was going well when one morning some ten days later, Kinyras and Dayonis were wakened by a blare of trumpets. He rose hastily and Hasvan entered with the tidings that King Erili had arrived.

3 At Helefka.

# CHAPTER XI

# THE KING'S WILL

inyras hastened to the chamber of Dayonis, where her woman was already busy preparing for the toilet. With a gesture he dismissed her, then stooped over the couch and took the yawning girl in his arms. 'Sweet, Erili has come and you must make yourself your lovely best. Keep your chamber until I send Hasvan to you. Our fate indeed lies in the balance and I have much difficult work before me. Aid me, Dayonis, with all your woman's wiles. First we eat and then I take him to inspect the lines. Have an excellent feast prepared by our return and be ready to enslave him as you have captured me.'

She laughed, clasped him about the neck with her bare arms, kissed him and sent him forth with good promises.

Kinyras, with several officers in attendance hastily summoned, met the King as he approached the precincts of his house. His greeting ws the essence of good humour and cordiality and the commander's spirits rose in consequence. They embraced and, dismissing his suite, Erili took Kinyras familiarly by the arm and they turned to enter the house together. 'Feed me, old Snail, for I'm famished and have a thirst which a Khemite would envy. Well, how goes it, comrade and brother?'

'Nothing could be better, sir, and your long-desired presence puts the key-stone to my gratification.'

Erili made an elaborate gesture. 'Away with ceremony, man. Let's eat and drink and talk like old brothers-in-arms.'

Hasvan had spread a hurried but adequate meal and the two men seated themselves at table, while the slave filled their cups of his master's best vintage. The King drank long and thirstily, though first he poured an oblation, then set his cup down with a bang and smacked his lips freely. 'It does a man good to relax, Kinyras. I find these cursed Karpasians, with their tricks and manners, like a halter round my neck at times. I'm a soldier and the camp suits me best.'

At a blink from his master Hasvan put the food ready and retired, leaving the men to serve themselves.

'Ah, that's better,' Erili sighed, watching the slave depart with a nod and a smile. 'Good fellow, Hasvan, and trustworthy.'

'To the death, Erili.'

'Tell me your news.'

'Tell me first, have you seen the envoys?'

Erili looked up from his dish and paused in his enjoyment of the fare provided, to shake his head reproachfully. 'Would you turn my food sour on my long-suffering stomach? They can keep, like ill tidings.'

'But you've seen them?'

'Not until two days ago, when I returned to Karpas after a prolonged survey of the line... and a little hunting. But more of them, later.'

Kinyras gave him an exhaustive account of all that had happened since last they met, while Erili listened with great attention, eating very rapidly and hungrily the while. Later the two went to the wall, their only attendant a little slave-boy to run and carry messages, if necessary.

'Your stockade is finished,' exclaimed Erili, in great satisfaction and no little surprise. 'Excellent! Truly, you can make men work and work willingly, old friend. That's a great gift. Now you're building in stone... on a new plan. You're full of strange gadgets, though I have little faith in them. They tell great things of your staveros. I just see it later.'

'You shall see a match shot this evening, if it please you.'

'It does, indeed, and I will give my brooch to the winner.'

Kinyras, much pleased, called up the boy and set him with a message to his lieutenant, bidding him prepare the match.

They walked further on, Erili's keen eyes missing nothing as he criticized and commented on all he saw. The boy returned, breathless from his errand, and fell to heel again, on his best behaviour, grinning with delight every now and then at the honour conferred upon him between periods of portentous solemnity.

'New thoughts, new ways, they have their uses, though the old and the familiar please me best, I confess. How are these walls of yours to be built? Have you plans I can see?'

'Come back to my house and I will explain in full.'

Erili assented and they returned. Seated at the largest table with the plans laid before them, Kinyras showed his scheme to build the wall in sections, having it twelve feet high and three feet thick, with a twenty-four-foot tower rising at every two hundred feet of length. The back of the surface was purposely left rough, so that later, as more stone became available, an addition could be built on of the same dimension, duplicating it in depth, height and strength. By this means there was little limit to the wall's capacity of strength. Its position would be forty feet behind the stockade, so that bowmen manning it would help in defence of the stockade.

When this wall had risen to thirty-six feet in height it would be pierced with loop-holes. In time he designed to add chambers at the back, so that the garrison could actually live in the wall they were defending and maintain a hotter fire through loop-hole and from the parapet. Temporarily, a wooden parapet would crown the wall, adding another five feet to its height, from which stones and other missiles could be dropped on the heads of the enemy which had reached the foot, without the defenders exposing themselves.

Erili was much impressed by this meeting of the difficulty of a weak point. He had taken many cities by rushing the walls under a heavy arrow fire, by means of scaling-ladders, and by constructing small pent-houses against eh wall in which were men vigorously picking away the stones, while the defenders above were too occupied in beating off the enemy to notice these tactics. The shelters, once in position, could be attacked only by the besieged exposing themselves on the merciless fire from below by leaning perilously over the parapet. But the parapet which Kinyras had designed was built out from the wall on beams, between which the rain of stones down upon the enemy below would be most disastrous.

'They look good,' Erili said, leaning back from his chair and taking a deep draught from the wine cup beside him. 'Here is to their success. If we had a year's peace you could finish them.'

'The enemy have been repulsed at all points even with the poor means of defence at our disposal,' Kinyras reminded him quietly.

'True, brother, but what avail your efforts and mine, if Hange strikes us in the back, as he will if he can?'

Before Kinyras could reply Hasvan entered to prepare the meal and all opportunity for private talk was in abeyance. Besides, Erili loved his food and such tidings as he bore could very well keep. They would look better on a full belly. At a whispered word from his master, Hasvan stepped to the door of the adjoining chamber and a few moments later Dayonis entered. Erili scrambled to his feet, surprised and perturbed, making a soldier's salute as his host presented him to the Princess.

Dayonis and her woman had spent the hours of the morning in devising the most devastating toilet they could jointly imagine, and the result was shattering upon both men, as Dayonis was acutely aware when she bowed to Erili and extended to him a white hand whose fingertips were delicately tinted with a concoction from the root poederos. The dazzling fairness of her skin and the ripe redness of her mouth were emphasized by a judicious application of Egyptian khol to her brows and lashes.

Her garment was simplicity itself, whose cut and

arrangement was so skilful that its beautiful lines and folds revealed and enhanced her figure. It was a miracle of cunning and dyed in a rich shade of blue, so that the hue of her eyes was accentuated. Her hair, which had received hours of attention, shone like a ripe chestnut, and fell in bunches of glossy curls about her white neck, confined by the straphos of gold and silver and green ribbons, tying the hair in place. She had bathed and rubbed her body with unguents, so that a subtle perfume of mingled roses and violets clung about her and wafted out with every movement. Upon her wrists and ankles were bracelets of beaten and worked gold, which made a soft tintinnabulation as she moved. Her feet were bare and artificially whitened with white led, which she had refrained from putting on her face with an admirable restraint. Her toes were coloured with the poederos and steeped in Egyptian unguents and her bare arms were laved in an extract of sweet mint.

Such was Dayonis when she appeared before the two men, outwardly very calm and regal, inwardly bubbling over with delight at her beautiful new woollen dress, so cunningly girdled with plaited ribbons of gold, silver and green to match her straphos. Never before in her life had she been barbed like this and she paid just tribute to the cleverness and excellent taste of her woman. Here was no peasant princess of a barbarian race, thought Erili, but a highly cultivated lady, fit bride for Pharaoh himself.

Sedately she walked to a little table, upon which lay two wreaths of varied flowers and iwth them she solemnly crowned the men, then seated herself at the table, with a gracious air invited them to their chairs. She enjoyed with hidden delight the sensation she had created and which, for a moment seemed to have robbed their tongues of action and doubled the activity of their eyes. They drank and she pledged Erili with the sign of the brotherhood.

'You have made the Princess free of the brotherhood, Kinyras?' Erili observed, and his eyes, tearing themselves away from his hostess for a second, questioned of his comrade, 'Was that wise?'

'She earned it in battle, where she saved my life. So had she served her apprenticeship and been tested.'

Erili bowed to her in acknowledgement. "Tis not easy for a man to think of such grace and beauty in the bloody business of fighting. Yet they say that your country-women are great warriors. Is this true, Princess, or merely a traveller's tale?'

She laughed her happy, seductive chuckle and at the flash of her lovely teeth through the ripeness of her full, parted lips, Erili's eyes blinked involuntarily.

'They say many things. They say I am a witch!' she retorted gaily.

'I'll dare swear you are; could wile a bird off a bough. Poor old Slow-but-Sure is a lost man. I receive that clearly.'

'And who is he?' demanded Dayonis, ogling for all she was worth.

'Our friend here, the Golden Snail, the Dreamer of Dreams.'

She drew a long breath, and her eyes glowed. 'So that is what they name you, Kinyras? I am glad to fight beneath such a banner.'

'Then you look like a goddess and fight light a man?'

'Aye, and more,' cut in Kinyras, enthusiastic. 'You shall see my lady shoot at the butts. Will you shoot for the King's brooch this evening, Dayonis?'

'Aye, that I will, and carry it off, too, sir. So look to it,' she cried merrily.

And that evening, clad in her short green tunic which barely reached her thighs, her red curls tied up in a green napkin, her white limbs flashing in the level beams of the declining sun, she kept her word and bore away the prize. Erili was fascinated by this slip of a wench and the more he looked at his mission, as yet undiscovered to Kinyras, the less he liked its appearance and savour. He tried to divert his attention by that other fascinating toy, the staveros, which performed wonders before his incredulous and admiring view, so that he must, perforce, be converted from his scepticism.

After the shooting match they returned to the house and Dayonis retired to her chamber, leaving the two men to discuss affairs of state. Her woman brought her supper of dried fruits and nuts, with wine, and Dayonis dismissed her for the night. She then dragged her couch in such a position that she could see and hear plainly all that went on in the adjoining room through an artfully disposed fold in the leather hanging which covered her doorway. It was a hot night, she stripped herself and lay bare upon the soft furs of her couch, munching, drinking and listening intently, her thoughts sombrous, her heart heavy with apprehension. Was she to be cast out to Pharaoh, to spend her life in the dangerous glitter of the Khemite court for a few years, then, when youth was gone, to be sold as a slave to the highest bidder? Was that her fate?

Must the advancing years be nothing but a dread and a scourge, while she decreased in value like an old garment? It was a bitter thought and she turned it about and about in a luxury of depression, savouring all its acrimony. Would Kinyras stand firm, remain faithful to her? Could she expect it? Fantastic notion! All her native savagery of independence urged her to fly, stark, with nothing but a bow for her defence, and the strength of her will alone restrained her. Even the restriction of clothes was irksome to her humour of fretting impotence and she had cast them impatiently from her.

Kinyras, too, was heavy with apprehension. The mere fact that Erili shirked coming to the point of his mission boded ill. The two men ate in a tense silence which was pierced with spasms of comment upon trifles, until Hasvan retired. Kinyras then filled his guest's cup with his best wine and charged—
'These envoys, sir, what of them?'

Erili sighed, looked reproachfully into his host's questioning eyes and braced himself to the unpleasantness before him. 'They're well enough... drunk night and day for the most part. They acknowledge they enjoy themselves to the full.'

Kinyras shrugged disdainfully. 'I saw some such. In Khem they feast much, with slaves carrying litters to bear their masters home when drunk, so I've heard tell.'

'Aye. Then priests arrive bringing mummies with them, urging the revellers to contemplate them and the time when they, too, will descend to the shades. This takes the edge from thirst, doubtless,' he laughed, and quaffed deep of his own cup. ''Tis said Pharaoh despises drunkards whom he sends up-river to the land of Punt, which, by all accounts is far worse than Hades.'

Kinyras spat contemptuously, all his hatred of Khem surging within him. 'In many ways a despicable people,' he scoffed, 'priest-ridden and spied upon, paying blackmail to the priest-hood to free themselves from spying and being reported to Pharaoh for drinking to excess. A pretty land, upon my word!'

Erili nodded and laughed sardonically. 'Well, I've plied them well with all the drink and pretty women they can stomach and they're in no hurry to depart. They are happy and send despatches to their general, which I have had heavily censored. My man Yakub is a Hebri, who loves not Khem, but who can read and write fluently in their tongue. He was a scribe in the Temple of Ammon and a clever fellow into the bargain, but one day went fowling with the throwing sticks... curved affairs which return to the hand when thrown in the right way. He killed a cat. They worship them.'

Kinyras whistled. 'And he fled?'

'By the gods, yes! He has even with me for years and seems devoted. When the despatches were submitted to him he saw they were written with a certain stiffness, words being used which had little relation with the body of the message.'

Kinyras scowled comprehensively. 'Secret writing?'

'You have heard of it? Yes, every seventy word put together made a secret message, telling of the weak places in the wall, and other matters too.'

'May the gods blast them!'

'What else would you have? Yakub changed those secret words, reporting that the walls were of immense strength and to refrain from attack at all costs until their numbers were greater.'

''Twas well done, sir, but what was the other matter of the

message?'

Erili glanced round cautiously and bent across the table, lowering his voice, so that it was only just distinguishable to the listening ears of the girl beyond. 'It spoke of the man named "the Servant of Pharaoh", who was to continue stirring up the people against "the wicked ones"... us, as I view it, and Hange.'

Kinyras bit his lip and after a brooding pause, asked anxiously. 'What said Yakub to that at your direction?'

'Bid Pharaoh not to be too trusting as the Servant appeared to be running with hare and coursing with hound.'

'Good. Now what of Hange?'

'He is swaying the Council against us and you in particular. Word has got through to Karpasia of you and this girl, Dayonis, and the long and the short of it is that she is to be returned to Khem. Hange has inflamed the populace, urging that she is a stranger and has no claim upon Karpas for protection, that many good Karpasian captives will be given up in exchange for her and that she is the sole cause of the Khemite invasion. Everywhere, at his instigation, the people go about shouting, "Must we suffer the terrors of war for one who has already enslaved four thousand of our people?"'

Kinyras pished impatiently and scuffed his feet in an impotence of irritation. 'Lies and rubbish!'

'Doubtless, but the mob will believe a lie like this at the bidding of their leaders and their own secret wishes.'

Kinyras brooded, silent.

'You know Hange. He hates us and no trick, no lie is too foul for him to stoop to, that will work us harm. I know he's in league with Khem, that he's "The Servant", but how to prove it? He has long been searching for a weapon against us and now he has found it in Dayonis. Moreover, he has told the mob that now we have built such strong lines Karpas has no further use for us, and can defend itself if necessary, and if this girl is given up the necessity will go with her. Even our own men are against her and distrust her, saying she has bewitched you. She must be given up.'

Kinyras struck the table with a furious hand. 'I refuse

utterly. I have given my word that she shall be protected. She is
my guest. I will never betray my sword-comrade.'

Erili smiled slyly to himself. 'She is very beautiful comrade,
brother. Can this be the soured old Kinyras I've fought and
caroused with for the past twenty years? She has indeed worked
a miracle in you, but such toys have no weight in assemblies.
Will you behave like a love-smitten boy? The Gods sends us
wonders, but this beats all! I'll send you a dozen of the loveliest
maidens in exchange for this one.'

'No!' thundered Kinyras, flushing a deep purple with
hatred of Hange and love for Dayonis.

Eerily dropped his bantering tone to one of a deep seriousness. 'Kinyras, be reasonable, I beg for the sake of old times.
We must stand together. Hange will stir up the people to
mutiny against us and we cannot hold the wall against Khem
without and rebellion within.'

'Do you command me, sir?'

Erili placed his hand affectionately in a rough way on his
companion's arm. 'That question does not arise. We are comrades in arms, brother. I do but bid you remember all that lies
at stake.'

'You are King,' Kinyras reminded him, sternly.

'Ah, sure! But only in name, friend, only by sufferance.
Had I been ten years at the task all would be different, i would
act for you and to good purpose.'

'Thanks, brother,' said Kinyras, much softened. 'I take the
will for the deed.'

'But now, to save all our throats if not your own, you must
give her up.'

'Never!' declared Kinyras, through set teeth, grimly. 'To do
so is to dishonour the brotherhood.'

'Be sensible,' the other urged, flushing a little at this last
thrust. 'Give her up, finish these walls, then take your men and
raid the cities until you have her back again. I'll give you men
and leave, on the word of a brother and sword-comrade. If you
retain her, the Karpasians will turn against us, slay as many of
us as they can and drive the rest of us forth. The Princess will

be left defenceless and sold into slavery. What then?'

'If I raided all the cities in Orphusa, could I find her?' demanded Kinyras, in impassioned misery. 'She will be sent to Khem and can I, with my few men do aught against the might of Khem? No, we can die together if the god's will. I have served under you for twenty hard years. I owe my life to you, would give my life for yours gladly. I will do everything else for you but this.'

Erili, much moved, sat staring moodily before him. Kinyras saw that his face was lined with care and that he looked much older than when he had spoken with such stern fire in the Council only a few months ago. Obviously he was searching for a way out of his tangle. At length he spoke. 'What alternative is there?'

'Let me take my ships and go away with a few men.'

'And leave the wall, all your hopes, your schemes for security? Take time to think, Kinyras. I can hold them for some days. You think this wench loves you? Well, who should know better than you by now what a woman's love is worth, weighed in the balance against his fidelity to his brothers and the State? You've had experience.' Kinyras shuddered and Erili observed him. 'This is a vital matter. You think she loves you? Well, let us try a little subtlety instead of this impassioned and bull-headed resistance. Supposing we send her to Hange. You know him. If he thinks she is yours... and he knows she is so... he will instantly want her for himself. His constant boast is that when he sees a woman loyal to her mate he never rests until he has made her disloyal. Upon him then will rest the onus of the decision, whether to surrender to Khem or to retain her as his own probably possession. He will stop at nothing to attain his own ends. While he is making excuses to Karpas for retaining her, and also to Khem, we shall have time to build the wall. Let us make Hange fight for us, work to attain our ends, instead of fighting him with opposition and so act as tools in his hands.'

Dayonis, hearing this, was roused from her black brooding, to a secret titter of delight at the project. It so fitted in with the tune of her own mind. She saw herself luring this hated enemy with every wile known to her, yet holding him off until he was crazed with desire for her. But would Kinyras yield to this most reasonable and subtle of schemes? She listened, breathless for his reply, straining forward on her elbows, her face alert and eager, her eyes green as the panther's whose form her own lithe body resembled. The ominous silence of her lover gave little promise of ascent.

'If the wench truly loves you, Kinyras, she'll be staunch, stand the test, work for us with all her clever wits, all her ravishing beauty. If she does not love you, what do you lose?' Erili continued, in silky persuasion.

Kinyras was in torment. He knew that what Erili proposed was a wise and suble measure and one which should appeal to him. Yet his whole body, soul and mind was strangely and inexpressibly revolted at the suggestion. To expose the woman he adored to so much peril was unthinkable. Why should he feel like this about a woman, no matter who she be? He could not explain himself to himself, to say little of making his companion understand. 'Dayonis is my wife, Erili. I would sooner have my limbs hacked from my trunk than willingly harm a hair of her head. We have mingled our blood.'

'She will be faithful, I'll wager my head on't, and work miracles for us into the bargain. At the slightest whisper of danger to her, you shall march to her rescue, I swear by the brotherhood.'

'That is the one thing you should not ask me. She is of the brotherhood herself. She should be under your protection.'

At this Erili looked a little askance. 'She has not taken the great rite,' he objected.

'She has fought naked at my side and has mingled her blood with mine. That makes her one of us.'

'She has sworn no oath to me as leader. If she had I would order her to go upon this dangerous mission, and she must needs obey me. I wish to find a way out of this coil and must think of the good of the whole army. "It is expedient that one should die for the good of the whole army",' quoted Erili, impressively.

'I cannot give her up,' Kinyras repeated, his voice sounding dull with obstinacy, his face grey with stress and misery.

Hearing him, Dayonis shrugged, yet glowed. To be so worshipped was a miracle from the blessed Gods themselves, and was a greater thrill even than the prospect of encountering and defeating the hated Hange. She was a woman first and a schemer second, and all the woman in her took fire and ached in response to her mate's indomitable pride and delight in her. They had promised her a defender whom she would love, but who would not love her, yet here was her own devotion to the man returned to her with an equal measure. During the silence which followed, in which Kinyras worked his thoughts at a tremendous rate, she lay, lulled in a sweet trance of blissful desire.

The voice of her beloved roused her. 'Erili, I too, have a plan, which I beg of you to consider well. It is that you make my brother Zadoug commander-in-chief of the forces and of the line in my place. You know his metal and he knows my projects, my schemes for building and defence, backwards and forwards, in and out. In this matter he is my other half.'

'That could well be done. Proceed, old Snail.'

'Give me leave to take my ships and Dayonis, to go raiding the enemy's coasts. By such means can they be diverted from attacking the line. Proclaim that I have revolted against your authority, that I fear the enemy's might and have deserted before they can attack me, have fled away by sea.'

'There is something in that,' the other conceded. 'Say on.'

'Time is on our side. In a week or two Dayonis will be forgotten and the truce is a godsend to us. Keep the envoys amorous and drunk, until they die of a surfeit, or some jealous lover ends them with a knife. Every day that passes our strength grows, in defence and preparation.'

Again Erili nodded, thinking deeply.

'But if the envoys are permitted to return, they betray our true weakness and the secret of the staveros, which by the greatest ill-chance they have seen at very close quarters. From their description the weapon can be made by craftsmen of Khem and so our greatest advantage is lost. What will Khem then care for truce or treaty? Amasis will *promise* anything because he is a frightened man, suspected, nay accused of conniving at the escape of Dayonis. If he fails to recapture her there is no need to speculate upon his fate, and while it is approaching him more time is gained for us. Then again, if we give her up Khem will soon raise an Aghirdian army through her and bring it against us.'

'And if we do not give her up we shall have the whole Karpasian army to fight in addition to Khem,' Erili grunted.

At that moment, Hasvan, who was on guard at the outer door, entered.

'Well, what is it now?' burst from Erili, impatiently.

'Majesty, one Yakub craves audience.'

'Bid him come, Hasvan, and hasten.'

The slave withdrew and almost on the instant a Jew, a lank, dark man with long curling ringlets, a beak of a nose and a small, twinkling, intelligent black eyes came in with a curious mixture of cringing and self-importance. The beholder felt that one of these two bearings would immediately dominate him once the humour of his lord was assured.

'You're here, Yakub?' exclaimed Erili in a maliciously impersonal manner, purposely keeping the man in doubt and watching him shrewdly.

Yakub ran forward and knelt, bending his head, but fixing the King with his piercing little eyes. 'The envoys have sent another letter, Majesty. In the secret writing it says that The Servant of Pharaoh will have fires lighted along the coast as arranged from the first moonless night. Where the fires end, that is the place.'

'Is that all?'

'Yes, lord.'

'You have done well, Yakub. Withdraw now until I summon you.'

When they were alone again Erili, who had been pondering the message with little profit, turned to Kinyras. 'You're a ship-man, what meaning do you read in it? Shall it go through?'

'If no secret messages go through the enemy will grow suspicious. This dispatch should go unaltered.'

'But its content, man!'

'This clearly indicates an attack by sea, perhaps a landing of large forces for rear assault, which would prove ugly for us.'

'It might mean a fleet, or one ship bearing a message, or to aid the escape of the envoys,' suggested Erili, hopefully.

'That, also. It's an old trick of theirs to kindle fires on dark nights to indicate a safe anchorage, the ships following the line of the blazes to the end, where lies their objective.'

Erili burst into a short, discomforted laugh. 'This looks as though we must perforce adopt your plan. The gods fight for you, Kinyras, and what you wish you obtain. We must watch, but also we must have ships at sea to catch them. Well, you go, Old Snail, but what of the girl? She comes with me?'

'Not so. She comes with me, Erili. She speaks Khemite and I must have an interpreter.'

'But if the girl is gone I have no excuse to hold the envoys. They will betray our weakness. The truce is too valuable to throw away lightly. Every day we grow stronger while it lasts.'

'Aye and there's the matter of the staveros, too. Not one has been captured by the enemy.'

'A prideful thing to boast, Kinyras. So the girl goes with me.'

'Nay, that she does not!' cried a vibrant voice behind them.

They swung round from their wild wrangling in astonishment, to find Dayonis. Unable to endure their interminable argument longer, she had sprung from her couch, snatched a cloak and leapt into the fray. She was laughing with joy, her eyes dancing with excitement, her milky shoulders gleaming from above the green garment, perhaps intentionally.

She moved to her lover's side. 'Majesty, the way is easy. My lord Kinyras has rebelled and defies the authority of all. He has flown to his ships, setting a seal and a guard upon his house until his return. You send relays of messengers, some of the highest in the land from Karpasia, but they cannot effect an entry and you detain the envoys until my lord's return. Delay,

delay is all we need. The envoys will stay so long as they think I am here behind the lines.'

'Oh! Oh! Oh!' grumbled Erili, secretly pleased as Dayonis very well know. 'What chance has a man against a red-headed woman? I'm defeated all along my line.'

'Then that is agreed upon?' cried Kinyras.

'What choice have I against you two? I'll order you to return to Vanner Hill, deprive you of your command and install Zadoug. As soon as I have gone, come back, put guards upon your house, muffle yon red-head in a cloak and carry her to your ships. I'll send Hange for her. All our men hate him and he will infuriate them still further against him.'

Kinyras was much moved and knelt at his King's feet. 'I will never forget this clemency, sir. I go to lure the ships of Khem and then to ram them.'

'Nay, Kinyras, old comrade, never kneel to me, man. Give me your hand and wish me godspeed, as I do you, for my task is more difficult than yours. Lady, I salute you.' He drew Dayonis to him and kissed her upon the brow. 'Now, get you to your chamber and lie close hidden. Everything depends upon your discretion and obedience.'

Submissive, tired and impressed by his kindness and humanity, she obeyed submissively and without a word. Then Erili assumed a forbidding demeanour and raised a great and angry shout. 'Ho, there! Hasvan! Yakub! Summon my guards!'

Erili's suite, hastily roused by the agitated slaves and the furious commotion which their King was making, came running, the sleep still in their eyes. Never had they seen Erili in such a passion. Soon the room was full of gaping men, while outside others hastened up, forming a dense crowd lit by flaring torches. Kinyras stood by with folded arms, trying to look angry and dignified, but only succeeding in appearing sullen.

'My lord, Kinyras,' Erili addressed him in a loud, angry and contemptuous tone, his voice booming out to the listeners beyond, 'I deprive you of your command for your insolence and disobedience and set it upon your brother. Soldiers and men of Karpas, my lord Zadoug is now commander in chief of the force defending Karpas and to him you will render your obedience. Lord Kinyras, you will return to your post at Vanner Hill, and if you are a wise man we shall hear nothing of you but your strict attention to your duty. Captain Baruk, you will convey my instructions to the lord Zadoug. The rest disperse.'

In silence the crowd melted away, awed and full of curiosity and wild rumours of the quarrel between the king and the general, while Yakub sat writing at Erili's dictation and Kinyras departed to collect two lieutenants and some baggage.

In an incredibly short space of time Baruk had gone in one direction, Erili in another and Kinyras towards Vanner Hill. The three departures were almost simultaneous and the gaping crowds watched them in subdued excitement, which rose to a pitch of incredulous amazement when, half an hour or so later Kinyras returned, assembled certain captains about him, gave them implicit instructions and then, accompanied by Hasvan, set out for Stronglas.

When they had gone perhaps two miles and just before the crack of dawn, a strange, closely muffled, slender figure ran out from a clump of bushes and scrambled upon the spare beast which Hasvan was leading. This done in a complete silence and with the utmost speed, the little cavalcade galloped away.


Dr. Groves, standing by the bed of Denvers with Mina in anxious attendance with Mina in anxious attendance, knew now for certain what he had suspected from the first, that here was no case of catalepsy. The only difference between Denvers' state and that of normal sleep was that he showed no signs of awakening. Since the marked change in his condition of several nights ago, he had been as talkative as formerly he had been silent. Mina was a pale shadow of her former blooming self, knowing not which was the more nerve-racking, Robert's deadly silence which had marked the early stage in his calamity, or this later one of an almost perpetual stream of inexplicable speech. 'Oh, doctor, what is the matter with him?' she exclaimed distractedly.

'I'd give anything to know,' he admitted candidly. 'It is the most amazing case I've ever encountered.'

'I cannot give her up, Erili. Dayonis goes with me. I have given my word that she shall be protected. You are king, Erili. Do you command me? Even so, I will not give her up. To do so is to dishonour the brotherhood, and the Banner of the Snail.'

'He is delirious,' said Mina.

Dr. Groves reached again for his patient's hand and he shook his head. 'No. His pulse is normal and his temperature, too. There is no sign of fever.'

'But he has eaten nothing for over a week, now. Doctor, he can't go on like this.'

'That is the extraordinary thing about it... he can and does go on, not only maintaining is strength but getting stronger. He is in a better physical condition now than he has when you first called me in to attend him.'

'But there must be something we can do.'

'I can get another opinion. He may be suffering from some tropical disease new to medical science, Mrs. Denvers.'

At this advice Mina hesitated. Neither she nor Hank wanted any publicity given to the case. 'Is his life in danger?'

Again the doctor shook his head. 'Frankly, no.'

'Is he mad, then?'

'He sounds as sane as you or I, and I believe him to be so. He—' Dr. Groves checked himself and remained silent, compressing his lips and frowning intently at the figure on the bed.

Denvers was giving words to an almost frantic passion for Dayonis, expressing his fears for her safety. 'We must feel to the ships, Dayonis, my beloved, and ravage the fleets of Khem.'

'What were you going to say, doctor?'

'He is undergoing some astounding experience, almost as though he were living in another life. I don't wish to sound fantastic, but—do you believe in reincarnation, Mrs. Denvers?'

'No—o. I've never given it any serious thought. Do you?'

'Hardly, but... well, shall we have that second opinion, ma'am?'

'Is it absolutely necessary? Will it do any good?'

Dr. Goves shrugged. 'So long as he shows no loss of vitality there is no real necessity and as for doing good, well, in my opinion it is only paying a big fee to puzzle another man. I believe he will waken naturally—when he is ready. I'll send in a nurse, if you like.'

'It doesn't matter,' Mina answered tonelessly.

When Groves had gone she resumed her seat beside the bed and gazed intently at Denvers. There was some curious change in him. Even in this strange sleep he looked alert and masterful. Misery no longer oppressed him. What had caused the change and who was this Dayonis, of whom he spoke so much?

Mina had her own ideas about Robert's talk of his king Erili, his enemies and the wall. His mind was for ever in the past, set upon ancient armies and fortifications. There was little wonder he should speak of them in his dreams, but Dayonis, this girl was a very different matter. Who was she and where had he met her? Mina felt a curious sense of mortification when he spoke her name because she could not hear it without feeling of discontent and humiliation.

# CHAPTER XII

# OUT ON THE GREAT SEA

ayonis unwound the wrappings from her about her head and drew a great breath of relief. The dawns come up very early when the year is still climbing and near its zenith, therefore not a soul would be stirring for at least three hours. She might ride unafraid, because undetected. 'So, we are away at last. Kinyras, how you men's tongues do wag. After listening to you and Erili I never again shall believe in the superior talking power of women.' She threw back her head and laughed, and Kinyras favoured her with a sour look and a grunt in the darkness. 'Now, where do you take your boats?' she asked, airily disregarding his portentous solemnity.

'Right out to sea, out of sight of the coast,' he responded, deciding it was useless to sulk with her and having no marked desire to do so. 'By daylight. There will be a look-out on the mast and I shall keep the crest of Stronglas in sight.'

'And the fires?'

'Erili will have three lit and at night I shall come in close. The last flare will bring them straight on to the rocks, when I shall attack. Is that good strategy, my princess?'

Not heeding the note of irony, she answered provocatively that it would pass at a pinch.

'They are no sailors and hate the gray-green, as they call the sea. Their ships are built only for rivers and to carry cargo. I would not go to sea in one of them myself. We shall keep out of the way, only putting in to shore for provisions, or if Erili needs me urgently, when he will light four fires on the summit of Stronglos. So we have arranged.'

Daynois was silent a moment or two, pondering what she had heard. Finally, she spoke her mind, cooly. 'Well, I will go with the sips, but it will be to raid Salam after we have sunk the Khemite fleet. We will have many good fights, my Kinyras. Perchance we may free enough Karpasian prisoners to pay my ransom. Maybe we shall win the great adventure, Death, but we will live whilst seeking it.'

'You have spirit, my Dayonis, perhaps too much, but it will be curbed somewhat when you are swathed in our three cloaks like a mummy, to be carried aboard between Hasvan and me.'

'I care not what you do with me provide I may be at sea and fight. Did I not tell you, Kinyras, that ere a month had passed you would be in rebellion against your King, for my sake?'

'Pish! I go on an urgent errand. There is no revolt, you slut!'

She laughed and he sulked, or pretended to, well content to be with her and to know he was carrying her to comparative safety. In less than an hour they reached the mouth of the Kastnon and could see the little fishing village, with one of the ships, the Sea-Horse, lying to at the jetty. The larger ship, the Dolphin, was at sea on patrol duty. Kinyras looked round for a suitable hiding place for Dayonis, while he and Hasvan descended to the harbour. After all, dignity could not suffer and much comment would be roused if the commander in chief were to be seen helping his slave to carry a bundle aboard. They found some dense bushes, into whose cover Dayonis promptly slipped.

Hasvan, the every-ready, produced a carpet from the baggage. 'Look, mast, if my lady will consent to be rolled in this we can tie it with cord and stuff the ends with a napkin, so.'

This was done quickly, and with the end where her head

came left open the roll was thrust out of sight under the bushes, while Kinyras and his slave ran down to the jetty. Though small, the little harbour was a busy one, and they found crowds of men hurrying backwards and forwards, carrying stores to the ship. Staying only to send a swift boat to the Dolphin, ordering her to meet the Sea-Horse on her outward course and to send a messenger to recall such of the crew as were away working on the fortifications, Kinyras called a couple of men to follow him and the four returned to collect the baggage.

Hasvan carefully extracted the carpet from the bushes, peered inside to encounter the glittering eye of the Princess and hastily masked it with a shawl stuffed in the end. 'Away with this, instantly, to the ship,' he commanded impressively. 'Bear it with care, for it is our lord's most cherished possession, no less than an image of the blessed Astarte herself. Give heed to it, lest unutterable curses fall upon ye.'

So was Dayonis conveyed to the awaiting boat, shipped aboard the Sea-Horse and stowed in the cabin, where she was quickly liberated from her suffocating prison by Kinyras. Being very tired and cross, promptly she threw herself upon the couch and slept. Meanwhile, the ship, laden with stores for the Dolphin, put to sea and it was almost midday before the big vessel was sighted. Once more rolled in the carpet did Dayonis tranship to the great galley and lie hidden in the cabin until the Sea-Horse had unladen.

Excited and happy, unmindful of her disgruntled lord, Dayonis issued forth and began to explore the battleship. The crew expressed no astonishment at her presence, for Hasvan had employed them elsewhere when the general came aboard and in no way was she connected in their minds with a roll of carpet.

Dayonis had been in fishing-boats before but never in one of such a size and grandeur as the Dolphin. Her length was a matter of one hundred and twenty feet, carrying thirty oars a side. She was painted vermilion, built for speed and strength with a high freeboard so that she might weather a beam-sea without swamping, or the continued necessity for bailing out. Somewhat snubbed in the bows yet rising to a good height in the forecastle, affording room for a body of archers, when she was in action, she terminated in a curious snake-like prow, while below the water-line she projected a blunt beak, bearing a rough resemblance to a dolphin's head in bronze, above which a large, fixed and glassy eye was limned. Her stern rose in a high curve, canoe-shaped, giving ample protection to the steersman and standing-room for another company of archers. The mast of pine, with its two fore and two back stays, was strong enough to support a great crow's nest, which was furnished with heavy throwing-spears feathered with leather. Cast from that height they would pierce any armour or shield, however stout.

The Dolphin carried one big, square sail made of thin canvas, sewn into rectangular sections with strips of leather and furnished with a ring at each intersection for purposes of reefing. The ropes were of stout, twisted ox-hide. Above her gunwales stout wooden bulwarks surmounted with a high rail upon which was hung hides and shields in time of action protected her rowers from arrows and her warriors standing in the waist of the ship, while from the mast a heavy net was suspended to the sides which, when stretched and covered with wet sea-weed, prevented boarding and kept out arrows and fire-balls, though it was easy enough to shoot from beneath its cover. The rowers sat in the hold on raised benches, with a gang-way down the middle, where sat the overseer who set the pace with his drum. The oars were fixed in leather loops.

Dayonis, here, there and everywhere she should not be, found several large earthenware jars and poking into them with excess of curiosity, discovered to her horror that they contained a number of snakes. Flying from these in detestation of the creatures, she cannoned into a sailor, who explained they were to be flung on to the enemy ships, there to wreck their reptilian wills. Terror turned to laughter and she ran chuckling to Kinyras. He had by now swallowed and digested her 'I told you so,' of a few hours back, and was happy and eager to set out with her on a tour of inspection and explanation.

They came to the great crane he had invented for the hoisting of heavy bundles of spears and of vast stones to the crow's-nest, the slip-hooks on the yard-arm, which raised huge leaden weights and dropped them from that height upon the enemy craft alongside, with such force that they would drive through deck and keel and sink her. This last device made boarding almost impossible except at bow and stern. Dayonis enquired anxiously whether it was still his well-persevered secret, to be reassured by an affirmative. She shuddered to think of such arms being used in turn against them.

He explained the use of the netting, showed her the large catapult amidships for hurling great stones, the two arblasts for hurling spears to an immense distance, so that they drove through bulwark and the men behind it. Then there were the grappling-hooks for boarding, long poles with sharp cutting-hooks affixed, with which to tear down rigging, jars of liquid fire, lances twenty-four feet long wielded by several men and which could pierce both shield and armour when an enemy ranged alongside, chains to reinforce rigging to prevent it from being cut in counter-attack and lastly the goliath ram, sheathed in bronze, which could crack a ship's sides like a hazel-nut beneath a hammer.

'These are mighty and terrible wonders,' she observed in aw-stricken tones when she reflected that they could as well be used against her as for her. 'Kinyras, let us at once find the enemy and use them upon him first. Let us ram and sink him without delay. I long to see them work!'

He laughed joyously, feeling his spirits rise as the deck heaved beneath his feet. He was in holiday mood, glad to escape the stress and anxiety of the wall and to leave it in Zadoug's competent and trustworthy hands, glad to feel the wind in the sail, on his cheek, to watch the dance of the sun on the deep blue lipping sea. 'Easier said than done, my Dayonis.'

'Why?'

'Becaus the Khemites are bad sailors, used to and liking only their great river. Their ships are built of heavy timber, dovetailed together without ribs, excellent for such sailing, where they are scraping along the sand most of the time, but it means a shallow draught, flat bottom and a low freeboard, long, overhanging bows and sterns. All these are good for river work on the Nile, but at sea these long bows weigh down, are slow to recover and plough through large waves, shipping much water, instead of riding free.'

'Oh!' says Dayonis, trying to look wise as an owl.

With twinkling eyes Kinyras pursued gravely his theme. 'A low freeboard spells exposure to arrows of steersmen and warriors alike, and a constant bailing out if they encounter beam-sea, and swamping in very rough weather. The shallow, rounded bottom without keel only permits use of the sail when the wind is dead aft. So they have to wait days, even months for a calm enough sea, or depend upon constant use of oars alone.'

'And your ship is not so built?'

'My ship! The Dolphin!' echoed Kinyras, wildly staring at such a supposition and finding no words in which to refute the impious notion. 'No, lady, she is not!'

'Then do they not fight on sea?'

'Yes, but in great fleets, not in small numbers. It is only this precaution of sailing in such fleets which prevents Orphusa from becoming mistress of the seas, but they have such few ships, though far superior in every way to those of Khem, that they would be crushed by numbers alone.'

Dayonis pondered this vexed question for some moments in silence, then asked another and obvious question. 'Why has not Khem fewer and better ships? Surely such would be to her advantage.'

'For many reasons, but chiefly because she is an old and conservative country, over-influenced by tradition, and with deeply subtle inner workings amongst her labourers. Certain laws protect these workers and give them power to form leagues, so that they can make decisions for themselves.'

Dayonis opened her eyes very wide at this. 'But are they not slaves, born to labour and to obey?'

'Some, yes, but not the master-builders, whose object in life is to get as much work as possible and who reason amongst themselves in this wise. "If such ships as we have built since the beginning of time were wrecked when they venture forth to sea, so much the better for us. We must build more and still more to replace them".'

'And the crews?' Dayonis laughed.

Kinyras shrugged and spread his hands. 'The remedy lies in their own hands. They may band together rand refuse to go on the Grey green in unseaworthy ships.'

'But this is the policy of madness, spelling naught but loss.'

'Doubtless the Priestcraft are at the root of the matter, influencing the builders by religious bans. The Temple has set its seal of approval on the first ships that were built. The gods have blessed them. To improve upon the ancient design is an impiety, implying that both gods and priests are dullards not to have obtained the best at the outset. So it is ever with new and better things, my love. The Temple damns and bans because it would lose its power if it did not.'

Dayonis pouted and frowned at this. 'How you do hate the gods, Kinyras. Have you no fear they will blast you?'

'No, I fear them not at all, because I know and love their Justice and their mercy. And because they are Gods, they know my mind. What I hate is the mockery put upon them by those who pretend to serve them in their Temples, filling the people with lies and follies in their name.'

Dayonis glided out of the argument with her accustomed ease. 'Long may Khem build and sail ships, say I. The more of them which are swallowed by the Grey Green, the better for us.'

So passed the day, then as night was falling Kinyras ordered a course to be set for Salam, which they had seen frequently from the hills and again from the sea, though none but Dayonis had been there. She had visited it with her father before it had fallen into the hands of Khem. She made a map of the coast, which Kinyras pronounced to be excellent and most useful. Upon which Dayonis coaxed him to give permission for the performance of certain rites, she declaring that she felt power coming upon her.

He consented with due solemnity, unable to refuse her, though when it came to a question of one of his oarsmen being sacrificed he stiffened.

'Only one lazy one,' she pleaded.

'There are no lazy men on my ships,' he told her sternly. 'Have done, lady. Human sacrifice is an abomination, of which I will have none. Content you with two black sheep.'

'Perhaps you are right, O Kinyras,' she sighed, submissive for fear of utter prohibition. 'I shall need assistance, yours and the master's.'

Again Kinyras frowned, not altogether liking the thought of Kinuis being witness to her mumbo-jumbo, but she persisted and for the sake of peace and quietness, he yielded, and she flew away, as happy as a child given a favourite toy to play with, to make her preparations.

The great cabin in the ship's stern was cleared of furniture, only two chests being retained with which she prepared two altars. Upon these were placed several big, shallow bowls. She next drew a large circle upon the floor with red paint, setting the smaller altar with a brazier in the centre, the larger outside, and ringing the circle with little lamps set a foot apart. When the time drew near she summoned her assistants and the sacrifices were driven in.

'We must cast away our clothes,' she announced in a hushed voice, as she slipped deftly from her one garment and her sandals.

Silently the two men obeyed her, while she took the sacred stone from her neck and laid it on the smaller altar. Prayer, in an unknown tongue, followed next and a command to her assistants to hold the black sheep. Midnight was not approaching and, with her sword in her right hand and holding a magic wand in her left, with one blow she severed each head from the animals, whose bodies were placed on the outer altar. The wand, the sword and a small figure of herself as enchantress, rested on the inner altar and her assistants were bidden to enter the circle with herself. Holding the two severed heads she marked both herself and the men on breast and forehead with blood, devoting them to Jaske.

With the bloody necks of the slaughtered sheep she marked out a broad, inner circle round the celebrants and placed the heads on the small altar. Then, with a fire drill, she lit the lamps and kindled a fire, chanting all the while in her secret language and pacing the circle in antithesis to the progression of the sun. Next, lighting the brazier, she cast into it many roots and herbs. A dense, choking and stinging smoke arose while, unheeding its discomfort, the two men knelt clasping hands, one each side of her, with instructions not to lose contact until the ceremony was over. Dayonis then knelt between them with her arms on their shoulders, bidding them to support her body with their arms. So with the circle complete, she explained that, as she went into the trance she would bend over the smoke and breathe it in, bidding them breathe no more than was possible and to guard her from falling face forwards into the fire. 'Mark well what I say and lose not contact else shall I waken ere the magic be complete. Remember, every spoken word has its meaning.'

Impressed in spite of himself, Kinyras inclined his head in answer, and once more she prayed to Jaske to aid her, bending over the brazier and inhaling deeply. Some seconds passed, when she began to speak in a slow, strained, dream-like voice, very different from her normal tones.

'I float over the great sea. I see Kaddam, unchanged, yet not the same as I knew it. Hatred and disquiet and tyranny are rife, the hands of the conquerors are heavy upon the people. They are weary with their labours and they throng the streets, their hearts and minds full of rebellion, but the men of Khem are there in their thousands. We can do nothing there.'

For a moment or two there was a pause, then the curious flat voice droned on: 'I rise again, I am searching, I see Salam. There are many Khemites, they are having a festival. No, it is a funeral for which they prepare and in two days they will for the great procession. All the troops of Khem will walk in it. Chebron, the Governor, is dead and they will take him across the great lake. All will follow because it is lawful to make accusation against him and his life has been bad. All will wish to see if any dare to speak against him. The citadel will be left under a very small guard and the slaves will be penned in their barracks with but a few to watch them. The Khemites know that starvation and hard work have crushed them beyond the point of revolt. We can attack the citadel with success, we can release the slaves from their pens...'

Wreaths of pungent smoke drifted through the red walled cabin, shrouding the kneeling figures of the celebrant, in veils of bluey vapour, so that they look like ghosts, and the circle of lamps burnt in a little circle of steady flame but in a strange etiolation, as though they, too, were but spectres of flames. Every now and then the brazier leapt to a long thin column of yellow and purple fire as the voice of the enchantress rose from the level of her monotonous chant, sinking when it fell again to be lost in a new denser cloud of cyanic reek, which wrought itself into strange, disturbing shapes, lurking in the dim and distant corners like monstrous shades from some sinister other-where.

Kinyras endured the ordeal with a grimness of fortitude characteristic of the man. His eyes ached and smarted with the stench, the acrid fumes nearly stifled him, he felt stupefaction to be imminent and his whole soul rose in rebellion at the discomfort. Himself a true psychic whose natural power had been cultivated through a period of many years of self-discipline and rigour to the highest pitch, he felt nothing but the bitterest, contempt and distrust of such methods as these, and inwardly marvelled at the success of the ceremony. A glance at Kinuis, however, shoed him the reason for it. The master was so completely absorbed, so devoutly and whole-heartedly at one with Dayonis, that their combined animal magnetism was overwhelming and set aside his own steely, intellectual criticism and disapproval as easily as a stone club wielded by a giant could beat down and blunt a rapier however keen.

The voice of the Princess died slowly and almost at the

point when he feared insensibility would overcome him, she swayed forward and would have fallen into the fire had he not pulled her away and so broken contact with Kinuis, who staggered back , gasping and choking. Seizing the brazier Kinyras staggered with it out on the deck and cast it into the sea with a venomous satisfaction, then returned and dragged his companions out of the murk into the sweet night air, under which they very soon revived, Kinuis rose and lurched aft, while Dayonis sat up, knuckled her eyes like a child and began to cough.

Kinyras gave vent to a surge of angry impatience. 'Hark ye, mistress, it's the last time ye play these tricks aboard my ship. I'll have none of it.'

'Eh?' she answered, still bemused and not comprehending.

'Turning my cabin into a shambles and a pickling den!' he grumbled. 'A pretty fine state of things!'

'Said I much?' she asked, after a considerable pause, occupied by both mostly in coughing and gasping and wiping their eyes.

'Aye!' growled Kinyras, 'a hell of a screed.'

'Tell it me, Kinyras, my sweet love,' she implored in such a dulcet tone that his disgust evaporated as his head cleared, and a sense of humour reasserted itself.

'You accomplished marvels, my Dayonis. You described an occupied city, Kaddam, and a Khemite funeral procession. Methinks you might have sat under the cool stars and have done as well.'

'You mock me!' she sighed, the darkness hiding the glow of anger and mutiny in her eyes, now wholly green, 'but tell me word for word, what I said.'

He complied and she sat silent, turning over the words in her mind. 'The citadel I know, it is a strong place, but of the lake I am ignorant. There are several, but the nearest is three or four miles distant from the city.'

'A likely place enough and suitable for the Khemite custom, which none may escape, not even Pharaoh himself. When the dead are embalmed, his mummy case is placed in a casket and drawn on a sledge to the lake and if there is no lake then one is made, so that all Khemite cities are so provided. There sit judges, with power to deny sepulchre if accusation is made against the deceased and the case proved. But, if the accuser cannot prove his case then a fearful vengeance falls upon him.'

Dayonis considered this information for a moment or two, while Kinyras looked out over the moonlit sea, his arm clasped about her waist, her head resting upon his shoulder. It was a night for lovers and talk of death and burial incongruous.

'It is sure, my lord, that none would dare arraign Chebron, he his life never so evil and the matter of it simple of proof. His family never would suffer the disgrace of refusal of sepulchre and the accusers would be sent to the mines for their pains. Yet the opportunity for a raid is god-sent, Kinyras, for curiosity will carry most of the population to the lakeside.'

'But is it true or only a smoke dream?'

'Catch a fisherman and ask. I never knew Jaske to lie to me.'

Kinyras sat erect with a jerk and squeezed her hand in the act of doing so, so that she called out in protest. 'Your wits work, no matter how smoke-bemused, sweet. What you say is true, and there is point half a mile west of Salam, with a fishing -village at its foot, where a ship may lie hid from the town. Tell me more of this citadel, be exact as your memory will allow.'

'The walls are but forty feet high, the moat dry and only twelve to fifteen feet deep.'

'But too far from the sea to carry long, scaling ladders. The great gates will be well defended, but is there no small postern, through which goods are carried and from which lovers slip at night to woo their girls?'

She shook her head, smiling. 'I know of none.'

'Some strategy must serve... a messenger coming from Pharaoh, or from his viceroy, Amasis. He would arrive in a chariot, accompanied by an escort, lit with torches and demand entrance at the citadel gates. The question is, would he be received with due honour into the fortress, while messengers were sent to the acting Governor, or would he be denied, kept outside until the Acting Governor arrived from the funeral rites?'

Dayonis turned to him eagerly. 'Not so is the messenger of Pharaoh used. Pharaoh is a god and his messenger would be received with great honour.'

'Good, then all we need is a chariot and horses and someone who can speak Khemite.'

'I can speak well enough to shout, demanding admission. They had me taught carefully enough, first for Amasis and then for Pharaoh himself... spit upon his name!'

For yet a little longer they sat there, murmuring endearments, exchanging caresses beneath the Cyprian moon, then, judging the cabin to be clear of smoke and again habitable they returned to it, to find that Hasvan had restored it to its former neatness and comfort during their absence on deck. Dayonis sought her couch with sleepy yawns, while Kinyras sought Kinuis, to give him instructions to catch fisherman, from whom they would extract as much information as he could supply.

At dawn Hasvan roused Kinyras, whispering that two fishing boats had been sighted and their owners seized and brought on deck. Their craft, two poor, crazy coracles of wickerwork covered with skin, were fastened alongside, while the men stood shivering in the presence of Kinuis and their tongues so paralyzed with fear into dumbness. Under promises of money and transportation of themselves, families, goods and possessions to Vallia, a town well within the Karpas border, they agreed to everything Kinyras desired. They were full of gossip about the funeral, knew where to lay hands upon a chariot and horses and, hating Khem, would willingly pilot the noble captains into their little harbour behind the point of Salam, provided they might be conveyed to safety as promised. The funeral was to take place that same night.

Accordingly they were returned to their coracles and allowed to fish, though kept under strict surveillance and their catch was bought, making an excellent meal for the ship's company. Meanwhile active preparations went on aboard for the night's raid and when the time ws come the Dolphin and Sea-Horse were taken in and moored to the little jetty, enough men being left on board to sail them out to sea in case the raid failed, the rest were landed in the ship's boats and the coracles.

As a precautionary measure the two fishermen were bound and gagged in accordance with plan and the party marched towards the town from which came the rolling of many muffled drums, the wild screaming of flutes and the blare of trumpets as the funeral procession formed and wound its way to the distant lake. On the outskirts of the town they raided several promising looking houses where they found chariots but no horses.

Here was threatened frustration at the outset, all available animals having been taken for the funeral procession. A brief, whispered consolation took place and they decided to comb the district for horses. After a fretting delay three were at length found, all of differing colours and heights. The two likeliest were chosen, a pail of whitewash discovered at the instigation of one of the fishermen very quickly transformed the unmatched team into a pair of white steeds used by all Royal messengers of Khem.

During this raid, which had been for the most part upon empty houses, their inhabitants having gone forth to the funeral, they had collected much costly raiment and trappings. In some of these one of the crew was arrayed to represent the envoy and beside him in the chariot stood Dayonis, dressed as a page, bearing the banner of the Snail, upon which had been sewn various pieces of gaudy cloth in red, green and blue, its folds draped so as to conceal the occupants of the car as much as possible.

A party of men as guards marched in front, carrying torches which had purposely been made smoky and held so that, while lighting the way, also they dazzled the eyes of the observers, and the smoke trailing behind obscured the rest of the crew following as a guard of Khemite warriors and holding their spears high to make them appear as the long pikes of Khem.

The procession started out and as they walked behind,

Kinyras and Kinuis, discussed their operations. The Dolphin and Sea-Horse had been left in charge of the mate, whose orders were to put instantly to sea should the raid end in disaster. At all costs must the ships be saved. In case of adversity the members of the raid would try to escape and lie hidden, seeking the coast at night, when their signal would be three fires lit in the form of a big triangle, with a flare at each point. The mate was to lie off all day and to come in for three successive nights in search of signals.

If they succeeded in entering the citadel and overpowering the guard, Dayonis was to remain by the gate, while the other two, dividing the remainder of their force in half would release the slaves and hunt for treasure.

'Is all clear, Kinuis?' Kinyras asked. 'Immediately the gates are opened we attack the guard while you hasten to the slave pens. Not a soul is about and it seems we may count on a measure of success, providing we can be speedy. The smallest delay will spell disaster.'

'You may depend upon me, sir,' Kinuis replied, in a gruff mumble. He was a man of few words, but lusty action and what he lacked in loquacity he made up for the quickness of wit.

They reached the great gates of the citadel without encountering a single wayfarer and blew a loud and imperative blast upon their trumpets, imitating the Khemite call. The trailing smoke from the torches hid the absence of an escort of chariots and Kinyras and Kinuis too their places at the end of their men.

Dayonis, almost completely sheltered behind the folds of the banner, yelled lustily for admission. 'Hasten, you dogs, hasten!' she bawled. 'Open to the messenger from the Son of Heaven.'

Behind the gates was the sound of hurry, a reply came from the Khemite trumpets and slowly the enormous doors began to move. It was a tense moment. Kinyras ran a rapid eye over his following, noting that while the torches flared over the company lighting all their glory, the smoke hid the hinderpart.

Gradually, foot by food, the gates opened and as soon as

they were back far enough the raiders rushed in. There was a sharp hand-to-hand encounter between the guard and the men under Kinyras, who so attacked the defenders that Kinuis was able to get by unobserved with his small force and hasten in search of the slave pens. Dayonis leapt from her chariot as soon as it had entered the fort and lent considerable assistance to Kinyras in rounding up and cutting down the guard. A search discovered a few more of the slender garrison left on duty and these, too, were despatched without ado. Hastily stripping the dead the invaders dressed in their costumes and were sent off by Kinyras to support Kinuis, only a remnant being retained to guard the gate and to help him in his search for treasure. A number of prisoners in the dungeons were released, together with many household slaves. The business of looting the citadel progressed merrily.

Meanwhile Kinuis welcomed the reinforcement sent by Kinyras and ordered the newly dressed party to run in advance to the slave pens, shouting to the guards that they had word of a rising. The doors were thrown open and the Khemite soldiers rushed out to discover what was the trouble. To overpower them was not difficult. A sharp and bloody fight, ruthless while it lasted and giving no quarter on either side, soon reduced the guards to nothingness, when the raiders ran with their flaming torches, opening up the pens and driving the slaves, of whom there were about five thousand, forward to the citadel court-yard, Kinuis left three men behind to fire the pens and all adjacent buildings at a given signal, then to hasten to the gate without loss of time.

Kinyras was equally successful. In the armoury he found a good store of arms of every description, nor was the treasury empty. He was joined by Kinuis and the question of what to do with the liberated slaves now arose. Their only hope of safety lay in flying to the hills of Aghirda. Climbing on a table which had been hastily brought for the purpose, Kinyras, surrounded by torches held high so that their light illuminated his face, addressed the mob of scared, liberated captives, and while he spoke others of his men went about amongst them distributing the arms looted from the armoury.

'Slaves,' shouted Kinyras, 'ye have been restored to liberty, but unless ye would be caught and slaughtered like sheep, ye must make for the hills of Aghirda. Two of my men, who know the country, have volunteered to lead ye.'

A hoarse cheering broke out from the half-dazed prisoners, which subsided as Kinyras raised his hand for silence. 'Three things alone will save ye from worse than slavery under Khem. They are Speed, Courage and Obedience to your leaders. Unity is strength, unity alone will enable you to survive your difficulties. The Khemite army stands between you and Karpas, so that was is barred to you. The hills and forests claim you, where lies food in abundance. I will give you two hours before I fire the citadel. The army is occupied with the funeral, unsuspecting of danger and in no hurry to return. Dismiss, march in order and the blessing of the merciful gods go with ye.'

At that moment a peal of trumpets sounded without the gates and an appalled silence fell upon all those within. Kinyras instinctively raised his hand and in obedience to the quiet, commanding, controlled gesture, all sense of panic was subdued. He turned to Kinuis. 'Can it be the return of the army?' he asked in a low tone, to which the mast silently shook his head. 'at least we can sell our lives dearly. Open the gates!'

Thus bidding the gates were cautiously unbarred and Dayonis stood in the aperture to find a genuine Royal messenger and his escort, awaiting admittance in a frenzy of impatience and demanding the reason for his delay in most uncourtly language. Murmuring apologies the gates opened wider and the *cortege* swept in, to be fallen upon and demolished without ruth, only the messenger himself being spared.

While the envoy was sullenly explaining his mission to Kinyras the slaves marched out. The envoy bore messages of condolence to the family of the late Ban from the Viceroy, and various instructions to his successor. He was quickly and securely trussed up and placed under a strong guard for later conveyance to Erili.

The slaves, deeply imbued with the habit of obedience to

discipline and order, had marched quietly and with incredible speed out upon their new life. When the citadel was cleared of the last of them, Kinuis recalled his three men and returned with the rest of the raiders to the ship, with orders to embark the fishermen, their families, goods and chattels and to have all in readiness for putting instantly to sea directly Kinyras and Dayonis arrived at the jetty. Presently they, too, had gone, bearing their prisoner with them blindfold, and only the man and the girl were left in the deserted fortress. Horses stood tethered by the gates, waiting to bear them to the jetty when their task was accomplished.

Elated with success and laughing at the false alarm raised by the genuine messenger, together they climbed to the highest look-out of the fortress and turned towards the distant lake. There on the horizon they could see a great flare of light. The hour had approached midnight and they sat down to their vigil. Kinyras pointed ahead. 'When these lights begin to streak towards us, then must we set about our task, Dayonis. The longer we can give those slaves, the better their chance of escape and the more crippling the effects of our raid upon Khem.'

'Dawn will be here in two hours and a half, we should be gone by then. That will give them three hours' start and they should do much with it. Oh, Kinyras, if only we have the power of gods and could take the whole army of Khem prisoner as it marches back here, all unsuspecting of what lies before it.'

'A pretty dream, my princess, but like most women, you are greedy. We have done enough for one night's work.'

'Oh!' Dayonis heaved a profound sigh of longing, 'I wish I might lure them all to the secret temple of Jaske, which he made among my mountains.'

'What then, sweet?' Kinyras smiled, one eye watchful of the distant enemy, who as yet showed no signs of return.

'Jaske would choke them for me!'

'A useful enough god, is your Jaske,' was all the comment Kinyras made. He took the despatches brought by the messenger from his breast where he had thrust them and turned them over. 'These may be as useful, my sweet sorceress, if only we could read them.'

She shook her head regretfully. 'I cannot help you there, Kinyras. The writings of Khem are hard to read. We must send them to Erili. You hope for some token of the treachery of Hange?'

He nodded, turned them over once more and replaced them in his tunic. The next moment she had caught him by the arm and was pointing southward. 'See, they are preparing to return.'

It was even so. Dawn was nigh and the distant glare had become disintegrated, where the vast concourse was breaking up.

'We have yet half an hour,' he said calmly, preparing to descend.

They ran hither and thither, thrusting flaming torches into prepared bundles of straw, firing concealed places first and leaving exposed out-buildings to the last. They had discovered a small postern and through this they led their horses with just enough room to get them through the narrow entry, leaving the great gates barred. Kinyras mounted Dayonis, muttering– 'If fortune is with us, they will spend some time in gaining admittance, before they discover what has happened to them.'

She sniggered in appreciation of this and with an ironical gesture towards the distant Khemites, they turned their asses to the jetty. A short and safe ride brought them to the village just as dawn was cracking the east with a crimson streak. A good breeze from the land sprang up and Dayonis shivered in the cold air. A cock crow, was answered by a second and a dog set up a persistent baying.

They slipped from their asses and set them free, ran to the water's edge where a boat was waiting for them. At a whispered word they were aboard and skimming lightly towards the Dolphin, whose bulk soon loomed ghostly out of the grey mists of morning. The ladder from the stern was lowered, they boarded, the great square sail slowly filled with wind, the fifty rowers bent to their task with a will and soon the Dolphin was flying before the wind, out to sea and safety.

From the land there came a sudden uproar as the advance guard of the Khemite army returned to their citadel, to find it a roaring pile of flame.

Dolphin and Sea-Horse made for Kastnon River, keeping a sharp look-out, but there was no signs of fires along the coast. The two ships were woefully crowded, for beside Khemite prisoners and the envoy, there were many Karpasians who had been captured and enslaved, besides the fishermen and their families, with all their household good cluttered about them. Ships so encumbered could not possibly be in trim for fighting and to rid themselves of their unwelcome passengers became the first urgent necessity.

Accordingly, when daylight had fully come, Kinyras put in to shore again, disembarking the fishers first. What to do with the slaves was a problem, but he solved it by sending them under escort to Witend, with orders to keep them all closely guarded and to preserve the secret of their arrival so that no word of what happened could get through to Hange. This done he breathed more freely and turned his attention to the envoy, who sullen and furious, stood mute before him in the great cabin, his dark eyes glowing with a malevolent hatred of the degradation which had befallen him, and of his capture.

Dayonis urged upon Kinyras the propriety of sacrificing him to Jaske, but he waved her aside and after the better part of an hour's futile questioning, he sent the man together with hid despatches under a strong guard to Erili and put out to sea again. The ship's cook had prepared a savoury meal of fish steeped in milk seasoned with sweet herbs and of this the three fighters partook hungrily, then went up on deck to seek some well earned rest.

# CHAPTER XIII

# HIDING THE TREASURE

Dayonis lay under an awning of rich dye on the deck of the Dolphin, watching the sunlight play upon the waves. And as she watched she smiled in spite of her fatigue. She had settled herself there to sleep, only to find the excitement of the raid upon Salam still held feverish possession of her mind. When she closed her eyes scenes of the previous night flitted before her like magic pictures and she must live over again the breathless rush of those fast crowding incidents.

To her presently came Kinyras and she started up on her elbow to gaze at him eagerly. 'Well?' she inquired.

He threw himself down beside her on the mattress. 'A rich haul, sweet. What shall you do with your share?'

'Bury it,' she answered him, promptly. 'And as soon as maybe.'

He laughed, stroking her arm with his knotted forefinger and looking up into her eyes. 'Where, my pearl?'

'Ah, that is another matter. Let us consider of it. And how we shall accomplish it in secrecy, also how much is my share?'

'A matter of six mule loads, or so, for all mine is yours and shall be set to the task of freeing your country.'

Unwonted tears misted her eyes as she flung herself with passionate gratitude into his arms. 'The gods are good to me,'

208

she whispered huskily. 'I thank and bless the gods of my fathers.'

Kinyras held her tight, surprised to feel her body trembling against his. For long they lay there, silent, while his eyes, ever watchful, searched the waters. But they were empty, save for the following Sea-Horse and a few fisher coracles on the distant horizon. After a while she spoke again, releasing herself from his embrace, her emotion quelled, her keen mind recovered its poise. Reluctantly he let her go, for it was not often she was in the melting mood.

'The possession of this treasure gives us a great advantage, my love, and the day of the freedom of my country draws near. With it I am no longer the wretched castaway whom you rescued. The means to fight is mine and I must send messages to this effect to my people. The question is how?'

'A delicate, perilous mission, demanding absolute loyalty and devotion. Whom can we send?'

She scowled at a gull flying low over the ship uttering its melancholy cry, as though she would capture it and force it to obey her need. Her hands struck together in her impotence, then suddenly her face cleared amazingly and she was all beaming smiles. 'Ammunz!' she almost shouted, 'he is well of his wounds by now and girding at his inactivity, I'll wager.'

Without a word in comment Kinyras and signalled to the look-out on the Sea-Horse to draw nearer. He was answered by a shout. Then, clapping his hands for Hasvan he sat down again. The slave came running.

'Sit,' Kinyras commanded and, as the man obeyed, he resumed in a cautiously lowered town. 'Hasvan, you will board the Sea-Horse and bid the master draw in as near to land as he dares. If the coast is clear you will land with all possible secrecy, procure an ass and ride with all speed to camp. There you will find the man, Ammunz of Aghirdi, and bring him hither without delay. On your way back you will collect six beasts to transport the treasure, for to-night we bury it on Stronglos. You will lie hidden in a suitable spot near the sandy beach of which you know.'

'I know, master.'

'Good. Unless I see enemy flares to warn me off I shall come in two hours after nightfall, when you will be waiting me. But if there is danger... and you will use your eyes and ears to good purpose, Hasvan... you will warn me by fastening a fire to a staveros bolt and by shooting it into the sea.'

'All is clear, lord. This poor slave will spend himself in your service.'

'I know it, Hasvan. It is now the eighth hour and if all goes well you have ample time. Gather news and impart none.'

The Sea-Horse drew alongside and Hasvan departed upon his mission. All day they cruised, keeping a keen lookout and all day the smoke from the burning citadel rose like the incense from some giant sacrifice, dense and black at its source but driving in filmy veils across the deep blue of the summer sky for miles. Both Kinyras and Dayonis watched it with ever increasing satisfaction, never seemed to grow tired of watching it, or of contemplating what it implied through all the length of the golden day, until the sun sank and the peril of their new enterprise lay immediately before them.

Night came, deep, starry and moonless, breathless, still, hot, even upon the unrippling sea. Not a fire winked upon shore, not a sound came from the sleeping land as the Dolphin drew nearer and nearer to the strip of sandy beach. The treasure, securely sewn up in bags of strong hide, was lowered to the awaiting boats and they drew cautiously inshore. As the keel touched sand the prow was grasped by a shadowy hand out of the darkness, another joined it as the boat was pulled strongly beyond the tide-mark.

"Master, we have come,' said the cautious voice of Hasvan and Kinyras knew an immense relief.

'My daughter?' demanded Ammunz, tentatively, looming out of the darkness, to which their eyes were by now accustomed, so that they could make out a darker blotch near by, which represented the awaiting donkeys.

Dayonis greeted her foster-father affectionately and the two withdrew to a distance, which she told him of the raid and of the mission to Aghirda which he was to undertake. The sailors loaded the asses with the treasure and Kinyras consulted with Hasvan. Apparently there was much discontent among his men at his banishment and this was a disaster neither he nor Erili had foreseen. The whole camp from end to end of the line was seething with rebellion and Zadoug had his work cut out to preserve order.

So much had Hasvan gathered during the short time at his disposal, and it was bad enough to set Kinyras cursing. But there was much to accomplish during the night's scanty hours and he could waste no time in probing the matter now. With a sharp call to Dayonis he urged the team forward as the last ass was laden and the party set out for Stronglas, leaving the sailors to guard the boat and to await their return.

Slowly the sure-footed little beasts found their way over the loose, rocky ground to the foot of Stronglas, upon whose summit Kinyras had decided to bury the treasure. He intended to build a fortress here when the wall should be completed because the natural advantages of the place would afford protection to his ships lying in the mouth of the river Kastnon.

At the foot of this hill the river widened on its southern shore into a small bay, opposite which lay swampland. The Kastnon narrowed again before it found its way to the sea, so that an isthmus of rock connected the hill with the little fishing town of Kastros which, perched upon its cliff, and reached by steps cut in the rock, overlooked the sea, and it was across this isthmus that the little string of animals felt their cautious way until they reached the cliffs of Stronglas.

Here at the foot they halted and in artful place of concealment between the base and a great rock. Ammunz unmasked a dull fire. With a little blowing it soon sprang into flame.

'Have a care!' warned Kinyras, sharply.

'We have tested it, master,' Hasvan hastened to assure him. 'It can be seen neither from sea nor land. We must mount here to the crest above.' He pointed to a place in the rock where the two men had spent the time of their waiting in hewing rough steps. By the crazy light of the flickering flame Ammunz scrambled up the face of the cliff like a mountain-cat and soon a rope of stout hide, which he had wound round his middle, was dangling from the top. Kinyras fastened it round Dayonis and by its aid she clambered up beside her foster-father, Kinyras following next while Hasvan covered the fire again with damp seaweed and swarmed up almost as nimbly as Ammunz, leaving the beasts tethered below.

Up on the cliff-top the wind from the sea cooled their panting heat, while the light from the stars sufficed to relieve the place from absolute darkness. They were on a small plateau of the rock, which was covered with a carpet of short, thick grass, strewn with large and small boulders. Ammunz, who was possessed of a ready tongue and wit, had contrived to learn something of the dialect of Karpas and, walking beside Kinyras, he said, pausing to stamp upon the ground. 'Much rock here, lord... digging difficult.'

'But the rock has been split by earthquakes, and in the cracks is some depth of soil,' Hasvan interposed eagerly. He was as excited as a boy over this expedition of burying the treasure and his energy seemed to be inexhaustible.

'You have found it, good fellow? Are you cold, lady?' Kinyras turned to Dayonis, who padded silently beside him.

She, too, was excited and laughed a shrill denial. 'Jaske has made the cracks. Jaske will protect my treasure.'

'It is here, master,' said Hasvan with an air of pride.

Ammunuz was already kneeling beside a great boulder which formed one of a semicircle and in the cleft between it and its neighbour he had hidden another fire, upon whose glowing embers he blew until they crackled into flame. By its light Kinyras and Dayonis looked about them. The spot was as good as any and easily distinguishable by reason of its position amid the rocks.

'The Gods have guided us to this place. Dig!' cried Dayonis, and Hasvan and Ammunz fell to work with a will, producing the tools they had hidden. 'I will watch from the north side, while do you take the south, my lord.'

She walked to the edge of the cliff where she would have

overlooked the swamp had it been light and sat down. The turf was soft and springy and she conscious of fatigue. Not a sound could be heard but the burble of the river below. She sat, watching the bespangled sky, breathing in the soft, scented air. Presently the stillness was broken by a low, fluty note as two nightingales in a distant wood began to sail and whistle to each other. She listened in a rapture of delight unconscious of time. In those primitive days, when men rose at dawn and slept with the coming of darkness like the animals, there was little danger of interruption, especially when the work was carried out with secrecy and dispatch. Her watch was but a perfunctory one, though her ears were instinctively attuned to the slightest various of the stillness about her.

It was therefore a startled girl who leapt to her feet when a hand was laid suddenly on her shoulder, even thought it proved to be Kinyras. Her anger flew out at him, all the more because she had not heard his approach. 'In gods' name why creep up upon me like an enemy?' she stormed.

'To catch you napping, sweet, as I did. Admit it.'

'Spy!' she hissed.

Again he laughed and kissed her roughly, receiving a sounding slap in the face for his pains. 'You hell-cat!' he barked, nursing the injured cheek with tender fingers, 'you've nearly blinded me.'

'Oh, my Kinyras, never say it!' she mourned.

''Tis nothing. Will it please you help us, Dayonis? The hole is dug and we must needs haul the treasure up the cliff-side, and time presses.'

'Willingly!' she hooked her arm in his and together they returned to the place of hiding.

Ammunz and Hasvan had descended the cliff and the weary business of hauling up the loot was begun. It took some time, during which they toiled and sweated as the getting and harbouring of gold alone can make men toil and sweat, until the load was lifted and stowed in the trench. Then, because dawn was perilously near both Kinyras and Dayonis began to help cover in the hole with a will, working with feverish haste and energy in this race against the sun. With the coming of daylight there was every chance of some shepherd-boy wandering near, but task was completed at last, the turf smacked down over the disturbed earth and some great, loose boulders rolled over the spot with infinite labour by the three men. Ammunz stamped out his fire and panting, exhausted, dripping with sweat, the four slid down the cliff side just as the silver crack appeared in the east.

Hasvan drove off his donkeys, while Dayonis and Ammunz exchanged farewells.

'The Gods go with you, Ammunz. You know what you have to do and none could do it better. Guard yourself, my father, be secret and wary. I will invoke Jaske on your behalf and pray him to keep you safe.'

He sighed. 'I mislike leaving you here alone, my daughter. Together we came and together I hoped we should return, but the gods have willed it otherwise. Perils surround you and my heart misgives me.'

'I am in good hands,' she reminded him, gently.

He shook his head, seemed about to speak, changed his mind and left her abruptly. With a slight chill of misgiving she watched his tall figure trudging wearily away through the gloom. Kinyras approached her and she threw off the feelings with determination. After all, what had she to fear? The tide was coming in, its soft lip, lip against the rocks was inviting, and she began to discard her garment. 'I am sick with heat and weariness, Kinyras, and so must you be. Come, let us enter the sea and refresh ourselves before we return to the boat.'

As they ran together naked over the sand down to the ghostly sea and gave themselves up to its cool strength, all her fears vanished in the exhilaration of rapid movement. She swam and dived like a fish, nor did Kinyras lack behind in prowess, and they played in the water together as happily and irresponsibly as children. When they came out, the first red beams of the rising sun were level over the waters and as she emerged from the spume about the rocks, they fell upon her white body and lit her with an unearthly radiance. Her long hair, dark and dank with water, clung about her snowy limbs like mahogany snakes.

Kinyras, who had gone in first and was sitting on a rock, watching her, drew in his breath with a sharp hiss of wonder at the sight. 'You look like Astarte-Astagartis herself,' He whispered, as she came up to him.

But Dayonis, in no mood for worship, seized him by the hands and forced him to run and dance over the sands in order to dry themselves. The vitality of the wench was amazing, though she was sedate enough as they returned to the Dolphin.

All that day they cruised again, drawing in to the coast as heretofore when night fell. When they were near enough in they saw a number of large fires. This looked like the signal for which all had been watching and a quiver of excitement ran through the whole ship's company. Kinyras and the master consulted together, an order was shouted and the Dolphin gathered speed, flying like a sea-bird along the coast for some thirty miles, noting that at regular intervals great blazes had been kindled, the last of which marked the site of a large beach, an excellent landing place.

'Oh-ho!' exclaimed Kinyras, the lust of battle swelling in him, 'This looks like action at last, praise the gods! Here we draw in, my merry lass!'

Dayonis, as eager as he, shared in the disappointment when, having done so, they found nothing; but a yell from the look-out reported that another fire had just been lighted further along. Again they hauled out a sea and ran for another ten miles, observing another succession of fires, at whose termination they once more drew in cautiously. Here Kinyras recognised a small bay which, while looking innocent enough and tempting, he knew to be full of submerged rockers.

Kinyras ordered a boat to be lowered and went ashore. While they were yet a little way off a voice hailed them in Khemite. It came from a fishing-boat and it bade them keep straight on. In a few strokes they were alongside her, where they found Yacob, with two of Erili's men dressed as fishers.

'Lord, the King is here with a large body of troops and

sends you greetings. He has news for your lordship.'

'Hasten then and bring me to him,' he commanded tersely.

The two old companions in arms met eagerly. 'It is good to see you again, old Snail,' Erili exclaimed, clapping him on the shoulder and giving him a friendly shake as he led him so, a little apart. 'How goes life with you, Kinyras? Well, by the sound of your voice.'

'And you, sir?'

Erili smothered a curse and a groan. 'Not at all to my liking. I am smothered in a network of intrigue, which does not suit my soldier's habit. I long to cut myself clear with a few good strokes of my sword.'

'Hange?'

'Aye, may the gods, blast him eternally.'

'Have patience. They will, or we will, if they neglect the business.'

Erili laughed. 'Upon my oath you speak with some confidence. I wish I could feel as much.'

'I feel it. What of the envoy I sent to you?'

'Oh! That business was well done, Kinyras.'

'Due to the wench, not me. She saw it all in her magic smoke, as she calls it.'

Erili scuffed an impatient foot in the sand. He did not like to encounter anything which he could not explain. 'Has she powers of magic, think you?' And as he companion did not immediately reply, added, 'More wit than power, I fancy.'

'It serves her well... and us, Erili,' Kinyras growled, not wishing to discuss the matter.

'True, I grant you. 'Tis a pity such a snarl entangles the girl.'

'What of the envoy?' the other reminded him.

'Yacob has read the despatches. They contain orders to the Ban of Salam to move with all his men to the Karpasian lines. The point of attack is unidentified because they used a Khemite name; but every man capable of marching and fighting is to go, leaving only the oldest to supervise the slaves, who are to be confined to pens on reduced rations so that they are too weak with privation to revolt. The young and strong who might lead a revolt are to be put to silence.'

'Is that all?'

'Yes. It may mean an attack or but a reinforcement of their line, but I have sent a warning to every commander. I, myself, cannot move until this danger from the sea is over or averted.'

With a little more talk, they parted, Kinyras to return to his ship, Erili to his camp. The steady patrol of the coast went on and the following night again the fires were sighted and at last there were ships outlined against their blaze, a great fleet sailing along abreast of them towards the little bay. Swiftly and joyously Sea-Horse and Dolphin prepared for action and long, sinister, eminently seaworthy, they bore down on the rear of their unsuspecting foe.

It was a very dark night, well suited for the raid contemplated by the Khemite fleet, which depended upon Hange for safe guidance by means of the fires to their objective, and never doubting that those they now saw and followed had been lighted by him. Slowly they approached the point where Erili and his men awaited them. Kinyras, rejoicing grimly, saw them clearly silhouetted against the immense blaze on the beach and drew in close for a rearguard action.

The Khemite fleet sailed on with an arrogant confidence in the close formation which was their wont and which now was to prove their undoing. As was inevitable the van struck the sunken rocks and the frail keels of the vessels were ripped out on their serrated edges like so much match-boarding. At this moment Erili attacked, sending showers of arrows into the densely packed men on the wrecked ships. The surprise was complete and the confusion fightful. Escape was out of the question, for one ship followed so closely upon another that it was impossible to divert the course, and those behind came on so swiftly that they were upon the rocks before the fate of the leading ships was comprehended by the rest of the fleet.

Now a mighty clamour arose, the whang of the continuous flight of arrows from the shore, the shrieks and groans of wounded and terrified men, for the Khemites feared and dreaded the sea, the roar of the ingoing tide, the cracking and rending of timbers as the boats were driven on the rocks, the cries of drowning men who in their desperation struggled amongst themselves and made the confusion still more desperate and deadly, the shouts of Erili's men plunging into the sea to attack the attackers.

It was the sweetest music in the ears of Kinyras and hearing it he attacked the rear. Bringing his slinging machines into action charged with barrels of blazing tar to which graplines were attached by short lengths of rope and hurled them with a frightful effect into the enemy's closely packed formation. At the same time his arrow machines kept up a heavy barrage of fiery darts, which had the effect in the blackness of the night of perpetual showers of shooting stars. So accurate was the aim of the throwers that barely one in a dozen went astray, or fell harmless into the sea, and soon many ships were ablaze, the hideous roar and crackle of the flames adding to the panic.

The confusion of the Khemite fleet was now complete, which apart from its immobility, was so heavily laden with men that the archers had no space to draw their bows and must needs stand inactive like sheep awaiting slaughter. Added to this terrible disadvantage the Khemites could not see their enemy while they themselves were clearly outlined against their guiding fires, and the blazing ships.

When the barrage had taken due effect Kinyras ordered all oars double-banked and to prepare for ramming. Rushing in with incredible and deadly precision, Dolphin and Sea-Horse rammed with smashing force, retreated and rammed again, keeping up the shattering process with incredible energy. The slenderly built Khemite craft cracked like hazel-nuts beneath the feet of elephants, and not only those which suffered the direct impact were stove in, but the rammed acted as rammers in their turn, to the utter demoralization of all concerned. When the rear was all but pulverized Kinyras attacked the centre with an equal success and so the demolishing of the enemy went on until dawn when, in the growing grey light the Khemites began to see what they were about and such as were capable of the effort made a dash for safety and got away. Nothing but exhaustion of every kind of ammunition prevented Kinyras from giving chase and as the Khemite archers could now see their targets and were putting up a good running fight, he could not ram in face of the volleys of arrows with which he now faced. Moreover his oarsmen were weak with fatigue, so he anchored and let his men sleep their fill.

This firest experience of the sea-fight left Dayonis somewhat discontented and pouting because there had been no opportunity for hand to hand encounters, for daring exploits of the spectacular quality so dear to her soul. The delight of Kinyras, which shone through all his weariness and hunger as he sat in the cabin eating an enormous meal, at which she picked with exaggerated delicacy in order to express something of her pique and of which he took no notice at all, not only exasperated her, but wounded her as well. He had put her so completely aside, seemed to forget her existence and she found time to wonder at the difference between men and women. Kinyras lived his life with complete whole-heartedness in isolated compartments. When he fought he was nothing but a fighter, when he loved her he was purely her lover, when he planned his wall he was obsessed with it to the exclusion of everything else, while in her the merging of each facet of her nature was so subtle as to be imperceptible.

'It would seem that the pleasure of a fight at sea lies with the master of the ship, the commander in chief of the forces defending Karpas and the men who work the engines,' she commented acidly.

He swallowed a huge block of goat's-flesh with a gulp before he could answer her. 'Experience will mend your idea, Dayonis.'

'Let us hope so.'

He snatched at his wine cup, drank deeply, smacked his lips, uttered a prolonged 'A-A-H!' of supreme satisfaction and rose, laughed good humouredly, chucked her under her chin, from which she jerked it away pettishly, laughed again, yawned, stretched, flung himself upon one of the couches, and almost immediately was snoring in concert with his exhausted men.

Dayonis crept up on deck to ponder things and to reason herself into a better and more generous humour. So she lay under her awning, thinking her thoughts bitter-sweet, watching the sunlight glancing on the blue water, listening to the lip of the waves against the sides. The ship was very quiet, even the look-out man nodded occasionally in his crow's nest, for nothing was in sight but a school of dolphins, whose gambles amused her until they, too, swam off, leaving that immensity of silence and loneliness for her contemplation.

Presently she, too, drowsed until a yell from the look-out roused her with a start, to find that it was evening and a boat was being rapidly rowed towards them.

# Chapter XIV

# THE LINE IS BROKEN

inyras was on the deck before the boat reached them. A rapid glance at his love assured him she had recovered her wonted good-humour. He noted the fact with satisfaction and relief, for she, too, had her lessons to learn, the first and foremost of which was the fact that she was a woman whose place in the creation of things she must fill. Tenderly he thought of her youth, but experience in him sometimes irked at the lack of it in her, and folly he could not abide, in anyone.

She was standing looking at the advancing boat, shading her eyes from the level sun with her hands. He went to her, put an arm around her shoulders, smiled down at her fondly and drew her towards him. She glanced up at him from beneath her thick lashes. 'My brave soldier, my Kinyras! Thank the Gods you are unscathed,' she said, smiling and yielding deliciously. 'It is Erili who comes yonder.'

It was indeed he, attended by one officer only. The ladder was lowered and he ascended, Kinyras extending a welcoming hand which was grasped cordially.

'Greetings, sire, and welcome to my poor ship.'

Erili smiled, but made a gesture of depreciation. His kingship, though he had urged it with so much persistence for reasons of his own, sat somewhat exasperatingly upon him, particularly when the company of his old comrade and favourite. He missed the freedom of his camp-days. 'Leave ceremony for its fit occasions, brother,' he growled, and turning to his officer, who was still on the ladder, bid him curtly wait on deck, then taking Dayonis by the hand he kissed her on the brow with some satisfaction.

Kinyras called for wine and fruit to be brought to the cabin, and Dayonis would have returned to her mattress, but he would have none of it, nor did Erili wish her banishment.

There was little need to ask for news, for Erili had the air of a man well pleased, and directly they had seated themselves he spoke. 'We have succeeded, Kinyras, and the loss inflicted upon the enemy must be enormous. There was as many as a hundred and sixty ships sailing in the Khemite fleet, carrying some two hundred men each, which we have destroyed. Those which escaped were few. Many men swam ashore and these we took prisoner.'

Kinyras drew a deep breath of relief and the eyes of Dayonis sparkled fiercely. 'Good!' they exclaimed in unison and Erili smiled at her, finding her good to look upon at that moment.

'What say the prisoners?' Kinyras asked.

Some of the satisfaction left Erili's face. 'Little. None of their higher officers have been taken, unfortunately, and those petty officers whom I questioned and who spoke under persuasion, only knew that they had orders to sail along the coast. The land troops were ordered into action, it seems, by the higher command upon the assumption that the line would be unguarded at that point and that, once past and landed, the occupation of the whole country would be naught but a matter of marching in.'

'May Jaske visit them with his everlasting torments,' came in a fierce little hiss from the excited girl.

Erili exchanged an amused glance with Kinyras, who raised his heavy brows and muttered—'Hange!'

'Without doubt.'

'But, sir, now we should have the means of making crow's meat of him,' Dayonis burst in, eagerly.

'I wish I could think so, lady. I have established by careful enquiry that the fires were lighted by men of the regular Karpasian troops, which the Council had insisted upon being kept in Karpasia to protect the town. These, upon pretended news of a coming invasion from the sea, had been reinforced, and had been ordered to occupy certain points, of import along the coast, where landings were possible. Their instructions were to light the fires for the purpose of sighting any attempt at a landing. By so doing the troops were convinced they were honestly defending their native land.'

'But the instructions!' Kinyras fumed, 'How and by whom conveyed?'

Erili shrugged and spread his hands. 'By words alone, by one of Hange's men, acting under secret orders.'

They were silent, digesting this bitter intelligence. After a moment or two Erili resumed—'Servants of Hange and men of his party were guarding the place of last night's attack, a well sheltered bay some five miles from Karpasia, excellent for the purpose. Unfortunately, we cannot prove this treachery and already he is making capital of our victory, telling the people that he and the Council had foreseen the invasion by sea and had frustrated it by strongly guarding the coast.'

Kinyars was speechless with rage at this, and stood as he had risen to reach for a new wine-jar, his jays clenched, one shaking hand resting on the table. He could do nothing but glare into the hot eyes of Erili. After a moment of consuming passion, which was terrible to the watchers, he recovered himself by an effort, got the jar, placed it on the table and reseated himself. Only his white face betrayed the recent storm. 'Hunt this rat out I will!' he declared in such a deadly tone that Dayonis shivered in spite of herself. There was something terrible to her in the anger of Kinyras, so different from her own gusty squalls.

'Aye, on that we are all agreed, but how? One thing may comfort you. I have cut off Karpasia, passing word along the line that every man, woman or child who tries to pass the guard I have set between the line and the coast is to be detained. I have ordered the Karpasian troops to stay at their posts. This means that these men who lighted the fires are still on the coast and must needs stay there or betray themselves.'

'Excellent, oh, most excellent, Erili,' cried Kinyras. 'all that remains now is to smell them out?'

'True, but how? Who can do this difficult and delicate thing for us? It will take time and much cunning and the man who does it must be bone loyal and have his wits about him. None of our men can leave his post and Zadoug is taking your place. You are known, Kinyras, and so am I. Whom then, can we send?'

Erili looked hopefully at Dayonis as he spoke, for here was a coil which a woman's wit might well help to untangle.

'Ammunz would serve, but him I have sent to Aghirda,' she answered reflectively. Their hopeful faces fell again and each thought with some desperation. 'But what of Hasvan?' she continued after a lengthy silence.

'He has the cunning of seventy demons and would be cut in pieces for me, but he is known, too well known,' Kinyras objected, with a gloomy shake of his head.

'But not if he grows his hair long, wears a beard and has one eye tied up. What say you, my King?'

'Princess, I believe you have solved our riddle. Trust a woman's wit to find a way out, if way there is.'

'By the gods he shall have his freedom if he scotches this snake,' Kinyras cried.

'And a twentieth share in the treasure,' added Dayonis, 'A freed man needs the where-withal to live, or his servitude is in better case.'

They laughed and Kinyras summoned his attendant. The slave came running, and Hasvan eyed him attentively.

'Hasvan, you are unkempt. Your hair is like the plumage of an eagle and you have four day's growth upon your chin.'

The man made a deep obeisance and looked most supplicatingly at his master. 'Pardon, lord, but what with the watch and the fight and one thing and another I...'

'Nay, good fellow, I know, I know. I did but plague and as

it turns out it is a most lucky chance, for I have another mission for you, a difficult and dangerous mission. Listen.'

Lowering their voices almost to a whisper for fear even that isolated spot was not safe for their secret plans, they talked long and earnestly, explaining the matter. Hasvan who had all the cunning and intelligence of his race highly developed, found the proposed adventure one after his own heart. Fear was unknown to him and he had a lion's daring. He was to be put ashore that night to follow whatever plan his ingenuity might suggest to him and the exigency of the moment. When he had anything to report he was to fire into the sea at night, at a given spot, a staveros bolt, to which had been attached a flare, when Kinyras, who would keep a strong look-out for such, would draw in as near as was safe while Hasvan came out to the Dolphin in a coracle.

Erili departed, leaving master and slave still talking, but when Kinyras spoke of the guerdon of his service Hasvan was almost reproachful. 'But master, my live is yours; your lordship has been good to me and always merciful. I need no reward.'

'But good service and devotion must meet with its just recompense and such it will be. All depends upon you, Hasvan, for unless this wretch can be confronted with the proofs of his crimes and pulled down from his high place, the whole country will be sacrificed to his treachery. It is his live or ours.'

'I will remember always it is my beloved master's life or his,' said Hasvan solemnly. 'And if I cannot find proof enough to hang him, I will creep behind him and stab him where he stands.'

'That too, might serve, and we will consider of it, but I would prefer to bring him to public justice.'

So Hasvan was put ashore in the darkness of the night, with money concealed about him and a bundle of assorted garments both rich and lowly, tied up in a napkin, to try his fortunes as a spy.

Meanwhile the patrol of the coast went on and the next day Kinyras sailed towards the Kastnon river, watching for stragglers of the Khemite fleet, but finding none. He must reload his ship with missiles, of which his store had run out. About midnight they had located a fire in that direction, but it was not until he ran in close when day was breaking that he saw that the one blaze was actually four, set in a row in order to be distinguished from the sea and was in fact the recall signal. Shortly after they were met by a small boat bearing a messenger with a letter for Kinyras from Erili.

> 'Come at once. They broke through Witend's line late last night. This is a breach of the truce and every effort must be united to drive them back again. Keep Dayonis out of sight, for Hange has been inflaming the minds of the people against her and if she is seen the breach of the truce will be attributed to her presence and the horrors of invasion laid at her door. In her absence she may be forgotten. Bring all the men you can spare and come to Hap Hill. We are mustering there and will strike at the enemy down the line of Witend's wall, to try to retake as much of it as possible.'

Kinyras sent back the messenger with tidings of his immediate departure and went to inform Dayonis. She announced her intention of going with him, but he was in no mood to waste a moment upon her and gave her her orders as sharply as to one of his lieutenants. 'You will remain on board, lady, in command of the ships in my absence. Some eighty of the Khemite ships have escaped from the battle of recent event, and an attack by them at a time when every man is needed to drive back the invaders from the wall, would be fatal to our cause. Farewell! Until we meet again.'

With a salute he turned, walked out of the cabin and had gone ashore before she had time even to feel flattered at having a definite mission of her own with which to deal.

Kinyras set out along his line towards Hap Hill, collecting all the men who could be spared as he progressed. He found trouble brewing everywhere. Hange's spies had been broadcasting dissension where possible, declaring that the sole reason for the invasion was because the Strangers were harbouring Khemite subjects, that all this trouble arose through one miserable slave-girl and a foul and accursed witch to boot, winding up with the assertion that if this one girl was given up there would be peace between the two nations and a life-long friendship. The only way to overcome the evil was to refuse to fight or to carry out any war-work.

This insidious doctrine came as a very welcome theory to men weary with building and holding the line, and to mothers and wives fearful for the safety of their menfolk, as women always have been since the creation of the world. The fact that the invasion had begun before the advent of Dayonis and would continue after her passing, until the whole of the island was in the hands of the enemy, was cheerfully ignored.

The agitators spoke the Mercenaries fair, urging that it was an unfair proposition for them to do all the work of defence for a people who were already talking and thinking of making a separate peace. It was impossible for the Mercenaries to hold the lines unaided and therefore the best course open to them was to offer themselves and their services to the enemy, who could use them to advantage in any of their numerous wars waging at the moment. Their Captain Kinyras had very cleverly deserted them at the right moment and gone off plundering on some private venture. Why stand by one who had already betrayed them? Why not open negotiations with the Khemites?

The result of this sedition was much unrest among the Mercenaries, while the Karpasian militia had almost all deserted in a body. But news of the invasion had terrified them and some had returned to duty. The return of Kinyras was welcomed by the older men, but the younger sulked, asserting that he had left them to fend for themselves. They were in an ugly temper.

Kinyras found that all his authority had lapsed. He had to defend the lines while at the same time he must move large bodies of troops to beat back the enemy. Much talk ensued, and Kinyras spent himself in argument and persuasion, with the result that the Karpasians promised to get their men to return to duty only if they were sure of being backed by the Strangers. The Mercenaries for their part felt the broken line was an irretrievable disaster and that their wisdom and safety lay in staying as near to sea as possible, where their retreat lay open to them.

After much discussion Kinyras succeeded in inducing a number of the elder men to accompany him. The further he went up the line exhorting the men to follow him, the nearer he got to the fighting, where men realised the seriousness of the situation, the more successful was he. At Monagra Hill he met Witkind with a number of men, from whom he got the latest news.

It appeared that the guards Kinyras had set upon his house on Gypos Hill had been attacked several times by bands of the Karpasian Militia instigated by Hange. Kinyras hurried thither, releasing the guard, who were a welcome addition to his company. A number of fugitives from Aghirda, hearing that their Princess was in the house had made their way to it, but as the guards refused admittance according to their orders, the men of Aghirda camped on the hill and then the house was attacked, beat off the Karpasians, returning to their camp when the fight was over and at all times demanding to see their Princess.

Kinyras had learnt enough of their language from Dayonis to make himself intelligible to them. He collected them and after talking to them well and eloquently, led them to the house, broke its sealed and entered, convincing them that he spoke truth when he said that Dayonis had fled to his ship for safety and was now occupied in raiding th eKhemite fleets. There was something about Kinyras that conveyed his upright-ness and honesty of purpose to his listeners and they agreed to follow him and to join in this war, knowing it was the wish of their Princess that always they should take the field against Khem when opportunity served.

This reinforcement of three hundred sturdy mountaineers was a very welcome addition to his company. They were all archers, drawing the bow to the ear after the manner of Khem, though being bigger and stronger they could outshoot the Khemites and could shoot further and with more force than the Karpasians. After much talking and diplomacy, Kinyras eventually got together a fair-sized army and advanced upon Hap Hill. As he marched he kept a sharp observation of the Khemite lines, but no movement pointing to an attack could be seen. He learnt that large companies of troops had marched northward, probably to reinforce the position which had recently been gained, but as he approached nearer to his objective he could see parties of the enemy on the march, of whom all the men who could be spared were being sent north.

The road he had made enabled him to speed his advance, but unfortunately it extended only to the boundary of Witend's line and progress slowed down again. Beyond the boundary he found many of Witend's men who had fled up the hill and the garrison of the little fort on the shoulder, the commander of which, on hearing of the breach in the line, had marched all his men north, making a very good defence along the crest of the hill and so preventing the enemy from widening his front. He had rallied many of Witend's men in their flight and recruited the shepherds dwelling on the hill, all of whom were excellent slingers. After several determined attacks upon his position the Khemites had decided it was too strongly defended and had withdrawn.

From this sector it was easy to see the broken line, pierced from the distance of about a mile. Witend had made his lines from the cliffs on the north of the hill down to a swamp in the valley below, serving as a natural defence, and continued it from the northern edge of the swamp until it joined up with Zadoug's section. This defence seemed strong enough, but the night of the attack on the Khemite fleet had been planned for a double advance and a large force of the enemy had crossed the swamp, advancing through its centre on floats and had made a determined rear attack. The surprise had entirely successful and so silently and effectively executed that a flight of arrows in the back of the Wall's garrison had been the first indication of their approach. Once the breach was made the attackers were soon masters of the line as far as the cliffs, though the crest of the ill was denied them.

From the top of the hill could be seen the extent of the Khemite advance inland, a matter of several miles, whose trail was blazed by devastated villages and burning houses from which the smoke curled lazily into the summer air. Kinyras viewed the sight with rage and hatred against the miserable cause of it all, the traitor Hange. Afar off a little party was coming towards him as rapidly as circumstances would permit. It must be Zadoug, but messengers from Erili distracted his attention. Erili was advancing to the rescue with as many men as he could muster with all the speed he could achieve and the spirits of Kinyras rose at the good news. With the Aghirdans, the shepherds and the remnant of Witend's men, his own force registered some two thousand men.

Zadoug came up and the two brothers greeted with a silent grasp of the hand. Zadoug felt bitterly this breach in the line during the absence of Kinyras, though it was due to pure fortune of war and to no carelessness on his part, or that of the men under his command. 'Congratulations, brother, you have accomplished wonders. I wish I could make as good a report, but you see how it is, old Snail.'

'Nay, lad, never take it to heart. We have a daring and ingenious enemy to fight. Let us accord them the honours of war and set about remedying the business. You must return to your line and keep a tight grip of your men and the Karpasians under your charge. Our danger lies from Karpas more than from Khem. With them we do know what to expect. If you can smell out any of Hange's men, string them up out of hand as an encouragement to the others. I shall attack downwards along the lines, keeping the enemy busy and preventing him from advancing further inland, giving Erili time to bring up his men. Farewell for the present, Zadoug, and if I fail protect Dayonis as far is lies in your power.'

'I will, Kinyras. Where is she?'

'Still on the Dolphin. I gave orders to Kinuis to keep her

out of mischief as far as possible.'

The brothers parted and according to his plan Kinyras attacked, rolling up small bodies of the enemy and advancing perhaps half a mile before he met with any serious resistance. The ground was in his favour as it descended the hill, the slope gave his pikemen the advantage and their furious charges wrought immense havoc. The staveros bowmen had the whole Khemite army below them and could rake the opposing regiments armed with copper falchions, spears and maces, with deadly volleys of bolts, before which the Khemite spearmen fell like reaped grain. Kinyras was facing three times his numbers, but most of the Khemite bowmen had been transferred to the West and this gave him a further advantage. Later the enemy rallied a large body of men and put up a furious resistance, but even so by the evening Kinyras had retaken three quarters of the lost line.

The ground from thence to the swamp offered him none of the advantages of the hill-side, but sloped gently to the swamp's edge. To remedy this defect he retreated to a small line of cliffs some three hundred yards back and halted for the night. Both sides were exhausted with a long day's fighting and though the enemy brought up large reinforcements during the night, no attack was launched. In the morning Kinyras received a few reinforcements and many bundles of staveros bolts, quantities of which he had expended in his action. Indeed he had been only able to continue his advance owing to the fact that his men had been advancing and thus were able to retrieve most of the bolts fired during their furious charges.

During the night Kinyras had set up rough breastworks of brushwood so that when the Khemites attacked in the morning his men were well protected, and the long Khemite shields though arrow-proof, were useless against the staveros bolt. Kinyras fought on with a light heart, reflecting that all the enemy's reinforcements came from within their line, knowing that they were expecting help from Salam, of whose fate they as yet knew nothing. Even so, their attack grew in violence as troop after troop was brought up comprising companies of slingers and pikemen. Kinyras repulsed their furious onrushes by rolling heavy boulders down the hill, though in order to do this the breastwork shelter had to be abandoned.

So the fight went on, swaying now backwards and now forwards, with varying fortunes on either side and definite advantage to neither, until a messenger came from Erili reporting that he was attacking to the east and driving the enemy back slowly. Further, the Karpasian regulars and militia were in force and behaving well. Erili had given orders that the enemy must be held at all costs.

So far so good and Kinyras held on with a grim determination. All day long parties of men had been coming up over the hill to his help, but soon after noon a thousand of the Karpasian militia came in to reinforce him, and their arrival put new heart of grace into his tired men.

Meanwhile more and more Khemites arrived from the interior, but they, too, were weary, weighed down with loot and unwilling to fight. Though they came on repeatedly, they had to be driven to attack with great whips of rhinoceros hide and their charges lacked punch through having to advance over mounds of their own dead and wounded. As the day wore on they became more and more dispirited. They knew their attack had failed and their one idea was to escape into safety, carrying their loot with them. Kinyras, old campaigner as he was, sensed this and after the last big assault had failed, he ordered a charge and advanced almost an eighth of a mile, where he halted and made a hasty defence of earth and dead bodies. It was little enough, but with shields gathered from the field laid on top, it kept out arrows. With this advantage gained, the edge of the swamp was under staveros fire.

Kinyras remained on the high ground from whence he could see Erili's banner waving distinctly, barely a mile away. The Khemites were striving to hold their line, but were steadily being forced back by him, giving ground all the while. A shout from one of the shepherds distracted his attention from this gratifying sight to where the man was pointing across the swamp. Furious fighting was taking place there, a party of the enemy who had been cut off by Erili were striving to break through by the further side of the marsh and were attacking the other section of Witend's line, whose garrison laboured under the disadvantage of having to defend its wall from the wrong side. They were fighting hard, but the attack was heavily forced and seemed likely to succeed.

While Kinyras watched, cursing and helpless to assist, a band of men swept down the hill with a rush, striking the Khemites on their flank and driving them down the hill into the swamp. They bore a banner in their midst, which hung limp in the hot air, clinging about its pole, but as it moved he saw its emblem, a red dragon on a white field. It was Zadoug's banner and his men pursued the Khemites into the marsh, where the reeds and the tall grasses swallowed them.

At the moment Erilie made a mighty charge until his left flank reached the slopes of Hap Hill. Kinyras ordered his staveros bowmen and a band of shepherds forward and with as many of these as he could spare from his main action, advanced until he was behind the enemy's right flank. The sudden and unexpected volleys of bolts and sling bullets from behind made Khem waver, and when Erili charged again the flank crumpled, broke and ran. Behind their line fresh troops formed and the rout was stopped, but now the Khemite centre was exposed and was forced to retire, losing many men in the action. While the reformed flank was under the fire of Kinyras from the hill, the rear ranks of the Khemites faced round and kept off the worst of the fire with their shields, but all the time they were losing heavily, and, attacked from both sides, were forced to retreat to fresh positions.

Once more Kinyras poured in his destructive fire and the Khemite commander detailed two regiments to attack him. Bravely they stormed the hill with heavy loss of men, but as Kinyras was not strong enough to resist, he ordered many great boulders to be rolled down upon the enemy, which crashed into their densely formed ranks, ploughing through and sweep-ing away many of them. When this manoeuvre was executed he retreated about three hundred yards up the hill, reformed and again opened fire, countering their charge with a second avalanche of rocks. Three times did Kinyras so retreat, when the Khemites, seeing the futility of the whole action, wearied and retreated in their turn.

Meanwhile Erili was slowly pushing back the enemy, whose front was being dangerously narrowed between the swamp and the foot of the mountain. The rearguard of the Khemite right flank attempted the ascent of the mountain, and Kinyras knew that if he was successful in this assault of the height, he could never be dislodged. Swiftly he gave the word and every man engaged rushed helter skelter, without any effort at formation, to get above the Khemites and foil the attempt with each rock and stone which could be seized and hurled or rolled down upon the advancing forces, before shooting them down. In this curious race the men of Aghirda easily beat the heavily armed Mercenaries. Mountaineers all, unencumbered by armour and having only a shield, a bow, a sword or a knife, they covered the ground like wild cats and being also very strong, each used to fighting single-handed, they had set great rocks in motion upon the enemy, long before Kinyras and his men, with the accompanying Karpasian militia could join them.

The Khemites came on under a covering cloud of arrows, in a dense formation, but the tumbling boulders made them open out their ranks. With plenty of room they managed to dodge the advancing rocks though, through being used to fight only in close formation they were unable to adjust themselves rapidly to a new condition and consequently their charges lacked punch. Lack of courage was no fault of theirs and moreover they were ten men to the defenders' one. Soon the supply of loose rocks gave out and nothing was open to the Mercenaries but to retreat up the hill to fresh ground, where there were more boulders and twice was this done before the attack slackened. To his relief, Kinyras saw that Erili had pushed back the main Khemite army still further and their rearguard action must cease if it was to avoid being cut off.

As the rearguard fell back to its main body on the plains, Kinyras seized his opportunity to execute one of his lighting rushes and so converted the dignified retreat of Khem into a sudden and unbecoming rout. Once more he found himself above their right wing, in a position to harass them with his long-range staveros fire. The supply of bolts had long since been exhausted, but the Mercenaries discovered that they could use the Khemite arrows, which they collected in their advance, with good effect if with no great accuracy. As they were firing into a great mass of men, this was not important since each arrow must necessarily find a human target somewhere.

Now in touch with his body again, Kinyras found with delight that Zadoug had crossed the swamp by means of a causeway he had built of Khemite dead reinforced with bundles of rushes. They had now a chance to cut off the enemy's retreat and messengers were hastily sent off to Erili to ask him to send up his reserves. Speedily the answer came in the shape of companies of Mercenaries advancing over the hill. Two thousand men reinforced the joined lines of Zadoug and Kinyras, between the base of the hill and the swamp and a thousand more manned the old line on the crest. These comprised the extent of Erili's reserves, but they were fresh while all the troops engaged in the day's fighting on both sides were exhausted. As dusk fell Kinyras made his dispositions for the night and both camps slept the sleep of utter weariness.

While the Mercenaries rested in grim satisfaction, the Khemites were filled with disquiet and a brooding sense of disaster. Their grate attack had failed, the might of their unconquerable arms had experienced the humiliation of being foiled at every point and driven back by a mere handful of men. Reinforcement from Salam had failed and worse calamity still, they were cut off from their base. But if the troops murmured of disaster, their commanders were confident. They had every reason to believe that a great army had been landed from their attacking fleet and might be expected at any moment to smash back and annihilate the troops which had been driving them all day.

If this pleasing fancy comforted them over night, it did not appear so rosy in the morning when they discovered that a ditch had been dug and a palisade built between the swamp and the foot of the hill, effectually blocking their retreat. Food was scarce, their men hungry and dispirited and though Erili refrained from making any move, the Khemites attacked as a matter of policy. They always attacked.

As the Khemites advanced they found their right flank and centre exposed to a heavy staveros fire from the hill, while their left was galled by archers hidden in the reeds of the marsh. They were driven back with little difficulty.

Opinion amongst the command was divided at the council which followed. One high officer argued—'Our men are exhausted. If we stay here the men of Salam must come to our rescue. They will attack the outer palisades while our men are resting and then we shall launch a joint advance, attacking this insolent enemy upon two sides, with the army from the fleet marching to our assistance. While we remain we keep the army of this paltry foe occupied.'

'Nay, with submission, not so, sir,' another rose to object. 'We have no food to enable us to await rescue. We must save ourselves. The army from the fleet is plundering and drinking, if calamity has not befallen it and it lies drowned in the great Grey Green. If it was approaching we should have had word of it ere this. We must make a massed attack and break a way through. We must deal plainly with our men, tell them that the armies from Salam and the fleet have failed us and are not to be expected, and that each man must now fight for his own life.'

'The gods have stricken you with madness, sir. If this thing is done then we are utterly lost, for the men will be too dispirited to fight.'

So the dispute went on, back and forth, while the army languished in semi-starvation and only half-hearted sallies were carried out. Soon it became known that the officers were in conflict of opinion and the morale of the troops sunk lower. Desertions began to be frequent, many seeking refuge in the swamp only to be drowned, others surrendering in large bodies.

Kinyras was anxious to get private speech with Erili, for he was curious to discover how the King had contrived to come to the rescue with so large a company of Karpasians. The position at his front was such that he could now leave it in safety for a few hours and mounting Baal Selah he rode over to the royal camp.

Erili received him gleefully, being in a high good humour, the reason for which he hastened to disclose. 'Here you are at last!' he exclaimed with relief, when they were alone, 'I have desired your presence much, Kinyras.'

'And I yours, Erili, for certain things have puzzled me exceedingly.'

Erili laughed and clapped him familiarly on the shoulder. He was in a very hearty mood. 'I can guess them and I will tell you. When i discovered that our friend Hange had been sol solicitous for the success of Khem and had contrived that the Karpasians' forces were so split up and disposed in diverse places that the capital was left undefended, I secured the written order for this manoeuvre, with its seals attached.'

'I being to perceive,' Kinyras grinned like a delighted boy and Erili grinned back. The King shouted for wine and poured generous bumpers. 'Let us drink to the speedy downfall of our honourable coadjutor.'

'And then?' Kinyras prompted.

'Yakub, but the aid of his copy, provided me with a fine set of orders from Hange and the council, commanding all troops to follow me in the defence of the frontier. Simple!'

They spent some time drinking and sharpening their wits at the expense of Hange. It was sweet to have cut the ground from under his feet, thus, for in the nature of things he dared make no outcry about the matter.

Kinyras regarded his friend and sovereign with admiring delight. 'The Karpasians have proved themselves fine fighters, Erili.'

'You speak truth. They have borne the brunt of this attack, for I used them in the front of the battle.'

'And I. It seemed wiser to save our own men for future

emergencies as far as might be.'

'So I deemed. Three quarters of them are dead or wounded, but by the grace of the gods, they have saved their country, as is fitting.'

'And the envoys?'

'I shall seize and imprison them immediately upon my return. The truce was deliberately broken and my way to that end is now clear. This business has much strengthened our hand, Old Snail. We have beaten the enemy, whose treachery is patent, and the people will now listen to me. I shall make much of the aid we received from the Aghirdans, give them half the credit of victory.'

Kinyras laughed. 'Khem has not yet capitulated,' he remarked.

Erili made an airy gesture. 'A matter of days only. The green boughs will be fluttering under our noses before we can say "shoot".'

'They have shot their bolt, I think.'

'Not a doubt of it. And now your red-head. How goes it with her? I shall tell the Council that she summoned her Aghirdans to your help and that should turn the tide in her favour. What I need is a legion of barbarians who will obey my orders without question.'

'She has already summoned such and they will follow her. She is their lawful queen.'

'That may be disputed. I hear tell of other claimants. Why do you not marry her?'

'That will come in time, please the gods, but only in her own country, where are certain sacred stones necessary to the ritual. I have urged that we, too, have our ceremony, but she will have none of it, declares no true marriage may be formed in the absence of these stones.'

'Oh, these women and their whimsies, how they tie up a man. Thank the gods I am subject to none of them.'

'The situation is strange,' mused Kinyras. 'She is my wife in all but ritual and is content to live so, deeming it no harm. Yet a marriage ceremony performed by any rites but her own she calls an insult and a mockery.'

'Well, she must have her way, it seems, but hark ye, Kinyras, let not a whisper of these "powers" of hers get about, or she is lost. The Karpasians have a great hatred and dread of witchcraft and will inevitably demand her death if she is known as a witch. Mark it, she has the power to ruin not only you and me, but all our men.'

'Yet some strange power she has, and has used it to our help.'

'Discourage its use, forbid it, set your face firmly against its practice. It is an order, Kinyras.'

'I do, Erili. I see as you do into the matter and from the first its danger has appalled me, but she is hard to move from her set purpose and is a true believer in herself and her mission. Such rites as she has held and I am forced to countenance one here and there, have been done in secret and only in the presence of those whom I trust.'

'I know. 'Tis easier to hold a wild cat than a woman, or to turn her from her purpose. Do what you can.'

'I will.'

'Return to your wall, Old Snail, and build as hard and fast as you can. That is your work, while mine is to outwit and pull down Hange and subdue the Council.'

'Sooner you than me, Erili!' Kinyras laughed, as they clasped hands and parted.

Erili had been right in his conjecture. On the third day from their meeting the Khemite officers ordered a massed attack, but only the Khemite troops obeyed. The Nubians, of which there were many regiments, had revolted. The General ordered them to be driven forward, but the resisted and turned at bay. They were attacked, other auxiliary troops came to their rescue and Kinyras beheld the novel sight of a miniature civil war carried on amongst his enemy under his very nose. Khemite discipline won, but of the army of thirty thousand which had menaced the wall, only three thousand could stand and the next morning this remnant sent in the green boughs of surrender.

So far so good, this was a respite, but not the ending of danger. Truly there was cause for some rejoicing, for the might of Khem had been brought low in the field and her cunning in statecraft foiled. This was a double blow to her pride, which must and would be revenged at the earliest opportunity. Therefore was there a feverish activity all along the Karpasian line, to make the most of this breathing space and prepare for the coming menace. All that military skill and foresight could accomplish was done in the disposal of troops along the wall to the best advantage and once more the Karpasians worked with a will at the defence, having learnt their lesson from their recent terrifying experiences.

One of the most difficult problems awaiting solution from Kinyras was the disposal and treatment of the Khemite wounded. The hospital he had organized was already crowded with his own men. The trouble lay not so much with the badly wounded, they would die inevitably, though it might be more merciful to dispatch them at once. Certainly it would be more economic to do so, but it was the slightly wounded which caused the problem. If they were left to lie among the dead they would kill all who chanced to pass by.

It was Zadoug who settled the matter by building a stockade on the edge of the swamp, where he herded all the Khemites who were likely to recover, supplied them with food and water and left them to tend each other's wounds. All the wounded Karpasians and Mercenaries had been brought in and tended as well as possible in the circumstances in the rough hospital set up by Kinyras. First aid had been given on the field by laying leaves or threads athwart the wounds, so giving the blood something to congeal upon and stopping the bleeding temporarily, before binding up with shreds of garments. But when these men were moved haemorrhage started again. From the villages round Karpasian women were recruited who had some slight knowledge of leech-craft, but whose remedies consisted of the steeping of certain roots, supplies of which were limited. Parties of men were sent out in search of these roots and when they were found and collected, a fair distribution had to be made.

Kinyras, restored by circumstances to his old dignity and authority, set out as was his custom, to survey his line. Everywhere he found the most satisfactory signs of renewed progress and good will. When he reached the plains he rejoiced to see that the whole Karpasian militia had returned to duty, scared thither by the recent happenings. Activity, re-established cheerfulness, greetings and words of praise for himself and his men, met him at every step. Such a state of affairs could not but put him in good fettle, both with himself and the world. At last he came to Vanner Hill and reaching the crest, saw a small party coming towards him up the other slope.

He sat staring, mechanically checking Baal Selah, his heart quickening with mingled sensations of joy and anger, for in their midst he saw a red head which could belong to but one person, and even as he gazed Dayonis waved both white hands in greetings.

# Chapter XV

# Taken Captive

I t was sweet to look upon her lovely face again, exquisite joy and pleasure to clasp her once more in his arms and to kiss the pouting red mouth, but his orderly, stern soldier's mind could not stomach the disobedience. Yet, what could he do? Nothing but sit like a stature on Baal Selah, refusing to advance one inch to welcome her.

She was full of excitement of their meeting and of all she had to tell him. Still in his arms she burst forth into animated speech. 'Oh, Kinyras, my sweet lord, I have much to tell.'

'Why are you here, Dayonis?' he began sternly.

'For the reason that I longed to be with you once more my love, as I knew you were longing for me,' she whispered ardently, her lips on his ear.

What could he do in answer to this plea but kiss her again with a growing passion and forgive disobedience on the spot? 'Foolish, foolish wench, you might have run into the worst terrors from which I have striven to save you.'

'Nay, I knew better, my beloved, or I would not have ventured. We have raided Capo Di Gato and the Khemite temple of Bast, the Cat-Headed one, where we found great treasure. The men are full of delight.'

Kinyras said nothing since he could not approve and would not scold. The place had no military significance and the destruction of the temple was against his principles for it did but enrage the priesthood and anything in the way of a senseless persecution he abhorred. 'What of Hasvan?' he whispered.

'Not a sign, not a word,' she murmured back.

They returned to camp where her countrymen clustered about her with an extravagant joy, but when she questioned them they knew little of what was happening in Aghirda, being of those who had dwelt close to the Karpasian border. They told her that there were rumours of many holding out against the Khemites, whose army, though large and mighty, could not penetrated the fastnesses of a mountainous country. With this Karpasian war to distract them, they could not discipline Aghirda so thoroughly as they would have done had there been peace.

The chief spokesman, a giant of a fellow with huge limbs covered with strong red down, clad in goat-skin, bare-footed and grasping an enormous bow, with a large quiver bristling with arrows slung at his shoulder and his long, red locks curling about his neck, looked a truly formidable sight. Mighty he was in strength and endurance, but his intelligence was not in proportion, and savagery usurped reason in his mind. Fixing his glittering green eyes upon her with a curious mixture of devotion, expectation and latent menace, he continued—'Much could be done if a message could be sent and a secret gathering-place appointed in the mountains. But the task of a messenger would be full of peril and who will risk his life when he once has saved it, or when the need does not arise? 'Twould be simple folly. You, my lady Princess, have much magic in your power and can send the message by magic.'

There was a murmur of assent from the half-dozen forbidding barbarians assembled. Like all mountain dwelling people they were no cowards, but they were extremely cautious. Used to the storms and rigours of nature in her most dangerous aspects the perils of their daily life was such that only the stoutest courage, endurance and prudence enabled them to survive, but the impulsive daring of the plainsman who, surviving in more amenable conditions appears bolder through ignorance, was unknown to them.

Kinyras, sitting on a large mole-hill, elbow on knee and chin on palm, saw that the moment was fraught with danger and crisis. Dayonis had been brought with startling suddenness face to face with the point in her life when everything she stood for was challenged by a witless savage, when she would either lose the adherence of her people and her country with it, or cement them to her for ever. Was she quick enough to perceive this and to comprehend all which was at stake? He could give her no help, for to betray the slightest emotion by look or sign would be fatal before the watchful cunning confronting them. He sat immovable as he had sat on Baal Selah a little while before, gazing thoughtfully on the ground.

Dayonis rose to her feet with a superb gesture, raising her right arm, and her slender figure seemed to tower above the great men as she said in a low, full voice—'Dare you to tell **me** how the magic of the High gods of the Mountains shall be used, O men of Aghirda?'

It was enough and they shrank like children before the majesty of her deportment, seeing which she broke into a kindly smile, but finished scathingly—'Such messages were sent long ere your witless heads could devise the means. Already the men of Aghirda are gathering and meeting in secret places and if they are not, then it is because Aghirda has offended Jaske beyond forgiveness.'

At the bare thought of this they fell on their knees in supplication. 'Pardon, O most gracious, most Holy! Intercede with Jaske for us and avert his wrath from falling upon us and our country.'

Now she held out her arms to them as though she would gather them into her embrace and murmured like a cooing dove—'Always am I doing that, my children. I live but to restore our land to its former freedom. And with this good lord's help, and your own, and the blessing of the High Gods, we will do so yet.'

Kinyras now rose, laid his hand upon his sword hilt and raised his right above his head in affirmation. 'I will do so,' he said simply.

The Aghirdans in turn knelt at the feet of Dayonis, swearing a solemn oath of allegiance, kissing her hand, and Kinyras they acknowledged as their chief and leader. When they had filed off, and the lovers were along, free from observation, Dayonis trailed her fingers across her brow, where her curls clung damply, and drew an enormous breath.

'A near touch, my Dayonis,' murmured Kinyras. 'You are indeed fit to be the bride of Pharaoh.'

She looked at him without answering, angry to think he had been witness to such a scene. Kinyras took the opportunity to repeat to her the message Erili had sent her, which she took very ill indeed.

But Dayonis would not be resentful for long and her mind was too acute not to perceive the wisdom of Erili's comments and advice. He was a man old in strategy and experience and she must be guided to a certain extent by his policy. Without his help and the backing of his Mercenaries she was powerless, and even though as the bride of Pharaoh she might enjoy great power, the enmity of the priests would be an ever-threatening danger and one which would engulf her in the end. Aghirda, her own country and her own people, were dearer to her heart than her ambitions, and she greatly loved a fight. If she became Pharaoh's bride, power would last with her only until the priests pulled her down, or she was assassinated. And if she escaped both priests and secret murder by miracle, then there was the tragedy of waning beauty to defeat her far more surely than either of the two former. So long as she was young and lovely, so long only could she retain her power, but as Queen of Aghirda she need fear nothing but invasion from hostile enemies. There she could use her powers without let or hindrance and be worshipped as goddess and queen over her people.

For a while peace once more settled down over the line and building went on apace. The opportunity was seized again to send out wood-cuttings under a strong escort and many scouts at the outposts, to fell and haul in great logs for future use. It was pleasant to look out from the crest of Hap Hill and to see the plains below once more unencumbered by the hosts of Khem. Hearts all along the border beat more lightly and hands worked more willingly for the sight.

But Kinyras knew that this happy state of affairs could not last and his warning went up and down the line to this effect, but with a better result than formerly. Not only had the Karpasians had a taste of the quality of the Mercenaries, whom they had come to love, but of the formidable might of Khem, and of what conquest would mean to the country. For the whole length of the line and for many miles inland, there was not a man, woman nor child but would slave at the defences from dawn to dark without any bidding from the commander. Whatever treachery might be afloat from Hange and his party in Karpasia it dared not show its face nor breathe a word in the borderland.

So passed a month of quietness and torrid heat, in which men sweated at their labours and grew thin, then one evening just as the last of the cutters were passing through the great gates with the ox-teams, a cloud of dust appeared upon the horizon. Kinyras watched it, knowing only too well what it signified. A great sigh seemed to go up from the line as men strained their eyes and their ears for the first sight and sound of what they knew was coming. Nor had they long to wait before another Khemite division had sat itself down before their walls. A howl of rage and excitement went up from the defenders, and many of the Karpasian officers, urged on by their men, came in a body to beg Kinyras to lead them immediately to attack the foe, so eager were they to be at their enemies' throats and beat them backward home. It took him long to convince them of the better policy which lay in letting the enemy exhaust himself with repeated attack, while the defenders hived their strength and resources in a steady defence.

The enemy flaunted himself proudly and boldly to the intense irritation of the defenders. He launched a series of attacks which never were pressed home and were easily repulsed. They were in reality feints which instantly put Kinyras so much upon his guard that a word of warning was sent along the line to the effect that Khem was either searching for a weak spot from without, or awaiting some planned treachery from within the wall itself.

The effect of this was to keep up the vigilance of all concerned to such a pitch that it resulted in a message from the commander of the little fort on the shoulder of Hap Hill, built on the spot where the shepherd lad had long ago scaled the cliff. The commander reported that his guard had seen two men dressed as shepherds come to the bed of the dry torrent the night before and lower a rope. The watchers lay still behind their bushes while two men ascended the rope and conversed with those who had lowered it, and then disappeared the way they had come. Before the guard could attack these strangers with their rope, they had disappeared, melted away like snakes into the darkness of the night.

One of the guard had pulled the alarm-string, which summoned the patrol. Asked why they did not immediately attack, the two men answered that they thought it wiser not to alarm the enemy at that juncture but to wait further developments. Kinyras hastened to investigate the matter. The rope was found attached to a strong root and neatly coiled, hidden away under a big stone. So he placed huge cauldrons of hot water, which were kept at boiling point by little concealed fires of charcoal, in the bed of the little stream.

Every preparation to give the enemy a fitting welcome had been secretly executed by darkfall. Towards midnight the two bogus shepherds were again faintly discerned by the starlight descending the hill, but before they reached the ambush awaiting them something startled them and they fled. A flight of arrows pursued them and one fell, shot in the leg and him they took prisoner. Examination showed he was no shepherd and he was taken away for future interrogation. Kinyras had recognised him as nephew of Hange and he sent him to Dayonis under a strong escort, with a letter to her in which he revealed to her the man's identity, urging her to set six of her Aghirdans to keep him fast until he could return and inquire into the plot.

As this was accomplished a call was heard from below. Two of the guard, dressed as shepherds, lowered the rope as on the former occasion, and helped a man over the top of the cliff, while a third, nicely placed, hit him on the forehead with a hammer, stunning him instantly. He proved to be a Khemite in full armour and was followed immediately by another, who was treated in a similar way. In all nearly fifty men were so captured before the alarm was given by one who saw his danger and shouted to the rest before he was struck dead by the hammer, but though answers in Khemite were given to the questions shouted from below, the false accent was detected, and no more could be induced to draw near. Believing a large body of men to be climbing the cliff, Kinyras ordered all the prepared cauldrons to be emptied down the bed of the runnel, which once more flowed, though now with boiling water! Yells and howls accompanied by thuds of falling bodies came from below as the climbers fell from rock to rock.

Sounds of fighting from the south caused Kinyras to abandon the runnel and hasten to the fort on the shoulder, which was being attacked in force. Under cover of the night the ditch had been filled in and when he arrived the enemy had obtained a foot-hold and were over the parapet. They must be stopped at all costs. Desperate fighting followed and as fast as they drove them back the Khemites came on again. The fort was the key to the whole Karpas position and Khem had seen the follow of spectacular attack from inland. Hap Hill must be taken at whatever sacrifice and once that was occupied the Karpasians would be outflanked and their conquest assured.

In the belief that their men were climbing up the runnel and would seize the crest of the hill under cover of the main attack, Khem charged with a will, only to be met with an iron resistance just as success was in view. Khem was on the wrong side of the stockade once more and Kinyras was charging with an incredible fury, shouting like a mad man, fighting like a whirling demon. The night resounded with horrid cries, fierce animal noises as enemy met enemy, the ring of sword on sword, the whirr of arrows and the thud of maces falling on the quilted helmet of Khemite or the bronze-bound shields of the Mercenaries.

Yelling 'Charge! Charge! The Snail, the Snail. Strike for the Snail! Charge!' Kinyras hurled himself over the remnants of the broken stockade, followed by his men. 'To me, the Snail, to me!' If he could drive them down the hill the garrison would seize the chance to start repairing the breach made. Khem was flying, down the hill, over the ditch filled with the bodies of their own dead. 'The Snail, the Snail.' The slope was in the defenders' favour, their big swards whirled. The delight, the fierce exultation of feeling them bite deep into the flesh of Khem! Bite deep, bite ever deeper, while the stockade was mended. Filthy, prowling wolf, seeking to devour the helpless and the unprepared, learn your lesson! Strike, strike, onward and downward, down and back to the plain without halting!

It was time to retreat, but they were still flying. Strike, strike for the Snail! One blow more, and another, and yet another. For each blow here a stake was fixed in the stockade. Strike! Strike for the Snail.

But the rout had stopped and a new company had come to its relief. Yet strike! A mace struck him, descended again. A searing flash as of lightning blinded him and he sank down into blackness and oblivion.

It was many hours before consciousness returned. Water was being dashed in his face and he awoke to nerve-wracking pain. A hoarse command, which he did not understand, came dimly to his slowly reviving mind, a whip cracked, cutting most vilely into his tortured muscles, he was jerked to his feet and stood swaying, seeing a blurred flare of torches. A fiery agony played in his arms, which he now realised were tired by the elbows behind his back, and his feet were bound so that he could take but a moderate pace. He was naked.

As his mind and sight cleared he knew that he formed one of a long chain of captives, each tied by the wrists to the man behind and before him. Beyond that his awareness did not go, for the pain in his head was still so acute that he could do

nothing but endure it and stumble along blindly. When a halt
was called, when food and water was thrust upon him he
rested, ate and drank mechanically. When certain of the
wounded, too likely to recover, were impaled upon stakes set in
the sand, he barely heeded or speculated upon his own fate,
and when the party was divided, the young going one way and
the older another, his apathy still persisted.

So passing several days in inconceivable misery and excruci-
ating pain. He longed inexpressibly for death, but this blessing
was denied him by his iron constitution and former healthy
life. Slowly re recovered, his strength revived, his wits
functioned normally, desire for life returned, plans for escape
began to germinate in his mind. He heard whispers about him.

'We are going to the mines and shall never see the blessed
sun again. The elder men always go to the mines.'

These words echoed and re-echoed through his brain and
he thought of all he had ever heard of the mines in the
interior, the copper mines which supplied the world and which
were in the hands of Khem. There was only one thing for
which he thanked the gods and that was his hidden identity.
Had they known he was Kinyras of the Wall, as he was called
amongst the enemy, he dared not think upon his fate.

The weary marching went on interminably, the ache of
wrenched muscles prevented any concerted attack upon the
warders, who, armed with the cruel whips of rhinoceros hide,
scourged those who flagged, and emphasized the wisdom of
obedience.

At last the mines wer reached and their slaves' duty of
carrying cut rock and ore out of the workings assigned them.
Kinyras descended a shaft some thirty of forty feet deep, upon
whose sides footholds had been cut. His companion slipped
and fell, and, being pronounced by the overseer to be badly
hurt, was promptly struck by a mace over the head and his
dead body hauled to the top by the rest of the gang and cast
aside to rot on a heap.

'Short and merciful!' mused Kinyras, as he used extra
caution and arrived safely at the bottom, to find a number of

galleries converging at that spot from every direction, of the same height and width of six feet by two, along which tiny lamps were set at intervals. At first Kinyras could not see, but in a few days his eyes grew accustomed to the darkness. Because he was too tall to carry sacks he was set to bailing out the water which lodged in the bottom of the mine.

The mine was drained by a shaft sunk to the lowest depth, into which all the galleries ran. Above this shaft another gallery had been cut, communicating through a barred door with a small chamber of about ten feet square, which had been built over the top of the shaft and which contained the winch placed at the shaft's mouth. On one side of this room was a raised ledge, upon which sat an overseer, with his whip, and a guard.[1]

Three men toiled at the winch, hauling up skin buckets of water through the shaft while a third emptied them through the grating provided for the purpose in the heavily barred door. As Kinyras sat in the wet beside men who were covered in loathsome sores owing to the perpetual dampness, for ever pulling up these buckets with a wearisome monotony, his thoughts dwelt continually upon escape and the means to it.

His engineer's mind fastened at once upon the probable method, the gallery and the grated door through which the water escaped. Whither? It must go somewhere, and if the door held not the key to freedom, why was it so strongly barred and why was the chamber so heavily guarded?

But the miners never left the mine having once entered it. They ate, slept, worked there in the everlasting darkness pierced only by the little points of lamp light. They were chained by the feet with heavy bronze chains, they were guarded by ruthless brutes who were incorruptible because the wretched slaves lacked anything wherewith to corrupt them. Nevertheless, whispers of escape went the round of the four in the chamber under the very noses of their guards. They worked in shifts of six hours each and when they were relieved slept in the prison above, cut in the solid rock and built with the stones thereof.

At last murmured persuasion covered by the clank of the

winch prevailed and the four agreed to make the attempt. The grinding of the rivets of their chains went on interminably against the stone walls of the prison, all through the hours of sleep, softly, stealthily, until they could be punched out, when they were wedged in position to prevent discovery. The day was fixed and the hour drew near when they were to return to duty. The old shift came down the shaft which led to the sleeping quarters, followed by the guard. The guar dof the new shift ascended first and seated themselves upon their ledge, the miners following, while the old guard remained at the foot until the last man of the new shift had started to ascend, when the whole relieved party marched away.

With nerves keyed up to the last pitch of endeavour the three men of the new shift clambered up the shaft and took their seats at the winch, working secretly at their rivets as they pretended to haul. The moment of crisis drew nearer with the ascent of the bailer. He toiled slowly and was shouted at by the guards for his pains, suddenly seemed to slip and threw up his arms, wildly clutching at a foot of each of the guard and dragging him from his ledge. Useless were their shouts, unheard above the rattling of the winch. Chains were off in a second and they were brained, their dead bodies cast aside and their arms seized.

In a dead silence the four listened breathless for signs of commotion from below, but all was quiet. Trembling with mingled joy and excitement at the success of their plan so far, they set the winch going again, for to cease bailing meant the immediate flooding of the mine and investigation of its cause. While two hauled and the third emptied, Kinyras attacked the door with a sword and soon succeeded in opening it, finding it led into a small gallery. After a whispered consultation with his fellows he took the lamp to explore, leaving them to work in the darkness.

Slowly and cautiously he crept along the gallery, which stopped short in a few paces, the water flowing to the left. A little further he saw a pale beam gleaming upon the water and hastily returned to leave his light in the doorway while he pursued the running water, upon which the moon was shining. Soon he was in a deep cutting beneath the open sky and advancing cautiously he found the ground sloped and the moon's light glinted upon the arms of a sentry. The mine was drained by means of a ditch cut into the hill, and an adit.

Kinyras returned to his comrades and while they talked they worked their hardest at the winch. Their plans made, they unshipped the winch and jammed it in the mouth of the shaft, wedging in the bodies of the two guards as a further barricade. They must be out and away, or dead, before the stoppage of the bailing was discovered and the guards on duty at the pit-head warned.

Hastily arming themselves with sword and mace, they came quickly and silently to within a few paces of the unconscious guard, keeping well in the cutting's shadow, while one dislodged a stone. The sentry turned and the mace in the hand of Kinyras struck surely and shrewdly.

The man dropped without a cry. His arms were seized and his dead body flung into the water. The four were free.

1. This mine and bailing may still be seen at Yero Khemuti, near Lanaca. The name seems derived from Khem.

# CHAPTER XVI

# KING CINYRAS OF PAPHOS

everal days later Kinyras and his companion, a Phoenician from Schelmi known as Bael-poor, were approaching Paphos in the south of the island. The others of the escaped party had been men of the mountains from Trudos and had returned to their homes. They had explained that their people did not love strangers and would inevitably sell Kinyras and Bael-Poor back to Khem. 'Nay, brothers, that is an ugly trick!' expostulated the Phoenician and the party had straightway split in two.

'Undoubtedly Paphos is the place for us,' Bael-Poor was saying, continuing the conversation which had occupied him and Kinyras for some time. 'She has a King whose will and strength are known, one who always serves as a mighty god from the mainland as High-Priest.'

Kinyras was not much interested in the King or his god, though he knew that Khem, to whom the kingdom was subject, respected foreign gods, having a belief that they had much power in their own territories and were best left alone. 'It is a port?' he murmured reflectively.

'Yes, with many ships.'

This was much more satisfactory, for where there was a busy port there was every chance of smuggling himself aboard some ship going north and so reach the Karpas again.

As they approached the district they learnt that Paphos was split with faction. A rival family to that of the reigning monarch had attempted to unseat him, but this had failed. The Tamiradae had, however, set up a Temple to their goddess Hera in opposition to Ashtoreth, goddess of love and fertility, and so high had fanaticism run, so big a flowing had the Tamiradae that an excited mob had destroyed the temple of Ashtoreth, whose High Priest had raised her another some ten miles distant from the city.

Kinyras learnt that this revolt against Ashtoreth was purely a commercial one. The Tamiradae were wool merchant-princes, owning also large dye-works, and their object in setting up Hera was to force the people to wear more clothes, saying the true gods, of whom she was a powerful representative, abhorred the sight of the naked human body and therefore if the people would win her approval and blessing they must clothe them-selves in as much woollen goods as a man or woman could wear. As the Tamiradae employed great numbers of workers in spinning, weaving and dying, these very naturally looked with favour upon any scheme which would promote trade and increase work. Hence the following of Hera was numerous, energetic and powerful, while that of Ashtoreth, who loved nakedness, though equally powerful in numbers, was indolent and good-humoured, content to worship without strife but very determined not to wear more than was proper in hot climate.

Fashions in Paphos at the moment ran to every form of extravagance commercial ingenuity could devise, voluminous skirts for women reaching to the ground, swathing and furbelows to the neck and as many of them as could be crowded on, the more the better since the goddess loved and blessed him or her who carried most upon the back in the way of dyed woollens.

Meanwhile, the King Cinyras had built his new temple to Ashtoreth and in order to prevent another attack from the Tamiradae was forming a temple guard. It was in the neighbourhood of this temple that Kinyras and Bael-Poor found themselves and they thought it would be wise to seek enlistment in this company. Kinyras had by now grown a thick bushy beard and was in no danger of recognition. The Khemites had recently conquered the country and upheld the authority of the King, well enough pleased to divert the people of Paphos from rebellion against themselves by secretly fostering the feud between Tamiradae and Cinyradae.

'Then, 'tis agreed we join this temple guard?' asked Kinyras as they finished a midday repast of fruit, which Bael-Poor had purchased from an adjacent farmstead. Their bronze fetters had been of great value and eagerly bought by the country people when offered for sale.

'Report has it that the goddess Ashtoreth will herself arise from the sea to avenge the destruction of her Temple. If we join in her defence much blessing will accrue to us in consequence.'

'Assuredly,' Kinyras assented, 'it will be a sad blow to the followers of Hera if such should happen. I heard that they will not suffer one to bathe in the sea unless fully clad.'

Bael-Poor uttered a rude noise most uncomplimentary to Hera and her addicts.

'Yonder is the place, I fancy,' said Kinyras, pointing to the horn-crowned columns of a fair temple rising on the cliff overlooking the sea. 'Let us hasten thither, my friend, for the sooner we are numbered amongst its guard, the safer for both of us.'

Bael-Poor assented heartily and rose energetically from the shade of the cedar in which they were stretched to issue once more into the blinding heat of the sun. In a little time they arrived at a large court of polyangled stone fenced about by a hedge of twigs, within which rose the two columns they had previously remarked. A round altar was set between these pillars and behind it rose the shrine, a massive tower-shaped building having two wings supported at each end by a column of stone and ornamented by a parapet of stone cut at the top into a conical design and terminating in a dove at each corner. In the centre of the sanctuary the shrine lay, concealed by a veiling curtain and approached from the court by three shallow steps, before which lay a tank of water containing fish. Upon the parapet over the doorway was cut a large crescent, between whose cusps was a star. Between the horns of the two outer columns was suspended a great garland of roses, and from a small circular building on the left came the constant cooing of doves. The birds fluttered about the court filling the air with their murmuring, while in the shade a number of young men and one or two girls idled, others looking from the doorways of a cluster of hits as the stranger approached, though none seemed inclined to do aught but stare.

Bael-Poor addressed the youth nearest him. 'We are strangers who seek enlistment in the Temple Guard,' he informed the youth concisely.

The young man stifled a yawn and smiled tolerantly before he murmured to a companion—'Two more fools seeking death in a hopeless cause, my Adonis.'

Kinyras frowned and Adonis ceased his chipping at a stone to ask—'Whence come you and whom seek you, friend?'

Bael-Poor, who for reasons of his own strove to hide his real identity, owing to his misused dexterity with a knife and in his not too remote past, replied ingratiatingly—'I am Mikel, from Syria.'

'And I am Kinyras, from Ascalon.'

Adonis glanced at him sharply, ignoring Bael-Poor, and after a comprehensive stare, said slowly—'Sir, my father is within a doubtless would speak with you. I will take you to him if your comrade will wait her.'

So saying he led the way through a wicket inside the enclosure to a shady corner, wherein sat a big, dignified man clad only in a scarlet loin-cloth, lazily throwing corn to the doves, which fluttered about him and from whose wings a subtle perfume filled the air, while creating a pleasant breeze about him. His dark hair curled crisply about his temples and he was handsome in a swarthy way, with shrewd, brilliant eyes of much beauty and a healthy red colour in his cheeks. His nose was large and beaked, curved with extreme delicacy in the nostril and his mouth was large, moist, well cut, bright-hued and most voluptuous. This imposing personage was too occupied at the moment with a dove which had perched upon his outstretched finger, to whom he spoke in caressing murmurs of endearment and to which it replied with pretty cooings and motions of its head, to pay any heed to their approach. But as they came up the bird flew off and the man turned his head in their direction and smiled with great charm. 'Well my son?'

'Sir, I bring a stranger who tells me his name is Kinyras, from Ascalon.'

The man stared and rose to his feet, motioning Adonis to withdraw. Kinyras, from the various signs, judged he was in the presence of King Cinyras, of whom he had lately heard so much.

'Is that indeed so? Then whence got you that name, friend?'

Kinyras smiled, and when he smiled he was most attractive. The king, seeing it, visibly warmed to him.

'Why, sir, from my father.'

'So! And the name of your father?'

'Herman.'

'Eh. And your mother?'

'Rhiam. They named me after my father's favourite brother, his youngest, who left us when I was but a child to go to the wars.'

'Hm! And what became of him?'

'that, sir, I cannot tell, for the Mercenaries attacked us when he had been gone but a while, killing my parents and my three sisters and taking my younger brother and me prisoner.'

'One further question. Tell me also the names of your unfortunate sisters and brothers?'

Somewhat staring Kinyras compiled, wondering if it was the custom of the land of Paphos so to examine strangers. He answered patiently—'Anietis, Mere and Racha, and Zadoug, sir.'

'I remember them well, pretty little innocents.' The king came close and took Kinyras by the chin the better to study his features. 'You have your father's face, and he was a handsome fellow, though he had not my inches. Well, well, I have deemed you and Zadoug dead with the others these thirty years. Do you not know me now, boy?'

'Can you indeed be my uncle, sir? 'this very strange a happening if you are.'

King Cinyras let out a great laugh and released his newly-found nephew's chin. 'No stranger than you should be yourself, but men think ever that their own happenings are the strangest. Gods, but it is hot to-day. Sit with me in the shade yonder and I will set my doves in motion again, so that the breeze from their wings may cool us and the perfume with which they are anointed be sweet in our nostrils. But first, wine and fruit. Ho, there!'

The king set up a stentorian bellow for wine, which was brought on a small, low table of wood inlaid with ivory, an elegant trifle of fine craftsmanship, as were the cups, the bowl of fruit and wine-jar. He returned to his mattress in the wall's shade, inviting Kinyras to sit beside him. 'Come, tell me what the gods have sent you of good and ill in the past years.' He dipped his hand into a skin containing corn beside him and scattered a few grains, when immediately the doves circled about him. 'I keep my pretty innocents in motion by this simple expedient and while they have this usefulness they please my eye.'

The languor of the hot summer afternoon was upon Kinyras and he would gladly have slept but he complied with his uncle's request and gave him a short history of his life and its recent events.

'So you would serve our lady of Ascalon? It would be a useful blind until such time as we can smuggle you hence to your wall again. You should know, Kinyras, and if I did not acknowledge the fact, your shrewdness and knowledge of affairs would discover it to you speedily—my kingship is but a name. I came hence after roving hither and thither, found the land good and to my liking and established myself with a band of followers. Others equally adventurous came from time to time with their families and we grew into such a prosperous colony that we attracted the greedy eye of Khem. Who can withstand her might? Had you been beside me, nephew, all might have been different. Even had we been united as a people our fate might have been better.'

'These Tamirade... I have gathered somewhat of them in my journey thither.'

'Huxters defiling the gods with their trafficking, and vile heresy. They have driven forth my lady from the city and set up a false stranger in her stead, because forsooth, her body lacks the loveliness of my lady Ashtoreth's and she must needs cover it with many wrapping to hide its unworthiness.'

Kinyras laughed and his uncle cocked a shrewd eye at him. 'It is a foul lie, nephew, put about to sell their wretched merchandise and to force the people to buy more and still more clothes.'

'But there is a limit to buying,' the younger man objected. 'If a man goes beyond his fortune he falls into debt and what then can it profit the merchant? There is no wisdom in it.'

'So have I declared many times, until I go purple in the face with saying it, but the Tamiradae are a jealous sect and the prevent my people from worshipping with persecutions, so that, being timid and of a peaceful nature they neglect their rightful lady.'

Kinyras could well believe that in the matter of growing purple in the face his uncle spoke the truth, for his visage was darkly inflamed as he spoke and lightnings kindled in his eyes, though he still continued lazily to cast corn to his doves. 'It is a dog's life!' the King pursued discontentedly, 'and I long to be back in Ascalon. Sometimes I dream of returning, but Myrrah says have patience until the tide turns again in our favour.'

'Myrrah?'

'My daughter, boy, my daughter and your cousin,' was the somewhat impatient explanation. Like many others King Cinyras thought himself of sufficient consequence for people to know as much as he knew of himself without being told. Then, in his former indolent, good-humoured tone he added: 'She tarries in the city watchful of our interest, sending me reports from time to time.'

He glanced idly about as he spoke, but his eyes became

fixed upon some object in the sky that gradually grew into a pigeon, which, circling several times over the court, flew into the cote. The youth Adonis, who had returned to his former occupation, now rose up again with some eagerness and ran into the cote, from whence he reappeared with a small roll of papyrus in hand. This he gave in silence to his father who, after making the cousins known to each other, examined the roll. Kinyras saw that it contained a written message and could but conjecture that it had been fastened in some fashion to the bird, who had been trained to fly from one destination to another.

While he was turning over in his mind the marvel and usefulness of this, at the same time giving a polite ear to the pleasant words of welcome coming from his cousin Adonis the King slapped his thigh resoundingly and beamed round with an alert satisfaction. 'From Myrrah, and a message of good I import. You have brought me luck, my boy. The people are turning to me once again and this iniquitous system of extortion has broken down, even as you forecast a moment or two since, nephew. The people have got so deeply into the merchants' debt that further credit is denied them and what is more, both work and pay have been pledged so far in advance for goods, that more is produced than can be disposed of. The warehouses are full, the demand for cloth is falling ever lower, and in consequence the workers are being dismissed. These fellows, idle against their will and harassed by debt, are now crying out against their masters and the false goddess, and calling for me, their King.' He struck himself on the breast and assumed a martial look.

'Your tidings are indeed gratifying, sir, but the manner of their coming puzzles me somewhat. Adonis here brought your message from yonder dovecote. Do you make the very fowls of the air cat as messengers, uncle?'

'Aye, aye. You are the first to penetrate our secret, Kinyras,' smiled Adonis. 'The birds are sacred to the goddess, who brings messages from her to my father. He will now prophesy to the people who need some stirring into activity, methinks.

What say you, sir?'

'Cease your prating, boy, lest the fate of all scoffers fall upon thee,' returned his father, with immense dignity. 'I shall, as you say, communicate the message of our lady to her people. Could the birds have brought it, had it not been her will?'

Adonis smiled knowingly. 'As you say, my father, it is her will and she looks kindly upon us once more. To her be thanks. We cannot too soon set about her behest.'

King Cinyras gathered himself together with majesty, closed one eye with great solemnity upon his nephew, so that Kinyras was ignorant whether it was part of a grave rite or merely a token of confidence in himself, or a repudiation of Adonis, rose ponderously and not without difficulty, and strode magnificently to the gate of the enclosure.

At the imperious clapping of his hands the works looked up from their languid pursuits in a dispirited manner. The king raised his right hand and spoke his mind, thus—'Our lady has filled me with her holy inspiration. She bids us return to Eryphrae to rebuild her Temple.' He glanced keenly from one to another of those nearest him, then closed his eyes, tilted his chin to the distant heavens and assumed a rapt expression of wonder and adoration, which failed not to move his audience. 'Hear the words of our Lady Ashtoreth.

'Take your ways back to the city. My people have had a change of heart and are crying for me. I will come shortly in my splendour to chasten the impious, to gather all men to my worship. Let him who will be deaf to my summons be for ever accursed. For a sign I will tell you. The people will abandon the temple of Hera, the false, and will congregate once more in my courts. Thus I have spoken.'

For a moment or two longer he stood there so, impressive and dignified before his gaping audience, while one by one they fell upon their knees, when he blessed them with great solemnity and dismissed them. Kinyras and Adonis had knelt one on each side of him as he began to speak and they now rose to their feet, awaiting the next phase.

It came quickly enough. The priest and mystic very

suddenly became the man of action and dropped the prophet for the soldier. 'Come, hasten! There is no time to be lost. Collect your weapons and bring out my chariot. Cease gaping like fish and think not to-morrow will do as well as to-day. Come, dispatch!'

Seeing that their King would brook no delay, the people became galvanized into action. A handsome chariot of wood reinforced with bronze, low in the axle, oval-fronted, its pole terminating in a cap and hooks of bronze, quickly appeared. Others let in a fine pair of blood stallions and coupled them in. A guard turned out, weapons were produced consisting of spears and swords, a standard unfurled and a line of march formed. The King entered his chariot and gathered up by the reins, making a very stately and imposing figure. By a courteous gesture he motioned his nephew to stand at his right hand. With a word of command to the slave to release the horses' heads. Adonis sprang in and the team bounded forward with a jerk which nearly over-toppled Kinyras, who was unused to chariot-riding and thought that what it achieved in dignity it lost in comfort, and longed for his little Baal Seleh. The road was rough, the horses mettlesome and the mode of transit most uneasy. Kinyras imparted his thoughts on the subject to his uncle and cousin, who both laughed. 'It passes my comprehension why a man should be judged the more dignified for being perched in such a contrivance, rather than go upon his two feet, but so it is and to such opinion the exalted must bow.'

'The gods preserve me from exaltation, then,' cried Kinyras, clutching wildly at the side of the car as the right wheel plunged into an unusually deep cavity in the road, while the horses, high courage from much good eating and resting, started madly.

The King controlled them with a steady nerve and when he had brought them to a standstill, said over his shoulder to his nephew—'As you say, our two feet will bear us with more safety and dignity, at least until we reach the outskirts of the city. Adonis, lead the nags and if we meet any coming this way, stop and we will again assume the guise of dignity. It will but look as though we had alighted for some purpose of adjustment.'

So saying King Cinyras stepped out upon the road followed by his nephew and the two marched contentedly in the hot afternoon, the king in great spirits, Kinyras affecting more cheerfulness than he felt because his thoughts were ever with Dayonis. It was not long before his astute elder had divined his hidden uneasiness, and upon enquiring the cause, Kinyras unburdened his mind, telling him of all which had chanced between the two since she had flown to him for protection at the wall.

'Assuredly we must contrive your return as speedily as you may be,' said Cinyras. 'But I shall be sorry to see the back of you, lad. You were always my favourite.'

Kinyras expressed his hearty thanks for this kind opinion and saw that they had come to the city's outposts. The king resumed his place in the chariot followed by the cousins, and their state progress continued. The town stood on the shores of a little bay in a naturally good position for defence. Two reefs formed excellent protection for shipping and in the absence of rock a low wall had been built, though wherever possible every advantage had been taken of the cliffs to construct a rampart, these being scarped on the outer side, and the stone excavated used to build the connecting wall between the two reefs. When this wall had been raised high enough it would form a formidable defence, but as it now stood it could serve only to keep out bandits.

Kinyras expressed his approval of what he saw, but his uncle fell into a grumble, and began to sneer mightily in his discontent. 'I began to build good walls, only the accursed Tamiradae foiled me, declaring that preparation for war inspired the will to flight. The truth of it was that, while the people were building walls they had no desire to cumber themselves with the many wrappings of the Tamiradae, whose profits diminished accordingly. Therefore did they raise a fine outcry against my wall, and therefore did we fall victims to the encroaching Khemite. I tell you, Kinyras, the more I see of men the more do I like and admire doves.'

'I would have made short shift of your Tamiradae,' Kinyras objected grimly.

'Aye, you are right there, Kinyras, I had more than a mind to do it, but hesitated between this policy and that, to the undoing of us all. I am between two stools as the result. We pay a small tribute to Khem and she uses our port for her ships before she rounds Cape Arna to get to the mines. We trade much with her an dit pays her maintain a friendly footing with us.'

'True, but if we fall and Aghirda is finally subdued, what then, uncle?'

'There is little doubt of the outcome. Khem will seize us forthwith and those mutton-headed sons of asses cannot see what is before their snouts. They think that because they desire a certain consummation it must necessarily be forthcoming in perpetuity and cannot see that Khem's greedy eyes are upon the whole island, and where her eyes fall there will her fingers clutch, sooner or later.'

'Aye. Vast forests and rich mines. The country is indeed full of wealth.'

'We have mines of pretty stones here, in the hills, which Khem buys of us at the moment; soon she will take them. I do what I can, quietly, you understand, because the Tamiradae oppose me at every turn.'

'Subtlety, eh?'

'Nothing else will serve. I add to the walls here and there and in their neighbourhood I have given fine sites to the Tamiradae, knowing they will build their temples of stone. So that other large buildings should be raised in the adjacent positions, I secretly put about the suggestion that it would be advantageous to the Tamiradae if their spinning and weaving quarters and their dye-works were built by their temples. The whisper reached them and promptly they seized the land, I making a loud outcry. They have built the working quarter of great stones quarried from rocks.'

Kinyras laughed and glanced admiringly at the tall man beside him.

'If I can sway the people to my side I can turn those buildings into sound defences within a month, but I fear my Myrrah flatters herself and me. The people have been pulled this way and that between the Tamiradae and Cinyradae, and are heartily sick of both. In order to avert this final catastrophe I have shunned the town. The last time I appeared before them they cast fishguts at me.'

The laughter of Kinyras became a roar, in which his uncle freely joined until the tears fell from his eyes. 'Fishguts!' he exclaimed, wringing the tears from his lids by shutting them very tight and blinking rapidly, 'think of it, lad! But it was done by the Tamiradae, trying to force me to charge the crowd with my guard. Fools and sons of fools!'

'Certainly they lack wit.'

'They spread monstrous reports about me and Myrrah, because I love the wench. Cannot a man love his children, especially his daughter, and such a clever witch into the bargain? She has more craft and cunning in her smallest finger than in the collected skulls of the Tamiradae, though I must say she assumes rights of direction over me in my exercise of certain rites of our Lady of Love, which I see proper to celebrate and with whose interference no parent could stomach, daughter or no daughter!'

'What then, my uncle?' smiled the nephew.

'Why, the celebrations take place at a distance,' said the King, waving a vague arm calculated to embrace the universe.

A silence fell, while Cinyras ruminated on certain triumphs over cunning opposition. 'What the eye seas not the heart grieves not. Still, Myrrah grieves, and when she grieves her tongue wags unconscionably, but not so much as if she had seen. Yet is she a good girl.'

They had by now reached the town's gate. With a flourish of trumpets the guard turned out, appearing genuine in their pleasure at their king's presence among them. Some crowds had collected in the streets among which Kinyras saw, with a twinge of uneasiness, enough Khemites to cause disquiet, though he did not greatly fear recognition in his present exalted company. The people cheered here and there, and those who were silent seemed to be so rather from policy than from hostility. To the relief of all no fishguts were thrown.

They drove slowly and with immense dignity through the streets down to the wharves, where a number of little merchant ships of Phoenician build and several much larger Khemite ships, were moored, though these latter did not appear so well adapted for deep-sea traffic as the handy little craft beside them.

The king pulled up and pointed to a rock in the sea at the entrance to the harbour, upon which he had built his palace. It was connected to the mainland by a long narrow timber bridge along which they walked. 'They must needs swim if they would reach me there,' he explained, with a smirk of satisfaction at his own cleverness. 'Also I could fortify it in a measure without raising too much questions. As it is, it protects the breakwater from the inroads of pirates, and neither the Tamiradae nor the Khemites wish to have their shipping plundered. For this purpose I can maintain a small garrison. Hither comes my pretty darling to greet and welcome her old father.'

A tall girl, clad in a richly-dyed robe of purple linen, came running towards them. Her black, glossy hair was dressed in a number of small curls and bound by a fillet of gold. She ran with the grace of an antelope and the king nudged Kinyras in the ribs as they watched her approach.

'Said I not she was a gem, my boy?' he exclaimed delightedly. 'There's action, there's grace for you. Match them if you can.'

Kinyras liked the man's delight in his child, and he watched his cousin Myrrah with interest. She was indeed a beauty, a delicate, refined edition of her father. Her face had the dusky beauty of a freshly ripened nectarine, her eyes beneath the black, fine line of her brows, large, lustrous and softly beautiful, while the strong, lovely curves of mouth and child showed her one well fitted to command. Her head was small and she carried it with a haughty grace. She was every inch a princess and Kinyras felt proud to claim relationship with such a pearl.

Myrrah clasped her arms round her father's neck and kissed him with stint. 'You received my message? How good it is to see you here again, my father.' She seemed to have no eyes for any but the king, but when she had released him from her embrace and saw Kinyras, she frowned slightly. 'A stranger!' she exclaimed, none too well pleased.

'A friend, one whom I knew and loved in Ascalon long ago.'

'You are welcome, sir,' said she, briefly, responding with an inclination of her head to the soldier's salute Kinyras accorded her.

She fell behind with her brother and Cinyras took the opportunity to whisper to his nephew—'I will inform her of your identity later. Spies are about me constantly and I cannot trust even my own guard.'

Myrrah, having held a whispered consultation with Adonis, now came forward showing a disposition to be more friendly. She plied Kinyras with questions of the mainland, which he found difficult to answer. She was eager for news, having many friends there, but her father made a certain sign with his hands and she ceased abruptly, skilfully changing the subject.

They entered the precincts of the palace through a low, narrow postern cut in the solid rock, against whose foot the waves of the sea lapped lazily. A broad, handsome terrace confronted them facing south-west and behind it the low, stately structure of the palace rose. It was built in stone of any immense solidity and the expert eyes of Kinyras quickly appreciated its capabilities as a fortress in an emergency. Its proportions were handsome and just, and of its strength there was no doubt whatever. The dull, greyish stone, with its massive pillars and open courts surrounded by various dwelling rooms hung with curtains of rich and many hued dyes, made a dignified and beautiful picture, set in the midst of the sea dancing and sparking like a sapphire in the sun.

Here the king dismissed his attendants and drawing Myrrah to him he kissed her and then glanced round the place with a sigh of satisfaction. 'Ah, child, but it is good to be here again. And now for news which will arouse your curiosity. Kinyras here is my nephew, whom I left long ago in Ascalon and whom I thought was dead these thirty years.'

Myrrah was very much surprised and looked at Kinyras with a new interest. 'You are very welcome, cousin, and you come at an opportune time. You look a proper man and the soldier cries aloud in you, to a discerning eye. We can use such as you, Kinyras.'

'Yes, you are speaking to a great soldier, Myrrah, no less than the Commander-in-Chief of the Karpasian Army.'

At this Myrrah opened her fine eyes very wide indeed and viewed her cousin with respect and admiration. The fame of Kinyras and the wall he had built in Karpas had been the talk of the whole island whenever there were Khemites to speak of it, and already whispers of the defeats of Khem in that quarter had drifted through.

'But how come you here, cousin?' she asked, glancing rapidly round to see that no one was within earshot. 'If your identity was known to the Khemites there would be short shift for you.'

'True, lady, and for that reason would I depart, as swiftly and secretly as may be.'

He told her briefly of the incidents which led up to his presence there and she gaped at him in wonder, while she eyed him with an undisguised admiration. 'What dauntless courage, what ingenuity!' she exclaimed. 'Kinyras, you are a man after my own heart. But come with me and I will take you to a guest chamber, where you may bathe and array yourself befittingly with such garments as my father can provide.' She turned to the king. 'Sir, the leaders of your party with assemble here at nightfall to take council together and to partake of a feast to which I have invited them in your name. We must prepare ourselves, and you need rest and refreshment in order to appear at your best, sire.'

'So-ho! Business first and feasting and pleasure to follow,' cried Cinyras, as delighted as a child at the prospect of a party, 'was there ever such a girl for cunning.'

Myrrah did not reply, but motioned to Kinyras. He followed her to a paved inner court from which guest and living rooms opened on all sides. 'Make yourself at ease here, cousin, until you are prepared to join us later. I beg you to excuse me, for I have much to communicate to my father before his followers arrive.'

Saying which she hurried away and Kinyras took the hint to keep to his chamber until summoned. It was pleasantly cool in his room, which opened on to the sea and he cast himself upon the couch beneath the window with a sigh of weariness and relief and soon had fallen asleep. He was roused about an hour later by the entrance of a slave, who came with suitable garments and the offer of his assistance. At the meeting in the council chamber, to which he was presently summoned by the king, and bidden to seat himself on his right-hand, he was an amused spectator of Paphos party-politics, and reflected how closely it resembled that other meeting in Karpasia, which now seemed so remote. There were the same prosy speeches, the same difficulty in coming to the point. Once more it was a question of building a wall, he discovered, and listened with interest.

Discontent was rife in the land because the Tamiradae, having overproduced, were faced with the acute depression and were forced to discharge large bodies of men daily from the Fabrica. Each unemployed man went home to a family seething with mutiny and hence the swing-over to the king's side once more. Unfortunately for King Cinyras he had not the wherewithal to pay men to remain idle, nor money for wages if he employed them on fortifications. Nothing remained but to levy a tax, and the question then arose upon whom it should be levied.

At length, after much wearisome discussion back and forth, it was decided to levy it upon all who held land within the town, and this was mostly held by the Tamiradae. This decided, an edict was then drawn up, whereby every man, woman and child over fourteen should work on the fortifications by compulsion for ten days at a stretch, but those who wished could buy exemption from the task by paying the wages of two men to take his or her place. This suggestion came from Myrrah, who took a very active part in the meeting and for whose wit and address Kinyras felt a genuine admiration. By this clever device of exemption they at one stroke rid themselves of useless labour from those untrained and secured additional funds for the work.

The council broke up in high good humour, and repaired to the feast, which was spread on the terrace overlooking the sea. It was a hot and sultry night, and the moon was at the full. The Cipriots used many lamps in this part of the island, shallow saucers of pottery, pinched together at one side to form a lip, in which the wick was placed, one end floating in the oil. This oil used for burning was heavily scented with various perfumes, and in the still night air the wicks burned with a clear steady flame. The broad terrace was furnished with tables laden with all the delicate cooked meats and cakes, choice fruit and wines which were both home produced or brought in by the Phoenician traders, and with reclining couches and chairs for the guests. Pretty slave-girls sat about the terrace with little bowls of corn, whose duty it was to keep the perfumed doves circulating above the heads of the guests and so create a scented breeze.

When the feasting and drinking were at its height a number of lovely dancing-girls whirled on to the scene, their slender limbs ceiled in the most gossamer of Tyrian webs and whose dancing ravished what little sense was not already destroyed by wine. Dancing was their excuse rather than their profession and very soon every man present had pulled a girl down upon his knee except the king, who had achieved two, with a third waiting in the offing. Several of them paid Kinyras special attention as the guest of honour, but he was in no mood for them. Dayonis filled his head and his heart.

Seeing him repulse them and noticing how little he drank, Myrrah, who had been keeping a stealthily watch upon her lord and father, now abandoned him to the safety of numbers, and insinuated herself beside Kinyras. He felt the warmth of her young limbs against him and turned with some impatience to discover the Princess, in a very on-coming mood.

'You drink little cousin, is not the wine to the taste?'

'It is excellent, Princess, too excellent for a poor soldier, who needs his wits about him in time of stress and danger.'

She pouted, her dark eyes beseeching his, looking most adorable. 'There is no danger her, Kinyras.'

He laughed. 'Indeed, but I think there is!'

She laughed with him, very softly and alluringly so that Kinyras felt there was some virtue in his faithfulness to Dayonis at the moment. 'Surely even a soldier knows that the night holds other things than alarums and excursions? Has the stone of your walls penetrated your heart, Kinyras, or do the soldiers of the Karpas despise the sweets of life?'

'I have but lately married a wife, cousin, and anxiety for her welfare in my absence holds all my thoughts. You must pardon my discourtesy.'

'And is she too, so faithful?' mocked the Princess, with slyness, sending a bewitching side glance which told him she had not yet abandoned all hope.

'I trust, so,' he answered bluffy, 'If not I'll know the reason why.'

Again she laughed teasingly. 'And how will my lord know?'

'You have me there, Myrrah, but I think better of your sex than you do yourself.'

'Because I know it better, but tell me of her. Has she beauty?'

'Much.'

'And has she wit?'

'Aye, one equal to your own.'

'But courage—has she that, too?'

'Truly, yes. She saved my life fighting naked beside me, armed only with a sword.'

'And is she by chance a great archer also?'

'Indeed, yes.'

Myrrah smiled and nodded, looking at him curiously. 'Why,

certain am I that you speak of that witch of Aghirda, of whose beauty men rave, even here. Tell me, is she Xanthos 1, or Pyrros 2, as reputed? Some say the one, some the other.'

'She is Pyrrhos and her hair of his deep red gold curls low about her even to the knees. Her body is white as milk and her eyes sometimes blue and at others green, like the sea. She is a very goddess and her name is Dayonis.'

'Aye, so I have heard, and other things about her–that she fights like a man and devours her conquests without even cooking them first. Now, that seems to me unsavoury, Kinyras, and she must have good teeth, for men are tough in flesh as well as in heart.'

''This a foolish lie and she eats like the rest of mankind, as do her people. But, unlike you cousin, she has tasted the hardships of war, when, if there is no fire, men must eat raw flesh or go hungry.'

'So, she saved your life, Kinyras? Well, I like you well enough to approve her for that timely aid. When you have driven back Khem from your wall and greed Aghirda from the enemy, I pray you, Kinyras, to come hither to aid my father and to bring your Dayonis with you. In the meantime you are eager to return to her, I can see.'

'She is wild and impetuous as a young stallion and I fear greatly for her safety when I'm absent from her side.'

'And with good reason. Would you return to the Karpas or to Aghirda?'

'Either would serve my purpose, Myrrah, and if you can aid me I will fulfil your request when my duty elsewhere is accomplished, and I am free to choose my own action once more.'

'If you were a sailor I could help you better. I have a friend, one Atreus, a Cretan, who fled from his native island when the great trouble came and his country was devastated. His family fled to the island north of Cyprus, to the Isle of Roses, or Rhos 3 as they call it. His ship is now in port.'

'I have ships of my own, cousin, and have worked on them. I could serve as one of the crew in any ship going north, and when we came into Karpasian waters I could contrive to fall overboard without detection of intent, or I'm a Khemite.'

She laughed at the scorn in his tone. 'Then all can be arranged. Have patience, Kinyras, and your return to your Dayonis shall be accomplished as soon as lies in my power.'

'You miracle of sweet kindness!' exclaimed he, fervently. 'I know not how to thank you, nor how to serve you.'

Myrrah glanced round and frowned at what she saw going on between her father and the single dancer who now remained with him. During the preoccupation with Kinyras the King had contrived to make his selection and to rid himself of the girl's two companions. 'Save my foolish father from the harpy by engaging him in discourse about himself. He will then talk until dawn,' she remarked acidly.

His glance followed her irate one and he shrugged. 'Of what use to interfere between a man and his pleasures, whatever they may be?'

But the Princess had risen to her feet and stood glaring angrily at the offenders. 'I will not have it,' she stormed, in a savage undertone. 'My father is a dotard in such matters and brings discredit upon his head and his house. Of what use is it for me to fight for his rights if, by his unguarded conduct, he gives credence to all the monstrous scandals urged against him by the Tamiradae?'

'But they have the wits of goars and the tongues of old women,' Kinyras objected. 'Why heed their clatter?'

'Because they inflame the people against us, accusing us of bleeding the poor to pay for our licence and extravagant orgies. These girls are not to be trusted, they hunt with the hounds an drun with the hare, and are naught but spies sent here by the Tamiradae, only my father will not heed my warnings. I have proved it many times. Come, Kinyras, ais me if you be sincere.'

Just like a woman, grumbled Kinyras to himself, to demand the impossible, but he also rose and watched her determined stride across to the King's couch as he followed her slowly. She paused before the culprits, flushed and determined Cinyras was engaged in slobbering over the girl's shoulder, and he did not look pretty.

The Princess tapped the naked arm encircling her father's neck with a delicate and disdainful finger, whose long and pointed nail was highly coloured and polished. 'Begone!' she exclaimed, in an urgent whisper of command.

The girl turned a languid head, her lips grinning insolently, and she laughed with scornful impudence. The next moment two strong little hands descended upon the gleaming shoulders, the spear-like, henna-tinted nails bit deeply into the soft flesh and the culprit was literally wrenched from her pray and spun with such violence that she went whirling across the pavement to fall in a whimpering heap at the edge of the fountain, whither Myrrah followed her, the King watching with a peevish indolence.

Kinyras sauntered up and stood between his uncle and the two women, while the king poured himself more win from the jar of painted pottery at his elbow. He had been drinking heavily, but his nephew observed that he could carry his win well and showed no traces of drunkenness.

'You see! It is as I told you, nephew. Coming between a priest and his sacred rites. 'Tis not decent.'

'Myrrah declares the girl is a proved spy.'

'Aye, so she always says. Old wives clack, Kinyras. I weary of it. But drink up, lad.'

Kinyras could see, however, that the mere breath of the word had rounded up his uncle with a jerk, and though he lolled back carelessly in his corner of the couch, he kept a wary eye upon what was happening at the fountain. The girl was led away between two men-at-arms, and Kinyras speculated whether a loud splash would herald her fate. He strained his ears for the sound, but his uncle was still grumbling in a monotone. 'The Tamiradae!' he ejaculated with huge scorn, 'by my right hand they will exhaust my patience ere long. If the religion of joy and happiness takes hold their reign will be over. Therefore are they afraid of me and my religion, for it would set our young men and maidens to dreaming instead of working, or if they worked it would be at work under the blue sky, not to toil at looms, or to by the expensive garments the

Tamiradae sell.'

Kinyras made inarticulate noises of assent, his ears still agog for that splash.

'A young man who loves beauty never will be a clever merchant, a good slave-driver or make a fortune in the Fabrica. What to the Tamiradae means success in life, would to him be a life spent in drab and dreary wastefulness.'

'To the slavish mind a slavish pursuit,' Kinyras observed.

'Beauty is aristocratic, hated and feared by the servile, yet beauty has been at the command of kings, lovely women, fine jewels, great houses, lavish furnishings. The slaves, huddled together miserably in wretched huts, have grown to hate all which reminds them of their oppressors. For them, the beauty of the naked woman speaks but of the women of kings and nobles, and of the sweat of toil which they must endure to produce these luxuries, so they see not the beauty of nakedness and they hate it. For the same reason do they hate an army with its beauty of young men, its bravery, music, and banners and shining armour.'

'Yet Khem will seize and over-run all countries which have not an army. The Tamiradae must be mad.'

'You speak truth, nephew. They fear I shall rouse a strong and manly spirit in the young men, so they deny me an army. They would rather the whole nation was enslaved. Having the spirits of the slave, they will suffer no hardship in slavery because, such is their hatred of aristocracy, they think slavery will be common to all, and the spirit of beauty and freedom will die together.'

'Surely, sir, you will not suffer this calamity without a desperate struggle?'

'No, Kinyras, I will not. I am not such a fool as they deem me. I was a match for the Argives, and I can use my wits against a handful of merchant scum.'

'The Argives?' Kinyras repeated, interested.

The King chuckled and refilled his cup. 'Aye, did you not hear of that, my Kinyras? They cozened me on an occasion into a tight corner, when I was forced to enter into a treaty offensive and defensive, plague take it. Came the war with Troy, when they called upon me to supply them with fifty ships of war, with full crews and warriors to boot. So, what did I do?'

'Sent them?'

King Cinyras winked prodigiously. 'One ship with forty-nine clay models on board, furnished with full equipment, also in clay.'

In spite of himself Kinyras laughed himself sick at this. His uncle joined in and the terrace echoed with their shouts and chokings. 'Fortunate for you the Argives were fully engaged elsewhere, my uncle.'

'Aye, but the levy was iniquitous and the promise stolen from he. However, I sent King Menelaus a beautiful suit of armour made by my own smith. Two or three times I struck it with a hammer and told him I had had a hand in the devising thereof. Methought he would view it with a greater favour, so.'

'And did he?'

The King nodded. 'He received the gift with much delight and laughed over the business of the ships. The Argives can laugh at themselves, it seems. Moreover, they had tricked me and they knew it.'

'How, tricked you, into so grave an obligation?'

'By sending an embassy and some beautiful women. We trade much with them, you must know. I gave a great feast in their honour and one of the women, Lias, was a lovely, a friendly, wench. Many of the Tamiradae were present and there was much clamour, all talking together, while the witch, Lias, plied me with drink. Presently I heard a shouting, "Drink! Drink to the fifty!" and Lias filled another cup, holding it to my lips, saying, "Drink, pledge the fifty." I was drunk, Kinyras, fast losing what little sense I ever had. Freely I confess it, and it taught me a lesson in sobriety.'

'Sobriety?' echoed the nephew, with a glance and a smile.

'Yes,' the king insisted, with dignity. 'I can carry much and keep my mind clear. This episode taught me never to go beyond that point again.'

Kinyras bowed to conceal another smile. 'Proceed, my

uncle.'

'I drank to the fifty and Lias said, "Come, i will help you to bed." Who would refuse such a courtesy, or what followed? In the morning Myrrah was angered and you have just seen what anger in her means. She was enraged, storming at me that I had pledged my word to send fifty ships to the aid of the Argives, who would attack Troy. You see I was tricked, so I in turn tricked.'

'Which puts a better complexion upon the matter, certainly.'

'Ah, my boy, there was more to it than that,' the king proceeded, with an unctuous satisfaction. 'Myrrah, it seems, had enslaved the affections of a handsome young Greek, had plied him with wine and taken him to bed with her. This is her method of discovering what is plotted and hidden against us. She declares it is the only way in which to worm secrets from the breasts of plotters.'

Kinyras laughed.

'She discovered that the Greeks had sent Lias and their presents of potent wine for the purpose of hoodwinking me, while one of the Tamiradae, a leading councillor, had agreed and contracted with the Ambassador. Whereupon, having upbraided me for my drunken folly, she attacked Lias with a knife and drove her forth, with a slashed face.'

Kinyras made no comment and the other continued. 'Later the Council came to me in a body, Tamiradae to man, declaring that I had done well to intervene in so just a war, but as they were the party of peace and had no men to fight, I must send all my fighting men in order to keep my royal pledge. I dismissed them with what dignity I could muster and went to consult with Myrrah. All their pot was now clear to me.'

'You are fortunate my cousin, sir.'

'You say well and truly, dear lad. I am,' the king beamed. 'She was calmer and informed me that the young Argive had confessed he had undertaken to murder me at the instigation of the Tamiradae when the ships were dispatched.

'Treacherous hounds!'

'Aye! The near prospect of death sharpened my wits and inspired me with an excellent notion. Sailors, as you well know, are pleased to have small models of ships set in their tombs. We make many such here and trade with them, they being known as Ships of Paphos. Therefore I sent off the one galley with a cargo of forty-nine models to the Argives. I had promised fifty ships of Paphos and I sent them.'

'And your wit does you credit, my uncle... cunning matched with cunning, that is what pleases me. But your talk of ships reminds me that my cousin Myrrah has spoken of one Atreus, who will by chance be persuaded to employ me as one of his crew.'

King Cinyras answered with a prodigious yawn. 'That will keep until morning, when we shall all be in better trim to plan with safety. To bed, nephew, and lend me your arm. Though my head is still clear, my knees are none of the steadiest.'

Kinyras complied willingly. He was weary and the fumes of wine sickened him. The guests to a man had long ago succumbed and lay peacefully snoring upon their couches, where they would remain until dawn, when their slaves would be admitted to carry them away home.

He was astir early in his impatience to plan his escape and to be gone, but had to wait some hours before the appearance of his uncle and cousin. The terrace was cleared and restored to its customary good order, one table being sent for the morning meal with fruit and wines in a shady corner. Here Kinyras waited and drowsed, watching the sparking sea with lazy eyes and dreaming of Dayonis until his host and hostess appeared, when it transpired that Myrrah had also risen early and had set about his business immediately.

'Myrrah, my wonderful, has already seen Atreus, who comes here soon. You are to sail as a mariner in his ship and he will engage you as a pilot with special local knowledge. Rhose is his first port of call and six months will elapse before his return, when all will be forgotten if the Khemites are curious. Your station will be in the bow, so that you can choose your place for disappearing overboard.'

279

'Nothing could be better. How can I thank you, cousin, or show my gratitude?'

Myrrah smiled, a little sadly. 'Of that he will not speak. It is my delight to aid a brave man and you are one after my own heart, Kinyras. I could wish fate had been kinder, but you must go. My father and I part with you with deep regret, cousin.'

'Yes, that is so, nephew, but you will come again, we have your pledge for it, and with that must be satisfied. Meanwhile, as a parting gift, there is a basket of doves for you, which have been trained to carry a message. So can you communicate with us.'

'Atreus will put in for water at the end of land, and leave this cage of doves as an offering at the Temple. There will be nothing strange in that, though if you landed there would be much gossip,' Myrrah explained, seeing Kinyras looked perplexed. 'But if a strange pilot fell overboard at that point and was drowned the day before the cage was landed, the mishap would pass unnoticed, beyond an offering of doves being made to the gods and prayers offered for the unfortunate pilot.'

'All is now clear and if I am caught and tortured you may depend upon my silence.'

'The gods forbid! When you wish to write, tie your message to a bird's foot and set it free. Keep the young in a good place until they can fly, and train them to carry by taking them to a distance and setting them free. They will return to their cote by instinct and if the distance is gradually increased they will fly at great length from one spot to their home.'

'The miracle is simpler than would appear at first blink,' said Kinyras.

'All miracles are equally simple,' announced the priest-king didactically, with the conviction of knowledge and frequent practice.

'To guard the secret well is of the utmost importance,' Myrrah warned, 'set up a small temple to Our Lady of the Sea on some advantageous rock, where the presence of these doves will be accounted votive offerings and so escape unusual attention. When you have trained a brood, send them to us and so we shall establish communication between us over great distances.'

They were interrupted by the arrival of a tall, red-skinned man, whose slender loins proclaimed him a Cretan. Myrrah greeted him with a kiss as Atreus, introducing Kinyras as her cousin. The two men saluted and eyed each other keenly. Satisfied with what they saw, their greeting was cordial. 'Your cousin must bear a name, lady,' Atreus reminded Myrrah, with a smile.

'To be sure. He is Etrenoros of Ascalon, who unfortunately has enemies amongst the priests, also Khem pursues him.'

'I understand, sir, that you would reach the Karpas and wish opportunity to get ashore there. All shall be arranged if I can but convince my crew that you are truly a navigator.'

'Ask me what you please, Atreus, and I will answer to the best of my ability.'

Much relieved and pleased at the proposition Atreus began forthwith—'How, then, do you set a course at night?'

'By the world-spike. 4'

'Ah, but how do you find it?'

'By following the two outer stars of the Wine-Dipper 5 which point to it.

'Good! You know something, Streneros, 6 I can perceive. Now, tell me. It is a dark night and you expect to land or you are out of sight of land, in strange waters. How can you proceed safely?'

'By having a man up the mast to look for shoal-water is one way, but a better is to let out the anchor-stone a hundred fathoms of line. If then you get shoal-water it will bring you up. Some speed is lost, may be, but for the sake of safety the sacrifice is worth while.'

'Ah, you are a Phoenix 7, sure enough!' exclaimed Atreus, delighted, and slapping him on the back. 'Do you in truth know the Karpas?'

'Indeed yes. I live there.'

'I will take you upon one condition and it is that you swear by Our Lady of Ascalon never to betray my help to those Khemite dogs, should they catch you.'

Kinyras readily took the oath and the bargain was struck, King Cinyras undertaking to supply his nephew with some baggage to carry on board in order to convince the crew of his genuineness as a pilot, such baggage to be left behind when he went overboard, and would by sea law be divided among the crew.

1. Golden
2. Red haired,
3. Rhodes.
4. The Pole Star
5. The Plough. The Big Dipper.
6. A Sailor
7. Tanned skin, i.e., a real sailor.

# Chapter XVII

# THE TRAITOR IS UNMASKED

But one thing troubled Kinyras when he embarked upon the ship of Atreus and that was the calm, untroubled summer nights, with the unfavourable aspect of the moon for his purpose of escape. It was at the full. However, he was not the man to be deterred for such a cause. He instantly set about convincing his companions in the crew of two things, that he was a heaven-born navigator, specially gifted by the gods in that way, but dull-witted to the point of imbecility in every other.

In spite of these latter defects, he quickly gained the rough liking of the crew, who in their short acquaintance became genuinely concerned at some of his stupidities, none of which could possibly harm aught but himself. For instance there was the matter of the coil of hide-rope which he insisted upon keeping in one particular spot in spite of all protest, and in which he was for ever getting his feet entangled. Yet, notwithstanding the patient explanation from Atreus downward that such would cause disaster to him, he was too stupid to heed his danger or their friendly warnings.

And such in the end it proved to be... a death-trap. They had rounded Cape Gato without mishap, where the temple being built to Bubestase, the Cat-Headed one, roused their ribald mirth at the folly of Khem in worshipping such beasts, passed Salem and arrived at the Kastnon river about midnight when the catastrophe happened. How he contrived the mishap was ever a mystery, but Kinyras the Steerer, the fool, steered close in shore to prove his cunning at the helm, tripped over his pernicious coil of rope and plunged with a whirl of arms and a heart-rending yell for help into the calm sea, to sink like a stone. Once he rose to the surface at some distance from the ship—they said there must have been a strong current sunning at that spot—waved his arms and beat the water frantically, appealing piteously for the aid, and sank again. A man who could swim sprang overboard, unable to resist the entreaty, but though he swam round for almost an hour, while the rest of the crew and the mast at the gunwale stared, gesticulated and shouted a dozen contrary directions, Kinyras was lost. The next day they put in to land for water, made a votive offering of a cage of doves to the Lady of the Sea, offered prayers and sailed away.

To Kinyras, the art of swimming under water had been his chief accomplishment from his boyhood days, but as he sped rapidly shoreward below the surface of the calm, summer sea, he wished he had not taken such trouble to conciliate the crew and been so successful, or that they were less humane. But the tide was flowing in, and he could float upon his back every now and then to regain his breath and so landed without mishap and without detection. He landed near Andrea and within a day had arrived on the outskirts of Karpasia.

On his way thither he learned much and found that common talk was all of his wall, which had now grown to one of uncommon strength. The Khemites were still sitting down before it, but refrained from attack and were building big houses in the vicinity of their lines. An excellent harvest had been gathered, and the new King Erili was in great favour with the people, who publicly acclaimed him their saviour. Hange still had a good following, but among the less reputable. Ugly whispers, which memory of his former great power and sway yet permitted to be no more than murmurs here and there, began to circulate concerning rumours of his having tried to sell Karpasia to the enemy. All this lent wings to the feet of Kinyras, but it was as he sat drinking and listening in the common-room of an ordinary, a low hovel, a mile distant from the town, that he heard news of his beloved from the lips of some disgruntled toper with a grudge against the Law-giver, cursing him roundly, both for his crimes real and supposed, and for his association with that misbegotten, red-headed witch from Aghirda.

Fuming with secret fears and suspense, it was some time before, by skilful manoeuvring, Kinyras could segregate the babble, and persuade him to speak more freely. Though half in his cups, the man's wits were by no means drowned, but at length Kinyras wormed his way into his liking and confidence when the murder was soon out. Damastes' daughter, her whom they misnamed the Princess Dayonis, was the paramour of Hange, was seen publicly in his company and known to frequent his house. The foul witch had destroyed the senses of the Law-giver and it was through her that he had betrayed the country. Hange was known to be irresistible with women and had quickly bent the red-head to his will. Subsequent probing discovered the fact that this man's wife, a young and beautiful girl, had been stolen away from him and seduced by Hange, only to be cast out in the depths of winter to perish of exposure and want.

When the full tale was told Kinyras sat for a moment numbered by the force of his blow. He had been so sure of the love and loyalty of Dayonis and now to find her doubly treacherous, to him and to her country, was more than he could endure without betraying his feelings. His companion glanced at him curiously from time to time and at length ventured to whisper, in the wild hope of getting another to do what he himself dared not—'Vengeance, master, vengeance, is the only salve for deep wounds.'

Kinyras started. The man's words were as a flame to oil and suddenly he was a roaring furnace of fury. He would strangle Hange with his bare hands, choke the like from him and wring the slim, white neck of Dayonis as easily as he would that of one of Myrrah's doves, before he fell upon his own sword.

The man was easily persuaded to show him Hange's house and to furnish him with a sword and shield, for Kinyras might have to fight his way before he could attain the presence of his enemy. The man stole away, promising to return with the weapons and to signal his approach. In less than an hour Kinyras heard the yap of a smitten cur and slipped outside to find his companion waiting with the promised arms. Whence they came he did not ask and together the two stole through the darkness until they came to a high earth wall surrounding a large garden. To scale it was easy to his hard-bitten nimbleness.

'I can do no more,' whispered the man, having brought him to this point. 'She is there, as I have seen. Go straight forward through the trees, when you will see a light. That is your goal.'

'I thank you, friend. You shall be rewarded. What is your name?'

'Gato.'

'Go to Erili, the King, Gato, in the morning. Tell him of the service you have rendered me this night and say that the Snail left your reward to him.'

'Nay, master, I need none. Your vengeance, if you carry it through, suffices me.'

'Nevertheless, go,' urged Kinyras, as he turned to clamber up the wall.

When he reached the summit he took the sword and shield from Gato and slithered to the ground. Some little distance away through the trees he could discern a crack of light and for this he made. In the darkness he could see the black shadow of a low, large, rambling house of one storey, behind which the moon was rising. It was a still, fine night, and no servants seemed to be on guard. It was in accordance with the arrogance of Hange to suppose he was immune from danger, that none would dare to attack him.

Cautiously Kinyras crept toward that crack of light which he soon found came through the chink of a partially closed shutter to the window of the room built at the corner of the house, and left unfastened doubtless because the night was sultry; Kinyras approached and applied his eye to the crack, and getting a complete view of the room. A fine supper of cakes, bread, mutton, fruit and wine was spread before a low couch, upon which Dayonis and Hange reclined, apparently upon the best of terms with each other. At the sight of her the blood of Kinyras beat heavily in his throat and flooded behind his ears, so that he swallowed thickly and could not see, but presently this devastating swirl of emotion subsided and his vision cleared. The room was richly furnished, mostly with articles and fabrics imported from Khem, and it was lit with many small, Cyprian lamps, whose scented oil burned brightly infecting the air with a sickly languor. Through a door opposite could be viewed a spacious inner court, planted with flowering shrubs and many roses. On one side it was open to the rising moon, in whose pale beams the flowers gleamed ghostly. A huge, fair moth flittered into the room, playing about the red curls of Dayonis and they made great sport of this, she affecting fear, he pretending to catch it.

'See, my Dayonis, the light of your eyes has drawn him hither and he singes his wings in the flame of your hair,' cried Hange, making certain passes with his hands, so that they came very near to her white breast.

Kinyras watched these ploys grimly, fingering his sword, while in another section of his brain the words, hovered, like the fluttering insect in the room.

'The moth with singed wings doth singed return, her loving light conquering her fear and pain,' and even at that tense moment he found himself wondering whence they came, or at the strange tongue in which the words formed themselves.

'Nay, sweet lord, business before pleasure. There are matters of grave moment awaiting our discussion. When they are passed, then can we give ourselves to the joys which should be ours.'

She lifted her ripe lips to his and yielded to his hot clasp with an abandon which fired him, but when his mouth was near to hers she eluded him with a provoking laugh and a

287

sudden, lithe movement which took her to the edge of the couch. The next moment she was upon her feet and had drawn up a chair to the opposite side of the table and seated herself. Hange, thwarted and almost beside himself with passion and the desire for conquest, was yet forced to submit. Cross the table and seized her hand in his fiery grasp and she suffered it to remain with a languishing look, while her tongue uttered crisply—'Now, sir, what of Pharaoh?'

'He is still demanding you of Amasis. He, desiring you for himself, temporizes, while the impatience of Pharaoh grows. He had but seen you, what...'

'But Amasis?' she recalled him, tapping upon the table with one white forefinger, yet tempering her asperity with a seductive smile which completely lulled him, so that he went on—'Amasis? He was the power behind the throne, of Royal blood and leader of a strong party in Khem, with designs upon the great throne itself. Pharaoh Totmes smelt this out through his spies and sent Amasis hither as viceroy to conquer Orpheusa. This has Amasis not accomplished, nor has he delivered up to Pharaoh your lovely self, my Princess, thanks to that accursed of the gods, Kinyras.'

'Speak not of him!' cried Dayonis in a high excited voice.

Hange leaned toward her, a scowl on his owl's face, his mean eyes glittering. Dayonis instinctively withdrew until she was leaning against the back of her chair, panting, the palms of her hands pressed down hard upon the table.

'Is that dog, that offal, still in your heart and mind, Dayonis?' he whispered menacingly.

Almost immediately she recovered herself and relaxed towards him, eyes downcast, lips softly parted and dewy as she wheedled—'Should I be here, Hange, were that so? But in my country we deem it an ill-omen to speak abruptly on the dead, and without a more subtle approach.'

He, too relaxed and for a while they gazed amorously into each other's eyes, the lamp standing on the end of the table, softly illuminating their faces for the benefit of the silent watcher at the window. He, knowing what Dayonis could be in the act of love, was for a moment or two deaf and blind by the swirl of an agonizing emotion and when he recovered some what Dayonis was still dulcetly murmuring, 'Amasis, what of Amasis?' to recall her reluctant lover to the matter under discussion.

'He will die, and already have the messengers of death been dispatched from Khem with Pharaoh's orders. His crime? Treachery to the throne and disobedience.'

'And the next viceroy of Orpheusa, Hange, my lord adored one, is he appointed?'

'My beloved, I can wait no longer; I am consumed with fire and impatience for your sweet body. Give me my life, or I perish.' His avid face was thrust almost into hers, his hot breath stirred her curls, his clutching fingers mauled her breast.

She cast a hurried glance over her shoulder at the opened shutter, gently removed his paddling fingers and held them in hers before laying his hand palm downward upon the table and covering it with hers. 'But, my beloved, I shall be lost in the joy and rapture of our contact and my mind will be clouded. Inform me of this matter first, I beseech your sweet grace.'

He could not resist the pouting lips, the witching eyes, and answered, though with the utmost reluctance, seeing she would not be utterly wiling until her whim was granted—'The next viceroy of Orpheusa must be a man with no material interest in the affairs of Khem, be no warrior, and without an army. He must be a native of the land and able to commend himself to her peoples. Therefore has Pharaoh deigned to look upon me, his slave, for the office, and the price of my service to him will be yourself, my Dayonis.'

'Dear heart, may that time come soon! But the wall, my Hange, the Mercenaries, Erili, the King, what of them?'

'Within a week will they be overthrown. My party is strong, my captains posted. At a signal the King will be dispatched, the chiefs of the Mercenaries seized and strangled, the wall will be in my possession and I shall be master of Karpas.'

'Your schemes are indeed well laid,' she breathed.

'Thanks to much which you have told me. Without your

aid I could not have accomplished so much so quickly. And now, my Dayonis! Now!'

She rose, still smiling, her hand pressing his down upon the table, her smile of acquiescence a bedazzlement to his seething senses. The light of the lamp illuminated the luscious green of her simple tunic, glinted in the gold of her curls and gleamed upon her pearly skin. Hange, watching her avidly, moistened his dry lips with his tongue and his breath came whistling with desire.

The next moment everything happened in a whirl to the bewildered onlooker. With two bounding leaps Dayonis had reached the shutter and torn it open and the next Kinyras had hurled his sword at Hange, hurtling forward to stop her. The weapon missed him by the barest space, to fall harmless in the middle of the room. Before Dayonis could get through the window, Hange had seized her and a desperate struggle ensured between them. Neither spoke as they wrestled strenuously, the girl trying to slip from his clutching hands. Kinyras leapt into the room, and seized him by the throat from behind, though not before Hange had let out one piercing shout for help. As Hange released her, Dayonis scrambled out into the garden and screamed through the window, 'Fly! Fly!' ignorant of the identity of her rescuer, and it ws not until he came into the light of an over-hanging lamp that she recognised him. 'My Kinyras, my Kinyras. Oh, my sweet love, beware!' she shrieked, tears of joy, excitement, and fear streaming down her face. 'Fly! Never heed his vile carcass! Come, before it is too late.'

'Wait until I've stifled the breath from this carrion. Run to the wall, Dayonis,' he answered, his fingers like an implacable ring of bronze tightening about the lean scrag of his enemy.

But she disobeyed, still standing there and yelling to him at the pitch of her lungs, while the voices of servants, bidden on pain of death to keep away from the chamber and its environs by their master, were heard approaching. Kinyras tightened his grip, and at one and the same moment two servants appeared in the doorway and the head of Hange fell suddenly forward limply. Hurling the body from his in the path of the nearest slave, so that he stumbled and fell, Kinyras plunged through the window, found the hand of Dayonis outstretched to him and pulled her after him without a word. They reached the wall, and he threw her up roughly. She scrambled into safety and lying at full length along its top, reached down to help him up beside her, nor did they pause in their flight until they had reached the safety of Erili's house.

With an equal and breathless haste did Dayonis tell all she had learned from Hange, and it was not until Erili had made the rapid decision to arrest all Hange's followers at present in the city and issued orders for its immediate execution, that the lovers had time for themselves or for the wonder which consumed them for all that had happened to each other during their separation, and for the joy of their reunion. To Kinyras, the rapture of finding Dayonis loyal to him in spite of what he had recently witnessed, the reaction from the misery of that hour spent at the window, the bliss of feeling his arms about her again, was compensation for all he had suffered in the interim.

The night passed in the exchange of news. Dayonis had been in Aghirda, where she had accomplished much. Her people knew of her safety and the whole nation was hers to a man, ready to rise and die for their freedom under her leadership when she gave the signal. She had stolen secretly back to Karpasia to consult with Erili, full of her former plan to entrap Hange into an admission of his guilt and treachery to the people.

In the morning came tidings of Hange's death which, while giving complete satisfaction, somewhat altered the complexion of things, robbing them of the vengeance they had planned in publically accusing their enemy and bringing him to trial before the Council. The pleasure of attending his subsequent hanging had to be dismissed. Nevertheless, Erili was determined upon exposing his villainy to the Council, who only too often had thwarted the monarchy by upholding Hange and his policy, and Erili was resolved to tighten his grip on the situation now so favourable to himself and his plans. Accordingly, an immediate meeting of the Council was called, but an accountable delay occurred in this project by the absence of most of the councillors from the city. They had gone to attend some religious festival which would be in progress for several days.

Meanwhile an unusual and brooding silence seemed to have descended upon the community and the city was strangely quiet. People kept within doors, or when they went abroad, hurried silently to their destinations and went swiftly about their business. Kinyras was preparing to accompany Dayonis back to Aghirda. Food for the approaching winter was their great problem and the two were much occupied in planning and organizing supplies. As soon as they had given their evidence before the Council they would start for the border. They would travel secretly, riding upon two asses which Erili had provided and which stood waiting in their stalls at the rear of Erili's house.

So passed three days, days of that strange, brooding quietness, which was vaguely oppressive. The weather, too, was unusually hot for the time of the year and the parched land cried out for the rains. A vague unrest seized upon Kinyras and he itched to be gone into Aghirda, where he could have Dayonis to himself, where their marriage would be celebrated in the sacred fastnesses of Jaske, and where his activities could be fully engaged in organizing the Aghirdan army. Idleness was abhorrent to his nature.

At last they came to the evening of this day and darkness fell. On the morrow the Council was to meet and by midday they would be started on their long journey. Supper was brought in by the slaves and they sat at it long, Kinyras and Erili discussing some knotty point of military strategy, Dayonis occupied with a bunch of luscious grapes, which he plucked languidly from their stem and popped one by one into her mouth. Suddenly there was a stir, a curious sort of dull murmur, like the rushing of wind coming from a great distance. Erili went to the window and saw the far sky lit by a steady glare, which had nothing to do with the rising moon. 'Look,' he called Kinyras, pointing. 'What do you make of that, my Snail?'

Kinyras studied it a moment or two and shook his head. Dayonis quickly joined him. 'It appears like the light from a multitude of torches,' he said at last.

'So I deemed it. What is toward now? And the sound?'

'The shouting of a great multitude.'

Erili nodded. 'Perdition seize it! My very bones warn me there is nothing good for us in this. How now?'

He sung round as there was a scurry of footsteps in the court outside and his body-slave came bursting into the room without ceremony, to fall gasping at his master's feet. 'Pardon, my lord!' The man was to spent with running that he could utter no more.

'Lie awhile and take your time, so will you be the more speedy in the end,' Erili commanded.

The man obeyed, lying there relaxed and there was no sound in the room but his laboured breathing. Dayonis was seized with an intolerable and strange apprehension and moved restlessly about the room, padding silently as a caged pantheress. For a matter of twenty seconds this went on, until she was arrested by the man's voice, strained and urgent and still weak with his great fatigue. 'Lord, Hange is not dead. He but feigned death the better to work against you, sire, and my lord Kinyras. These three days has he been stirring up the priests and people against my lady Dayonis here, and even now a great multitude draws near to seize her and him, to burn and torture for witchcraft. I was on the far side of the city and heard him with mine own ears addressing the people.'

Dayonis visibly paled at the news and Erili and Kinyras stared at each other, in silent dismay.

Presently the King spoke. 'You have done well. Summon the captain of the guard hither and then go you to the stables and take the two asses to the great cedar by the white stone. You know it?'

'Yes, master.'

'And you, Kinyras?'

'I, too, sir.'

'Excellent! Now despatch.'

The man scrambled to his feet and hastened out.

'Kinyras, there is not a moment to be lost. Arm yourselves and fly on foot to the trysting place. Go by all the secret ways of the city, for it you ride you will surely be stopped and taken. I will defend the house and hold them for as long as may be. Hasten and the gods preserve you.'

Dayonis opened her mouth to protest, but Kinyras seized her roughly by the wrist, thrust a knife into her hands and found her bow and a quiver of arrows, which he strapped upon her back. Then buckling on his armour, he found helmet and sword, took his shield and pushed her through the window into the garden, all to the accompaniment of hasty directions from Erili to the captain of his guard, who had orders to send a squad of men by a devious route to seize all Hange's household and burn down his house during his absence with the mob. The clamour from the advancing people, the glare from their torches grew louder and brighter with disturbing rapidity, and Kinyras feared the house would be surrounded before they could get away.

Even as they ran across the garden to the postern in the wall, they were followed by the men who were to guard and hold it at all costs, but they were too late. As they slipped into the narrow lane beyond the gate, half a dozen men came running towards them, some bearing torches, all armed with spears and knives and shouting—'The witch escapes, brothers. Burn the witch, burn her.'

With a hasty order to the leader of the postern-guard Kinyras closed the door and heard it bolted and barred behind them. 'Now, my Dayonis, stand firm and we have them nicely. Take my shield and strike shrewdly.'

Coolly they awaited the onslaught, which being by fanatical priests and civilians, was a disorderly rush, with no thought to their rear. Two to six were long odds and it might have gone badly with Dayonis and Kinyras, especially as those with torches were clever enough to use them as weapons of offence, had it now been from two of the guard who climbed the wall and fell upon them from behind. Te whole party were quickly dispatched and the death of each assured before Kinyras and Dayonis, grasping hands, sped lightly down a network of alleys, out of the city towards their trysting place, knowing by the clamour behind them that the attack upon Erili had already begun and that there was no time to lose.

# CHAPTER XVIII

# THE MARRIAGE IN THE TEMPLE OF JASKE

Events had moved so rapidly within the last hour or two that all their plans were set at naught. Kinyras and Dayonis now found themselves fugitives from the worst form of religious persecution, hiding by day, creeping cautiously forward towards Zadoug's encampment by night, while the witch-hung swept fiercely up and down the country.

The Karpasians were a very superstitious people and a great fear and hatred of witchcraft was ingrained in the mind of the nation. Though the popularity of Hange was of the wane, immediately he raised the hunt and the smelling out of witches, all his rumoured misdeeds were forgotten for the time being, and he was able to sway the priesthood and the mob as he wished. That this hunt was fierce and thorough they had ample evidence from time to time, and were forced to proceed with the utmost caution, so that a week had elapsed before Kinyras was able to crawl through Zadoug's window one dark night when his brother had retired to rest. 'Zadoug!' whispered Kinyras, urgently, 'Zadoug.'

His brother was in his first sleep and took some rousing. 'What is it?' he muttered drowsily, 'Who calls?'

'It is I, Kinyras. Waken, Zadoug, waken.'

But that was the last thing Zadoug ever wished to do, once

he slept comfortable, and he muttered—"Tis a dream come to plague me. I am always dreaming of Kinyras. Be off, I say, and leave me in peace.'

But Kinyras would not be denied and soon Zadoug was awake, embracing his brother convulsively, shedding a few irrepressible tears and stuttering with joy. He had heard of the return of Dayonis from Aghirda and the resulting witch-hunt, but no whisper of his brother had reached him, and Erili did not dare to send him word.

When the first pleasure of their reunion had died down a little, Kinyras was eager for news of what had happened during his flight and hiding.

'Erili very soon had the situation in hand and the town quietened, but the mischief had spread to the country, worse luck. He dispersed the mob, seized Hange's household slaves, and burnt his house to the ground, but the lawgiver had disappeared, nor has he been seen since.

'Hiding, eh?'

'Aye, biding his time. We shall have no peace in the land until we've assisted him to a dance in mid-air, brother, and for my part I'll string him out of hand without warning or trail, if I catch him.'

'But the Council?'

'Have met, Kinyras, and Erili has laid the matter of his treachery before it. But Hange still has a following amongst those who seek to gain by his favour and advancement, though three parts of them are against him and strive to have him apprehended. So the matter rests at the moment. And now, brother, are you for Aghirda, or do you return to the wall? And how did you escape from Khem?'

Long they sat, talking in whispers, while they discussed the ways and means of raising revolt in Aghirda. And when that was over there was the marvel of his escape from the mine and of his meeting with Cinyras of Paphos to be related, all of which entertained Zadoug mightily.

'Old Cinyras King in Paphos, eh? Who'd have thought it, Kinyras? And we had deemed him dead these many years past.

Marvels will never cease, but, oh, brother, it's good to see thee again. Old Snail, I thought I'd lost thee, and my heart has been heavy with bitterness since the day of the fight until now. And Dayonis, she was like to go mad with grief when he discovered you'd been taken.'

This was sweet hearing to Kinyras and his former doubts of her filled him with remorse.

'But the difficulty is to get you both into Aghirda. You are safe enough with all that growth about your face, but what of her red head? How can that be hidden?' They pondered the problem for some time in silence, until Zadoug suddenly slapped his thigh and cried—'By the gods, I have it! For some time past I have been sending food across the border by a secret way, and a train of asses laden with trashed corn packed in packets is even now preparing. The baskets have been found lighter than bags of hide and are large enough to conceal a man, much less Dayonis. Go, brother, and bring her hither before the moon rises. She can lie hidden here until the convoy sets out.'

It was risky, but Kinyras thought it might be done. Accordingly he crept away to the spot where he had left Dayonis. Fortunately, she was as skilled as he in the arts of hiding and stealing away on a journey unseen, and for two whole days did Zadoug hide them until the food convoy was ready to take the track into Aghirda, for it was little better. It ran north, about a mile back from the great wall to the point where the fortifications terminated in the natural cliff. From here it proceeded still towards the coast until abruptly it turned left and wound away through the hills upward, to be lost in the fastnesses of Aghirda. The Khemite line was weak here, so it was simple to get past their patrols at night. Hitherto the question had been one of the safe transport of the grain, but now food became of secondary importance to that of human life, and the plan of campaign must be different. But how? How was suspicion to be avoided? Zadoug and Kinyras turned hopelessly to Dayonis, who shook her head.

After much thinking, rejecting one scheme after another, at

last she spoke. 'I have it. Bands of my people will be hunting in the hills and instructions must be given to hand over the convoys to the first party of hunters it encounters. See, my Kinyras, I will give you my magic stone, which you will show for a sign to the chief of the party. By it he will know that I am near, and will yield you his obedience. Do you therefore, Zadoug, put Kinyras as the second in command of the convoy, to take charge and to bring back the asses and baskets after the armed guard has delivered it up to the first party of Aghirdan hunters we encounter. They will return to you, leaving Kinyras to go forward with the convoy.'

As no better plan offered, this was adopted and Zadoug took Kinyras to the granary, there to superintend the loading of the grain, formally making him responsible for the convoy under the military officer. When the last of the baskets were loaded and corded, Zadoug made a great parade of sealing each one, and having them placed by the granary door, ready for loading in the small hours of the morning, for the team was to start with the first crack of light in the sky. Work for the day then being over, the doors were closed, and fastened.

It was an easy matter for Dayonis accompanied by the two brothers, to slip into the granary some minutes before the slaves appeared for loading the convoy, for one of the baskets to be emptied and herself secreted inside with the seals reaffixed. Kinyras marked the basket with a dab of red paint, and saw which animal bore it and himself led it to the head of the column, never letting its head-rope out of his hand.

The column started, Kinyras leading, five slaves following, the military escort bringing up the rear. Concealed in his loin-cloth, Kinyras bore the sacred stone of Aghirda, while its owner lay cramped and sweating in the basket, cursing Hange with every breath she drew. The way seemed infinitely wearisome and he was beset with anxiety for his love, fearing she would die of suffocation, or shriek aloud with the cramp. And as for Dayonis herself, during that terrible journey she sometimes thought that death for witchcraft was preferable, yet hour after hour she endured until her mind sunk into an apathy.

Slowly the day declined and with every step the track now became rougher and progress more slow. The wild beauty of the scene made little impression upon Kinyras, harassed as he was by fears, and he barely saw the many hued hills richly lit by the evening light, nor the purple grandeur of the distant mountains. Doggedly he plodded on, eyes eagerly seeking some signs of men, but the country was incredibly lonely. Just as he was facing heavily the almost certain prospect of having to encamp for the night, and wondering by what device he could afford relief to Dayonis, a big stone rolled down from the hill beside them and the next instant a man's head appeared, thrust cautiously round the edge of a rock some hundred feet above. Almost frantically Kinyras made the secret sign and gradually the owner of the head emerged upon a narrow path which led downwards, followed by his six companions.

They made a savage enough looking party with their manes of ragged red hair of varying shades and their rough garments of goat-skins clumsily fashioned. Kinyras advanced halfway to meet their leader and stood waiting, seething with secret impatience, while the man leisurely picked his way from boulder to boulder, ignorant of any need for haste. Kinyras had only a moment, for the officer of the guard was coming up from the rear, and he must witness nothing unusual. Standing with his back to the oncoming soldier, Kinyras again made the secret sign and beckoned urgently, then drew forth the magic stone, held it up by its string and concealed it again, just as the officer took his place beside him.

Seeing this, the Aghirdan began to leap forward having recognised the stone, for where that was, there also was his queen. Kinyras saw that his eyes scrutinized each face keenly, then returned to his own with an enquiring look. Kinyras pulled his leading ass forward with a significant return glance and laid his hand as though accidentally upon the basket in which Dayonis lay concealed.

The man was quick to comprehend, especially as Kinyras then touched the spot in his loin-cloth where he had again hidden the Stone. Kinyras, who was to act as interpreter for the officer, now presented him to the Aghirdan and the convoy was formally handed over. Compliments were exchanged, when the officer suddenly decided that he would here encamp for the night and march back to the lines at dawn. Here was a complication and a fresh delay in rescuing Dayonis, but Kinyras dared make no protest.

The Aghirdan agreed without blinking an eyelash, saying he knew of an excellent position for the purpose. He pointed to a barely indicated path leading away on the right and said a few rapid words to one of his companions in an undertone, then taking the officer familiarly by the arm led him away to view the site, while his adjutant seized the leading ass by its head-rope and led it away round a bluff in the opposite direction. Kinyras gave a hasty order to the slaves to follow the soldiers with the camp equipment, saying he would stay by the asses. Soon the party were out of sight among the rocks and Kinyras flew after Dayonis.

He found the second Aghirdan disappearing into the mouth of a small cave, which would be just enough to stable the convoy. In less than a minute he had got the basket open, and had lifted Dayonis out, laying her tenderly on the ground. She had fainted, and for a moment or two he feared she was dead of suffocation. Meanwhile the Aghirdan was putting stones in the empty basket and refastening the seals. This accomplished, he stolidly led the ass back to its fellows.

Kinyras carried Dayonis deeper into the cave and began gently to rub her limbs. She soon revived and declared all she needed was to stretch herself and sleep off her weariness, urging him to return to the camp, bringing her food and drink later. Thankfully he obeyed and the rest of the night passed without mishap. The guard set off on the return march at dawn the next morning, taking the slaves with them, and Dayonis was free in Aghirda, safe among her own people, and none the worse for her gruelling experience of the previous day.

The party of Agnirdans they had met were out hunting Mufulon, the wild sheep of the mountains. At her bidding they took charge of the team and the party started for the interior.

'Now, my Kinyras, we will go to the Temple of Jaske and I will show you many wonders. There shall our marriage be celebrated, if you are still of the same mind.'

Reveiving ardent assurances of this, they started out for the place. The two were in holiday mood and they loitered, happy only to be in each other's company after their long unhappy separation and the anxieties of the past week. Towards evening hey came out on a ridge above a deep valley, where Dayonis pointed to a little cleft scarcely three feet wide, which appeared to split the whole mountain side. 'That is the entrance to Jaske's temple,' she informed him.

'This!' he exclaimed, incredulously, 'Why, I can step across it at a dozen places.'

She smiled at him in a superior way, as though he was a doubting child. 'You will see, my Kinyras, old doubter!' and she pouted.

'Oh, I believe you, my love.'

Meanwhile a stout hide rope was being fastened round her shoulders and to his dismay Kinyras saw her lowered into the cleft by one of her men and disappeared, where he must needs follow. Soon he, too, was swinging dizzily at the end of a rope, until his feet touched a ledge and in the gloom he could just discern the figure of Dayonis, awaiting him. 'Can you see, Kinyras? If not, wait until your eyes become accustomed to the murk. The way is dangerous.'

Gradually her pale form became clearer and the dizziness left his head. 'Lead on!' he commanded, briefly.

She seemed to flit lightly before him, like a moth, and cautiously he felt his way until the ledge broadened out to the mouth of a large cave, where a swirl of smoke and the acrid scent of burning torches smote his nostrils. A chatter of voices proclaimed a crowd of people before he saw them, men, women and children, as many as a hundred of them, who started and fell silent when their Queen appeared suddenly among them. Dayonis raised her right arm in greeting. 'Hail, my people! Once more I'm among ye.'

They parted to make a way for her, murmuring greetings as the queen and her companion passed through to emerge upon another ledge. It led along the edge of the crack, which penetrated to the very depths of the earth itself, surely to the world's axis, Kinyras thought, averting his eyes hurriedly from the abyss. Beyond was another cave of enormous dimensions in which was assembled fully eight hundred people, and at whose upper end a rough kind of throne had been chipped from the surrounding rock. Some daylight did indeed penetrate the crack, but it was more an appearance of light than an actuality and a number of small lamps of earthenware burned here and there, embellishing the oolitic limestone of the walls with little cones of yellow flame.

When the assembly saw Dayonis a mighty shout went up, which rumbled and echoed through the cavern and from the throng two or three pushed their way clear and came towards her, the first of whom was Ammunz. Prostrating himself before her, he kissed her feet and, bending, she laid her hand upon his head, bidding him rise. Again the people acclaimed, and would have pressed forward in their excitement and curiosity, but springing up Ammunz shouted and waved them back with wild gesticulations, until a broad road was made down the middle of them, leading to the throne. Ammunz took her by the hand and led her down the lane amid the awed and breathless silence of the throng, Kinyras following close at her heels. Whome they were halfway to the stone Dayonis stopped dead, struck by a sudden thought, seized Ammunz by the elbow and whispered in his ear. He bowed his head in acknowledgment and dropped behind beside Kinyras, whom he too detained by murmured words, While Dayonis slowly and majestically walked to her throne and seated herself. When she sat the people fell upon their faces with one accord and Ammunz led Kinyras away for a private conclave. A man, who looked like a priest, brought a sceptre and presented it to her with great ceremony.

A body of men, powerful fellows armed with a spear, sword and shield, had now grouped themselves about her, and the while assembly waited for her to speak. At length, after an impressive moment or two, in which her busy thoughts raced, she raised her sceptre and her voice rang out clear and penetrating. 'Rise, my people, and sit upon the floor and listened to my words.'

There was a great rustle as they obeyed, and when this died down she proceeded—'As you know, may be, I have been absent from you, seeking counsel of the High Gods in my country's extremity. Jaske, the Holy, the Mighty, has spoken to me, saying, "I have heard your voice, my daughter, and the supplications of my people. Your cries have not been in vain. You bear upon your neck the Sacred Stone, which I gave to your forefathers in olden days, promising aid in time of trouble. Upon the stone is carved the figure of a man, armed with an unknown bow, which he points at an enemy. Go you into the Karpas and there will you meet him, the Rescuer. He will save you from your greatest danger, bringing you by strange means back to your people. He will show the people how to make a mighty army and he will lead them to victory over their enemies, even over Khem. Aghirda shall be free, and you will take this man to husband, for he is the beloved of the gods. It is my will."'

She paused, while hundreds of pairs of eyes were fixed unwinkingly upon her in awe and wonder. Seeing the favourable effect of her words, slowly he raised her hands and took the sacred stone from her neck, holding it out before the people. A gasp of astonishment and wonder when round. 'See, here is the stone, bearing the portrait of the saviour of Aghirda. Let one man out of every hundred step forward, that he may view it and witness amongst ye.'

After some little murmuring, fluster and hesitancy, at length eight or nine men assembled before the throne, looking sheepish and fearful. Dayonis solemnly motioned them to approach and to each showed the stone. When this identification and verification of her truth was over, they returned to their places and once more Dayonis raised her hand for silence and immediately received it.

Amid a breathless hush she continued—'I obeyed the command of the Mighty Jaske and all fell out as he foretold. Peril dogged my footsteps, and in my greatest need Jaske sent the Stranger, His Beloved, to my rescue. He brought me back to Aghirda from the midst of my enemies. And now I present him to you as your saviour and my husband to be.'

She clapped her hands and at the signal Kinyras walked in from the direction in which he had disappeared, but with what a difference! Gone was the bush about his jaws and the thatch upon his head. With hair cut and smoothed and crowned with a high, bronze helmet, cheeks flushed and tanned with the sun, he came towards them with a lordly stride. He was stripped of clothes, carrying only a bronze shield and a great sword, while an attendant carried a staveros. His tall, sinewy body glowed with health, the muscles rippling under the shining skin, which had been rubbed and polished with oils, while a delicate and subtle essence wafted from him as he moved. With his fine, free soldier's carriage and the easy swing of his bronzed limbs as he advanced, he looked every inch the beloved of the gods, which Dayonis had recently christened him, and she viewed him with mingled feelings of relief, satisfaction, and pride.

Kinyras, who had to thank Ammunz for the success of his hasty toilet came leisurely before Dayonis and halted, raising his spear high in salute.

She rose from her seat, ranged herself at his side and together they walked forward a few paces nearer the people. 'This is my lord Kinyras, the chosen of Jaske, to be your saviour and my husband. Give him your welcome and allegiance, my people of Aghirda.'

A mighty shout of approval rose. The people of Aghirda had accepted Kinyras without question.

He raised his hand for silence and made a short address, a speech which, by its brevity and directness, won their hearts. 'Men and women of Aghirda, food for the winter will be assured to you, and in the spring I will lead you against your enemies. In the meantime you must labour to make the arm which will give you victory and of which I alone hold the secret. And when you have made it then must you learn to use it. Pick out from amongst you twelve of your most skilled smiths.'

Wild cheering followed and in the excitement Dayonis led him away to show him the wonders of the caves, and to prepare him for their marriage, which she informed him would be celebrated that night. Dayonis led him during this exploration to a further ledge of the chasm, which seemed to end in space. Kinyras sickened at the sight and drew back involuntarily, and she laughed.

'Those who follow Jaske must have a steady head, Kinyras. But see, I will lead the way and do you follow with care, for one false step will hurl you to destruction many hundreds of feet below. Put your right hand against the opposite wall of the cleft, so, and let it take your weight while you feel with your foot for the niche or the further side of this buttress of rock, so.'

Kinyras followed instructions and found that, when once shown, the passage was not difficult. The ledge continued without further obstruction and led to another large cave, where a matter of thirty women were occupied in boiling some decoction in clay pots over fires.

'It is Helleboros,' she explained, 'a deadly poison and a Royal secret and not healthy for everyone's knowledge. It sometimes happens that a man becomes irksome, from this cause or that. My father's sceptre has spikes upon it, which are dipped in the poison, and if any noise-some fellow became saucy and spoken him ill, then would my father smite him with the sceptre. Men said he died of shame. Maybe so, but the Helleboros helped. Staveros bolts dipped in this will kill if they do but scratch, and the Khemites must be driven from the country before spring, so that the sowers may go forth. Let them freeze here all winter, say I, but when the sun lures them out, then we'll have them with the staveros bolts flying. Can you tell me of a better way?'

'Let me see one of your forts first before I speak, and have ready a great store of the poisoned bolts. Let Khem bide until we are ready for them.'

Dayonis led him to a small cave, where she bid him rest and meditate until their marriage took place. She was retiring for the same purpose, explaining that the rites must be solemnized, fasting at midnight, but that a great feast would follow.

Kinyras told her in his arms and kissed her ardently. 'I care not what I do so that I may claim you at last,' he whispered. 'I have not waited and fought for you, beloved, thought I had lost you forever and found you again. Shall I complain now?'

'You do not repent? You are of the same mind?' she whispered, her arms clasping his neck.

'I love you, Dayonis. Body and soul I am yours to the end.'

Later she came to him and first tying a wet cloth over his mouth and nose and then over her own, she led him by a still more difficult and hair-raising path deep down into the mountain until they came to a small cavern, triangular in shape, having at its further end a fissure similar to that outside, only smaller in width. From it curled lazily fine whorls of vapour like floating veils of gossamer, which were drawn upward by the draught from what appeared to be a natural chimney in the rock above, and down which came enough light to create a wan illumination. Before this cleft was stood a rough hewn conical stone serving as an altar. The air was tainted with the odour of spilt blood which, mingling with the smoke from the hidden fires of the earth beneath, was very unendurable to Kinyras and made him sick to the soul. He found himself wishing that his love was less fond of smoke-stench. A number of white animals, sheep and goats, were herded in a rough pen, shivering with fright and bleating piteously, causing the bridegroom still more discomfort.

'Jaske dwells below,' said Dayonis, pointing to the fissure. 'See, to-day he is in a beneficent state and sends us fleecy messages of goodwill, but sometimes he is enraged and belches forth angry clouds, so that it is difficult to approach his altar, and when he is furious he leaps forth in fire and stones, so that none dare approach him.' Then she whispered, 'The secret

305

fastnesses where the stones I told you of, is below. A wet cloth is stretched over the fissure there, to filter the smoke, else we could not stay here long enough, though our mouths are protected.'

Kinyras nodded, misliking the place as much as the pleading animals, and wondering how they contrived to get them to such a place. They must have been lowered from above with an infinity of danger and difficulty. Ammunz and several great chiefs now joined them, with wet cloths over their faces, and the ceremonies began.

First Kinyras, as instructed, made offerings, saying, 'I bring you gifts, O Mighty Jaske. The Gifts of a Warrior. Here is my helmet. To friends lovely to behold, a terror to mine enemies. This Eager Sword, whose metal is worn in the fierceness of battle. This Curved Bow and its Quiver, but the shafts I do not bring, for them I have given already on the field of battle, to the hearts of men.'

Dayonis then shed her dress and offered it, saying, 'O Mighty Jaske, I bring you a woman's gift. Accept this raiment like the flowered purple of the mossy deep, studded with flowers.' Then a series of mysteries, incantations, exhortations and prayers, which seemed to him to last for hours, though they were much less, and of which he grew so wearied that at last his mind could no longer attend, and he followed blindly the whispered directions of Dayonis. Taking a curious object from the altar, very finely and delicately worked in bronze, she presented it to him, saying. 'Take this, my husband, and keep it for ever near you. It is a charm which will preserve you from your greatest danger. It will give you a new life for an old.'

Kinyras took it, saw it represented a snail and he held it in his hand until the rites were over. Nor did he think it strange that Dayonis should officiate at her own marriage. She, as officiating priestess, appeared to be marrying herself to him, but he cared not who performed the ceremony so that it was solemnized and she tied to him indissolubly, resolving that once he was quit of the place nothing in the wild world should beguile him into a second visit.

At length it was over and Dayonis, seeming little the worse for her ministrations, was smiling and happy, satisfied and very loving, which was all Kinyras secretly cared about. They re-ascended nearer to earth's surface, to his infinite relief, and spent the rest of the night in feasting and love. Breast to breast and bosom resting upon bosom and lips pressed to sweet lips. Her skin touching his. Then silence and sweet sleep.

Several weeks passed, in which the staveros was made with a feverish activity and thousands of bolts were fashioned and steeped in the deadly Helleboros. The autumn rains and winds raged wildly amongst the mountains without, giving place to the snows of winter, but within the caves the people were snug enough, sheltered from the fury of the elements. Wood there was in plenty and huge fires blazed, and the eyes and throat of Kinyras grew accustomed to the reek of smoke, and his sight to the dimness of these interiors, though he longed to be out and abroad, attacking Khem, who were sheltering in various forts they had raised in propitious sites. Kinyras learned that when the people of Aghirda had first sheltered in the mountain the Khemites had pursued and pressed them, but the ledges were so easy to defend that they had retreated, leaving them in peace and determined to starve the country into submission. During these months of inactivity he found plenty of occupy him at the butts which he set up, where the training of men in the use of the staveros went on hour by hour, and week by week. The strong and muscular Aghirdans were naturally excellent bowmen, and soon he had a corps of which he was justly proud, eager for battle and for the day when this beloved of their god should lead them forth against their enemies.

January was half through and the mountains deep in frozen snow before men and arms were ready, and Kinyras said to his wife—'Lead me to the nearest fort, Dayonis, that I may prepare for its destruction.'

Accordingly they set out and traversed the frozen snow for some distance until they came to a wide valley, at the upper end of which a strong fort was well set upon a little hill in a fine strategic position. Beneath the snow open grassland lay on every side for two bow-shots.

Dayonis expressed a deep disgust. 'This is called the Granary of Aghirda, and we cannot till the soil, for if we did they would but reap our harvest. See, they have felled the forest all round, to build their stockade and to prevent us from using it as cover.'

'But they have built of wood,' objected Kinyras. 'Why not an attack under clouds of arrows, to pile brush-wood against their stockade and burn them out?'

'I tried that before your return, but we suffered from a murderous arrow-fire through their loop-holes and as fast as we piled brush-wood they soused it with water, having built over a great spring, so that it would not light.'

He nodded. 'Aye, but then you had no staveros, now you will see a difference.'

They returned and set every available man to cutting brush-wood. Three days later, with an army of five hundred all armed with the staveros, they set out for the attack. It was bitterly cold, with a howling wind which bit into them as they advanced to the attack in the bleak dawn. Stealing cautiously down-wind, they were within half a bow-shot before they were sighted from the fort, each man carrying an enormous bundle of brushwood. Trumpets shrilled at alarm from within and a heavy arrow-fire was poured out at the Aghirdans, now a hundred paces distant, but arrows could not pierce those busy shields carried before, and the advance was continued to within fifty yards of the stockade, behind which the staveros men opened fire upon the loop-holes of the fort.

At such short range a miss was rare and though the Khemites were numerous and brave, this unequal duel was soon seen to be disastrous and a sally was made from the great gate on the opposite side of the fort from where the attack was in operation. The Khemite troop advanced at the double, forming up for attack and losing heavily during the manoeuvre. At length they were ready to advance, but their archers posted at the loop-holes, seeing the futility of their defence, had taken cover from the enemy bolts. Kinyras gave a sharp command

and the whole line of brush-wood breastwork, carried on its poles, with a sudden rush was piled at the foot of the stockade, and before the sally-troop could get round, jars of hot oil had been poured upon the mass of twig and the whole ignited. The stockade was blazing by the time the Khemites appeared, and amid yells of rage a rushing retreat for water was pursued by a grilling staveros and arrow-fusillade.

The spring was frozen and though the Khemites made balls of snow and hurled them into the flames they were useless. The leaping fires, fanned by the fierce wind, spread to the fort itself, and in less than an hour the remnants of the garrison were being pursued hotly down the valley, led by Kinyras and Dayonis.

So passed the winter in these sporadic attacks upon the isolated forts of Khem in the mountains of Aghirda, and in each case success followed. Kinyras discovered that he could feed his men upon the captured food and found this mode of like not only enjoyable, but suited to his love of a soldierly activity. The mountaineers were happy and satisfied. Their queen, under the direct guidance of god, had brought to them a hero armed with a wonderful weapon, and by the spring Aghirda was once more free. Only one or two forts remained operative, but they were beyond the borders of the country and the Aghirdans could view them with indifference.

All this time Kinyras had been training pigeons given to him by his uncle. He had managed to convey several promising young broods to Zadoug, with instructions to pass them on to barrios suitable posts, including one to Erili. By this means he had established a swift communication both with the lines and the capital. Moreover, he had trained Ammunz in the secret, so that in event of any fatality to himself and Dayonis, the news could be sent to Zadoug and Erili at once.

'Well, how's he now... any change?' Heyward held Mina tight, asking his usual question almost mechanically as he looked down into her upturned face, his eyes telling another and very different story.

'No, nothing,' she murmured, trying to wriggle free in a restive way.

His hold tightened possessively. 'Damnation! How much longer is this going on? I'm about fed up with it.'

'Well,' she demanded, acidly, 'what are you going to do about it?'

'What what's wrong with you, little girl?' he went on fatuously.

Mina squirmed. There was something hideously inappropriate in the term as applied to her age, which offended her niceness of perception and which she would never have noticed a month ago. 'Don't call me that,' she said tensely, 'I'm not a girl and you know it. It's sheer mockery.'

He released her to tilt her chin and force her to meet his injured gaze. 'You're app to pieces, dear. I don't know you for my little Mina. This business is getting you down.'

'Perhaps it is. Oh, Hank, if only we knew how it is all going to end. Sometimes it terrifies me to death. What is going to become of us all?' She began to cry with a desolate fashion.

'How d'you mean? You're coming with me, aren't you? I thought we'd arranged all that, long ago.' He released her and stood staring at her gloomily, his hands thrust deep into his trousers' pockets.

'Yes.' She hesitated and he marked the reluctant tone with an ugly frown, 'but what is to become of him?'

'Need that worry us?'

'It worries me dreadfully.'

'We needn't cross a bridge before we come to it. We're not ready to go, yet. And until we are you'll stop with him, of course. He's a damn nuisance, he always was, but his being like this fits in very well with our plans. At least he no longer bothers you with his moanings, as you say he used to.'

Mina felt an impulse to say so many things at this that she said nothing at all from sheer inability to select the most important.

Heyward went on in his sneering way which cut into her

bruised and frightened spirit like a whip. 'If you can't stand him any longer, why don't you clear out? It doesn't seem to make any difference whether you're here or not.'

She gazed at him in mute fear, pondering his utter heart-lessness, wondering whether ever it would be directed against herself. 'How can you?' she breathed at last in a frightened whisper.

'How can I what?' he echoed, and without waiting for her reply went on, 'Come, darling, don't snivel like that. Let's have a look at him. After all, he must do something sometime, and it may be at any moment.'

He strode into the bedroom, she as usual trailing behind, full of a mute protest at his presence there, yet unable to tell why she felt so resentful. Denvers was talking of Dayonis. Mina hated, for some inexplicable reason, unfathomable by herself, to stand beside Hank and listen to him. She lingered in the doorway, listening distastefully.

Hank turned to her with a laugh. 'Some bird, this. Come and listen. I always told you he was a sly dog, Mina. Just think, all the time he's been moaning about us, and pretending his life was wrecked, he's been carrying on with this bit. Why, he's up to the neck of it—it's as plain as a pike-staff.'

'He's dreaming,' she thrust in, hastily.

'Not he. This is a solid fact, if anything is. Can't you see how beautifully this lets us out?'

Mina's face assumed its most obstinate look. 'I tell you there's nothing in it,' she repeated stubbornly, 'it's all a dream. You can't attach any importance to what a man says in a dream.'

Heyward shot her an appraising look and burst into a shout of laughter. 'A dream! So are you, my dear! Why, God bless the woman if I don't think she's jealous! Here you've been telling him for months past to find another woman and leave you in peace and when you discover by chance he has done it long before you told him to, you don't like it. Doesn't that beat the band!'

It was so true and the idea of this other woman was so

hateful to her, that she could say nothing except comment scornfully—'What expressions you do use! Where do you get them?'

But her face was too ingenuous and she unable to hide her real feelings from so acute an observer and one who knew her so well. His face darkened as he demanded ominously—'Mina, what does this mean? Why are you jealous?'

'I'm not,' she denied, flaming out at him.

'You look it. Do you still care what he does?'

'You wouldn't like to think Mary had a lover all this time?' she fended him off.

'Mary? What on earth has she to do with this?'

'It's the same thing.'

'I can't see it. She would never dream of such a thing. She's one of the faithful souls.'

'Must you sneer at faithfulness? Yet you expect me to be true to you. And you don't like the idea of Mary having a secret lover to console her.'

He laughed awkwardly. 'No, I don't, but not because I love her.'

'Why, then?'

'Simply because one doesn't like to think one has been mistaken in a close relation all these years,' he offered defiantly.

'No, one doesn't!' she declared emphatically, 'and you've answered your own question, Hank.'

After this there was a moment's pause, during which they eyed each other warily. At length Heyward protested—'Mary means nothing to me, Minda, so don't run away with the idea that she does.'

Mina was aware of nothing but an immense desolation in which all her little world was lost and shivering. She began to cry again, bleakly—'Oh, Hank,' she wailed, 'don't let's quarrel. I'm so wretched and there's only you.'

In an instant he was beside her and she in his arms. 'My darling, don't fret. You mean everything to me and I want you. I always get what I want, Mina.' He jerked his head in the direction of the bed. 'You don't think a thing like that fool could stop me, do you?'

# CHAPTER XIX

# VENUS RISES FROM THE SEA

Spring was returning to Aghirda when a letter came by carrier pigeon to Kinyras. It was from Erili and its message ran: 'Come. Enemy massing for attack.'

All the soldier in Kinyras thrilled to this call and a longing to see his old comrades again possessed him, as he showed the message to Dayonis. She read it in silence and slowly, feeling an unaccountable reluctance to let him go. She looked at him keenly and saw his eagerness to be off. Stifling a sigh, she said resolutely—'They have need of you, Kinyras, and you should go. Of little use to drive Khem from Aghirda, as we have done, if she breaks thorugh the line and over-runs the Karpas. We are not yet clear of the wood, husband.'

'But you, Dayonis? It irks me sorely to leave you and it were not safe to take you with me.'

'My place is here with my people and who knows if Khem will not attack us at the same time, even though there is no evidence of the intention?'

'True, my sweet, by, Dayonis, swear to me by the flames of Jaske, that you will run no unnecessary risk. You are reckless, and thoughtless, too.' He knew he could formulate no more solemn oath for her.

She pouted. 'I swear, Kinyras, even thought I do not extract a like vow from you.'

'Knowing it to be needless,' he teased.

They parted tenderly. Kinyras went straight to Zadoug and found Erili with him on a brief visit from the city. The reunion was a happy one and all seemed in excellent spirits, giving him a heart-warming welcome. For upwards of an hour they gossiped, exchanging news. Erili was steadily gaining more and more of the good opinion of the people.

'You have done well, old Snail, extremely well,' he cried, slapping Kinyras vigorously on the back. 'By freeing Aghirda from Khem, you and Dayonis between you have risen high in the good graces of priests and people alike. No longer is she the penniless vagabond to be pursued and burned for witchcraft to provide a public holiday for the fanatical mob, but a high and mighty and courageous Princess, Queen of a valuable ally.'

Kinyras snorted, unimpressed, and Erili and Zadoug burst into laughter, exchanging glances.

'While you, my Kinyras, are the great general who not only planned and built the wonderous wall and made the great new arm, but the Liberator of Aghirda as well.'

'Faugh! All this stinks in my nostrils, whether as the stench of opprobrium or the cloying scent of adulation. One is as bad as t'other.' And he spat vigorously to express his contempt.

Determined upon plaguing him, Erili continued solemnly—
'also has it been noised abroad of your mighty connections in Paphos, where your uncle, the King is held in good repute and speaks well of you. I had this from one high in the Council, whose son has many ships trading with Paphos.'

Kinyras looked from one to the other, frowning. 'What talk is this? Tell me rather of Hange?'

Erili shrugged and spread his hands. 'Still at large and we make no great effort to find him—at the moment. Time is still of value to us and while Khem aspires to win by treachery what she cannot gain by honest fighting without great expense, so much the better for us, provided we know what are her plans.'

'Hange dead is less useful at this stage than Hange alive, is that it?'

'Even so. He is serving our turn admirably.'

'Almost it would be punishment enough for his crimes, did he but know it,' reflected Zadoug.

'Aye, did he but know it,' Erili agreed silkily. 'And in good time he shall know it.'

'But the enemy?' Kinyras exclaimed, impatiently. He had little stomach for diplomacy in his present mood.

'They have received large reinforcements by sea from Khem,' Zadoug informed him. 'The walls are now twenty-four feet high, the towers thirty-six feet and Khem is preparing to besiege us in force. They are constructing many Sows 1, either to conceal rams or to shelter sappers for undermining the walls, and these are so numerous that, in my opinion, they mean to attack all along the line at once.'

'Also,' Erili thrust in, 'they are making several vast earth ramps, with movable wooden barricades at either end.'

'Aye!' affirmed Zadoug. 'Daily we see the stream of earth pouring down the forward slope. They have put hundreds of men to this work, covered by the barricades.'

'And have you made no attempt to stop them?' Kinyras demanded, his frown deepening to a scowl at the impertinence of these unchecked activities on the part of Khem.

'The slinging engines are put to work and when they have got the range, account for many slaves, but they are immediately replaced. The ramps grow nearer and higher each day.'

'I have every reason to believe they are trying to mine the walls,' Erili added, gloomily.

Kinyras sprang to his feet, unable to remain longer inactive before enterprising tan enemy. 'If that is so, then can it easily be detected,' he asserted, 'I crave your leave, Erili. There is work to be done here, and without delay.'

Erili dismissed the brothers with a wave of his hand. 'I grow stale in this business of kingships, where tongues work in the place of heads and hands. The gods go with you!'

Kinyras hurried to the wall and viewed the activities of Khem from a sheltered outlook. He ordered bowls of water to be placed in spots where undermining was likely to occur, detecting by ripples on the surface where such operations were being attempted. Here he had small countermines dug, with charcoal fires set beside them, upon which large jars of water were kept boiling. When a min was about to break through, the countermine was filled with boiling water.

In this foiling of the steadily growing menace before them, a month went by on winged feet, until the day came when a Khemite prisoner was brought to Kinyras, captured in a raid while drunk. Vociferous and boasting, he waved his arms at the frowning general and shouted—'Mighty is Khem, unconquered and unconquerable! Your time is come, sons of dogs, for your witch of the hills is captured and your strength gone from you.'

Kinyras, gold as ice and feeling his heart like a stone in his breast, ordered the man to be sobered by constantly being plunged into a great jar of cold water. This done he was induced to speak less boastfully and more plainly by aid of a bow-string twisted around his temples, when it was found he knew very little beyond the fact that word had come through that the dreaded witch of the mountains, by whose wicked sorceries the constant defeats of Khem had been brought about, was now in their hands and was being sent to Khem to be sacrificed to the gods. So little did he reveal and no amount of twisting the cord would extract more.

He was taken away, leaving Kinyras to face the dire fact as best he might. Almost immediately a carrier pigeon came from Ammunz, confirming the tidings and stating that her capture had occurred at Lepithus.

'At Lepithys?' repeated Zadoug, who had received the message, 'That can mean but one thing. They will take her to Khem, but they must coast southward, since they will not risk the dangerous northern passage past Karpas.'

'Aye,' agreed Kinyras, heavily, in a daze of misery.

'That will take them past Curium,' Zadoug went on, eyeing his brother anxiously. He did not like this look of utter wretchedness and something must be done to rouse him from it, even though the hope implied seemed abortive to each.

Kinyras passed his hand across his forehead, as though he would brush away something which obscured his mental clarity and paralysed his initiative. 'But—w-will they call in?' he stammered, 'They are cautious sailors it is true, and coast when they can, but surely they will now expect a rescue and keep well out to sea?'

'But Paphos? They are in constant use of the port and if Old Cinyras cannot help, he is wily and will glean news.'

'Oh, I am going, Zadoug, never fear. I'll tear the heart out of every Khemite I encounter until I die in doing it, but I dare not hope to rescue her.'

'There I think you are wrong, old Snail, and to despair is foolish. Much is in your favour. Erili has made you a free man, to come and go as you please, to fight either on land or sea, as seems fitting to you. What more can a man desire? And your ships are waiting in harbour, ready to sail within an hour of your embarkation, or even less.

While Zadoug was speaking in his slow, deliberate and reasonable way, the mind of Kinyras was rabidly clearing. He was too much the man of action and resource to sink into a lethargy of grief for long, no matter how desperate the circumstances. 'Thanks, Zadoug, you are right, and I am indeed a fool. Time is on my side, for though they man send her off to sea at any moment, still am I depending upon their fear of the sea and of our little Cypriot ships, and that they will wait to collect together a fleet of warships.'

The brothers parted with a handclasp, and within an few hours Kinyras was once more aboard the Dolphin, having first sent out scouts among the fishermen. As they sailed along the coast they picked up these scouts from time to time, but no tidings were obtained beyond the rumour that the Red Witch of Aghirda had been captured, by whose arts the war was prolonged. Now the Karpas would be conquered and the war come to an end.

The rowers sweated, Kinyras in his agony of mind, rowing with them, and within three days they reached a little, secluded bay east of Paphos Temple, where some great rocks masked its opening. Here he moored his remaining ships, having sent three out to sea for scouting purposes, and in the evening slipped ashore disguised as a countryman, carrying a basket of foodstuffs. First he went to the Temple and soon found they knew nothing and from thence went on to the city.

Here he took up his station in the market place, where he soon found gossip and rumour circulating in the wildest way. He rapidly sold his wares, for he offered them cheaply and bought more, wandering aimlessly down the quayside. A large Khemite fleet was in the bay, forty great ships of war filled with soldiers. The quay was humming with activity, slaves loading the boats with provisions and water and every indication present that they were putting to sea speedily. Kinyras had prepared a few lines scratched upon a tiny roll of papyrus and presently he saw what he had hoped to see, his cousin Myrrah strolling upon the quay accompanied by her women and followed by a slave.

Kinyras approached and stood full in her path. 'Princess, blessed be the Doves of Astoreth, and thrice blessed Our Lady of Ascalon.'

This pious invocation instantly centred her attention upon him and after a sharp scrutiny, which told her little, and a puzzled frown, she remembered his voice, as he had counted upon her doing. 'Friend,' she said, mildly, 'let me see your wares.'

'Lady, I have here a tiny jar of the choicest perfume, sweet enough even for your beauty.'

'I will take it and if I like the contents I will buy more of you, if you will tell me your abode.'

'Alas, lady, I dwell not here, but come from afar with my unguents and scents, but I am staying at the house of the Golden Cock in the Crooked Street.'

Myrrah took the painted jar containing the letter and sauntered away without more words. The day seemed an eternity to Kinyras as he went hither and thither about the city, trying to glean tidings of Dayonis, feeling that she was near him secreted in one of these ships, yet fearing his hopes and wishes led him to the conviction rather than reason. At length night fell and a man muffled in a dark cloak, keeping his face hidden, came to his lodging. There were others in the room, but Kinyras drew him into a corner, where the man, letting his cloak fall from his face for an instant, revealed himself to be the King, dressed as a slave. Kinyras fetched a stool and his uncle seated himself with his back to the lamp, while he sat on the floor beside him.

'What brings you here, Kinyras? What ails you?'

Kinyras, with one wary eye on the door, explained the emergency in hurried whispered, his uncle nodding dolefully every now and then.

'Some big matter is afoot, that is certain. When the fleet arrived two days ago I went on board the leader's ship to welcome him, as is my custom. I discovered then that some secret thing was toward, of which I was to see and know nothing. But to-night I have prepared a feast for him and his officers, and when they return I will accompany him back on board—merely as a courteous mark of esteem, you understand. If I fail to find some indication of what we both suspect, write me down a lousy Greek and no mighty king in Paphos.'

'How can I thank you, sir?'

'Tut, nephew, we are kin, and I would do much for you, but I have little power. The city is full of Khemites and I dare not fall out with them. It would mean instant death if I did so, and I think they suspect me. I find they know of my kinship with you. They fear attack, I know, and are marching more troops hither, which arrive to-night. Already have they garrisoned several towers in the city.'

Kinyras made enquiry of the activities of the Tamiradae, which sent his uncle off into a long dissertation upon them and upon his own trials, all of which he had mentioned several times before, on the occasion of his former visit. He wondered why old men must repeat themselves and paid but little true attention, sitting with his elbow on his knee, gravely asking himself whether he, too, should fall to maundering in his eld.

'Prudes, every man jack of them!' spat the king, in conclusion. 'Well, I must return, but I will do what I can for you and your beauty. I'm getting old and these crazy swine are driving me into my grave. Wait here and I will come again to you, no matter what the hour. I have already sent off pigeons to call in all the men who are trustworthy.'

After his uncle's departure Kinyras settled himself in his corner to get what sleep he could. His fellow guests drank, quarrelled, fought and gamed through the live-long night, but at length they, too, slept and all was quiet, when the door was pushed open and King Cinyras lurched in. Kinyras hastened to support him, guiding him to his old place, where he deemed it wiser to seat him on the floor in the corner, with the two walls supporting him

He had been drinking heavily, but was by no means besotted. 'I did what I could for your beauty,' he hiccoughed. 'I did not see her, but I found they would not suffer me to approach the centre cabin. I had plied them all the night with much strong wine and this I will say for these swine from Khem, they can drink like men and not like ninnies, as do these Tamiradaen Sodomites.'

'Yes, yes! What then?' urged Kinyras, seething with impatience.

'All in good time, nephew,' retorted the king, with immense dignity. 'Well, where was I? Oh, yes, I had much ado to get aboard with them, for they did not want me, but I insisted and once there, we circulated more good jars. Then I called loudly for Khemite beer and abused them roundly when they assured me there was only wine to be had. Whereupon we guzzled more, to adjust that little dispute, when I had craved pardon. After that I had to embrace them all in token of renewed amity. One fellow eluded me, and as I made a tipsy rush at him to kiss him, I stumbled and fell over the top of the centre cabin, my sword slipping from its sheath and falling to the deck with a great clatter, but in that moment I contrived to drop another sword which I carried concealed in my cloak through the bars of the cabin window.'

'The gods bless and reward you,' exclaimed the tense listener fervently, and received a hearty embrace for his thanks.

The king chuckled, well pleased with his own cleverness.

'The old fool has never before been so full as this, they laughed and said, then they grumbled and bundled me overboard none too gently, nephew, carried me ashore and dumped me upon the quay. Now your beauty knows that friends are near and has also a weapon, by whose means she can seek death when all else fails her.'

The king paused, a little breathless, and a silence fell, in which Kinyras contemplated any amount of reckless and impossible attempts to rescue his wife. Were it not better to swim out to the ship, climb aboard, boldly batter down her prison door, clasp her once more to his breast and both of them die together in one last, long, desperate fight? Truly, yes, and that was what he would do, if the worst came to it, but life was sweet, and faced with the stark certainty of death, hope clamoured within him with no uncertain voice. Besides, when all heroics were said and done, the fact remained that he knew not on which ship she was held, nor could he find it in the dark, amongst a fleet where every ship was as like its sister as peas in a pod. He roused from these dismal reveries to find his uncle looking at him kindly and pitifully in the feeble light of the lamp. 'Take heart, Kinyras. All is by no means lost.'

'Can you tell me of the ship, sir, so that I could find it.'

The king shook his head. 'Put that thought out of your mind, nephew. It would mean certain death, and what has she to gain by your death? Nothing but the loss of her last hope. There are times, Kinyras, when it is harder and more courageous to live, and the path of death only the coward's way.'

Kinyras was silent and presently the king spoke again. 'I have sent a messenger to the captain of your ship, bidding him to recall all those at sea and to follow the fleet when it sails, to encircle them, harry them, keep them occupied, and telling him Dayonis is on the Leader's ship.'

'That is well!' exclaimed Kinyras, much relieved. 'Kinuis is a shrewd fellow and a fearless fighter. And the officers are very drunk, my uncle?'

'They drank as only a Khemite can,' the king assured him with a solemn hiccough. I was the only sober man among 'em.

And there was that in the last jar, a rare and precious wine, doctored with poppy juice, my boy, which I took with me on board, to ensure sound and happy sleep. They told me they sail at midday.'

'That gives us some hours, then,' breathed the distracted husband.

'My men will be coming in at dawn, when I'll provoke the Tamiradae to a riot and rouse the whole city to a fight. If Kinuis were to block the harbour mouth and attack the fleet at the same time, what with this scheme and the officers bemused with prepared wine, there should be a very pretty confusion aboard, in which you must try to reach the ship.'

'How can I distinguish it?'

'In the daylight easily enough. It is the spirit of God, moving upon the face of the waters, Nef, its emblem the asp.'

'I shall find it,' Kinyras assured him grimly. 'I will go to the quay-side at dawn.'

'In the meantime, try to sleep and Lady Astoreth send you sweet dreams. A wearied man is a helpless one, therefore seek sleep resolutely and I will do likewise.'

So saying he rose with difficulty and staggered to the door, leaving Kinyras to follow his advice to such purpose that he fell into the deep sleep of utter exhaustion as soon as he lay down again in the corner. Some three hours later he was roused by someone shaking him vigorously by the shoulder, crying urgently in his ear: 'Come at once, sir, come at once.'

He started awake and saw that it was a messenger from his uncle, and rising, he followed the man at a run and was guided to the back of the Palace.

Here they found the king waiting with three chariots. 'They've done us, they've sailed!' he shouted. 'Curse them, how they fooled me! Come with me. You must get to your ships to follow without delay.'

As he leapt in beside his uncle Kinyras saw that Myrrah and Adonis were in one of the other chariots, but there was no time for greetings. They drove furiously and as he clung desperately to the side of the rocking car, his mind was groping blindly for some means of rescuing Dayonis in face of this defeat to their plans.

Dayonis also at that moment was breathlessly waiting to put a cherished plan into execution. Ever since her capture she had been searching for a means of escape. After the departure of Kinyras for the wall, she had found life in Aghirda strangely dull without him, and to vary the monotony and being fired with an ambition to drive Khem out of the three forts remaining to her on the borders, had planned their attack and subjugation. With two of them she had succeeded, to her great elation, but with the gird the fortune of war turned against her and though the fort fell and the garrison were forced to flee for their lives, in a too ardent pursuit she was cut off and taken prisoner, and hurried by a series of forced marches on board this ship, where she had plenty of leisure to meditate upon her rash folly.

She supposed that hers was the fate of all oath breakers and that Jaske viewed the matter in a different light of her own. One might have supposed that he would overlook the crime, in view of the fact that she had driven the enemy of his country and hers far from their borders, but such was not the case. She had wronged her god and wronged her husband and, being now in the sorriest plight, was deeply troubled and repentant.

Her gloom had been profound and though she spent most of the time in supplications to Jaske for his pardon and help, he had turned a deaf ear. Nothing happened, her door was firmly fastened, her window secured with additional bars, which she heard hammered into place with the acutest dismay. Her food was brought regularly by a great Nubian, who could have smashed her with one blow from his little finger, she told herself, despairing.

Her cabin was comfortable, even luxurious, vividly coloured, furnished with a table, chairs, and a couch, to which was added a gaily painted wooden head rest. This, by reason of its hardness, seemed an additional insult, and she hurled it pettishly into a corner, being unused to the luxury, where it lay, mocking her with its gaudy hues. Of its extreme hardness she had ample proof, for she barked her shin on it twice as she gave a savage, flaunting turn when tigerishly pacing her cabin. Yet, for some childish folly, she would not stoop and pick it up, but kicked it bitterly and ferociously out of her way each time she passed, as a vent to the rage and futility that possessed her.

With her mind in such a swamp, it was not amazing that invention failed her, and it was not until she was wakened by a rumpus overhead that she knew the harbour in which they had anchored as Paphos. Amid the drunken babble she heard the name of Kinyras spoken several times, but soon realized that it was the King of Paphos and not her husband who had come aboard. Then came a foundering clatter and under cover of the noise a sword was suddenly dropped almost at her feet. Her wits cleared as if by magic, she read its message of hope and possible deliverance, and the next moment had snatched it up and thrust it under her mattress.

Gone now was the ferocious resentment, to be succeeded by her normal resourcefulness. Jaske had pardoned her and sent help. Kinyras had followed with his ships and sought aid from his uncle. Clever, admirable King Cinyras, how she adored him! She listened as he was bundled into a boat alongside and taken back to the quay, listened with a satirical smile to the foundering footsteps of the officers, to their fuddled words as they bid each other good night and retreated, as best they might, to their various ships, heard the stuttered orders of the Leader to the ship's master to sail down. Drunken swine of Khem! Glorious, mighty Jaske! He should have a thank-offering and that right soon, of the kind he liked best and if she had not the leisure for the proper rites, he would forgive that trifling omission in view of the emergency.

Then she fell to thinking of Kinyras in a glow of tenderness and remorse. Yes, she had indeed behaved very ill to him, causing him the greatest unnecessary suffering. No further sleep came to her and she lay, thinking hard, wondering how best she could get away. It was better to make one last, desperate attempt to escape, even though she died to the effort, rather than be carried a prisoner to Khem. Now was her chance, for once the fleet left Paphos harbour and reached the open sea, with all the will in the world Kinyras could not hope to accomplish anything with his small numbers against so great odds, with no advantage from hidden reefs and unpropitious coasts. No, whatever was done must be done quickly.

If she knew her Kinyras and his tactics, and she flattered herself that she did so, he would make some attempt upon the fleet as it was on the point of clearing the harbour. That was at dawn and it was almost at hand. The officers were drunk, lying snoring in their quarters, nor could they possibly be recovered in so short time. This meant that both vigilance and discipline would be relaxed, and, where in one way this was a great advantage, in another it might wreck her hopes. All now depended upon the slave who brought her food. Usually he was punctual to the second and as the first slanting rays of the sun pierced her cabin, so would he unbar her door. By that time her own particular ship should be just clearing the harbour. Would he come, or would he forget her in the excitement of getting out to sea and of the attack of the Cypriot ships? He must, he should remember her, she would force him to do so.

Sitting up on her couch she visualized his huge form until he seemed to be standing beside her in the flesh. Then she fixed her eyes upon his and willed him with all her might to bring her food at his usual time. And so she passed the hours between that moment and the second of his appearance.

The darkness of the cabin gave place to twilight and suddenly the ship and those about her hummed with activity. Naked feet thudded upon the decks, orders were shouted, there was the creak of cordage, the grating of heavy oars and, yes, at long last, the unbarring of her door. The slave was always so cautious that he shut the door before advancing into the cabin to the table. It was then she must strike him, when his back was turned to her. The hilt of the sword projected from beneath the mattress, ready to be plucked forth, but she needed something hard and heavy with which to strike him down. While waiting her eye fell upon the head-rest. It was, she knew now, not made of wood at all but of Oriental alabaster, which accounted for its hardness and heaviness. She put it on the couch and stood waiting, an angelic smile upon her parted lips.

The man stood in the doorway, his great red mouth gaping in a grin of delight. At first he had been terrified of the witch, until he found she was like nothing he had seen in the witch-doctors of his own or any other tribe. The sheer loveliness of her, banished terror, and his eyes now dwelt in fascinated delight upon her. 'I had almost forgot you, lady,' he said.

'And then you remembered?' she answered dulcetly.

'Even so.' He turned to shut the door.

She raised the heavy pillow in both hands and brought it crashing against the back of his neck at the base of his skull. Without a sound he sagged at the knees and crumpled side-ways, either dead or stunned. With an infinite difficulty she dragged him slowly into a corner, cut his throat and pulled the couch across, flinging her tunic carelessly upon it, so that the corpse was hidden. Then, seizing a napkin, she caught her hair at her nape, twisted it into a tight screw and bound the linen about her brows, so that all her betraying red glory was hidden. Then, taking the sword she opened her door a crack and peered out.

There seemed to be a considerable confusion and noise amongst the fleet, from what cause she cared not, and most of the company were at the moment crowded forward shouting, cursing, and very active. The pilot, seated on his raised post, was endeavouring to keep the ship clear, and the archers, usually stationed beside him, were absent, as he would not have been had the officers been on duty. For some brief seconds Dayonis saw a clear passage to the stern. It was now or never. She was naked, her hair was hidden and she had her sword for attack. If she sped lightly, in the rush she might escape recognition and it would be difficult to snatch at her naked body, which she had taken the precaution to oil well.

Without more ado she ran like the wind and so quick was she that she escaped attention, where everyone was hurrying somewhere. As she leapt beside him the pilot made a futile snatch at her, but she was poised for the dive and over into the sea before he could make a second attempt to catch her, and the betraying sword of King Cinyras lay at the bottom of the sea, never to bear witness against his treachery to Khem. Dayonis swarm under water until she thought her lungs would burst, rose to the surface, floated and dived again.

While he drove King Cinyras goaded his horses by a continual series of hoots and howls, well calculated to excite them at the verge of madness. He never touched them with the whip, though he cracked it repeatedly. The din was frightful, the lurching and bumping of the flying car unendurable, and what was the noise and the eccentricities of the motion, Kinyras thought he must have lost his wits and be in the storm-centre of same crazed delusion. How his uncle persevered his balance was a marvel, but he managed it with apparent ease, standing with his sturdy legs well spread and his body yielding gracefully to the movement.

After a drive of about ten miles they could see the Khemite fleet standing well out to sea with a good breeze behind it. 'Curse them!' yelled the King, to be heard above the clamour of his drive, 'this favourable wind prompted them to sail early. Where are your ships? I can see nothing of them.'

Kinyras, gazing hard, could see the rising sun lighting up a familiar sail. He pointed, his hand shaking with excitement. 'They are there, harrying the fleet. Bravo, Kinuis! Said I not he was trustworthy?'

As they came closer to the sea they could see that the fleet was in great confusion, but while they were eagerly watching and conjecturing, event nearer to hand claimed their attention. A great crowd was gathered upon the shore, among whom the King's quick eyes discerned the long robes, tall mitres and stately bearing of many Tamiradae priests. He pointed them out to Kinyras. 'Note their sallowness, their upcast eyes and downturned lips, they whey-faced, bean poles!'

He spurred his horses to a final spurt with an eldritch shriek. To the very verge of the crowd, where the people scattered before him as he pulled up with a jerk that sent the beasts back upon their haunches, pawing the air. One of the priests came forward, an angry glint in his eyes.

'What seek you here?' demanded the king, curtly.

'We come to worship our blessed Hera. Erglion, the seer, has been vouchsafed a vision. Our lady has told him she will come in all her glory from the sea and with her might drive out the foul superstition of Astoreth and her sacrilegious worship,' the priest answered malevolently.

King Cinyras was furiously angry at this insult and laughed his derision. He spat contemptuously and flourished his fingers very close the other other's nose. 'Fools! It is the Lady Astoreth who will rise from the sea, in all the glory of her beauty, and not the misbegotten and mis-shapen Hera, who must needs hide her deformity beneath a swaddle of garments.'

A dull purple mantled the cheeks of the priest and his hands clenched, while the people gasped and shivered at this blasphemy, looking to see Cinyras smitten beneath a thunder-bolt. But the sky remained untroubled and the priest controlled his rage, to reply quietly and steadily. 'Not so, king. It is the divine Hera who will come, and speedily.'

'And I say it will be Astoreth,' bawled the king. He turned to his nephew and whispered from the corner of his mouth, 'My men have come, but of what use are they against a fleet at sea?' Even as he spoke the ships slowly faded over the horizon, together with the ships of Kinyras. The king turned again to the priest, sneering savagely. 'And how will you tell, priest, whether the blessed visitant be Hera or Astoreth?'

'By the richness and beauty of her raiment,' was the loud and determined answer, so that those about him murmured assent and encouragement, and his words were taken up and repeated to the heart of the crowd.

Once more the impious and ironical Cinyras scorned him. 'So! Hera will rise from the sea, swathed to the chin in vesture of multi-dyed wool. And she will be dry as a bone, doubtless?'

'Most truly so, blasphemer.'

'Truly a miracle! And if she be naked, dripping with

sea-water? What then, priest?'

The goaded wretch suddenly lost his temper and bawled, so that his voice carried over the crowd—'Then is she most surely not Hera, but Astoreth, the lewd and iniquitous.'

Cinyras laughed in contempt and turned aside. He had bandied words thus with the priest while his thoughts were busy trying to form some new scheme to assist Kinyras, but he was spared the effort by a fierce excitement, which had unexpectedly seized the crowd, and a cry went round, 'The Goddess! The Goddess!'

'What cunning trick are these priests working now?' exploded the king, 'To me, my men!' He shook up his horses and drove them at the crowd, which scattered before them, and the troup which had arrived a moment or two before, followed him through the lane of people. They came out on the open shore where, standing upon a flat rock, bare in the beams of the rising sun, her red hair curling about her knees as she had shaken it from the confining napkin, stood Dayonis.

The king stared with starting eyes, unable for the moment to credit his senses, and Kinyras gazed in joy and rapture upon the beloved form which never again had he expected to see in this world. The people, who never before had seen such amazing beauty as this and to whom that red mane of curling locks, blazing a vivid gold in the sun, was miraculous among a black-haired people, hailed her with a loud voice and fell upon their knees in adoration and prayer.

'Dayonis!' breathed Kinyras, in an ecstasy of happiness and relief, 'Dayonis!'

At these words enlightenment fell upon the king and he rabidly emerged from his wild trance of amazement to a full grasp of the situation. 'Silence, nephew,' he commanded and drove to the water's edge.

The rock was still surrounded by the shallows of the ebbing tide and a hundred little sparkling wavelets curled about the rosy feet of Dayonis. The sun's level beams played upon her white limbs, lighting them to a flushed transparency, so that their warm blood glowed like rich wine in a fine porcelain vase, while every now and then spray from some larger wave bejewelled them with a thousand chromatic drops. Above her was the vast blue of the unclouded spring sky dripping down to the amethyst and gold of the sea, lit up with the glory of the rising sun. Before her the gilded sands, patterned in runnels silvering their way to the sea, gemmed with bright pools at the base of the dusky rocks, where streamers of weed hung lank, or trailed their bright hues upon the pearl and gold of the shore. Away to the northward, the Troodos mountains showed a purple smudge in a lavender haze, and the rocky foreshore merged into virescent slopes strewn with violet and narcissus, asphodel and the gold and purple of iris, timbered with great forests of cedar and walnut, and the sombre spears of the cypress.

'Astoreth! Astoreth!' shouted the king in a loud and triumphant voice as he drove, so that all the people heard him. 'It is not the much-clad Hera, but the blessed, beauteous Astoreth who has risen from the sea and comes to bless us and all this land.'

And the people, gazing wonderingly upon that entrancing vision, found courage to acclaim her—'Astoreth! Hail divine Astoreth! Aphrodite!'

Dayonis stood, one lovely hand raised to keep the hair from blowing into her eyes, and marvelled at the kneeling people. Her native sagacity warned her not to speak until she was addressed. The chariot, threading its way round the rocks, pulled up opposite her, the horses feet churning the sand at the water's edge, and the king descended.

Dayonis watching him curiously, undecided what to do. Her long and trying swim had exhausted her and for the past half hour she had been hiding amongst the rocks, resting and watching the retreat of the Khemite fleet. Her captors might well remain in ignorance until the time came for her next meal, which was not until the evening, when the fleet would be many miles distant and the officers unable to detect exactly where the escape had taken place. She had then come out of her hiding only to find a great crowd of people assembled on the shore. Apparently they had not noticed her until she clambered out of the sea and stood upon the rock to shake out her hair. She had lost the napkin, which was floating away behind her on the ebbing tide.

Maybe it was the custom of the Paphoans to kneel in greeting to a stranger, yet it was very strange! Undecided whether to go ashore amongst them, or to retreat to the outer rocks and bide her time, she hesitated, though looking not as though she hesitated, but stood there to reveal the glory of herself to the wondering and adoring people. At that moment the chariot flashed to the water's edge and the king alighted and knelt, and it was then that she saw Kinyras, with his finger to his lips, and a warning look in his eyes. She stared, silent, wondering.

'My goddess! Hail, O most divine Astoreth! When, in my vision this morning, you called to me and bade me hasten to the shore to greet your coming, I... words fail me in the sight of your beneficent Presence, Pardon, Lady Astoreth, my tardiness.'

Cinyras folded his hands upon his breast and bowed his head, and again the people shouted—'Astoreth! Hail, blessed goddess of the light!'

The eyes of Dayonis widened and darkened to a deeper blue as fear seized upon her heart. Here was blasphemy indeed, to impersonate a goddess! Dared she? Would not the outraged heavens themselves rain thunderbolts and the very flames of Jaske consume her? She raised her eyes to the blue above her and saw its clear and smiling beneficence. She looked at the man kneeling before her. He had raised his head and sent a keen, commanding stare deep into her eyes, before he bowed his head again and spread his arms wide in a gesture of reverence and submission. Then, holding out both hands to her he spoke again—'My lady and goddess, having risen from the sea to visit and bless your poor people for a space, ere once again you seek the realms of the blest, I pray you will ascend this chariot and come to your temple?'

If she did not so, if the people discovered the fraud they would tear her in pieces. She spread her arms wide towards the crowd, assuming her most noble and dignified expression. 'My people!' she said, giving the words that special significance which she alone could give and which she always found so effective in charming and subduing them. 'Blessings be upon your heads and the heads of your children, upon your homes and your labours.'

For another moment she stood, then slowly and without looking down put out one foot to test the depth of the water, found it reached only to her ankle and walked like Aphrodite herself through the shallows to the dry sand. At the gesture of the king that she should enter the chariot, she slowly shook her head, knowing she could not possibly retain her dignity in its uneven course. 'Nay, but I would walk amid the sweet flowers. Greetings, O King Cinyras, my priest and my friend.'

A shout arose from those nearby, which was taken up by the others until it became like thunder. 'A miracle! The goddess knows the king by name. Of a truth he **is** her priest!'

Dayonis waited until the hush which followed fell again upon the people, when she turned to Kinyras with her sweetest smile. 'And you, O mighty warrior, great builder of walls, whose destiny it is to bring peace and freedom to a suffering people, you, too, are called Kinyras and shall be blessed.'

This second speech so roused the people that they began to press upon her, but she waved them away, crying out with a sweet smile—'I love ye, my worshippers, but methinks you stink with sweat, and are unclean. Strip off your garments and cleanse yourselves in the purifying sea ere you worship me.'

Many rushed off at once to do her bidding, but others consumed by curiosity and adoration, deeming there was time enough for bathing later, remained to gape and wonder. At that moment there was a scurry of horses' feet and twenty Khemite chariots swept up. Their leader sprang out with drawn sword pointed at Dayonis, shouting—'Seize the woman for sedition and inciting to rebellion.'

The quick emotions of the crowd were roused at this out-rage. 'Blasphemy! Foul impiety! Blasphemous dogs, they would injure our goddess!'

For one fatal instant the Khemite officers hesitated, uncertain of their authority in the face of the national habit of non-interference with the religions of their tributary states, and in that moment the crowd overwhelmed them, demolishing the chariots with their bare hands and strangling their riders.

The king, whose keen wits and eyes had never for a moment faltered, saw in the whole incident of this appearance from the sea, the downfall of the Tamiradae with its worship of Hera and the rise of his own party, with himself at its head, justified, and restored as the High Priest of Astoreth. Even the most ardent worshippers of Hera were now converted, thanks to his altercation with the priest before the appearance of Dayonis. He now saw that the bolder of these Tamiradae priests ranged themselves on the side of the Khemites, he who had disputed with him awhile since, crying—'The Khemites are right. Seize the impudent impostor. Blessed be Hera!'

But even his own people turned upon him with cries of 'Blasphemy! Blasphemy!' and Cinyras bent upon him a very ugly look, exclaiming in a loud and threatening voice—'Did not you yourself declare but an hour since that Hera would appear in rich and wonderful raiment? And if the goddess was unclothed then would she be Astoreth. Behold the unashamed beauty and wonder of Astoreth! Out of your own mouth you acclaim her!'

By this time not one of the Khemites remained alive and their horses had miraculously disappeared, unobtrusively led off in various directions by interested parties. The indignant multitude would have executed summary justice upon the priest had not Dayonis, from motives of policy alone, intervened. She put herself before him and extended both arms. 'Nay, my people, forbear. I like not the bloodshed of priests, no matter whom they serve, and this man, it seems, hath proclaimed me Astoreth. By his testimony is he saved. Depart in peace, friend, and vex not my people nor me further.'

This incident deepened the ardour of the mob, who were prepared even to safe-conduct the priest in their excitement, if he had not taken his life in the hands and vanished, whither no one cared to discover. The crowd pressed closer and closer, each one anxious to view this wonder from the heavens. Presently the word Olympus began to circulate and soon everyone was whispering—'Olympus! The divine lady comes from Olympus! She is truly of the island and dwells upon the mount with other gods. Blessed be the Gods of Olympus who have sent us this wondrous miracle.'

Word by now had spread to the town of what was happening at Neo-Paphos, and already the most enterprising of those left behind were beginning to arrive in chariots. Cinyras calculated that before night-fall the whole population of Paphos would have arrived and not one adherent of Hera be left to vex him more. The more fanatical had but to look upon Dayonis in order to be converted to belief in her godhead. He had only the Khemites to fear and they must be settled speedily. He looked round for Adonis and beckoned him. The youth, who with his sister Myrrah, had ranged themselves close behind Dayonis, came up.

'My Adonis, go before us and prepare the Temple for our lady.' Then, lowering his voice he whispered some secret injunction, doubtless of some utterly sacred rite, thought the gaping multitude.

Adonis bowed low and with extreme reverence. 'I hasten to obey, my priest and king.'

He departed and a determined move was made toward the temple, but progress was extremely slow and the king fumed with secret impatience. He looked to Kinyras, but he was walking at his wife's heels, in such a daze of bliss that he seemed incapable of awareness of any but her.

At this moment Cinyras observed two of the priests of the Tamiradae, one of whom was the man whose life had been spared an hour ago. They had assumed the clothes of the people and removed their head-dress, but the king was certain of their identity. His guards were active in forming some sort of order from the existing chaos, forcing the people to walk in single file past the goddess and even as he watched, he saw them pushed into the line. Breathless he watched. Would his bemused nephew observe the danger in time. 'Kinyras!' he called urgently, trusting the tone of his voice would convey a warning, 'Kinyras!'

Kinyras roused at the call and looked at his uncle, who was separated from the little group by a dense pack of people. The priests approached Dayonis, knelt at her feet together and kissed the ground, as did the other worshippers, then, as they rose, drew swords from beneath their garments. But before they could strike Kinyras lunged at one with the drawn sword he carried and kicked at the other. The first was split through the midriff, the other staggered back into the arms of the guards and was literally torn in pieces by the infuriated mob, with diabolical yells of 'Blasphemy! Blasphemy!'

When this grisly incident was over the king forced his way through to Dayonis, raised his arms and cried for silence. 'So perish all blasphemers!' he ejaculated solemnly. 'And for this sacrilege must all the people assembled purge themselves. Before any many now approach our Lady Astoerth, each must cleanse himself of sin by bathing in the sea and come before her stripped of mortal clothing.' Then in a whisper to Kinyras: 'Thus we will ensure that no one comes nigh her with a knife on him!'

In an incredibly short space of time the whole crowd was diverted into the sea and never had those rocky shores witnessed such an orgy of bathing as now took place. Nor was the scene entirely peaceful, for many shrunk from any contact with the water, usurping the place of those who were eager, and cries and scuffling ensued. Meanwhile those about Dayonis took the opportunity to step out more briskly for the temple, the king giving orders to the guards to marshal the people into a double file as they came up from the sea and march them to the sanctuary.

As this was being done, more and more people arrived from the town, reporting that great rejoicing was abroad over the fate of the Khemite warriors. By careful questioning, Kinyras learned the persisting rumour that as they approached to lay hands on the goddess, the Khemites and all their company had been blasted where they stood. And Kinyras, with a glance at his uncle, gravely confirmed this statement. 'Such will deter Khem from precipitate action and give you time to be with your worshippers long enough to stamp your image deep upon their hearts, lady, before you disappear in a cloud of glory.'

Dayonis laughed and pouted. 'Must I disappear, my uncle? I find that being a goddess pleases me.'

'I fear you must, my child, though not too soon. Once you enter your temple you are safe for a few days. Whatever may be the thoughts of the Khemites, fear will hold them back for a while, and they have been taught to respect the sanctity of foreign gods. But they are wily, and will invent some ingenious device by which they may legitimately enquire into your authority, and if you fail to pass that test, then will a fearful doom await you for sacrilege. Nay, never look alarmed, my beauty. We will have you well away ere that befall.'

'And so I must go?' signed Dayonis, with a flutter of her lashes at him. 'You are unflatteringly eager for my departure, sir.'

'Not so, sweet, but there are many dead goddesses; is it your wish to be numbered with them?'

He pouted adorably and they fell to a whispered consultation of ways and means, which lasted until they reached the Temple. While Adonis had sent messengers to the city reporting the blasting of the Khemites, Kinyras had lighted smoke signals to recall Kinuis and his fleet. As they neared the temple the people began to return from the sea and those pressing upon her heard her call the king uncle. Word of this was bandied about. 'The king is the uncle of the goddess! What vengeance might he not have taken? Truly has he been forbearing to us.' And they looked upon him with awe and new reverence.

Instigated by the Tamiradae priests some of the bolder and less religious spirits among the crowd began to murmur at the lack of costume, uttering their disapproval with a loud voice, so

that the guards seized them and there was not little disturbance. Dayonis, becoming aware of this, called to them to hold
and bring the malcontents before her. She was instantly obeyed
and a lane was made for them, through which they were thrust
forward, when it was seen that most of the complainers were
priests in the dress of the laity.

Dayonis stood on the steps of the temple and addressed
them. 'My people, ye who would worship me and be truly
blessed, I command to cast aside your garments and to bathe in
the sea. Cleanse your bodies so every day and so will ye cleanse
your minds of evil thinking and all reproach. Let the life-giving
sun and wind play upon your naked flesh, thus and only thus
may ye come near my shrine.' She paused to gaze benignantly
upon the rapt faces upturned to her. 'Near here are two foun-
tains 2. Ye who would know the delights of love must come to
my temple, then make a pilgrimage to one of them, bathe in
the waters and drink of them. Ye who suffer by too much love,
seek ye the other and do likewise.'

Again she paused, noting the indifferent health of many
before her. 'Some of ye are sick of many diseases and are frail
of limb. Come ye first to my shrine from whence I will bless ye
through my priest and uncle, Cinyras your lawful King, then go
ye to the sea from whence I came, rest upon the shore in the
sun, let the waters of the sea cover ye and so shall ye be healed.

'Love and obey King Cinyras, who is my High Priest, and
all his line after him. If ye would have my blessing, see that ye
do this faithfully. Shed no blood upon my altar, but bring me
sacrifices that are meet, flowers, and fruit and honey from the
wild bee. Even though ye see me not, yet I shall be here, and
my voice shall be heard through my oracle by those who are
true and give me faith and worship.

'I hear my father calling me and my time with you grows
short.' Slowly, as if reluctant to leave them, she turned and
entered the Temple, going towards the great natural cone-
shaped stone which the King had brought with him from
Ascalon. Standing between the two pillars which flanked it, she
again faced the crowd that had managed to pack itself into the

forecourt, amongst whom were some of the Tamiradae priests still clad in their robes. Pointing to them she called them to her and hesitantly, shamefacedly, first one and then another cast forth his garments and fell on his knees naked before her to kiss her feet. Most tenderly and wooingly she addressed them— 'Be ye my priest also. Forsake your pale mistress Hera. Worship love and joy, light and air. Put aside your hatred and jealousy of my priest, Cinyras. All ye, go, make the pilgrimage to the fountain, drink of it and bathe in its waters, washing away all impurity of heart and mind, all wickedness and blasphemy against me. So only shall ye be worthy to officiate at my shrine, to preach glad tidings of hope and joy to my people.'

'Oh Blessed Goddess, we swear obedience to your divine behests,' they cried with fervour of conversation to the force of beauty and good-will.

She gave them a special blessing and they retired. Kinyras approached, fell on his knees before her and as he kissed her feet, whispered, 'Some Khemites come. Retreat father into the temple.'

He remained kneeling and she raised her arms high in blessing. 'My father calls yet again and I must heed him. Remember my words, O my people of Paphos. Love me and obey my laws and so shall the blessings of life fall upon ye and upon your children. Farewell, and my blessing be upon ye all.' Still with arms extended towards them and a smile of benediction upon her lovely lips, she retired slowly backward with much majesty into a smaller chamber.'

Adonis drew the curtain before the sanctuary and falling upon his knees began to chant many prayers in a loud voice, the people following his example.

When the curtain was drawn the king shut the door of the inner chamber and touching the stone wall in a certain spot a portion of the floor moved slowly back revealing a rough flight of steps leading to a room where several small lamps burned brightly. They descended and Cinyras showed her how to close the aperture by a similar means to that used above and in the same place beneath. The stone moved back and he pointed to a bar of stout bronze swinging from the roof beside the opening.

'Fix this into position, so,' he said, illustrating the method, 'and it prevents the mechanism working. Search the place as they may, they will discover nothing. I devised this secret security for my own safety, and rest assured it cannot be surprised. Stay quietly here and rest until I come to you again. Yonder is a net-work of caves leading through to the bay where Kinyras anchored and there lies your road of escape when the ships return, but do not attempt their intricacies unguided, for danger lurks and the sea is treacherous.'

'If the ships fail us?' she breathed.

'They will not,' he answered with decision. 'Kinuis has seen the signals bidding him return, and seemingly the Khemite fleet knows nothing of what has occurred so miraculously on shore. Even when your flight has been discovered they will know not when it happened and will suppose you sought death rather than escape. By midnight you should be aboard and off again, if all goes well.'

The king returned to the temple without further parley just as the party of Khemite officials drove up, followed by a regiment of chariots, who proceeded to surround the Temple. With all the dignity he could muster he stood awaiting their approach. 'Whom seek ye, masters?' he demanded.

'We hear strange rumours of a goddess come to earth and we must see her,' said the leader, glancing uneasily about him, fingering a copper falchion, which he had drawn.

'Ye seek her with arms?' commented Cinyras, dryly.

Hastily the man returned it to its sheath. 'Not so, O King. If she be a true deity we come to render her all homage and awe. As ye know, we of Khem respect all gods, but we must test their verity. If they are false we shall know how to deal with them; if true then will Pharaoh desire that such a goddess as yours should visit the land of Khem and accept of his hospitality, since he, himself, is a god and kin to all others.'

The king bowed low in acknowledgment and thought hard without appearing to do so. 'I fear ye are late,' he murmured regretfully. 'Our divine lady has departed, returned to sacred Olympus, whereon she dwells. But if ye will consult her oracle, I am her High Priest and will convey to her the invitation of the Divine Pharaoh and bring you her message. If ye bring suitable offerings she may deign to hear your prayers.'

'Nay, that will not answer,' the leader assured him stubbornly amid murmurs of assent from his companions. 'It is not meet to entrust our mission to another.'

'If you bring rich gifts to her shrine, then may ye penetrate to her Holy of Holies and in prayer there entreat the acceptance of Pharaoh's invitation,' the king bargained, 'but each man who enters must make a good offering of gold to the Temple.'

'Gold?'

Cinyras nodded very firmly. 'Aye. If ye would pray in the forecourt and have hope to obtain an answer from the soothsayer there, then must ye pay a lamb, but to enter the inner sanctuary the offering is at least a gold bangle. For that gift ye may ask the Oracle one question, though in favour of your lordship and his company, for two bangles three questions may be asked and answered.'

At this they withdrew to consult together, while the king clasped his hands meekly before him and threw back his head in devout contemplation of the sky, as though expecting a further visitation from that direction, which he watched them greedily from beneath his lashes. Rich gifts to his temple were all too rare and the gold of opportunity not to be missed.

'Extortionate dog!' he heard the leader mutter, fingering the bangles which adored his bronzed and bony arm and reluctantly sorting out the least valuable. Unfortunately he was a connoisseur and they all equally precious.

When all was said and done, the goddess might be genuine, and affronted. His hair crept upon his scalp at the bare thought, and hastily seizing the most valuable upon his arm, he plucked it forth and held it out to Cinyras, who emerged from his abstraction to grasp it firmly before he should change his mind. 'I and nine of my officers which to consult your oracle, asking one question each, but before we do so we wish to inspect all the temple buildings.'

The king bowed condescendingly. 'I am happy to assent. See all you wish, sirs. Ours is a simple faith and we conceal nothing. Lay your gifts upon the pedestal of her altar, cast off your garments and bring your weapons with you. Our lady is also a warrior and knows that a man love snot to be parted from his weapons.'

Once inside, the Khemites searched the building thoroughly, after which the leader went outside again to consult with the officer whom he had left in charge of his men. When he was about to re-enter, the king smilingly barred his way, hand outstretched. 'Another bangle, sir.'

'But this is outrageous—sheer robbery.'

'Not so, lord. It is the law of the temple, a bangle for each visit. But if you wish to compromise the matter, sir, five bangles of approved weight will entitle the donor to as many visits as he desires to make for three months.'

With an oath the man wrenched another bangle from his arm and strode past, furiously conjecturing how he could make good the loss in his next balance of the tax accounts. He had vowed to indemnify his officers by replacing the bracelets with which they were forced to part, and he scowled at the costly business. Surely he could classify it as investigation expenses? In any case, he, having paid twice, was entitled to ask three questions.

Cinyras, reading his mind very accurately, was in turn grappling with a difficulty. Solemnly he spoke the fear lurking in his mind as an accusation. 'Come your ways, lord, but remember one thing. Since my lady was mishandled by your people, she may not be disposed to smile upon the sons of Khem, but come your ways.'

When the Khemites assembled they found the priest-king anointing the great conical stone in the court with oil, while priestesses in all their stark beauty were arranging flowers in bowls around it. The leaser tersely stated their wants, to which Cinyras answered, after a thoughtful pause—'A long tiring journey has my lady taken this day from and to Olympus again, yet may she deign to answer one question, since you represent her divine cousin. Ye others who have paid your dues must come again, and if ye bring some small offering such as fruit and flowers, then will she answer your questions to your heart's desire. But come you, lord, into the sanctuary.'

The leaser swung forward with a military swirl of his hips, forgetting he had discarded his clothes, and was ordered to kneel on top of the trap-door through which Dayonis had passed recently.

The king fell on his knees facing a small cone-shaped representation of the goddess, saying solemnly—'Think deeply of your wish and pray devoutly that it may be answered. Speak not to me of your desire, but whisper it in your heart, promising the goddess a suitable gift if she deigns to hear and answer.'

A profound silence fell. Presently it was broken by a soft, sweet murmuring, appearing to come from the direction of the cone, growing clearer, a woman's voice. 'She whom you seek is not here. She came from the mountain, she has returned to the mountain. Seek not to find her path. Your eyes are held, you cannot see. When you are on her path you know it not. Venture not to test the powers of the gods of the Mountain. They are strong of old. Until you can cleave the sea like a fish, until ye can search the hills like an eagle, ye may not find her. Greetings, O Khemite lord, to my cousin, the god Pharaoh.'

The Khemite fell flat on his face and the whispering died as it had come, leaving the same profound silence.

'The oracle has spoken,' announced King Cinyras, in an awed voice. 'Had you the happy answer to your question? I fear not, if it is some girl whom you seek. Pursue her not if the gods say she is not for you, but offer a sacrifice and make pilgrimage to the waters of forgetfulness and hate. Pray there and drink of the waters and you will forget your love of this girl and desire her no more. Come ye and your men this day week with offerings and I will implore the oracle to speak further.'

Wearily the Khemite arose and went out, joining his

companions in the forecourt. He could do no more in investigation of this strange affair and signified his intention to depart forthwith, carrying his men with him.

Intensely relieved, King Cinyras politely and sanctimoniously accompanied them to the temple gates and watched them ride away, then returned to his sanctuary, to find his daughter Myrrah standing there, smiling, 'Did I not speak well for the oracle?' she asked mischievously.

'Exceedingly well, sweet. And I, too, have done well. Eleven gold bangles of the rich warrior's metal, none of your thin casing proffered for temple-rites, besides six hundred sheep, eight hundred goats and half a hundred oxen. Our fortune is made and we must build a great temple here. The Tamiradae have knelt and sworn to serve me here and the priestesses have so taken the eye of the Khemite warriors that all are preparing to become worshippers in perpetum.'

'The Tamiradae are defeated and their followers converted to Astoreth. Behold, it is a very great triumph, my father, and all due to that witch from Aghirda.' And Myrrah laughed long and loudly.

'That nephew of mine is greatly to be envied and with all my heart I hope they escape in safety to their own land.'

'I hope he does,' qualified Myrrah, devoutly.

1. Sows. Freat roofs on wheels to be pushed up against the walls.
2. Close to Paphos. Still believed in.

# CHAPTER XX

# VICTORY

They returned without mishap to the shelter of their wall two days later. There Kinyras found much work awaiting him. The siege was progressing with a feverish activity and the dreaded Khemite ramps were now within a bowshot and growing more menacing each day. The walls were being heightened with all possible speed to counteract this increasing peril, but Karpas lacked the labour available to Khem and once more the terror of conquest possessed the people.

Erili was now in supreme power and no longer need keep a watchful eye upon his council. When Kinyras returned he found the king staying in his house at Hap Hill. 'Never was a man more needed, Kinyras,' said Erili, with every sign of great relief as the two clasped hands. Then he turned to Dayonis, and his eyes and voice were cold and steely. 'Princess, I greet you, but let there be no more of these woman's ploys. It is a command lady. There is man's work to be done here and the fate of the people is at stake. You are a woman, and have been naught but a hindrance to the defence and the welfare of this land. You will therefore retire and employ yourself with women's work until the wall triumphs, or is broken. Kinyras, your counsel is urgently needed and, Princess, you have our permission to retire.'

He bowed in dismissal and regretfully Dayonis obeyed. She

felt the justice of his reproach and knew not how to express contrition. Erili was very angry and she was sorry to have raised his antagonism. She answered nothing, judging it wiser to await a more favoured opportunity of wooing him to smiles.

As she was about to withdraw he stayed her with a parting shot. 'One more thing, Princess. For your future guidance it is well to bear in mind that foolhardiness is not courage.'

She flushed to the roots of her hair and bit her lip. Never had a man spoken to her so contemptuously before. 'Your structure is just, majesty,' she murmured, and vanished.

Kinyras said nothing. Dayonis had broken her solemn oath to him and caused an infinity of trouble by so doing. Twice had she been the cause of his absence when he was most needed. He felt she deserved all the reproof she had received, which, coming from him, had not the weight Erili could give it.

The king glanced at him and shrugged. His anger was short-lived and he was entirely without malice. 'These women! They are sorry enough of themselves, but when they ape the man!... It is a likeable wench, and lively. I would not be too hard upon her, but there is a time to stand firm upon the feet, my Kinyras, especially when a man is plagued with a young and ambitious wife. A slipped reign wins no charge, friend.'

Kinyras laughed. 'You have spoken well and wisely and she must needs heed you, which is half the battle.'

They began to speak of more serious matters. Hange was still at large, awaiting Erili's attention when the pressing matter of the siege was settled. Hasvan had not returned, nor had any seen him. 'He will come back in good time,' said Kinyras, tranquilly.

'You trust him, then?'

'As myself. When I need him most, then will Hasvan appear.'

Kinyras went out to review the situation and ordered a number of new slinging machines to be made, setting men to work on them night and day until they were finished. With this reinforcement to those he already had, he maintained a perpetual bombardment of the barricades, battering down their walls and pouring in a heavy staveros and arrow fire upon the workmen, yet, because of the vast numbers of the Khemites, still the ramps grew, the bodies of the dead slaves helping to build them up. The barricades were rebuilt as fast as they were crushed. And now Khem began to widen her ramps, to mount slinging-machines upon them, thus causing much loss to the defenders. However, this widening took time and also there began to be a shortage of earth, so that it was impossible to advance and broaden at one and the same time. They must wait until fresh supplies of earth were brought up from the rear.

Thus the defenders were given another respite. Kinyras, for ever studying the problem of fortification, now saw that an inner wall must be built, so that as the ramps grew in size until they were above the outer wall, it could be abandoned and the besieged still be safe. Once more a fever of building raged in the Karpas and every available man, woman and child worked on the new wall.

From the height of his towers Kinyras could survey the enemy lines and saw preparations for a great attack being made. He saw them with satisfaction for, builder though he might me, he was first a soldier, and knew that nothing wears down a warrior's spirit like the long inactivity of a powerful siege. The menace of the growing ramps had wearied his men and given too much rein to idle fear and fancies. Some good, stiff, steady fighting would improve matters wonderfully, and from what he could see of the enemy's vast preparations, they, too, were glad to get down to bare hostilities again.

The ramps were now stationary, for earth must be brought from a great distance, some of it through dense forests. For the sake of sheer self-preservation the Khemites dare not break up the rich farm-lands of the plain for their purpose. What would it profit them to obtain victory at the price of certain starvation? A massed attack, a determined effort to break through at whatever the cost, were a better and wiser policy than obliterating farms.

So Kinyras argued to himself, wondering when the

moment for striking would come. Dawn was the enemy's favourite hour, but that night he was wakened from sweet and hard-earned sleep by his body-slave bursting into his chamber with cries of—'They come, they come, lord! Hasten, master.'

Kinyras sprang from his couch, followed by Dayonis, who bucked on his armour with eager fingers before she put on her own. But he stopped her instantly, giving her stern injunctions not to stir from the room that night, or at any other time to take part in the fighting. Then, seeing her angry dismay, he snatched her hastily into his arms. 'Nay, sweet, look not so. You are my life and soul, and if ill befalls you I am a crippled man. My work is here on the wall, to safeguard the lives of this people. Too long have I been a run-a-gate for your sake and you owe me this reparation. Who knows but this attack may be but a feint to lure you forth and seize you? Have patience and wisdom, my dear heart.'

With her arms round his neck and her lips on his she promised obedience, but so had she promised before, and as he went forth Kinyras gave whispered directions to his slave not to lose sight of the Princess until his return.

He hastened to the top of the nearest tower and looking out over the plain saw the Khemite lines humming like a bee-hive with activity. Thousands of torches flared below him, darting hither and thither in the darkness of the night. The clash of arms, the neighing of horses, the shouts of men ascended to him. It was extraordinary that they should make so much noise. He sent out spies and awaited the moment of attack. Hour after hour he waited, and he sent messengers to Erili. Dawn streaked the east and by its pale light he saw a regiment of chariots driving away, slowly. What in the gods' names were they about? Incredulous of what his tired eyes saw, he strained them further to the amazing sight of regiment after regiment, forming and standing at ease. For what purpose? Not so did Khem attack, with all this noise and bustle of preparation. Grimly he watched.

One of his spies stole in and was brought to him. 'Lord, they retreat.'

'It is a feint?'

'I cannot say, sir.'

'It is a feint.'

All day he watched them, sardonic and wary, laughing grimly at this child's play. What a fool must they deem him! And his dignity was wounded at this lack of esteem from this age-old enemy. Surely had he deserved better of them than this?

So he sat in ironic bitterness, until one spy more successful than the others came flying at him with great news. 'Thothmes is dead, lord. Blessed be the gods. Thothmes is dead! His sons are quarrelling about the succession. All Khemite troops are withdrawn from Orphusa for Khem is seething with rebellion, and Karpas is saved.'

'It is but a feint, man,' said Kinyras, contemptuously.

'Not so, sir. I overheard the Captains talking of it, and already were they taking sides.'

'It is a feint!' repeated Kinyras, obstinately. And continued to sit there, watching, until Dayonis came to fetch him to eat and rest.

For a week did Kinyras rule his command with an iron hand, keeping a steady look-out, preserving the utmost discipline, pressing forward the building of the second wall with feverish energy, waiting for Khem to steal a surprise upon him. Then came a dove from Paphos, confirming the news, with the story of a similar withdrawal, and his many spies came with the tale of a great embarkation and the sailing of an enormous fleet from Salamis.

Then did rejoicing fall upon the people of Karpas and a day was set for a great celebration of victory and thanksgiving to the Gods. The festivities were to be held on the scenes of triumph, at the wall, and the gates of the fortification were set open on that day and the people streamed in from the farms on the plain. From the interior of the Karpas great crowds of happy folk hurried along every road and pathway, to sacrifice to the gods, to feast and dance and to express the thankfulness, joy and relief from oppression and fear which had filled their hearts and lives for so long.

But, above all, did they come to render homage and gratitude to their saviour, Kinyras of the Wall, and all his officers and men.

The festivities started with solemn rites and sacrifices at the altar, which the priests had set up in a grove of cedars near the spot where Kinyras of old would lie on his back beneath the stars. In the immensity of dawn the people gathered, with offerings and prayers. When these celebrations were over the rest of the day was given over to merry-making and feastings. A town had grown up behind the wall and its narrow streets and unpretentious huts were festooned with garlands of flowers and branches of cedar. Every scrap of gay coloured rag which could be collected was hung out, and the people danced with wreaths upon their heads and round their middles, trailing ropes of roses, singing and clapping their hands to keep time to their tripping feet. Great jars of wine stood about and tables loaded with every kind of food and fruit available, while the sun poured down on them and they seemed not to heed its heat at all.

Through these scenes of rejoicing and goodwill came a tall Syrian of very powerful build, dragging behind him a bearded man by a rope tied round his neck, and whose hands were bound in the cruel Egyptian manner. These two struck a sombre note and the people made way for them in silence, asking whispered questions of each other and watching them as they made their way towards Hap Hill.

'Surely it is Hasvan, body-slave to the Lord Kinyras.'

'Well, 'tis no affair of ours!' and they fell again to their dancing and singing.

The house on Hap Hill had grown in size and a pleasant court had been laid out before it, in whose centre grew a large cedar. Roses now flourished here and spring grass was not yet withered in the heat. Here were assembled Erili and the chief councillors, the Princess Dayonis, Kinyras, Zadoug, and the captains of the Mercenaries. Servants were bringing out tables and setting them in the shade, while others bore wine-jars and foods for the feast.

Amongst these, Hasvan too struck the sombre note as he dragged his prisoner roughly before his master and bowed with his hands to his forehead. 'Master, I bring you the traitor, Hange, and the others I have tired up securely in a secret place, lord.'

Impossible to recognise in the foul, hair-covered, filthy nakedness of the wretch before them, the once debonair lawgiver. Kinyras looked and saw the sweat of agony on the man's brow. He remembered with a shudder his own torment when he had been similarly bound, as he was dragged to the mines, and he uttered the curt command—'Unbind him!'

Dayonis laid an urgent hand upon his arm. 'But lord...' and in his ear she whispered, 'Have a care, sweet Kinyras.'

Hasvan was staring stolidly, pretending he had not heard his lord's madness.

'Unbind him!' Kinyras repeated and whispered back to Dayonis, 'He is unarmed, what can he do amongst so many? I know how such thongs bite, my Dayonis, and Hasvan will watch.'

With equal stolidity Hasvan drew his knife from his belt, cut the thongs and restored it to its sheath. Hange stood dropping and then fell to the ground, where he lay in agony as the blood returned to normal circulation.

Erili, who had been talking to a distant group of councillors, now came forward, followed by his company. 'What is this?' he demanded.

'Hasvan, returned with his burnt offering,' Dayonis answered him, with her imputdent smile. She was now quite restored to favour and high in Erili's good graces.

He smiled and turned to Kinyras for elucidation.

'Hange!' said Kinyras, with a gesture towards the fallen man, half of pity, half abhorrence. 'Hasvan, speak.'

'Majesty, this man was hiding from your wrath and I tracked him to his cave in the mountains at my lord's bidding. He is a traitor to the Council and his country. While Khem beleaguered Karpas, this dog sold secrets to the enemy and showed them how they might land a great army in safety by following fires which he lit. This and much else has he done.'

'That we already know. Tell us how you took him?' Erili replied gravely.

Whereupon Hasvan began the recital of his adventures since the day when Kinyras had dispatched him upon his errand and, after the manner of their country and age he was a good story-teller and they excellent listeners. He had tracked first the men who lit the flares, had gone among them freely and learnt their secrets, then when Hange had disappeared, he had set himself to find him, stalking his enemy with all the cunning of his race and finally taking him by strategy, bringing him to their presence on that day because it was meet and fitting that the public enemy should be brought to shame on the day of public rejoicing.

While Hasvan was speaking, Hange was gradually recovering from the bad effects of his bondage. He shifted his position stealthily several times to secure greater ease, stretching his arms and legs to allow his blood to circulate more freely. With his face concealed, he lay listening to his captor's long-winded narration, hate swelling in his heart and seething in his brain. Must he suffer this frustration? Must his life be stamped out in this filthy manner, with all his many failures thick upon him? His one wish and hope was to wrest triumph from his enemy and turn it to dire disaster.

Craftily watching his opportunity and staking all upon one desperate chance, he sprang to his feet and in the one Simian gesture of inconceivable rapidity had plucked a knife from the nearest belt. A dozen hands seized him but not before he had hurled it with all his might at the breast of Dayonis. Kinyras had time only to fling himself before her with a sideways lurch of his body. Erili's dagger was out in an instant and he stabbed at Hange wildly in the long, disembowelling rip-stroke, and as Kinyras sank into Dayonis' arms he heard the Lawgiver's groan and saw him clutch at his belly and sink upon his knees.

Presently Hange raised his head and a strange silence fell upon all assembled. 'So, I have you, my enemy, at last! Your tormentors have no terror for me, Erili! Listen, Kinyras of the Wall! And mark well my words. We die now, both of us, but we shall live again and at the same time. Down through the ages will I pursue my revenge, not with the follow of dagger-thrust, but with the destruction of all you hold most dear. I have the powers of long sight and I see us, always in the same orbit, I the robber, you the robbed, of your faith, of your hope, and of the faith and hope of all who trust in you.'

He ceased in his wild raving and the awed, superstitious silence of the gathering seemed to increase. But in a moment it was broken by a clear, penetrating voice. 'Not so, Hange the lawgiver, traitor and murderer. By my magic I tell you, you lie. Kinyras lives. See, I say the words and I use my power. Already his wound has ceased to bleed and he grows stronger. And so shall it ever be. Down through the ages you shall prevail against him until the last moment, when he shall triumph over you, because he is a better man than you. Because he has been faithful shall he live and prevail.'

Dayonis finished speaking and bent over Kinyras. She took him into her arms and held him to her breast and as she laid her cheek against his, murmuring, 'Rest, my love, rest and grow strong,' he felt himself sinking into a delicious languor which gradually merged into oblivion.

# CHAPTER XXI

# ANOTHER VICTORY

The last day of Heyward's leave arrived and early in the afternoon he went round to say good-bye to Mina. He was entirely satisfied and self-congratulatory at the way events had favoured them. In his opinion fate had indeed been propitious.

Yet, every now and then, a haze of doubt beclouded this tranquility. Certain it was that Mina was changed and as this change in her grew, so did his passion for her, which had reached a resting-place, increase. There were moments when Heyward was no longer sure of Mina, and possibility of failure in that direction looked like a bad dream in the far distance.

But failure was a thing which he never would countenance. It was an instinct with him never to contemplate it and whenever it overtook him, which it did but rarely, it was his habit to sweep it behind him, to treat it as though it never had been. His facility for forgetfulness was truly amazing. He owed all his success in life, and it was considerable, to this habit.

So, when it crept upon him, he swept all doubt aside with no uncertain hand. Mina was overwrought and the past fortnight had been enough to try the nerves of the most unimaginative of women. With an unusual flash of insight Hank was able to see just exactly what poor Mina had been through. He was aware of this only because he wished to be, because by seeing it he was enabled to banish doubt and to

354

maintain that happy sense of satisfactoriness more or less intact.

Mina yielded herself to his passionate embrace of greeting with an acquiescence unknown to her of late. Hank was leaving England for Paris that evening. The tension of her mind had grown so acute, his heartless presence beside Robert's bed had become such a nightmare that, without considering all it implied, she was glad of the respite from present complications which his absence would give her. She consoled herself with thoughts of the letters they would write each other and with the future they would spend together, when all present ills should be past.

Some time they spent in discussing their plans, which remained unaltered.

'Any chance of coming out to have tea with me, darling?' he whispered, as he kissed her neck.

'I can't leave him,' she murmured.

'Oh, come on, sweetness. What harm can it do him? He's lain here for a couple of weeks now without a sigh of coming to himself, and it's not likely to happen in the next two hours, is it?'

'I wonder if I dare?' she hesitated.

'Of course you can.'

'After all, he's quite safe. I've a good mind to risk it, but I'll go and see first.' She rose from the couch on which they were sitting together and hurried into the bedroom. Denvers was lying on his back, his hand still clasping the snail lay on the eiderdown. He was silent.

Mina bent over him and listened to his even breathing. He gave no sign of consciousness. 'There's no change,' she said straightening and moving away. 'I think it's quite safe for me to go, Hank.'

'Righto,' Heyward answered, 'get your things on, then.' He, too, was peering down at Denvers as he spoke, noting the bronze object clasped in the inert hand. His curiosity with regard to this thing had always been of the acutest kind and he longed to take it in his hand and examine it. Several times he had tried to do so, but Mina had always stopped him with a sharp word. For some inexplicable reason she could not bear the thought of Heyward touching her husband in his present defenceless state. It was bad enough to endure the lash of his expressed hatred and the contempt he would pour down upon him, in spite of all her efforts' to check it.

Now, with Mina off her guard, the opportunity for Heyward to gratify his curiosity was not to be missed. Swiftly he bent down while her back was toward him and seizing Denvers hand in a brutal grasp he wrenched open the fingers and forced the snail out of them. It was surprising how hard it was to do this, how tenacious were the fingers. Heyward found his brow was clammy with sweat and his heart beating unaccountably hard, while the detestation he always felt for Denvers seemed to rise within him in an overwhelming tide. Heyward could have killed him where he lay with the greatest of satisfaction.

The effect of this violence upon himself was at nothing compared with its action upon Denvers. He yawned copiously, opened his eyes, rubbed them vigorously with his knuckles for a moment or two, yawned again with a gasping noise in his using manner and suddenly sat erect in the most natural way in the world. This action brought him on a level with Heyward's face and the two stared into each other's eyes. 'You, Hange! And still alive. They told me you were dead. Erili,' he bawled, 'this carrion is still ours for the hanging.'

Heyward sprang erect with a stifled exclamation, but it was Mina who provided him with the greatest surprise. She flung herself down on the bed beside her husband with a more impulsive action than he had ever known her to show, and he saw with a desperate rage that both her arms were around his neck.

'Oh, Robert! Robert! Thank God for this! Oh, thank God!'

Neither had he ever heard her call upon God before, nor show any awareness of His existence. Heyward felt stifling as he watched Denvers' arms go round his wife and hold her close.

'My beloved, my dear!' he murmured softly.

Heyward also noticed that his tones were stronger and more vibrant than of old. For a long moment there was a complete silence as he contemplated the two on the bed. At length, after what seemed an age to him, his voice broke in upon them harshly. 'Well, Mina, are you coming?' He had swiftly determined to ignore her too enthusiastic welcome of Robert back to normal life. Such a sudden happening was enough to harrow any woman's over-wrought nerves. The sound of his voice seemed to divide the two on the bed like a cleaving sword.

Denvers looked at him over Mina's shoulder, a long, peculiar look, which Heyward found it impossible to fathom. 'Ah, Heyward, it's you,' he said, slowly and deliberately. 'So I shall not Hange you after all, Lawgiver.' He laughed and shrugged.

'You seem to be quite yourself again, Denvers,' Heyward said stiffly, his owl's eyes nearly bolting out of his head at the sight of Mina still clasped in Denvers' arms and showing no disposition to come out of them. He saw that she was trembling excessively and that her husband held her very tenderly and protectingly.

'Oh, yes, I'm quite myself, thanks, Heyward, never felt more fit in my life before. I hadn't been sleeping very well. But this good, sound sleep has set me up wonderfully; I feel I can cope with anything, now.'

'It ought to have done,' Heyward commented with a sneer. 'You've slept, as you call it, for a solid fortnight on end, any-how.'

Denvers said nothing, nor did he evince the slightest surprise.

It was Mina who spoke. 'Oh, Robert, it was terrifying—seeing you like that day after day. I was frightened to death.'

'Were you, now? Why? You are usually so wonderful when I'm ill.'

'Yes, but this was different. Have you ever been like it before?'

'Yes, several times—before we met,' Denvers answered

carelessly and quite untruthfully.

She drew a deep breath. 'I hope it never happens again. I couldn't bear it if it did.'

'But you won't be here to see it,' Heyward reminded her, savagely. 'Well, Mina, what about it? Time's getting on.'

'Hank, do be reasonable,' she said pettishly. 'How can I possibly go now?'

Denvers held her by the shoulders, looking steadily into her eyes. She gazed back at him.

She seemed to have forgotten Heyward's existence and fury mastered him. All his passion for her surged within him and never had she been more desirable in his eyes. His feeling for her was like a spell cast over him, raising the primitive savage in him, which was always lurking just below the surface. He strode to the other side of the bed, seized her roughly by the shoulders, flinging off Denvers' hold to do so, and yanked her brutally to her feet. 'What does this mean?' he gasped, trembling.

A dressing-gown lay neatly disposed over the back of a chair beside his bed, and Denvers quietly reached for it, got out and put it on. He waited, tall and straight, and had a most unusual look of command as he stood tying the cord round his waist. 'It means, Heyward, that I've had just about as much of you and your little ways as I'm prepared to stand. Get out, before I kick you out. My wife is mine and I keep her. Understand?'

Heyward looked long at Mina and saw that the incredible had happened. He had failed. He could not get away quickly enough after that, in order to put that failure behind him.

As the door slammed after him, Denvers came up to his wife. 'You are at liberty to follow him, Mina.'

'I don't want to,' she said simply. 'All the time you have been—like this, I have been seeing things—quite differently. I have changed.'

'No, you have just gone back to what you always were. I knew you would, but I was afraid it might be—'

'I know,' she interrupted. 'Your letter—I read it—it was wonderful. Such faith! I do think great faith can save.'

'I know it can, Mina.'


Later, over their coffee in a quiet little Soho restaurant where they dined, she suddenly asked him—'Robert, who is Dayonis?'

'Dayonis?' he repeated vaguely.

'Yes, you have been talking about her constantly for the past fortnight.'

Denvers smiled. 'Oh, that? I had dreams. She was you, I think.'

'But she had red hair, and green eyes.'

'And I had black hair and black eyes, yet it was I. Yes, you are Dayonis, dear, and she is you. There is no doubt about that.'

'It was a strange thing to happen, Robert.'

'Do you believe in reincarnation?' he asked, and began to tell her about Rudolph Steiner's theory of group-reincarnation.


*Thotmes III of Egypt conquered Cyprus about 1450B.C., but at his death it seems to have been lost in some popular rebellion such as described.*

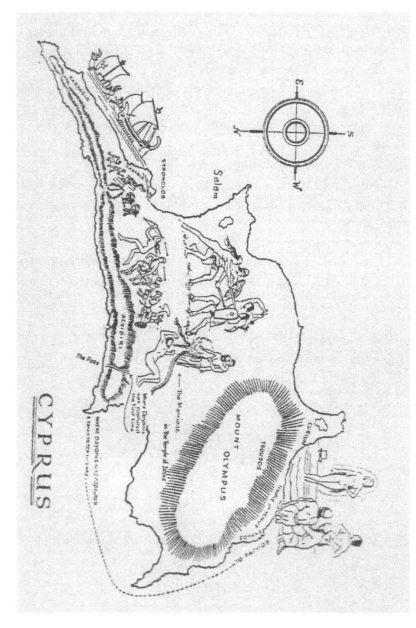

CYPRUS

DARK DRAGON PUBLISHING IS PROUD TO
ANNOUNCE THE RELEASE OF THE HISTORIC AND
CLASSIC FICTION NOVEL WRITTEN BY THE
FATHER OF WICCA
GERALD B. GARDNER.

FOREWORD BY PHILIP HESELETON

DELVE INTO THE WORLD OF WITCHCRAFT AND
HIGH MAGIC!

Jan, Olaf and Thur attempt to perform Ceremonial Magic at
a time when delving into these Arts could cost them their
lives. Unfortunately, they discover they are missing an
integral aspect to High Magic and are doomed to failure
unless they find the Witch of Wanda to initiate them and
train in the secrets of Witchcraft.

AVAILABLE ON AMAZON, INDIGO/CHAPTERS/,
BARNES AND NOBEL, AND ANYWHERE FINE BOOKS
ARE SOLD.

AVAILABLE FOR SALE FOR BOOKSTORES AND
OCCULT SHOPS THROUGH INGRAM WITH THE
FOLLOWING ISBNS:
Jacketed Hard Cover: 9781928104292
Trade Paperback: 9781928104308

# BOOKS

To see a full list of our amazing books,
please check our website:

www. darkdragonpublishing.com/books.html